Shattered Allegiance

◆

Shattered Allegiance

◆

Philip S. Woods

Writers Club Press
San Jose New York Lincoln Shanghai

Shattered Allegiance

Writers Club Press
an imprint of iUniverse.com, Inc.

For information address:
iUniverse.com, Inc.
5220 S 16th, Ste. 200
Lincoln, NE 68512
www.iuniverse.com

ISBN: 0-595-15692-4

Printed in the United States of America

This work is dedicated to all those level headed persons who strive, on a daily basis, to get along with their fellow man and prevent the events described herein from occurring. Hatred kills.

Introduction

◆

The violence is over now, but the unrest is not. The guns are silent, yet, the weeping remains. The final tally in cost of human suffering and, ultimately, loss of life will never be known. The number of deaths, in just eight months, already far surpasses the total numbers of dead attributed to the entire six years of World War II. Across the sea, old enemies eye us with newly fired intent. The pragmatists among us realize that an attack could come at any time. The security from foreign threat is, by no means, certain. Our ability to repel any such threat is even less certain. Out of the ashes, with, much like the Jewish settlers in the mid-twentieth century, one hand on the shovel and the other on the rifle, we hasten to rebuild our wounded nation. This time, hopefully, we will take special care to ensure that the horrors of this latest in man's conflicts are not repeated. The future is uncertain. There is trouble in the east.

Bits and fragments of new information continue to arise, daily, as investigators seek to piece together the puzzle of events that staggered this nation for eight terrible, blood-filled months. With every new finding, the underlying conspiracy becomes ever more evident. What, at first review, appeared to be nothing more than the sometimes anticipated natural escalation of racial hatred under extreme circumstances is, now, becoming more and more clearly recognized as a carefully contrived and orchestrated plot. As the pieces fall together, it appears, disconcerting as it may be, that the plot was fostered in the mind of one of this nation's most respected, influential, and wealthy capitalists. These new revelations clearly identify Martin Edward Hastings, the renowned American benefactor and philanthropist, as the mastermind behind the violence. Such a turn in the events has stunned the entire world, as well as this reporter. That such a prominent capitalist could be the originator, instigator and primary financial backer for such a heinous program of genocide as that which engulfed this country is unconscionable. That the man had a precise, well-executed and highly effective method of eliminating the African-Americans within the borders of this country is, now, undeniable. That he was not alone in his desire to kill every black man, woman, and child in the United States is the subject of this present work.

I have called upon all of my literary resources to compile the pages that follow. Time limitations were, of necessity, a key concern in the recording of the many events. The luxury of months of careful editing was not an available option. The names, except in rare instances, are the real names. The individual stories are the real stories, albeit, in certain areas, I have had to resort to a certain poetic license to describe and illustrate events as I, and other investigators, believe them to have occurred. I have adopted the novel format for the convenience of the reader. I have tried to capture the real horror, but realize, now, that doing such is an impossible task for any one man. Indeed, there are not enough words in all of man's languages to describe the length and breadth of the powerful emotions arising from the unfettered violence that rolled across the land and so savagely gripped and ravaged this nation. Each of us must deal with the pain in our own way, exorcise the demons at our own pace, try to learn from our experiences and, in the final analysis, put it behind us, label it history and press onward. I wish you success. Other enemies vie for our attention.

Amidst the broken ice floes off Greenland's northeastern coast, the NOAA research vessel slipped through the frigid, gray darkness and sounded the sea floor's depths. A solitary figure, well insulated against the sub-zero cold in arctic parka and multiple clothing layers, sat upon the ice-covered deck and gazed skyward into the arctic sky. Through thick clouds of his own misty breath, he watched the celestial presentation unfolding above. The beauty of the millions of points of flickering light and the majesty of the dance of the aurora borealis was lost upon him. The input from his optic nerve could not drown the thoughts cycling madly through his mind. Rigidly, he leaned back against the NOAA vessel's canvas covered dinghy and closed his eyes to the star-filled night. He was a broken man in a frozen expanse of solitude. Memories filled his head, propelling him into the past and a buffeting array of tortured visions of life gone by.

Dawn broke warm and pink upon a marbled, Alabama sky. There would be rain today, perhaps a storm. The teenager hefted another bale of hay across the fence to the absent stares of a handful of sturdy cows. A gray tabby cat purred and rubbed in familiar circles against his worn jeans. Today was the first day of his senior year in high school and he had already been up and working for the better part of an hour. Chores had to be done regardless of the day's designation. His name was Martin Edward Hastings, the only son of James Franklin and Julie Davis

Hastings. Be it in the hard Alabama clay, the sandy South Carolina low country, or the peat of Ireland, the Hastings had been farmers for as far back as the family tree could be traced. Farming was hard work and, being the only son, Martin saw more than his share of that work. But, he did not complain. Work, Martin had decided, like so many other things, was just a part of life that no amount of complaining would change. He would draw more water, hoe a few rows of vegetables, wolf down a quick breakfast and, then, make his way to school. His afternoon would be filled with even more work. Tomorrow, he would get up and do it all again. It was an unending cycle—a cycle to which he had long since been accustomed.

"Are you excited?" Julie Hastings asked, placing a plate of eggs and grits before him.

"About what?" Martin asked.

"Your first day back to school." answered his mother, "Being a senior is a big deal, after all."

"Yeah," Martin replied, "I guess it is a big deal. I don't know. Maybe, I'm a little excited. I can't really tell."

He did not go into what was really going on in his mind—thoughts of the last year in school, thoughts about the future, a future that did not include farming. There were far too many questions and so few apparent answers. Martin wanted more of life than a hand to mouth existence. He wanted success. He wanted to break the bond between him and the soil. Yet, his conscience questioned, how could he abandon his father to do all the work that farming required? What kind of son would he be to repay his parents by striking off on his own to make his own way? Silently, he ate his breakfast and pondered the future.

Julie Hastings watched her son as he ate. She could almost read his thoughts. She realized, without him having to tell her, that Martin had dreams—dreams that would, soon, carry him far away from the farm, far away from her. Mixed emotions accompanied this realization as her gaze shifted between Martin and James, her husband, across the table.

Martin's face was smooth and still bore the ruddiness of youth. James' face, by comparison, was hard and deeply lined from years of toil and worry; his thick hands were rough and heavily callused from a lifetime of laboring. Farming was James Hastings' life, the only life he had ever known. He would never understand why Martin could want to leave the farm. Julie had discussed the issue with him on countless occasions. Slowly, over time, James had resigned himself to the fact that Martin would, one day, be gone. But, that did not mean that he liked the idea. James, like his son, ate his breakfast in silence with his thoughts fixed on the day's work ahead.

Beyond the Hastings' breakfast table, outside the walls of the Alabama farmhouse, life went on without pausing to consider the subdued thoughts of a single family. Time whirred forward, through and beyond temporal obstacles. No barrier, however significant, could bar its passage. The collective whole had neither the time nor the inclination to spend any energy contemplating the worries of mere individuals. It was the 1960's and a period of pronounced uncertainty in the World. Life in the United States was certainly no exception. Racial tensions that had been building for a century were rapidly approaching an out of control level. Government agencies, the FBI and CIA among others, were, already, well out of control, piloted by power hungry megalomaniacs. It was a time when television and mass media carved for themselves seemingly indispensable niches in the lives of the expanding American public. News stories were being covered around the globe, complete with film footage.

The whole world had watched as President John Fitzgerald Kennedy and his pretty wife smiled and waved to onlookers lining a sun-filled Dallas street. The film continued to roll as a gun, or guns, snapped and the President's head popped. In the U.S., racial unrest was, temporarily, forgotten while the nation mourned the young President's passage. With the swearing in of the new President, a crusty good old boy Southerner, life got back to normal quickly—normal being a continued, crazy shift in the status quo. Traditional morality came under full assault on every front, and, consequently, American youth, unrestrained, was fast becoming something alien. Anarchy loomed on the horizon. It was a time of the disappearing crew cut, a quest for faster cars, James Bond, Mafia kingpins, and a space race. Technological advances were occurring at a staggering rate as, daily, the political, social, and scientific structure of human civilization, world-wide, was undergoing metamorphosis that would lead to, inevitably, who knew?

The U.S. Department of Education was one of the first to show the effects of the changing philosophies of the time. God and Judeo-Christian ethics, removed from the classrooms, were quickly replaced with a social concept of life—an 'I'm O.K. you're O.K., no one is responsible' society. Control shifted from the teachers in their classrooms to a central office chaired by an elected official. Curriculum changes, subtle at first, introduced alternate views of life to the nation's youth. Free from the restrictions of acknowledging an all powerful God, education officials were presented with a free hand in tackling life's issues. The molding of future generations began.

The American public stood by, offering only minor, periodic protest, as increasingly liberal content found its way into their children's text-books. Their were concerns elsewhere—a multitude of concerns. Over-shadowing them all, however, was an uncertain fear of impending nuclear doom. The weapons that were developed in the years since WWII were, the world's citizens were told, incomprehensible in their ability to destroy. With a push of a button, entire regions of the earth could be erased. First would be the blinding flash, brighter than the hottest midday sun, the boom mingled with the hell storm of the initial concussion wall. The ripple of man-made fury will level and kill every-thing in its path. But, just to make sure, it will turn on itself and rush back inward to fill the vacuum left by its forward passage. When the smoke finally clears, a dead, radioactive desert will have taken the place of once flourishing civilization.

There was, everyone knew, no defense against such weapons. Across the globe, nervous eyes searched the heavens for evidence of missile attack and the anticipated arrival of doomsday. It was a time not altogether dissimilar to a driverless, runaway carriage being pulled at an impossible rate by wild-eyed, maddened horses along uncharted, untrodden paths with its cargo, mankind, busily moving to and fro like insignificant insects content to ride along, oblivious of their plight.

For the U.S., a pseudo war sputtered and popped in the far off jungles of Southeast Asia, as Vietnam, a buzzing hornet since the late 50's, began to appear in the nation's headlines with increasing frequency. France had already suffered defeat there and, now, the U.S. was taking its shot. Why? There were no real answers. It was just another in a long list of conflicts falling under the general description of 'fighting communism.' It was us against them and that was all that was important; important enough to spend the blood of the nation's youth. Few Americans realized that the leader of the faceless yellow men the U.S. forces were fighting had been placed in power by the U.S. Not that such knowledge would have mattered much, anyway. There is much done in the name of the democracy that will never see the light of day. Had we not placed Japan back in the hands of its prewar leaders? Americans have always had a proclivity towards believing what their leaders told them. Regardless, ultimately, everything can be traced to the bottom line. The Vietnam conflict was a lucrative venture, which was quietly generating enormous wealth in the coffers of the international financiers. The American collateral for the venture was provided in the drained blood of the nation's young sons. Thousands surrendered their life's breath in far away jungles and fields for a cause that, now, as then, remains undefined.

Within the U.S. borders, Civil rights developed into a white-hot issue. Elijah Mohammed, Malcolm X and the Fruit of Islam were calling for revolution by any means. White man's oppression, as they saw it, had to end. Martin Luther King and a host of others were calling for the same revolution by non-violent means. Across the country, marches were held, protests were staged, and the message was clear. The time of the Negro had come and segregation of the races must go. The U.S. Congress bellied up to the bar and proclaimed that the races must meld for the benefit of the entire country, regardless of public opinion. Forced integration of public schools, bussing as it came to be called, was one of the proposed courses of action designed to facilitate the 'melding', and proved to be an action that would only serve to compound the craziness of the times. In some areas of the country, the mingling of blacks and whites was carried off without incident. In other areas, the transition was not so smooth. Years of deeply ingrained prejudice are not easily overcome. Whites in these areas lashed out against the sanctioned integration of races. One such area was Johnsons Gap, Alabama.

Johnsons Gap was a small southern town with a population of a little over 1,200. The town itself consisted of a food market, a courthouse, a fire station, a hardware store, a barbershop, and two churches all on a single, main avenue. It was one of those sleepy southern burgs where everyone knew everyone else, and the closest thing to trouble usually involved too much liquor on a Saturday night. It was, however, unique among most Alabama towns, in that, its black population was zero. Due to the new bussing laws, Johnson Gap High School became one of the many schools, nationwide, which were instructed to integrate. Johnsons Gap citizens, for the most part, were outraged. They were simple folk, content with life the way it was. They strongly resented the heavy-handed interference of the federal government. Citizens there, as elsewhere in the country, were convinced that the government had far overstepped its bounds. The integration order, naturally, sparked violent protest in Johnsons Gap. The citizens of the small town were not going to stand, idly, by and let the bureaucrats in Washington D.C. dictate how they were to live their lives. Rallies were held throughout the summer, threats were hurled, ultimatums issued, but, in the end, all of this did nothing to sway the Government's directive. The times were changing and the message was clear. You either went with the flow, or you suffered the consequences. Even Alabama's Governor had been powerless to stem the tide. The writing was on the wall. Segregation was going to end even if it took the mobilization of the National Guard.

The eastern sky was turning ominously dark as Martin arrived at school that warm, September morning. He had been able to see the crowd gathered before the school's entrance for the last several hundred yards. Now, he could hear the tumult. Four long, yellow, Bluebird buses pulled to a dusty halt in front of Johnson Gap high school with a sigh, belching thick, black diesel smoke. Martin sidled closer to the crowd and stood quietly by, watching, with curiosity, as the buses slowly discharged their wide-eyed black cargo. Hate-filled hisses, insults, and curses emanated from the crowd of white students, students' parents, and town citizens who had gathered, yet again, to protest the mandated integration of their school. Hate filled obscenities and threats bombarded the arriving blacks.

Martin had never seen so many of blacks gathered together at one time. Having spent his entire life secluded on the family farm, Martin had never developed a hardened opinion of his own concerning blacks. Apart from the occasional chance encounters, Martin had never been around blacks for any length of time. Standing there, under the ancient oak at the edge of the parking lot, he watched, with interest, the unloading of the more than 130 Negroes. He felt a strange sense of embarrassment as the crowd of whites, people he recognized, some of whom he knew well, viciously railed at the newcomers with undisguised vehemence and hatred. Amongst the crowd were a number of signs displaying cruel and pointed messages; the most common among them; 'Nigger Go Home!' Martin found it hard to comprehend that those in the crowd, those he knew well, those he attended church with every Sunday, could be involved in such a hate filled gathering. Unease settled upon him. He wondered how the blacks must feel about the reception.

Martin studied the dark faces. On some of those faces, he saw fear. But, not on all. Martin could not help but marvel at the courage demonstrated by these. Faced with the angry crowd, the explicit signs, the scathing insults, and the hate filled threats, it was only natural to be afraid. Yet, many of the blacks seemed to ignore it all. The whole group, as one, stared past the crowd and marched, silently, into the school building. Standing there in the September heat, Martin wondered if he would have had the same courage had the situation been reversed and it had been he that was bused to an all black school. The feelings he experienced there that morning were new feelings for Martin. They would remain with him for the rest of his life.

Lightening flashed, thunder cracked, loudly, and rain burst from the sky in torrential sheets. The falling rain pelted the earth with a fury that only a late summer, Alabama storm can produce. The crowd dispersed quickly, scattering for cover. The protest was over. Blacks were now a part of Johnsons Gap High School. Life would never be the same.

It was later, that same week, on Friday, that the fight broke out. It was just after the bell signifying the end of the school day. Martin was already in the schoolyard. Having physical education as the last class of the day afforded him the luxury of being among the first dismissed in the afternoons. He idled around waiting on his girlfriend, Kelly. Other students milled about. Most discussed their plans for the weekend. The conflict began.

"Why don't you watch where you're goin', you STUPID NIGGER?" The words tore through the hot, still air and filled the dusty afternoon. Martin, and all others in the vicinity, turned at the sound.

David Bullock, another senior, stood directly in the path of and towering over a younger black girl. His face was red with rage and his knuckles white against clenched, oversized hands. Without any doubt, Bullock was the meanest boy in the school. He was feared by many and disliked by most. He was unusually large for his age and had been able to pass for a full-grown man since the ninth grade. Bullock was an All-State defensive back for the school's football team for two years in a row. He had won the State wrestling championship for his weight class the previous year, and was expected to repeat that feat in his senior year. By the best of standards, Bullock was a bully. His school disciplinary record was replete with incidents of violence. He was not someone to tangle with lightly.

The confrontation had been brewing steadily all week. Bullock had been openly taunting the black students since Monday morning. He, like many others, had been deeply offended by having to share educational facilities with blacks. For the entire week, Bullock had been quite loud in voicing his disgust. He made no attempt to couch his racist views in what we would term today, politically correct rhetoric. His words were vulgar, his tone threatening, and his message was clear—the blacks were not welcome.

Everyone, teachers and students alike, knew that it was only a question of time before the hot, volcanic hatred of Bullock erupted. Sooner or later, one of the blacks was going to say something out of place and the keg would explode. Bullock was pushing for sooner. That afternoon, Bullock, also having physical education as the last class of the day, had waited in the schoolyard, alone. He had decided that the time had come. He was waiting on a target.

The final bell rang and a flood of students broke through the school's doors. Bullock watched them, searching. He spotted her, immediately. With firm lip and a fire flickering in his eyes, he watched the waif-like tenth grader as she exited the side door of the school and made her way across the school yard toward him and the waiting line of buses. She was reading a book, lost in its pages, and not paying any attention to where she was going. Bullock eased into her path and waited.

Her name was Louanne Walters. She was fifteen and the middle child of five, all girls. Like the rest of the blacks, she had not been happy about the bussing order. She did not understand why she could not go to the same school she had always gone to. Louanne had spent her first week at Johnson's Gap High School walking in fear.

Bullock continued to watch her and, when Louanne was within reach, he reached out, slapped the book from her hands and bellowed, "Why don't you watch where you're goin', you STUPID NIGGER?"

Bewildered, Louanne looked up. The white boy's eyes bore into her. The hate telegraphed itself clearly. The fear, having ridden her shoulders for the entire week, now welled up as terror in her frail body. Louanne apologized shakily, "I'm…I'm sorry, I shouldn't have been rea…"

Bullock did not allow her to finish the sentence. Lashing out swiftly, he slapped her across the top of her head with his open palm. Then, grabbing her right arm and twisting it, he spun her around and clutched her light body to his chest in a powerful bear-like hug. Confused, Louanne cried out in a mixture of fright and pain.

Martin watched in disbelief as Bullock manhandled the terrified, crying black girl. Another senior, a girl with large green eyes perfectly set upon a pretty face eased up alongside Martin. Surrounding her face was long, soft brown hair, escaped from the ponytail that fell upon her patterned, blue cotton summer dress. The dress well accentuated the hourglass figure of the young lady. Her name was Kelly Stevens and she had been Martin's girlfriend ever since the 6th grade.

"What's he doing?" Julie asked, nervously.

"Don't know." Martin answered, without turning his attention from Bullock and the black girl.

What was Bullock doing, Martin wondered. The black girl in Bullock's grasp was a small thing—petite, frail, and slightly, Martin thought, pretty. Bullock outweighed her by at least a hundred pounds. He was handling her like a rag doll.

"What a jerk!" Kelly exclaimed.

"So, what else is new?" Remarked Martin.

"Pleeease stop!", Louanne cried, "I'm going to miss the bus!"

"Tough luck, nigger." Bullock hissed. He applied yet more pressure to her skinny arm, "I'll stop when I'm damned good and ready, and not before. So you just keep your mouth shut."

Bullock swung Louanne around and motioned with a nod of his head towards the blacks gathering at the waiting line of buses, before offering. "Why don't you scream real loud, and maybe one of your big-lipped, jigaboo bucks will come over and rescue you."

A slight whimper was Louanne 's only reply.

As if drawn by a magnet, other white students began to gather around Bullock and his captive, delighting in the black girl's torment and smirking at the bully's remarks. Soon, they began offering degrading comments of their own.

David Bullock had taken full advantage of his physical attributes from an early age, and had used his size as a weapon of intimidation against those smaller than him ever since he had found out that he could. The look in his eyes telegraphed the joy he was experiencing by humiliating the black girl. He was secure in the knowledge that no one would dare to interfere.

Martin, as he watched the scene, felt a sudden, rising flood of emotion and sympathy for the helpless black girl. The taunts of the other students only served to intensify his feelings. Someone had to do something, he decided.

"Why doesn't someone do something?" asked Kelly, echoing Martin's thoughts.

"Hold these." Martin directed, handing his books to Kelly. "I'll stop the idiot!"

"No," exclaimed Kelly, eyes, suddenly, wide with fear, "I didn't mean..."

Kelly's words trailed off into silence as she, mechanically, accepted Martin's books. She watched with a mixture of admiration and terror as Martin marched off in the direction of Bullock, the black girl, and the delighted, growing crowd.

By this time, a crowd of blacks had gathered at the edge of the parking lot, hovering near the waiting line of school buses and sheepishly watching Bullock and his tormented captive. They were not making any moves to inch closer. The courage shown at the first of the week was, now, conspicuously, absent. The crowd of whites gathered around Bullock had grown substantially and many of these began to eye the black group menacingly. A few hoped the blacks would try to intervene. A few of these possessed the hope out of compassion for the suffering girl. Most, however, desired black intervention as an excuse to break out with fists, baseball bats, and pocketknives to settle the integration issue once and for all.

Bullock, noting the group of blacks gathered by the buses, twisted his prey's arm with new intensity, eliciting renewed cries of pain.

"You bunch of coward, nigger bastards!" Bullock yelled across the playground, "Why don't you come over here and get some of this?"

Despite the taunting, the blacks would not move away from the buses. Granted, some of the blacks present in the group wanted to do so, but the others restrained these few. Those doing the restraining knew all too well the potential consequences of confronting the white crowd.

"Well, monkey," Bullock returned his attention to the frightened Louanne, "Looks like your burr-headed buddies don't give a flying rat's turd what I do to you!"

Bullock grabbed a handful of Louanne 's braids and snatched her head around, forcing her to look at the group of blacks across the way. "Looks just like a bunch of monkeys at the zoo to me." Bullock hissed.

"How 'bout you, nigger? Do they look like apes to you? I don't know why they think they need education. Seems to me they should get back in the fields where they belong!"

Terrified, Louanne did not answer. The crowd howled with laughter.

"Let her go!" Martin ordered, simultaneously shoving his way through the spectators gathered about Bullock and his victim.

The air stilled. A strained, tangible silence settled on the schoolyard.

Bullock wheeled violently in his tracks, dragging Louanne with him, to see who would dare challenge his actions. When he saw Martin, his eyes narrowed momentarily. Then, Bullock emitted a rolling laugh.

"Well, well, well," Bullock chortled, "if it isn't puny, little Mister Straight A's' Martin Hastings come to the rescue of his little nigger girl-friend!" The silence dissolved as quickly as it had settled as the others in the assembled throng laughed heartily at Bullock's response to the intrusion. Some among the crowd began to offer retorts of their own.

"Uh oh! Look out David!" said one.

"You're in BIG trouble now, Dave!" said another.

"You better run, David." quipped, yet, another, "The Nigger Avenger is here and he looks pretty upset!"

Martin, ignoring the mockery, cast a quick glance into the eyes of the captive black girl. He found, there, the smallest glint of bewildered appreciation.

"You just keep your punk face shut, Hastings!" Bullock spat, no longer laughing, no trace of a smile remaining on his face. "I'm not let-ting go of this little nigger bitch for you or twenty just like you. If you don't want me to pound your eyes out, you best get gone, boy!"

Bullock twisted Louanne 's arm once more, causing her to cry out, again. With eyes filled with rage, he tried to stare Martin down.

Martin, unflinching, moved closer.

"That's enough, David." Martin announced. "You've had your fun. Now, let the girl go."

"No, Hastings," Bullock replied with a twisted grin. "I don't think so. I'm pretty sure there's a little bit of fun left in this pickaninny."

Bullock's free hand reached slowly around the front of Louanne 's dress and began groping at her.

"My, My," Bullock exclaimed as his hand continued to roam freely, "What have we got here?!"

To the delight of the other boys gathered around, Bullock grabbed the neck of Louanne 's dress and ripped violently downward, exposing her small breasts.

At this, rage completely enveloped Martin and, taking two steps closer, he boomed, with a voice he did not know he possessed, "I SAID LET GO OF HER, YOU USELESS SACK OF BIRD SHIT!"

The last of Martin's words echoed off the gymnasium wall as another, sudden, anticipatory quiet fell upon the crowd. There was going to be a fight. All could feel its impending presence in the electrically charged air. Was Hastings crazy, or what? It was a silent question that filled the heads of many of those present. Did he not realize whom he was confronting?

Bullock, enraged by the open challenge of the insignificant Hastings, shoved the now sobbing Louanne violently to the ground. He filled his chest with air in a practiced maneuver of attempting to swell to gigantic proportions in the face of opposition.

"O.K., Hastings! You nigger-loving asshole!" Bullock seethed. "Now, you've stepped in it."

Louanne, finally free from Bullock's grasp and with tears streaming in great rivulets down her soft brown face, climbed to her feet, clutched the tattered remains of the front of her dress to her chest and ran swiftly through the parting crowd and toward the waiting buses.

Martin watched her go, and waited until she reached the parking lot before turning to face Bullock once more. The crowd of students flowed into the gap left in the wake of the fleeing black girl. The circle closed

around the two seniors. Bullock reached out and gave Martin a powerful shove.

"I'm going to stomp your ass," Bullock spat. "You stupid piss ant!"

Martin, miraculously, managed to keep his feet under him as he was
propelled backward by the force of Bullock's shove, but did not reply.

Bullock shoved him again, harder this time.

Still, Martin would not go down.

"It's a little tougher when you're not picking on a little girl," Martin
asked. "Isn't it, David?"

With an enraged bellow, Bullock fell upon Martin in a flurry of flailing fists.

Once again, all silence was shattered as the attending crowd roared
instantaneous approval. The battle was joined.

The metallic taste of blood filled Martin's mouth, hollow thumping
pounded in his eardrums, and bright points of light danced excitedly
along his field of vision, as blow upon blow pelted him. Still, he would
not yield. He could feel the force of Bullock's powerful punches, but
they were not accompanied by any discernable pain. Legs unsteady,
arms like leaden weight, muscles screaming for oxygen, Martin continued to swing his own bruised, torn fists and gasp for air.

The two young men pounded one another with impassioned fury.
Bullock, despite his clear advantage in size and experience, was finding
that he was not immune to the effects of the fight. Although he had
experienced the same effects many times in his young life, there was
something different about this time—something unnerving.
Accompanying the familiar—the difficulty in breathing and the weari-
ness of the arms and legs—was a crazed confusion as to how Hastings
could be putting up such resistance. Bullock had never before met his
match in a fistfight. He had certainly not expected Martin Hastings to
present any sort of a challenge, but a challenge he was—and a formidable challenge at that.

Clothes torn and covered in dirt, faces bloody and full of rage, the two combatants rebounded off one another in clouds of dust, trading fading blows. The other students continued to move in a frenzied, ever-expanding and contracting circle about the two flailing seniors. Among those who now formed the dynamic arena, some offered advice or encouragement and effectively drowned out the calls of the few who urged an end to the fighting. Most silently watched in alternate degrees of vicarious participation. Martin and the bully went at one another like equally matched dogs, neither willing to yield. The two would pound one another furiously, pause momentarily to suck in great gulps of air, then hammer at one another again. In retrospect, it was a classic struggle: the one fought to retain his reputation, the other, to right an injustice.

Neither of the two appeared to have the upper hand in the fray when, suddenly, much to everyone's surprise, Martin found an opening and locked his arm securely and forcefully around Bullock's neck. Martin slumped to his knees, pulling Bullock's massive frame with him. Simultaneously, Martin wrestled Bullock's large head level to his own chest and, with newfound strength and intensity, began pummeling the bully squarely and viciously in the face with jackhammer force.

After only a few seconds, all resistance from Bullock ceased. Martin continued to hammer away at the bloodied flesh. It became obvious to all that the fight was at an end—to all, that is, but Martin. It was blind rage that now propelled his fist with piston-like strokes. A primordial rage he had never known enveloped him. Nothing but the absolute destruction of his foe would satiate that rage.

Martin's blows took on a mechanical precision as he raised his fist repeatedly and brought it down with full force upon Bullock's unconscious, torn and bloodied face. Martin showed no signs of stopping. The limp Bullock could offer no resistance to the repeated blows and, finally, it fell on others to intervene. Goliath had fallen. It took five other boys to break Martin's grasp, separate the two and allow Bullock to slump to the ground in a crumpled heap.

Martin, still full of the adrenaline which had fueled his very first fist fight, stumbled several steps before sitting, abruptly, on the dirt which was the schoolyard's surface. Tingling arms resting shakily on his head, he gulped air deeply, and paused only to spit blood. The crowd, completely amazed at the fight's outcome, slowly and quietly dissolved. The onlookers melted away, turning their backs on victor and vanquished alike.

Kelly, who had viewed the entire affair from a distance, walked quietly towards Martin. Tears of relieved anxiety and newly found pride streaked her pretty face. Martin was her hero.

Across the way, the Bluebird buses hissed and pulled out of the parking lot. In the rear window of the third bus, another tear streaked, this time, brown face, smiled slightly, eyes fixed on Martin and hands pressed firmly against the smudged glass.

———————————————— ◆ ————————————————

A whale surfaced nearby breaking the surface with powerful ease and expelling a cloud of salty mist. The sound wrenched Martin Hastings' thoughts back to the present. Martin watched the magnificent creature as it paused momentarily upon the icy surface, filling its lungs for another dive. Barnacles, affixed in patches to the huge mammal's body, glistened in the gray stillness. The memories came again as the tail raised high in the air, and the years rolled back as the great beast slipped, silently, beneath the waves.

The morning following the fight in the schoolyard, Martin could hardly move. Stiffly, he rolled out of bed and plodded to the bathroom. The face that met him in the mirror above the sink was not very pretty. Both eyes were almost completely closed, swollen in powder blue puffiness. His lower lip was about three times its normal size and split in two places. He gingerly touched it and, immediately, wished he had not done so. He looked at his hands. Those two efficient battering rams bore the marks of the fight, knuckles raw and torn, fingers swollen. But, the chores would not wait. Grimacing from the soreness, Martin went about his usual morning activities around the farm.

When he had finally limped his way in from school on that eventful Friday afternoon, Martin's mother nearly panicked. Kelly, who had accompanied Martin home, quickly quelled Mrs. Hastings' hysteria with a brief run-through of the fight as well as the events leading up to it. Martin put forth his best efforts in attempting to calm his mother's fears as well. after explaining as best as she could, Kelly, discreetly, withdrew and made her way home, leaving Martin to fill in the details.

"Somebody had to do something, Mom." He assured her, "There's no telling what Bullock would have done to that girl. It seemed pretty obvious that nobody else was going to stand up to him."

"Why didn't any of the other blacks step in?" Julie asked. "Surely, it was their place to do something."

"I don't know." Martin answered, "I guess they were too scared…just like everybody else."

"Maybe so, Martin," Julie agreed, "but, I can't tell you that I approve of fighting for any reason. I don't want any son of mine to be a brawler. It's just not gentlemanly."

She read a glimmer of hurt in Martin's eyes and quickly added, "Still, I'm proud of you for taking up for that little girl. David Bullock's been a bully his whole life, and, it's about time someone gave him a good thrashing. I just wish someone else had done it instead of you."

Martin smiled a little, albeit painfully. "Well," he said, "he certainly got thrashed—no doubt."

"That'll be enough talk about it." Julie admonished, "Now, you go get cleaned up before your father gets in from the fields.

She watched as Martin limped to the bathroom. Inside, her mother's heart swelled with pride in a son who fearlessly stood up to mindless bigotry and abuse. The pride was tempered, however, with the realization of what could have happened to her son at the hands of David Bullock. Such thoughts vanished, however, at the sound of the back door screen opening. James was home.

It took Julie only a few minutes to fill James in on the afternoon's events. His comments had, more or less, echoed her own. "That Bullock boy has needed to be dropped a notch or two for years."

Later, in Martin's room, James had told his son, "I'm proud of you for what you done, boy. A man's gotta stand up for what's right, no matter who it harelips. But, you best be careful around town from here on out. Keep a watch to your backside."

Martin looked at his father, his eyes questioning.

"Bigots'" answered his father, "have friends."

Saturday was a new experience in soreness and pain to Martin as he struggled to do the farm work. Sunday morning was little better. Martin was not as raw as earlier, but he was a great deal sorer. His lip had returned to almost normal size and was not quite as tender. His eyes, though no longer so swollen, had turned from powder blue to a darker, almost purple, hue. He tried to beg off church, but his mother would not hear of it.

Martin was the center of attention in his Sunday School class. Kelly was there. He was glad of that. Her closeness seemed to ease his pain. Martin allowed her to answer all the questions issuing from their curious classmates. Her pride was not concealed. The teacher, Mr. Long, said that although the Bible called for men to turn the other cheek, sometimes, actions like Martin's were necessary. He was not, he emphasized, advocating violence, but was merely pointing out that the open confrontation of injustice and evil can lead to extreme situations. Always, he instructed, try the soft answer first. Above all, he cautioned, pray before acting. During the sermon, Martin reflected on the Sunday School teacher's words. Prayer had been the farthest thing from his mind when he had waded through the crowd and challenged David Bullock. He had been angry. How righteous, he wondered, staring at the hymnals in the back of the pew before him, was that anger. It was an answer that alluded him. How far would he have gone, he also wondered, if the others had not pulled him off Bullock? Would he have killed him? A sinking sensation settled over him. Yes. He would have killed him.

The black girl whom Martin had defended was not in school the following Monday. She would not return to Johnsons Gap High School. The experience had been far too painful for her. Her parents sent her to

live with relatives in Ohio. It would take many years before Louanne
Walters would feel any semblance of security around whites. David
Bullock was not at school, either. It would take two more days before his
pride would allow him to return. Martin, however, was present—both
eyes, now, mottled black and ringed in brown. At least the soreness was
gone. Martin wore the black eyes as badges of honor.

The reception by the other students had been mixed, but better than
Martin had expected. Some students congratulated him. Others
avoided him. But, none openly confronted him. After all, if he could do
what he did to David Bullock, no one dared chance angering him. The
Principal, to Martin's amazement, did not call him or David Bullock to
the office over the incident. Naturally, the Principal knew about the
fight. Everyone, by now, knew about the fight. It was for political reasons that the Principal and the teachers chose to ignore the event. It was
in everyone's best interest, they decided, not to make an issue of it. All
hoped that, by ignoring it, the associated problems would "go away."
Integration was proving tough enough without fanning any flames. The
fight must be allowed to go officially 'unnoticed'. Martin met Bullock in
the hall on Thursday morning. The two passed one another without
speaking. Bullock averted his eyes quickly when he saw Martin and
ambled away without pausing. Over the weeks, the incident, like the
Principal and teachers had hoped, faded away into just another memory. Life went on.

In Johnsons Gap, Martin's senior year flew by. He, along with the
other senior boys, found his thoughts, if not completely focused on,
certainly, directed toward events in the far east. In ever increasing numbers, American boys were being drafted into service and whisked away
to the far off jungles to fight and die. At first, they went by twos and
threes, here and there, but as the pit opened and the violence escalated,
the young men started disappearing from the nation's communities by
the dozens. Whisked off to basic training camps for several weeks of
conditioning and small amounts of weapons instruction, most were,

then , loaded on planes or other transports for destinations in a steamy, green hell. The draft, recently reinstituted, became a thing to be feared—a life sapping behemoth. There were, Martin heard, those American youths that were, rather than answering the call to arms, fleeing the country. These Martin considered cowards. If he were drafted, he assured himself and vowed to others, he would go. Duty still meant something in those innocent days. As it was, Martin never had to test his vow. Fate smiled upon him and he drew a particularly high number in the man-eating draft.

Eleven out of the thirty-nine young men in Martin's senior class were singled out by government generated lot and spirited away to the military. David Bullock, one of this number, was pushed through boot camp, assigned to an Infantry battalion, and shipped immediately to the I-Corps south of the Demilitarized Zone. Three weeks into his tour, Bullock stepped on a Bouncing Betty (a particularly nasty anti-personnel mine) while on patrol northwest of Da Nang. At less than six months after his graduation from high school, Bullock lay twitching in the elephant grass and steaming mud, beset by ants and biting flies and losing blood. The slick arrived within fifteen minutes. Bullock was in a China Beach triage within an hour. The overworked surgeons did the best they could under the circumstances, but the damage was, simply, too much. Both legs had to be amputated just below the pelvis.

With time, Bullock recovered, as much as possible, from his physical wounds, but, the psychological injury of the loss of his legs was something he could not overcome. David Bullock died, a broken and drained shell, in a stateside hospital bed six months after stepping on the mine. His will to live had left him in Vietnam, along with his shattered legs.

Graduation came quickly, followed by another long, hot summer of work around the farm. In the Fall, came the inevitable. James and Julie Hastings hugged their son's neck at the Greyhound station three towns over from Johnson's Gap, his worldly belongings neatly packed in a time worn suitcase. The grades he had worked so hard to maintain throughout his years of school had earned Martin an academic scholarship at the University of Alabama.

Word of David Bullock's death made it's way to Martin at college. An indefinable sadness accompanied the tidings. The fight in the schoolyard between he and Bullock now seemed a lifetime removed, yet, Martin still remembered it like it was yesterday. Thinking back on it, Martin reflected that none of the black students had ever shown any indication of gratitude to him for his stand on the part of one of their own. None had ever sought to befriend him. All had treated him with the same degree of mistrust with which they treated the other white students. Martin tried to convince himself that it did not matter—that he did not care—that he did not need their gratitude. He would have made the same stand, he was convinced, for anyone, regardless of their race. Then, Martin had taken a great deal of satisfaction in the fact that, following the fight, Bullock never again bullied anyone else at the school. Naturally, there had been other, isolated racial incidents at the high school, but neither Bullock nor Martin had been involved in any of those. At the University, Martin was no closer to defining his feelings towards blacks than he had been at the first day of his senior year in high school. Blacks were, he had decided, not something to be feared or distrusted. They were, simply, different.

The years rode the cold wind, whipping across the shadowed ice and slapping at Hastings' numbed and tortured mind. In the biting, crisp air, the memories played clearer, the colors were more vivid, and the sounds were almost audible above nature's moaning. With Hastings' physical being rooted firmly in the present upon the frosted deck— his spirit and his thoughts roamed free to a more innocent time of decades past.

The college years went quickly for Martin. His holidays and summers were spent on the farm at Johnsons Gap helping his father with the farming during the day and visiting with Kelly in the evenings. His time on campus was spent in study, as Martin applied himself and excelled in his subjects like he had done throughout high school. His was a regular name upon the Dean's List for four years. Martin graduated on time, first in his class of business administration.

Two weeks after returning home, Martin Hastings and Kelly Stevens were married. The ceremony was small, a collection of family and friends gathered in the Johnsons Gap United Methodist Church. All assembled had known that this day would come. The two had been a couple for as far back as most could remember. Seldom was one seen that the other was not close by. Marriage was the natural step in the ordered progression of their lives. The newlywed couple spent the summer lost in one another, cut off from the outside world, in a rented cottage in Panama City, Florida. By day, they had the sun, the sand, the waves; and endless walks on hot, white beaches. By night, they had the unceasing, cool gulf winds riding in low with the breaking surf under a star filled sky. Rain or shine, night or day, they had each other. The time flew, yet remained eternal.

Following the honeymoon, Martin set his eyes on the workforce with robust energy. Kelly enrolled in a law program in Birmingham, while Martin began his job search. With a keen eye towards the world market, it did not take him long to zero in on the military/industrial complex as a means to produce appreciable amounts of money. After substantial research into the field, Martin secured an interview with a potential employer. The interview went very well and, on the call back, he was hired. Through dogged determination, indefatigable drive and no small amount of good fortune, Hastings climbed rapidly through the ranks of the well known and influential defense consultant and arms supply corporation. Fate, it seems, provided some assistance by sparing him from being called for the escalating military activity in Vietnam. Perhaps his position with the consultant group had played a significant role in that bit of good fortune, as it was among the few top line groups which provided very expensive, behind-the-scenes hardware, support, and guidance to a significant number of military establishments worldwide. It was a period when it seemed the entire world was scrambling to purchase the latest and most sophisticated in military hardware, and the organization for which Hastings worked was perhaps the foremost broker for such commodities.

That Martin was, essentially, a merchant of death delivering tools designed to kill did not weigh on his consciousness. He viewed his occupation objectively and rationalized that with or without his participation, the arms market would thrive. Kelly, immersed in piles of reading material for her law classes seemed to have no reservations about Martin's occupation either. From the money building in their joint account, it was obvious that Martin was good at what he did. Early on in his career, he showed a natural ability for closing a sale, regardless of the customer. By his third year with the corporation, Martin had become the all-time leader in sales. This was no small accomplishment given that there were countless salesman on the corporation's payroll that had been with the firm for two decades or better. Martin's services and contributions to the company's till did not go unnoticed, nor did they pass without reward. The salary and commission he collected during his years with the defense contractor were more than sufficient to keep him comfortable for the remainder of his life, but Martin was not one who could be satisfied with being merely comfortable. He wanted, he demanded, more.

After Kelly passed the bar, she joined a law firm in Atlanta, Georgia. The move was convenient for Martin, who spent a great amount of time travelling. Atlanta was a common stop for him and millions of other airline travelers. Martin and Kelly bought a house near Lakewood Park and set about turning it into a home. Time spent together became a precious thing to the two professionals. As their careers progressed, that time grew smaller, but their relationship was such that the separation, rather than driving a wedge between them, seemed to intensify their love for one another. Laura Chastity Hastings, their first child, was conceived during one brief rendezvous between trips. It was a rainy October afternoon in 1971. Martin had just returned from Ankara, Turkey and Kelly had just won a major anti-trust suit. Martin had two days to burn and Kelly, the entire weekend. The two never left their house.

Nine months later, Martin was in Tunisia as Kelly sweated and groaned and gave birth to seven and half pounds of red-faced noise. Laura was two weeks old before Martin held her for the first time. A broad grin coursed across his face as he watched the tiny life in his hands grip his finger. Tears of joyful pride welled in Kelly's eyes as she sat looking at Martin and their child.

"God, she's beautiful." Martin said, sitting beside Kelly on the couch and hefting Laura before him, oblivious to the line of drool extending from her small mouth and falling in droplets upon his trousers. "She looks just like you."

"Oh, stop it." Kelly returned, "All babies look alike!" She reached over and wiped Laura's mouth with a tissue. "Besides, she has your eyes and nose."

Martin looked more closely at his new daughter, studying her. "No." He stated, after a moment, "I don't see it. I say she's a perfect Kelly Junior." The room fell to silence apart from the small cooing of the couple's new baby. Kelly and Martin snuggled close and returned Laura's inquisitive stares. Sleep came and all three snored quietly in a pile on the living room carpet. The family cat kept watch at the windowsill.

Chasing the sun from meridian to meridian, Hastings spent seven days out of ten travelling. Today in Lima, tomorrow in Sierra Leone, the arms market was a fluid dynamic filled with a kaleidoscope of consumers and each customer had to be allotted the requisite amount of personal attention. Hastings had the ability to read situations and seemed to instinctively adopt the correct track on approaching and selling his customers. The wares in his product list were, by no means inexpensive. There were always other contractors, rooms full of other contractors, offering less expensive products. Customers were, of course, often aware of these lower prices and were tempted to route their dollars in the direction of these other suppliers. Hastings, with a head full of numbers, test results, and polished smoke, would, soon, show these customers the error of their ways. Using the touted quality of his products and their relative superiority to any others on the market, Hastings would defend the price he offered while, at the same time, playing upon the deep rooted, ubiquitous pride of the customer. They were free, he told them, to spend their hard-earned money as they saw fit. And, he counseled, if they thought that buying inferior products would be fiscally responsible, then, he assured them, he could, certainly, understand. They could, he would say, always rest in the thought that, maybe, they might never actually have to use the weapons. Usually, though not always, the customer would be persuaded by Hastings' pitch and place all orders with him. His commissions grew.

The massaging of the client base, while inflating Hastings' income, also took the lion's share of his time, leaving less and less time for Kelly and Laura. Even though Kelly had given up her law practice to be a full time mother and housekeeper, the time the married pair could allot for themselves diminished to only a few days per month. Yet, no strain on the relationship developed. The two eased into and out of these intervals as if nothing could be more natural. Laura was, most likely, confused by the arrangement, but who was to say, for sure, what one so young can and can not comprehend?

As Laura continued to grow, however, it soon became obvious to Kelly that her daughter was showing evidence of discomfort with her father's almost constant absence. Laura, normally active when Martin was home, would, in his absence, sit idle for long periods staring absently into the television, the aquarium, or, even, the carpet. Her appetite began to fall precipitously and she grew more and more of an irritable persona. When, at the age of three, Kelly found Laura crying softly, late at night, for the fifth time, she decided it was time to approach Martin.

It was after nine o'clock before they got Laura to give up her fight against sleep. But, they finally managed and, leaving her quietly snoring in her bedroom, Martin and Kelly made their way, on tiptoes, downstairs. Over coffee, in the kitchen, Kelly brought up the subject of Martin's frequent trips and their apparent effects on Laura. Martin listened intently and weighed options. Young daughters require a father's attention. Martin recognized this and, consequently, it did not take him long to decide to cut back on his travels for Laura's benefit. Money, he reasoned, though important, was no substitute for family. If Laura needed to see him around the house more, then, Laura would see him around the house more. Kelly smiled broadly and embraced Martin when he told her his decision. When he mentioned that Laura needed a playmate, Kelly cocked her eyebrows at him, thought about it for an instant and, then, smiled again. Martin returned her smile, took her in his arms and carried her out of the kitchen, through the den and up the stairs to their bedroom. Rebecca Miriam Hastings, the couple's second child, was conceived that night beneath the tangled covers.

When Rebecca was born, nine months later, Hastings juggled his schedule to allow him to be at the hospital. He helped Laura color pages in her coloring book, while Kelly sweated, groaned and gave birth to their second baby. Later, Hastings cradled the new arrival, holding her low for Laura to get a good look at her new sister. Laura's lip curled upward on one side as she gingerly poked at the bundle in her father's hands. She was not at all sure she was ready for a sister. Martin shot Kelly a quick glance, smiling at Laura's facial expression. Kelly returned the smile. The new baby opened its eyes for an instant and stretched a bit, yawning and pulling a tiny hand across its face. Laura's frown turned to an instant smile. Maybe a sister would not be such a bad thing. "Can she sleep in my room?" Laura asked, without taking her eyes off her new sister. "Do I get to feed her?"

Martin and Kelly laughed. Their family was growing.

Fresh pain fought its way through the chill and into Hastings' thoughts—a familiar worm that seemed to bore deeper upon every recurrence, exposing new nerve endings, twisting and turning, tormenting. The worm brought with it the memory of Kelly's death.

It was a warm, humid July evening in Atlanta. Kelly had left Laura and Rebecca with a babysitter for a day of shopping. Leisurely cruising the aisles in the department stores, Kelly allowed the stress of parenthood to dissipate and fade to nothing. Even though, she seldom purchased much, her periodic 'shopping' trips were essential, Kelly told herself, to the maintenance of her sanity. The hours she spent in the malls recharged her internal batteries and equipped her for her eventual return to the monotony of motherhood.

On this evening, Kelly had spent more time than usual wandering about the stores. It had been a particularly taxing week. Laura had picked up a substantial dose of poison ivy, somewhere, and had required almost constant attention. Rebecca, left to her own devices, found plenty to get into. In the course of three days, she managed to pour fingernail polish on the living room couch and carpet, break a porcelain vase, stuff two rolls of toilet tissue into the toilet, and give the cat a haircut. Kelly could not move fast enough to soothe Laura's misery and keep up with Rebecca, too. The poison ivy rash had finally dried up and gone away and Kelly had seized the opportunity to get out of the house for a little unwinding. The hours passed without notice to her.

Most of the shops were closing, or were already closed, as Kelly made her way to the almost empty parking lot with her few bags of purchases in tow. Oblivious to her surroundings, she fished for her keys in her purse as she plodded along towards her car. She failed to notice as the two black teenagers fell in behind her. As she inserted the key into the station wagon's door, the youths moved in on her.

Confused surprise filled Kelly's thoughts as the rough hand closed across her nose and mouth. An arm enveloped her and pinned her arms to her sides. Another arm appeared and finished unlocking the car door. Kelly watched, in mounting fear as the third arm opened the door, reached inside and unlocked the back door. Then, she watched as a black teenager climbed into the back seat of her station wagon.

"Open your mouth, Lady," a black, insolent voice growled hot and close in her ear, "and you're dead!"

Terrified, Kelly did not struggle as she was roughly pushed into the back seat in the direction of the waiting black teenager. She was able to see the second black youth as she sat down in the seat. A look of animal lust was fixed upon his face as he settled in beside her, closing the car's door behind him. Shock had settled upon her and the unfolding events took on a surrealistic quality as if time stood still and raced at once. She was in denial in the face of incomprehensible reality. This could not be happening, she told herself, This kind of thing only happened to other people, not people like her.

When the hands began to tear at her clothing, Kelly snapped out of the temporary daze long enough to attempt a scream. A clenched fist slammed against her temple halted the scream before it could gain any volume. Two more such punches knocked her unconscious.

Twenty minutes later, rough hands pushed her partially clothed body out of the station wagon as the engine roared to life. With a squeal, the two attackers exited the parking lot in the stolen vehicle leaving Kelly bruised and battered, lying in a pool of her own blood on the heated asphalt. Robbed, brutally raped, and beaten, Kelly died on the emergency room table two hours later at a nearby medical center despite doctors frenzied attempts at saving her life. The station wagon was located, the next day, abandoned on the side of the road in Newnan, Georgia. Apart from an eyewitness at the mall indicating two black men had driven away in the vehicle, there were no fingerprints or other evidence providing any clues in the case. Kelly's assailants had escaped and would remain unidentified.

Martin was in Greece negotiating the sale of a dozen jet fighters when he received the devastating news of Kelly's death. Hastings listened in stoic, numbed silence as the details of her death knifed their way through the telephone's receiver. The room seemed to spin. Colors expanded and folded in upon themselves. Dark shadows pressed in. Hastings' world tottered and caved in upon him. The phone fell to the floor.

In the days to follow, the flight home, the reuniting with his daughters, and the funeral, there were no tears or any other discernible outward manifestation of Hastings' grief. His countenance offered no hint of the pain that was ripping his heart. His face presented no indication of the depth of his loss and was completely void of the consuming anger that was already festering within him. The surface was untouched, but the currents beneath were being irreversibly altered and, in the places formerly filled with warm love for his young wife, a vacuum developed. Slowly, a cold darkness crept into the hollow depths and took powerful grip. Where once was love, newly created hatred found foundation and began to build in Martin's soul. There would never be another Kelly Hastings and the world, he decided, was going to pay for taking her away from him.

---------------------------- ◆ ----------------------------

A breath of cold blew along the back of his neck beneath the multiple layers. It was a cold deeper than anything the arctic air could match. The hatred was still fresh, even after so many years. Watching the ice floes slip by in the semi-darkness, Hastings realized the hatred would always be there. There was no salve for the pain of Kelly's loss.

Somewhere in those first few days after Kelly's death, another force, apart from ambition, took over the drive of Martin Hastings—a powerful and irresistible force born of the hatred for the black men that had violated and murdered his wife—hatred for the black race as a whole—hatred for inept authority which had allowed Kelly's assailants to remain free—hatred for an American justice system that allowed such atrocities as his wife's brutal slaying to occur and go unpunished—hatred and contempt for the American Civil Rights system—hatred born of frustrated anger—hatred fueled by disgust with a system that had gone awry. In Hastings' eyes, day to day life in the United States had been polluted with years of inequities on behalf of the NAACP, the ACLU, and other minority watchdog groups. Such groups, in Hastings' estimation, existed only to punish and, ultimately, destroy the American working man in favor of an unworthy, leaching class of people—a race that shunned productive labor in favor of welfare handouts. Such a system, Hastings surmised, if allowed to continue unchallenged, would spell disaster and, likely, doom for the capitalist system. Stone piled upon stone, hate upon hate, until Hastings had constructed an impregnable wall around himself. Prejudice built within him to such an extent that all of the world's problems were, for him, attributable to the black race. Hastings determined to do something about the problem. In his wounded mind, plans took form and began to arrange themselves in patterns—plans that would culminate in the complete upheaval of the United States.

After less than fifteen years with the company that had given him his start, Hastings resigned his chair on the executive board, cleaned out his desk, and struck out to pursue a dark course. The money was not going to be a problem. From his very first pay check, Hastings had invested a considerable share of his earnings in a diverse range of concerns. In the process, he waxed quite adept in his ability to nurture his money to work for him. Often sacrificing needs of the present for the promise of the future, Hastings was not averse to assuming the inherent risks of tying up so much of his money in speculative investments. Naturally, some of the ventures had failed miserably. However, a substantial number of the others had not. Among the investments that did not fail were included far-sighted gambles that ultimately paid huge dividends. These investments included computer and video technologies, telecommunications, real estate development and new research and development in a number of disciplines. Others of his investments were smaller gambles that had not required overly large capital outlays, but had, in the end, yielded similarly enormous profits. These included the acquisition of controlling interest in certain now well known fast food chains, several lucrative export/import enterprises, advertising agencies, furniture producers and retail outlets, engineering firms, research institutes, and various others. Hastings rotated the profits, turning them back into the investment loop and, before long, his profit margin began to grow exponentially.

In the late 1960's and early 1970's, in a series of sales to some middle eastern powers, Hastings arranged with the principals to have payment made in the form of gold. The majority of these deals were concluded with the acquisition of stacks of 32.15-ounce gold bars bearing the stamp of Johnson Matthey. Hastings would, subsequently, personally see to the exchange of the gold on whatever market offered the most favorable rate. In these transactions, he would retain his commission in gold bars rather than converting them to dollars. In those days, the price of gold hovered around thirty dollars an ounce. When the price of gold began to spiral upward, Hastings paid close attention. When the price hit $780 U.S. dollars an ounce, he converted his entire stockpile. In a single day he had secured for himself a two thousand and six hundred percent return on his investment. Martin Hastings was fast becoming a wealthy man.

Attention to trends and details gave Hastings a Midas touch. By way of his uncanny ability to choose the right investments, he amassed his first million dollars by the time he was thirty. In the years to follow, he devoted more and more of his time to the pursuit of even greater fortune. His devotion and drive paid off and, as the years passed, his wealth vaulted from millions of dollars into a billion, then billions of dollars, until, finally, any discussion of the wealthiest people in North America would, invariably, include his name.

Retail outlets, grocery chains, service centers, and various and sundry other businesses bearing either Hastings' name or business logo were to be found in every state and several foreign countries. His influence spanned geographical borders and accompanied him wherever he traveled, at home or abroad. Intelligent, unpretentious, even humble, he was held in high regard by most everyone he met and by hundreds of thousands of those he had never met. His benevolence, philanthropy and outward concern for his fellow man were renown. Always quick to assist those in need, Hastings was generous in providing assistance when and where it was needed. Over the years, many charities had benefited handsomely from his wealth. No, money would not be a problem. Hastings campaign of revenge would not lack financing.

Vengeance, I have, on occasion, heard, is a dish best served cold. The benefits of such reasoning are, it would seem, plural. One allays personal suspicion that would naturally follow any immediate retaliation, while, at the same time, lulling the recipient of the vengeance into a sense of relative security. Proper retaliation, regardless of when it is applied, requires planning.

Hastings wrestled now, upon the ice-covered deck, with the implications of the dark reasoning that had pervaded his being following Kelly's death. Hatred was not a gentle bed partner. It took its toll without apology, draining the life from the hater in slow but sure chunks. For Hastings, his desire to eliminate all blacks in the United States had never been a question of right or wrong. His was a crusade of necessity—a crusade in which he believed as strongly then as he did now. But it was the participation of the others that now invaded his consciousness. Hastings tried to convince himself that he was not rationalizing, that he was not shifting blame or trying to spread the responsibility. The facts were, after all, clear. The others, many others, had joined Hastings' crusade without reservation and had pitched in with enthusiastic zeal. At no time had Hastings applied undue pressure to any of these. He had neither threatened nor bribed—had sought no leverage. It was of their own free will that they had joined forces with Hastings. Without reservation they had embraced his

dark quest. And they had been good people by any reasonable measure. Right or wrong? Good or evil? These were relative concepts and,
try though he might, Martin could not evaluate his actions within
such loosely structured parameters. What had happened, simply was.
There was no more to it than that, and no degree of delving for
answers would change what was and what is and what was to come.

The scale of retaliation Hastings had conceived required more than
just planning. Logistics dictated, from the very beginning, that he incor-
porate some help with his dark campaign. He could not, Hastings realized, single-handedly plan and execute even a small percentage of the
operations that were forming and reforming in the command post of
hatred established deep within his being. Apart from the obvious, hands
on, field deployment and physical manipulation of the destructive
tools, there were an endless number of arrangements to be made and
far too many details to be worked out.

Hastings spent days into weeks pondering the potential consequences of approaching the wrong person and seeing his plans evapo-
rate before fruition. Absolute secrecy was required. Any premature leak
of his intentions and any planning would be for nothing. Sleepless
nights were spent as Hastings tried to work through the dilemma. By
this stage in his life, Hastings found it increasingly difficult to confide
in, let alone, trust anyone. A career of wheeling and dealing across the
globe had given him a healthy respect for the deceptive practices of his
fellow man. In the end, following all of his turning the problem over
and over in his mind, Hastings concluded that he would have to force
himself to trust. There was, simply, no other way to accomplish his
goals. That decided, Hastings turned to the project of recruitment in his
usual, thorough, business-like manner.

Hastings decided that a board of three to five confidants would be
appointed who would serve as, what he termed, the Planning Group. It
would be their responsibility to orchestrate his plans, to engineer all the
pieces to fall into place at the proper time and in the proper order.

Hastings began reviewing backgrounds of prospective members less than a year after Kelly's murder. By the time another year had passed, he had made his selections. Four names had arisen out of the dozens that had initially been selected.

The first name was the easiest choice. It was that of Roger Delong, Hastings' closest, most trusted friend and one time fellow employee. Hastings had first met Delong in the French Congo, in 1970, while both were on assignment with the defense consultant firm for which they both worked. The two had hit it off immediately, drinking their off duty hours away and generally raising hell. Delong had been with the firm a full three years longer than Hastings. He had an easy-going nature that Hastings found refreshing in the shark infested waters of the defense consulting business. Hastings was also impressed with his newfound friend's intelligence. Over the years, the two of them had been assigned to several projects together and their friendship gradually grew. In 1972, when the consultant corporation underwent major realignment and great numbers of employees were laid off, Delong's name had been on the list of those to be let go. Hastings had intervened immediately with the board of directors, threatening to leave if Delong were cut loose. The Board instantly reconsidered its decision and in addition to retaining Delong had even given him a substantial raise. No price was too high for the Board to pay in order to hold on to so great an asset as Martin Hastings. Delong was taken off guard by the raise, having fully expected to be fired like so many of the others. "See," he told Hastings, with relief, "Good work is always rewarded. If you'd get off your sorry rear and do something, sometime, maybe you'd get a raise too!" Hastings had only smiled. Delong never knew about his friend's intervention on his behalf.

When Kelly was murdered, Delong had stayed by Hastings' side through it all, and had taken care of many of the necessary arrangements for the funeral, allowing Hastings to spend time with the grief stricken children. When the insurance company had balked on paying off on Kelly's life insurance policy, Delong had paid a personal visit to the firm's corporate headquarters. The money, all two million of it, was deposited in Hastings' Atlanta account the very same day. Hastings had inquired numerous times, since then, what Delong had said or done to effect the insurance company's change of heart, but Delong had never provided an answer. One report that reached Martin had it that Delong had beaten the immortal hell out of the insurance company's Director and had promised more of the same if the policy money was not immediately forthcoming. Delong remained mute on the issue.

Something Delong said in the tortured period following Kelly's funeral that stuck with Hastings and played heavily in his selecting Roger's name for the Planning Group. The graveside service had just concluded and people, darkly dressed, dispersed in groups and singles. Nearly all approached Hastings, offering condolence before turning to continue their lives elsewhere. Hastings received them all autonomously—a shell of a man going through the motions of shaking hands and returning hugs. His thoughts were centered several yards away from where he stood. Those thoughts hovered somewhere above the contents of a metal coffin at the bottom of a hole excavated that morning by a backhoe. Hastings' life was in that coffin and, soon, when the cemetery emptied, that life would be buried along with the cold flesh of the once living Kelly. Emptiness descended upon him with confident familiarity.

Roger Delong watched as Hastings shook hands and nodded to the people milling about. Delong could see that Hastings was merely going through the motions. He saw the far away stare in his friend's eyes. Delong cursed God, if there was a God, he was not so sure, anymore, for allowing things like this to happen to people like Martin. As the last of the people ambled slowly away, Delong moved to Hastings' side.

"What say we vamoose, compadre?" Delong suggested, laying his hand upon Hastings' shoulder.

Hastings smiled lightly, but did not turn his gaze from the dark hole in the earth—the shadowed slit beneath the striped canopy, surrounded by green indoor/outdoor carpeting, rows of folding chairs to one side, mounds of floral arrangements to the other. Something inside Hastings wanted to crawl in the hole, to embrace the cold death lurking there, and wait for the soil to be poured upon him. How easy it would be—a logical cathartic therapy for the pain that plagued him.

"Or," Delong continued after a short pause, "we could just stand right here all day. Your call."

Hastings' smile grew, albeit only slightly. He was glad, at least, that Roger was making an effort to keep his sense of humor alive. "No," he answered, finally taking his eyes off the grave and turning to his friend. "I think I'm in need of a beer or two."

"SAH!" Delong answered in his best British Sergeant-major impression, simultaneously snapping his heels together and saluting, palm outward, fingernails resting on his right eyebrow. "Ale it is, then. Right away. SAH!"

The two turned their backs to Kelly's final place of rest and, with hands in pockets, made their way to the waiting car. It was then that Delong had said the words that took hold in Hastings memory. In the distance, three black funeral home laborers were waiting to descend upon Kelly's gravesite and hastily shovel the excavated soil back into place. The three men were leaning on shovels and laughing carelessly at something. As Delong watched the black men, his face became suddenly, uncharacteristically, red. Before thinking, Delong had mumbled angrily, "Damn Niggers! They should all be rounded up and shot!"

The words found immediate reception in Hastings' conscience. The suddenness of Delong's anger, however, had surprised him. He glanced at his friend, pondering. Delong, seeing the strange look on Hastings' face, had quickly recovered his equanimity and attempted to apologize.

"Oh!" Delong said, "Hey, I'm sorry, Martin. It's just that…"

"No, Roger." Hastings interrupted, "You don't have to explain any-thing. It's O.K. It couldn't be any secret that I feel the same way. There's nothing to apologize about." Neither of the two men had ever mentioned the incident again. Rebecca and Laura, Hastings' daugh-ters, already in the car with Kelly's mother, had, thankfully, not heard the exchange.

Two years to the day after Kelly's murder, Hastings approached Delong with the strange proposal. It was a Saturday and the two men were on the front nine of the consultant corporation's exclusive club in Palm Springs, Florida. Delong, a miserable golfer, had just double bogeyed the par three, number seven hole to bring his score to an even forty.

"Maybe if you opened your eyes," Hastings offered, "you'd do a little better there, Roj!"

"Yeah, Sure!" Delong replied, "Rub it in! What you don't know is that I purposely do bad just to keep from embarrassing you."

"Well," Hastings returned, "thanks. I appreciate that about you, Roj!"

The two had laughed lightly and boarded the cart for the short ride to the number eight tee. On the way, Hastings laid the entire plan on the line. Delong, incredulous, listened open-mouthed, but with-out comment, unsure what to think about the proposal. The two allowed another group to play through as they continued to sit in the cart and talk.

When Hastings completed his spiel, Delong had looked at his friend long and hard, his mind racing in a dozen different directions. Finally he had said, "You're serious aren't you, Martin?"

"Damn straight, I'm serious, Roger!" came the immediate reply. "I've never been more serious about anything in my life. I'm sick and tired of putting up with blacks and the strain they put on hard working people like us. If somebody doesn't do something, and quick, the bastards will drive this country into the ground and you know it!"

Delong considered his friend's words for another silent moment. "But, it' all so crazy, Martin!"

"Yes," agreed Hastings, "It is crazy. Downright maniacal, but it has to be done. It just has to and that's all there is to it. You know me. You know that I'm not about to go off on anything half-cocked. I've thought long and hard about this and I'm determined to go through with it. I'm not about to turn back now." He looked his friend fully in the eyes, "I'd like to think that you're with me, Roger."

Somebody let fly an expletive as they sliced their drive far out into the water hazard. Delong briefly looked in the red-faced golfer's direction and smiled. He was very familiar with the stretch of water, having lost many a ball in its depths. Finally, turning fully to face the anxious Hastings, he gave his answer. "Yes, Martin. I'll do it." He slapped his friend's leg for emphasis, "Hell, whatever you want me to do. I'll do it. It's crazy as all get out, but I'll do it." He extended his hand across the cart's seat and the two exchanged a firm grip. "But first," he continued, "I think I'll finish waxing your butt all over this course!"

Hastings laughed heartily, a relieved laugh, got out of the cart and pulled a 3 wood from his bag. "That'll be the day, you no golfin' reprobate!"

The second name on Hastings' list was that of another of his close friends. Lee Moore was a full partner for life in a California based law firm which had branch offices worldwide. The firm was established in 1946 by Moore's grandfather, Justin Neighbors Moore, a far sighted entrepreneur who saw an expanding world arising from a terrible war—expansion rich in opportunity for any who would reach out for it. Lee's grandfather had reached with both arms.

In December of 1941, Justin Moore was sitting at bench on New York State's Circuit Court. With his position in the community and his age, 52, he was not expected to answer his country's call to arms, but answer he did. He need not have bothered. Each of his attempts to enlist or be commissioned were denied, despite every effort on his part. For a man who was accustomed to having things his own way, the reluctance on the part of the government baffled him. One accumulates many strings over a period of eleven years as a judge, many unspoken 'IOUs'. Justin Moore had accumulated many such strings and, before his attempts at gaining admission to the war effort were over, he had pulled them all, and pulled hard. Still, he faced a stone wall. It would be many years later, twenty three, before he discovered, quite accidentally, the real reason for which he was denied opportunity to join the military forces preparing to go to Europe. By then, it was too late to matter, and the obvious mob connection was, although unsettling, committed to the past and not dwelt upon. It seems that, even though he was not on their payroll, some of Moore's decisions on the bench were of particular favorable importance to a, then, very powerful faction of the underworld crime organization. The illicit organization had no intentions of allowing such a judge to slip through their fingers. For two months, by means of political favors, cash payoffs, persuasion and outright threats, the organization managed to thwart Moore's every attempt at entering the military. In the end, however, the judge's tenacity and singleness of purpose touched a particularly high member in the clandestine organization and the campaign to keep Justin Moore in the states was terminated. The judge was, it was decided, by agreement, to be allowed to participate after all, but strictly in a non-combative role. His liberal ideas were too important to be allowed to die in some trench in Europe or some remote beach in the Pacific. Calls were made, and orders were issued.

In June of 1941, the U.S. War Department, ostensibly tiring of his repeated entreaties, offered Judge Moore a position in the U.S. foreign diplomatic corps. Moore jumped on the offer with both feet. The organized crime figures that had thwarted Justin Moore's previous efforts at joining the military neglected to attempt to block this move. It proved to be bad judgment on the part of the mobsters. Judge Justin Moore would never return to the bench.

Life in the diplomatic corps was, for Justin Moore, in a word, revealing. Following a short period of training in the U.S., he was shuffled to England for some on-the-job training. His age, his experience, his intelligence, and his ability to understand the big picture quickly earmarked Moore for some of the more significant assignments of the day. The assignments were many. Fortress Europe was a hornet's nest. The German Army held the continent and was proving to be everything it was purported to be—an unbending and deadly efficient military machine. The Japanese were, seemingly, everywhere in the Pacific and pressing. The future was precariously balanced. Moore studied the reports and the maps and was disturbed. Brave men were dying and he was on the sidelines, out of harm's way. The arrangement did not agree with him, but there was nothing he could do about it. His assignments, he was told, were equally important, if not more so, as those of the combat infantryman or the fighter pilot were. Diplomacy and politics, must, it was the generally accepted theory, gain the victory before the war could end. The mistakes of 1918 could not be repeated. The argument was not very soothing to the frustrated judge.

While other Americans fought and died, Moore spent the war shuttling around the globe meeting with representatives of virtually every nation on earth, which included some very secret meetings with representatives from Germany, Italy, and Japan. Traveling the world and seeing the war's impact on soil and man was an awesome experience for Moore. In the many meetings, with their long hours of exposure to and interaction with the various representatives, Moore witnessed a stark and revealing demonstration of human nature and drive. The revelations developed in him a renewed respect for and faith in the indomitable human will. His contacts grew with each mission. Friendships were established, and light began to dawn in his reasoning. Invisible networks, secure but non-binding, were seeded and fertilized. Frameworks were riveted in place.

It was not until the summer of '44 that the tenseness began to give way to optimism. Optimism continued to grow, its light flickering only slightly for a short period in December of '44 when the German threw fresh troops into the winter whiteness of the Ardennes. The Allies met the new challenge and, eventually, drove the advance backward over its own tracks. Moore's schedule calendar filled noticeably. When the Russians crossed the Vistula, talks at the various meetings shifted dramatically, transforming from open, over the table, group talks to quiet, splintered discussions in the corridors. Moore, perhaps better than anyone else, recognized what was going on in these hushed meetings in the days before Berlin fell. The world, the 56-year-old judge could clearly see, was being sectioned and the land was up for bids. The bidding began long before Enola Gay rolled off the tarmac and headed towards the Japanese mainland. Europe would have to be rebuilt. The world would have to be rebuilt. The cost would be staggering.

Moore, seeing the writing on the wall, took full advantage of his unique position in history to nurture and, sometimes, exploit the valuable contacts that he had developed over the years of the war. In the process, he built the foundations of a small empire. When the war in Europe ended, Moore returned to the States with head and notebooks full of ideas, plans, and rough drafts of a dozen already cooking, and several done, business deals. He did not stop in New York, but flew directly to, after a short stay in Washington for obligatory debriefing, Los Angeles where he established a law office. Six months later, the firm opened its first branch office in the U.S., in New York City. Four others had already been established. One in Tokyo—the first, and the remainder in Berlin, Geneva and Sydney. By the time Lee Moore joined his grandfather's firm, there were branch offices in 127 cities, worldwide.

Douglas Winton Moore, Lee Moore's father and Justin Moore's son, had also been a lawyer. He had graduated from law school third in the class of 1935. The Depression was not a hospitable place for attorneys in those days. Employment was not easy to find for anyone. Justin Moore told Douglas that he could arrange a job for him with no problem, but Douglas had declined the offer and, instead, sought and received a commission in the U.S. Army Air Corps in the fall of 1935. In 1939, he met and married Lee's mother, Karen. Lee, their only child was born two years later in the summer of 1941. Douglas was stationed half way across the world and was not present for his son's birth.

Karen Moore, no longer able to stand the strain of separation had appealed to Lee's grandfather. The judge, delighted to help his daughter-in-law, made a single phone call, and, the next day, Karen left her 5-month-old infant with her parents and flew to Hickam Field in Hawaii for a surprise visit with Douglas for the holidays. It was the special perk of being married to an officer who had a rich and influential father.

The joy of being reunited with his wife easily offset any anger Douglas may have had with Karen for calling on his father for assistance. Forgetting the world around them, the two spent the days and nights rediscovering one another. The happy couple were on their way to another sun filled day at the beach when the first of the Japanese planes began to pass overhead on a warm December morning. Death came quickly for both. Karen Moore would never hold her infant son again. Douglas Winton Moore had never held him.

Hastings had first met Lee Moore in Sacramento, California, in the late 1960's. It was a business meeting. Hastings had been instructed to meet with representatives for a group of particularly sensitive buyers. The weapons order was expected to be, the Board had emphasized, 'large'. So large, in fact, that the Board had recalled Hastings from another assignment to handle this one exclusively. In the end, the sale had not been so large after all—eight fighters, five helicopters, 2,600 small arms and some 2 million odd rounds of assorted ammunition. What had impressed Hastings about the meeting was Lee Moore. The young man led a team of four other, older gentlemen. Lee carried himself with poise and apparent self-assurance throughout the negotiations. He was good, Hastings noted. So good, in fact, that Hastings was unable to secure the degree of profit margin he had intended and to which he was accustomed.

In Lee, Hastings saw a bit of himself. After the meeting, Hastings invited the young lawyer for drinks and dinner.

"I must tell you, up front," Moore had warned Hastings at the offer, "that I'm not about to reveal the identity of my client no matter how much butter you throw my way."

Hastings had laughed heartily. He did not bother to tell the idealistic attorney that he already knew the identity of Lee's client. He had been able to spot government sub-committee jobs for years. Which committee, he did not know, but names and faces weren't important. He knew, from experience, that the money would be paid from black bag funds and the goods would be delivered. Then, the arms would simply disappear in the bottomless morass south of Texas.

The two men had eaten a modest meal, taken in a movie, and, then, hit the bars. As the rest of the city went to sleep, Hastings' and Moore's personalities clicked and the scotch flowed. They were thrown out of their third bar at 4:30 the following morning and had, only then, decided to call it a night. Hastings boarded a plane back to Atlanta and Moore made his way back to L.A. The friendship they established that night took root and, over the years flourished and grew.

With understandable nervousness, Hastings flew to L.A. and pitched his strange idea to Moore. Like Roger Delong, Moore was, at first, incredulous and, then, surprised at Hastings' proposal. When Hastings assured him of his sincerity in the matter, Moore had been more than a little apprehensive. Living in Los Angeles, the problems presented by an unruly black population were clearly evident to Moore. As a lawyer, he could also see the law's perceptible bias towards blacks. Despite this, however, he could not see the need for such drastic measures as those proposed by Hastings. Surely, there was another way, he had questioned Hastings.

The answer had been a quick and final, "No." There was no other way. The numbers, Hastings told him, would only increase. The drag on society would also continue to increase. It was a weight that the system could not bear. In time, Hastings assured Moore, the load would be too great, the black numbers would be too large—the country would tumble. The entire world's economy would suffer. The only solution was the elimination of the blacks. Sure, Hastings agreed, it was a harsh proposal, a dark undertaking, but one that was, without any doubt, necessary. It took the better part of the day and an even greater part of the bar's scotch supply before Moore was convinced. Yes, Moore finally agreed, the blacks have to go. He would do all he could, he told Hastings, to assist in the eradication, and damn the consequences.

Hastings now had two compatriots—men who could be counted upon to maintain silence while, at the same time, working to devise an intricate plan of genocide. Hastings turned his attention to a third candidate.

Senator Duncan Fowler of Massachusetts was only a city councilman when Hastings first heard of him. Fowler's name had been prominent in a series of articles regarding the political unrest over the broiling Vietnam issue. Fowler, it seemed, had drawn national attention to himself by withstanding the opposition, the majority opposition, to the face and calling for the continued support of the war effort. The city councilman had been firm in his unpopular, minority view. Hastings had predicted at the time, to none but himself, that if the councilman stuck with it, he would rise the political ladder quickly. The prediction proved correct. The notoriety of the councilman's unpopular stance propelled Fowler into the U.S. Senate in 1970. Even those who disagreed with his position on the war admired him for his steadfastness and had shown their admiration at the polls.

Hastings approached Fowler at a fund raising dinner. The Fowler name had deep root in New England, and carried with it respect. It also carried money. Duncan Fowler was well endowed with 'old money'. In a portion of the country known for its liberal political views, Fowler had remained steadfastly conservative. That the man had, in spite of his conservative label, consistently won the vote of the traditionally liberal masses in his bid for public office was a testament to his worth as a political force. Hastings knew that such a force would be helpful, if not absolutely necessary. Hastings had estimated correctly when he anticipated that Duncan Fowler would achieve high political office. He had also estimated correctly when he discerned that Fowler could be, not only trusted, but also relied on for assistance in carrying out Hastings' particularly ambitious, though dark, plan.

In addition to Duncan Fowler's character and abilities, there was another, more significant element which had attracted Hastings' attention. Fowler's son and daughter-in-law had been brutally killed by a black man on the streets of Boston. The black assailant had approached the young couple as they exited a downtown restaurant and demanded money. Fowler's son had complied with the man's demands, handing over his wallet and watch. Unsatisfied, the black man had leveled his pistol at Fowler's son's head and pulled the trigger. Before the limp body had fallen to the pavement, the gun had been turned on the young wife with equally fatal results.

A crowd of onlookers had viewed the event from the restaurant and were able to describe the assailant to the police. The man was apprehended later that night, less than three blocks from the scene of the murder. In the event, the police managed to effectively bumble the arrest, failing to read the suspect his Miranda rights. The murderer had walked out of the courtroom on a technicality, a free man.

The senseless death of his only son had rocked Senator Fowler to the core and left him with a deep-seated resentment towards blacks. The failure of the authorities to impose justice on the murderer had only poured salt on the open wound. If the established law could not deal with man, Fowler decided, then, he would. He vowed to take revenge. He waited four months—waited and planned. It was a simple matter to locate his son's killer. The man had not even left the neighborhood after his acquittal. Fowler rented the car using an alias and wearing a hairpiece, a false beard and mustache. He made the 150-mile drive to Boston in less than two hours. He parked the car three blocks from the spot where he found the black man lounging against the side of a building. The disguised Senator approached his son's killer purposefully, hand tightly gripping the .44 magnum revolver in his overcoat. A handful of other pedestrians passed on the dimly lit sidewalk paying little attention to the bearded white man.

"Give me your money!" Fowler demanded, stopping directly in front of his son's killer.

The black man looked at the stranger in disbelief, rolling his eyes and remaining resting against the worn bricks. "You got to be trippin', Home. I ain't got no money. Get out of my face with that noise."

The Senator pulled the revolver from his pocket and pointed it directly at the black man's face. "This is for my son."

The black man's eyes grew wide with fear. He moved to make a run, but was too slow. Fowler's gloved finger closed on the trigger and an explosion of sound boomed along the street. The heavy slug ripped into and through the black man's head, killing him instantly. His body slumped to the filthy sidewalk. Elsewhere on the street, people scurried for cover. Fowler spat on the lifeless form before him, dropped the revolver alongside the body, and casually strolled away.

The drive back to the rental agency took a little over three hours as Fowler obeyed all the speed zones, not wishing to be pulled over for a traffic infraction. After returning the car, Fowler took a cab to the airport where he removed his disguise. He placed the overcoat, the hairpiece, the beard, mustache, and gloves into a carry-on bag and bought a ticket to Washington, again using an alias. Safely back in his apartment inside the beltway, the Senator had laid back on the bed and reflected on the night's activities. The satisfaction of having killed his son's killer was not what the Senator had expected. Revenge had not assuaged the pain of his loss. Over the next few days, the Senator disposed of the various elements of his disguise separately and returned to business as normal. Back in Boston, the homicide on the sidewalk would remain unsolved. The gun was untraceable, there were no fingerprints, and, typically, no one had seen anything.

Fowler accepted Martin Hastings invitation to step outside for a talk at the fund raising dinner. Once safely out of earshot of others, Hastings had presented the proposition like he would any normal business deal.

The Senator, unsure he had heard correctly, asked Hastings to repeat himself.

"Sure." Hastings responded. "I know it sounds unreal. But, surely you must understand the risk I'm taking confiding in you?"

The Senator nodded his head affirmatively.

"The time has come," Hastings continued, speaking very softly, "to do something about this country's race problem. I propose to take the bull by the horns and initiate a program to take care of that problem on my own. It seems painfully obvious that no one else is going to do it."

The Senator nodded again. "Go on."

"In short," Hastings stated, "It's not something I can do without help. I propose forming a group of closely allied confederates to hammer out the logistics for a campaign of eliminating the black threat to our country. I want you in that group, Senator."

Fowler took another drink of his scotch and looked long and hard into the eyes of Hastings, studying him. The man was dead serious, he decided, after a moment.

Hastings returned the Senator's probing stare, wondering what must be going on in the seasoned statesman's mind. He prayed he had not made a mistake approaching Fowler.

A minute passed in silence. Then, another. Sounds of conversation and laughter filtered from the dinner hall. An airliner passed by, low overhead. Finally, the Senator smiled broadly. A flood of relief washed over Hastings, even before the Senator answered.

"Yes! I'll do it" The Senator reached out and grasped Hastings' hand, pumping enthusiastically. "Hell, yes. I'll do it. It's about time that someone did something!"

"Outstanding." Hastings replied, returning the Senator's beaming smile. "Now, I suggest we get back inside. I'll contact you tomorrow and we can begin discussing the details."

———————————— ◆ ————————————

A deckhand passed alongside, wrenching Hastings' mind to the present. He watched, absently, as the sailor eased his way forward along the surface of ice that was the deck. Even with the sea's surface calm, the boat continued to roll, gently, from side to side. The boat's movement made keeping one's balance on the ice more than a little tricky. Under alternate circumstances, watching the man slip and slide along would have made Hastings smile. Now, he doubted if he would ever smile again.

In September of 1980, the four members of the Planning Group met for the first time in a hunting lodge in Wyoming. The lodge, owned by Hastings, was miles from anything approaching civilization. Apart from the small staff, a cook and two caretakers, Hastings, Delong, Moore, and Fowler had the lodge completely to themselves. Careful precautions were taken by each man to ensure that their presence at the lodge was kept secret. Secrecy would, throughout the group's existence, remain the first priority.

The group spent the first day like any other group, socializing and catching up on the latest news and gossip. They went through the motions of going on a hunt, but none of them so much as chambered a round in their weapons. Flasks of bourbon were tilted with regularity as the stress of day to day existence faded in slow progression. It was not until after the evening meal that the four men turned to talk of the business at hand. The staff was dismissed to retire to their individual cottages and the Planning Group settled into the huge den. The men initiated their activities with a purposeful fervor. For the first time since before Kelly's murder, a sense of optimism found its way into Hastings' troubled mind. Under the blank stares of the glass-eyed taxidermist mounts surrounding them, the men began hammering out, with precision and interminable discussion, the preliminary details of a dark plan. Their consciences steeled against the consequences of their actions, the four men approached the task with cold, businesslike seriousness. The work continued late into the night.

For two more days, the group worked at formulating the rudimentary shell of a plan—the abc's of destroying a minority population. Instruments of mass destruction were proposed with no more emotion than one would exhibit talking about a favorite recipe. Estimated kill ratios were discussed with all the feeling present in a debate over air fresheners. When the weekend ended and the men departed to return to their normal lives, the structure of a workable plan was in place. Over the years to follow, the plan would grow by bits and pieces. The group would meet several times a year at a number of different locales. All of the meetings were, as much as possible, scheduled to avoid any possible link between the four men. As time progressed, less meetings were required as each man took a specific portion of the plan and assumed control over the logistics of that particular section. With the financial backing of Hastings, budget considerations were never factored into the planning. The group's members faced no limits in their acquisition of resources, apart from the need for secrecy. It became obvious to all the members, very early on, that the plan on which they worked was going to be a very workable plan—a very effective plan. The blacks were in for some serious hardship.

Kabul, Afghanistan, in April of 1982, was, understandably, not the safest place on the planet. The occupying Soviets and their puppet government, finding themselves in a particularly troublesome can of worms, had assumed a shoot first, ask questions later philosophy. It had become altogether obvious that the Mujahadeen were determined in their efforts to rid their homeland of the communist invaders. Their resolve was apparent on every front, as they continued to prove themselves as an effective force against the technologically superior, Soviet occupation army. Consequently, the rebel fighters were beginning to receive more and more assistance from sympathetic sources. Such assistance came in the form of arms, supplies and money.

Martin Hastings had been supplying the Mujahadeen with arms for three years. He had supplied them at a time when it was both unpopular and exceedingly dangerous to do so. With the recent fresh infusion of funds, the mountain rebels were calling for increased weapons shipments. Naturally, they turned first to Hastings, a trusted ally that had stood beside them when the rest of the world had turned its back.

The new weapons orders had prompted the clandestine visit of Roger Delong to the dangerous country. His mission was not one of hammering out the details of the, what promised to be, large shipment of weapons and ammunition, but was, rather, one of diplomacy. It was an assignment that Hastings could trust to no one else. Delong had accepted the task without the slightest hesitation or argument. Hastings knew, though Delong denied the charge, that Delong thrived on the intrigue. More than once, Hastings had called him "My own James Bond." Though Delong had denied the title and its implications consistently, he did enjoy and look forward to the cloak and dagger type assignments. Despite his advancing years, he relished the adrenaline rushes provided by living on the edge. To be in Kabul in 1982, negotiating an arms shipment with the opposition, directly under the noses of the Soviets, was definitely living life on the edge.

Delong and his interpreters had arrived the previous evening, complete with dusty beards and desert nomad garb, in the company of a small trade route caravan. Delong had joined the collection of travelers, camels and goats just across the Iranian border. One interpreter had accompanied him on his journey from Saudi Arabia to Iran. The second was already with the caravan. Delong sensed, at the first close up view of the caravan, that the next succession of days would be more of a trial than an exciting trek through enemy territory. The smell of the encamped assembly was powerful and not at all pleasant. Delong had dug in his pocket, located the tube of Chap Stick and rubbed the balm on his nostrils and mustache in attempts to break the smell. It had little effect. Curious eyes studied him from all over the camp.

Wars have come and wars have gone, but, throughout history, the caravan routes of the middle and far east have continued to be traveled. They are one of the few things on Earth that are genuinely timeless. For Delong, it was his first such caravan. It was an experience he would not soon forget. The trip had taken a full twenty days and nights and, along the way, Delong had learned much, often the hard way, of the exotic customs of the nomadic traders. In addition, he had developed a new respect for their vehicle of travel, the camel. After so many hours in the saddle, Delong was certain that he would never be able to walk straight again. The bite on his leg he had received early on the trek was taking its own sweet time healing. He would never again kick another camel, no matter how stubborn it might be. Once was enough. The camel had refused to stand as the group was breaking camp. Urge and curse though he might, Delong could not make the camel budge. Finally, out of frustration, Delong had delivered a disgusted kick to the camel's side. His nomadic travel companions had gotten a hearty laugh at Delong's expense when the obstinate beast had whirled suddenly upon him and bit a plug out of his thigh. Immediately after the incident, Delong had hopped about on one foot, clutching the offended, bleeding leg with both arms and voicing expletives he had not used for years, some he had never used, and many which he created on the spot. Through it all, the camel had merely stared ahead with its large moist eyes, and chewed casually on its cud. Or, as Delong thought, 'on the meat he removed from my leg'!

Delong sat now, cross-legged, in the teashop, flanked on either side by his interpreters, awaiting the arrival of the Mujahadeen contacts. The meeting was to be no more than a formality. Most of the details of the weapons deal had been worked out through a series of late night encounters beneath the desert sky along the route, as rebels had, by design, made contact with Delong's traveling group. This meeting was the diplomatic portion, a face to face exchange between the heavies. Hastings had sent his number two man. The Mujahadeen would also be sending someone of like power. In a region of the globe where important deals were more covenants than contracts, the meeting was mandatory ceremony.

That the meeting was risky at best, dangerous beyond any doubt, did not seem to be the smallest concern to these people, Delong decided. He was not sure if he would ever understand them. The air was thick with a mixture of both indefinable and distinct odors. The smell of unwashed bodies Delong had gotten used to over the previous weeks. The other smells—tobacco, spices, food cooking, animals, and other not so distinct odors—would take a little longer for his senses to adjust to. Despite the conditions of the day, the marketplace was alive with activity as traders plied their ancient art of buying, selling, and haggling. Delong delighted in watching the various vendors and buyers negotiating deals with exaggerated moans and gestures. It was, he had learned, all part of an age-old game. One did not simply approach a booth and purchase something for the set price. Such a breach in protocol would be an act of ignorant and inexcusable rudeness, a supreme insult to the vendor. Prices in the market place were, by unspoken rule, strictly negotiable. A sale often consumed much time as the buyer and seller drank strong tea, smoked stronger cigarettes, and bantered amounts back and forth, the one far too high, the other much too low. Invariably, the price would settle somewhere in the median and the sale would be consummated. Both the buyer and seller would feign that they had received the short end of the bargain, yet, both would be satisfied, or the sale would never have taken place.

How different these people were, Delong thought, as he sipped at his tea and studied the faces of those around him; so simple, so basic, and yet so complex. Befriend one and you have secured a friend for life. Cross one and you stand the chance of dying quickly, or, if the offense is great enough, very slowly. In a strange way, he envied them their existence. Free from the trappings of the western world, they could pack all of their earthly belongings in a matter of minutes and move on to more adventures. Mortgage payments, insurance payments, and keeping up with the Jones' were completely foreign in this ancient land. The U.S. could learn much, Delong decided, from these rugged individuals.

After what seemed an eternity to Delong, the rebel contingent arrived and took their places around the table. A curtain was drawn and guards were posted. The meeting commenced. Delong studied the faces of the three rebels before him. Each bore the scars of life in the mountains. Each, he was sure, was a hardened killer, but not like the death row killers of the U.S. No, these were noble killers, soldiers fighting for a cause that they held dear above any other—freedom. Delong allowed his interpreters to carry on the negotiations, speaking only when asked a question directly. The interpreters had been in Hastings' employ for many years and were familiar with the weapons sales operations sufficiently enough to handle the bulk of the discussions. Delong was aware that his presence was merely symbolic, but it did not take away from his sense of accomplishment or importance. He admired the rebels. Theirs was a difficult struggle against impossible odds, yet, somehow, they were winning. It was their indomitable spirit, Delong was convinced, that provided the advantage. The fire in their eyes clearly proclaimed that they would face death before they would accept defeat. With such singleness of purpose, Delong assured himself, the ragged bands led by these hardened men could not lose.

The meeting was over almost as quickly as it had begun. The curtain was drawn and the band of rebels melded into the marketplace crowds. The order had been placed. A price had been agreed upon and a delivery date and place had been set. There were no written contracts, no hand shakes, no lawyers. In this land, a man's word was his contract, and legalese was neither necessary nor wanted. This is the way to do business, Delong thought. After a space of a few minutes, Delong and his interpreters also exited the tea shop. The trio wandered about the various stalls in the marketplace, playing the role of interested buyers.

Later in the afternoon, near one of the gold booths, a passing man bumped roughly into Delong, almost knocking him off his feet. Instantly, one of the interpreters lashed out with, what Delong was sure, a barrage of damning expletives, condemning the offending man to an eternity of writhing, miserable agony for his mindless clumsiness. The man bowed deeply several times and apologized profusely.

"Please to be checking your valuables, Mr. Delong, Sir." The second interpreter instructed Delong, simultaneously unsheathing his large curved knife and holding it to the offending man's throat.

Delong felt about in his robes. Nothing was missing.

Satisfied that the incident had been an accident and not an attempt at pick-pocketing, the stranger was allowed to depart. Delong and his companions continued their browsing as if nothing had happened. The charade was a little harder for Delong to carry off, he being unable to shake the idea of what would have happened had the stranger actually stolen something from him. That the man would have been killed was without question. Justice was swift in this corner of the world.

Delong found the note, later that evening, when the trio had returned to their nomadic camp on the outskirts of the city. It was in the inner pocket of his outer robe. It was hand written and in English. The man who had bumped into him in the marketplace, Delong quickly deduced, had to have placed it there. There was no other explanation.

"Mr. Delong. I need assistance", it read, "Meet me at the well outside your camp, tonight. 10 p.m. Alone, or not, it's up to you." It was signed, "Desperate friend."

Delong looked at his watch. 8:20. His curiosity began to peak. A new surge of adrenaline coursed through his veins. Questions rebounded through his mind. It could be a trap. Or, if it wasn't a trap, who could have known that he was in Kabul. The note had been in English and addressed to him directly. It had to be a trap. The Soviets had discovered his mission and, now, they were going to arrest him. But that didn't make any sense. If it was true that the Soviets knew about him, they could arrest him at any time. They wouldn't have to arrange such an elaborate scheme as this. Finally, Delong decided he would meet the note's writer, but not alone. He arranged for his interpreters to secret themselves a short distance from the meeting place so as to keep an eye on what transpired. If there was trouble, they could take whatever steps they deemed necessary. Despite the strong urging on the part of the interpreters not to make the rendezvous, Delong had made up his mind. Curiosity was a strong force for Roger Delong.

At the appointed hour, Delong sat at the well's edge and stared into the night sky. The stars were present by the billions. A warm breeze tugged at his loose fitting robe. In the clump of trees, about seventy feet away, his two interpreters waited silently and watched. All was quiet, with the exception of an occasional call from night creatures. Were it not for the nervous apprehension that gripped him, Delong thought, it would have been a perfectly calm and peaceful night.

"So you did come." A voice said from the shadows.

The words startled Delong and he jumped to his feet with an exclamation. "Jesus!"

The man had appeared from out of nowhere. "No," the newcomer apologized, "it's only me." The stranger's smile was evident in the moonlight. He continued, "I'm sorry, Mr. Delong. It was not my intent to sneak up on you."

Delong narrowed his gaze and tried to make out the stranger's features. He was tall, too tall for the average Afghani, and, although clothed similarly to Delong, was obviously muscular beneath the loose fitting robes.

"That's O.K." Delong assured him. "I'm just overly jumpy, I guess."

"Quite understandable, under the circumstances." The stranger replied. "I wasn't sure if you would come."

There was a moment of tense silence as the two measured one another.

Delong broke the silence. "Who are you? How did you know about me?"

The stranger settled against the well and folded his arms. "My name," he began, "is Petyor Vasiliovich."

Delong was instantly on guard—A Russian.

"You must believe me," the man stated, "when I say that I am your friend."

"We'll see." answered Delong.

"I can understand your caution." the Russian continued, "Frankly, if the situation were reversed, I doubt that I would be here in your place. You are very courageous."

"Or stupid!" Delong observed.

"You mean, if this turns out to be a trap." replied the stranger, "I can understand that, also. But, I assure you that this is no trap. Besides, you have your friends in the trees should I turn out to be a marauding criminal."

The stranger's smile glistened in the moonlight. Delong tried to appear nonplussed.

"I am," the Russian said, "indeed, desperate and I do, sincerely, need your help. Or, more to the point, the help of Martin Hastings."

Delong was no less at ease, and feigned ignorance in his best theatrics, "Martin Hastings?"

"Please, Mr. Delong." the Russian pleaded, "Let's not play word games. As you well know, Afghanistan is not a safe place at the present. We haven't much time to talk, and absolutely no time for games. Suffice it to say that I know much about you and even more about your employer." He reached into his robe.

Instantly, Delong's hand went to the hilt of the knife beneath his own robe.

"Please, calm yourself, Mr. Delong." the Russian soothed, noting the flash of alarm, "I simply want to show you something."

With that, the stranger pulled out the identification card case and handed it to Delong who accepted the credentials and held them to the moon's light. "It's all in Russian," Delong announced after a moment, "I can't read it." He handed the case back to the stranger.

"It is my identification as a Major in the KGB, Mr. Delong." The Russian replied.

Chills hop-frogged the length of Delong's spine. He suddenly wanted to run away.

The stranger continued speaking. "I am assistant Directorate of operations for this region. That should give you some idea of how I know so much about you."

"Some." agreed a tentative Delong.

"Yes. Well," continued the Russian, "I will get directly to the point. I want out. To defect. I need help to do so. Martin Hastings can provide that assistance."

"Defect?" echoed Delong. He had not expected anything like this. His mind backtracked a bit, the unease subsided. "Why Hastings?" Delong asked, after a short pause, "Why not contact the CIA?"

"Please, Mr. Delong!" the Russian laughed robustly, sincerely. "Those monkeys are more pitiful than my own KGB. I would not trust them to wipe my ass, let alone save it. No, Mr. Delong, no CIA." The Russian sat down upon the brickwork lip of the ancient well and stared into the night sky for a moment before continuing, "Martin Hastings is, at the present, perhaps the most powerful western influence in Afghanistan. A man of his, let's call it unique qualities would be of great potential benefit to someone such as myself—someone who is looking for a way out. To reach him I have come to you. It's as simple as that."

Delong remained silent. He had dealt with the CIA on more than one occasion and, generally, agreed with the Russian's assessment. They were, without a doubt, if not monkeys, at least, snakes and were certainly not to be trusted. Delong also agreed with the Russian's assessment of Hastings being the most powerful western influence currently at work in Afghanistan. Although this was no great secret, it was, by no means, common knowledge. The Russian was obviously privy to at least mid-level intelligence. If, Delong thought, the Russian was not lying, if he truly was an Operations Directorate, then he would certainly have access to even higher intelligence. Delong's interest gained impetus. He kicked at the rocks with the toe of his sandal and asked, "Why should Hastings help you? What's in it for him?"

The Russian smiled slightly, "Ah, you capitalists. Always looking for the profit, no? All I can offer is gratitude, Mr. Delong." He saw the look flash across Delong's face, the 'are you crazy' look, and quickly added, "Gratitude…and a wealth of sensitive information concerning my country's operations in this God forsaken land." Delong's eyes lit up slightly. The Russian continued, "Information about weapons stores, capabilities and inventory, as well as helpful intelligence on troop numbers, placements and dispositions. Suffice it to say, Mr. Delong, that it is information which would prove to be of inestimable worth in the right hands."

Yes, Delong thought, considering the offer, the right information could prove to be very lucrative indeed, in more ways than one. The wheels began to spin in his mind. He was hooked. Delong stared off into the darkness and pondered the opportunity. It was several seconds before his eyes caught those of the Russian's. Delong could read from the look on the Russian's smiling face that his decision had telegraphed itself. Delong cursed himself for his transparency.

"How do I know," Delong asked the Russian, attempting to recover somewhat, "you can be trusted?"

The Russian's smile faded. He stood to his feet and shook the dust from his robes. "You can't know that, Mr. Delong. I can offer no proof of my sincerity, no collateral on your investment. All I have to offer is my word. I only hope that you and, more importantly, Martin Hastings can accept that."

Delong thought things over one more time, took a step towards the Russian, extended his right hand with a smile, and replied, "Fair enough."

The Russian accepted Delong's hand and shook it firmly. "Then you will inform Hastings of my desire?"

"Sure." promised Delong, "But, how can we contact you?"

The Russian waved his hand slightly, "Secure Hastings' answer first. If he agrees to assist me, you can signal me by painting a few of the weapons crates that you are sending across the border next week. A brilliant red with a single yellow stripe would be acceptable."

Delong was hammered again by the intelligence information possessed by the KGB agent. The color drained from his face. The exact details of when and where the weapons would be delivered had only been decided that afternoon. That the Soviets were aware of the details already was sobering. The walls really did have ears in this strange country, Delong thought, suddenly very paranoid.

The Russian, seeing Delong's countenance change, quickly interjected. "Do not worry, my friend. The details of your weapons shipment are safe with me. The traitorous worm who delivered the information to my ears is now food for the rats."

Delong studied the Russian's eyes. He looked serious. Yes, Delong decided, this was a man who could kill easily and without feeling. Whether or not he was to be trusted was not an easy answer. Delong preferred not to have to trust him, but when making deals of this nature, one does not, he realized, always get what one wants.

"When I see the signal," the KGB major announced, "I will contact Mr. Hastings. I look forward to meeting with you again." Without further word, the Russian stranger slipped away into the darkness. Delong watched him disappear into the still mountain night. Minutes later, the two interpreters joined Delong by the well. He told them nothing.

Delong's trip out of the country was much easier than had been the trip in. Traveling by car, he crossed the border into Pakistan without incident. From there, he was driven to India and, later, by jet to Turkey. Hastings was waiting for him in Izmir. Delong waited until they were alone before discussing his meeting with Vasiliovich. On the balcony overlooking the crystal clear Aegean, Delong broke the news.

Hastings listened with apparent interest as Delong related the KGB operative's request for assistance.

"What do you think, Roj?" Hastings asked, when Delong had completed the details of the secretive encounter in the desert.

"I don't know." Delong had answered after a short pause, "It's hard to get a read on the guy. He could be serious, or he could just be pulling our chain. You never can tell about these secret agent types."

"This?" exclaimed Hastings, "Coming from James Bond himself?"

"You know what I mean." answered Delong.

"Well," Hastings continued, thinking aloud, "if he were a bad guy, he could have taken you out in Kabul, but he didn't. That must mean something. It could be a game he's playing, but I don't think so. I say we should give it a shot. At the very least, we've learned that our secret operations with the Mujahadeen are not so secret after all. That information alone hurts the other side's cause sufficiently to suggest that our man's for real. In the future, we'll let our associates, in country, take care of any deals. No more trips to Afghanistan for you."

Delong was relieved, the adventure had suddenly lost its allure, for some reason. Hastings picked up the phone and ordered a bottle of scotch delivered to the room. "You take care of the message for our Soviet friend, Roger. Make it happen. We'll listen to his proposal, anyway. If it turns out that he's for real, we might be able to supply our rebel friends with more than weapons in their fight against the communists. God knows they can use all the help they can get." Delong nodded affirmatively. "But, first," Hastings continued, "get a shower Roj. And burn those clothes. You are a little on the ripe side there, pal!"

Delong smiled, "You don't like it? I call it Bedouin Boutique. It's very in."

The phone call came late in the evening. Delong shook Hastings from a sound sleep. "It's him." Delong announced. The simple message was enough. Hastings bounded from the bed and accepted the phone from his aide.

"Martin Hastings here." Hastings announced.

"Ah! Mr. Hastings." came the voice from the receiver, "We speak at long last. I'm sorry that there is no time for pleasantries. This line is only secure for a few more seconds. Later today, you will receive a package. In it you will find my proposal, complete with the assistance I desire of you. I thank you, in advance. Good-bye, Mr. Hastings."

"Wait…" Hastings said.

"Sorry," the voice answered immediately, "no time. I'll be in touch."

The click was evident and final. The connection was broken. Hastings handed the phone to Delong and rubbed along the base of his neck.

"What time is it, Roj?" he asked, not bothering to look at the wall's clock.

"3:20." Delong answered, checking his wristwatch.

"3:20!" exclaimed Hastings, "I'm going back to bed. Wake me up when the sun gets warm."

Delong smiled, "Sure thing, boss."

Hastings climbed back into bed and Delong exited the room, marveling at Hastings ability to sleep at times such as this. There would be no sleep for Delong. The excitement of the brewing intrigue set butterflies to flight in his bowels. 'Working with a KGB defector,' he thought, somewhat proudly, 'James Bond eat your heart out!' He selected a book from the many lining the room's shelf and settled back to read.

The package arrived later that morning. Hastings opened it in his office. Delong sat in a chair opposite the desk and looked on anxiously as Hastings placed the package's contents on the rich oak desktop. There was a note, a map, and copies of Major Petyor Vasiliovich's dental records. That was all.

The note, addressed to both Hastings and Delong, outlined the KGB officer's plan for defection. In two weeks time, provided Hastings agreed to the deal, there would be an accidental Soviet Hind helicopter crash in a remote corner of northern Afghanistan. Petyor Vasiliovich would die, along with three other Soviets in the fiery crash. Of course, Vasiliovich had no intentions of being on the chopper when it augured in, but he needed proof that he was, hence, the dental records. Hastings, with his wealth and influence would have no problem, the Russian major wrote, contracting the construction of believable facsimiles of the major's teeth. The completed teeth were to be delivered to a drop point in Pakistan within 10 days. Vasiliovich would arrange for their pick up and subsequent placement on the doomed helicopter. As for getting out of the country, the Russian agent wrote, he would handle that also. At the same time that the helicopter would be going down in northeast Afghanistan, Vasiliovich would be driving across the Afghani border to a predetermined location. The location was well marked on the map which had been included in the package. There he was to be picked up by Hastings' representatives at a designated time. If he were not at the location at the appointed time, Hastings was to assume that everything had gone wrong and suspend the operation.

Vasiliovich would, he wrote in the final paragraph, bring with him certain documents and other papers identifying troop concentrations and disposition, detailed maps of Soviet positions and the armament of those positions, current operational plans for the Soviet military forces and other such, he underscored, 'valuable' information. It certainly sounded valuable to Hastings, enough information, Hastings surmised, to allow his Mujahadeen friends to inflict a substantial amount of damage on their Soviet invaders. The note concluded with another premature 'thank-you' and a post script that stated Vasiliovich would phone later that same afternoon, 5:10 p.m., for confirmation of the package's delivery and Hastings' final word on the matter.

"Seems rather straight forward." Hastings commented after reading the major's note a second time. "What do you think, Roj?" he asked, leaning forward in his chair and handing the note to Delong.

His aide studied the note for a minute, enjoying the intrigue, before replying. "You're the boss. What do you say?"

Hastings settled back in his chair and half swiveled back and forth, his fingers clasped before his chin. The creaking leather had a soothing tone. "I say it's worth a try." He announced after a space of just less than a minute. "If the information he brings out is half as good as I think it will be, then the risk is definitely worth it. Hell! If it's even a fifth of how good it could be, and its accurate, we should be giving him money, too!"

"What if its all a trick?" asked Delong scanning through the note again.

Hastings stood up, returned the remaining papers to their packet and answered. "It may be, Roj. But even if it is, what have we got to lose?"

Delong did not have an answer. Hastings handed the major's package to Delong.

"Let's get hopping on those teeth, shall we?" Hastings prompted. Delong nodded and exited the office. The deal was done. Hastings would assist the KGB officer in defecting.

The phone rang at 5:10 precisely. On the second ring, Hastings answered. "Martin Hastings."

"Yes or no?" were the only words from the other end. The voice was the same as that of the morning call.

"Let's do it." came Hastings' immediate reply.

There was a short pause. "Got it…See you soon…and thanks." The phone went dead.

Delong looked on, questioning. Hastings shrugged his shoulders. "Not a very talkative fellow, is he?"

Finding someone to duplicate the major's dental work had not been as easy as Vasiliovich had indicated. It had taken three days to locate a suitable artisan, a particularly gifted German dentist. The price had been steep. The work would be complicated, the dentist had explained. Believable reproductions took time and sophisticated equipment. Besides, the observant German discerned, there was, in the words of the Bard, Unser Shakespeare, as he called him, something rotten in Denmark—something not entirely legal. The clients would, naturally, have to pay accordingly for such service. Delong had agreed to the inflated price and promised a bonus of fifty percent should the job be completed inside five days. The dentist had readily accepted, and, suspending all of his pending appointments, immersed himself in his laboratory.

The German was truly an artist. He was also, as many artists tend to be, a perfectionist. Night and day he worked on the project—settling for nothing less than identical replicas of the teeth in the reference records. On the fourth day, he contacted Delong. The German got his fifty percent bonus. Delong was pleased. Hastings was pleased. There were still five days to spare.

A week later, along the frontier marking the boundary between Afghanistan and Pakistan, a Soviet helicopter on routine flight was downed by Mujahadeen rebels. The two pilots and both passengers were killed in the crash. The subterfuge was effective. The Soviets found the fabricated remains in the downed helicopter. There were not a lot of identifiable body parts left in the scattered, blackened wreckage, but there were enough to identify Major Petyor Vasiliovich as one of the casualties. 530 kilometers away, the defecting KGB agent slipped into the compartment beneath the waiting car's rear seat and rumbled away to freedom.

Three hours later, Hastings and Delong greeted Vasiliovich as he stepped off another helicopter, on the deck of an anchored oil tanker. The Russian walked towards the two Americans, smiling broadly and breathing deeply the warm Arabian Sea breeze. When he reached them, the Russian extended his right hand in greeting. In his left hand, he carried a wealth of information. Delong eyed the briefcase as Vasiliovich and Hastings shook hands.

"Ah! Mr. Delong!" greeted the Russian, noting Delong's stare. "We meet again."

Delong accepted the outstretched hand and returned the firm grip.

"You wish to see the prize, do you not?" Vasiliovich smiled even more broadly and handed the briefcase to Delong. "I think that you will be most pleased."

"There'll be time to look at that stuff later, Roger." Hastings announced. Then, turning to the Russian, asked. "So, Peter. How about a drink?"

Vasiliovich quickly agreed, replying, "Ahh, Mr. Hastings. I can see that you and I shall get along splendidly!"

The trio spent the remainder of the day in Hastings' cabin, Vasiliovich reveling in his new found freedom and Hastings and Delong pouring over the information that the defecting KGB Major had secreted out of Afghanistan. The intelligence was better than Hastings had dared to imagine. The rebels would be immensely pleased. Vasiliovich had proven himself quite useful. As the days, weeks, and years passed, the big Russian would continue to prove his usefulness to Hastings.

Under the name of Peter McNair, the ex-patriate Soviet worked hard to demonstrate his loyalty to Martin Hastings. After three years of such steadfast, committed service on McNair's part and several months of serious consideration on Hastings' part, McNair was invited to join the inner circle of the Planning Group. The Russian had accepted the opportunity with genuine enthusiasm. Later, after even greater consideration, Hastings explained to the other Planning Group members that he was going to approach a sixth and final member. This member's identity would, for various reasons, remain a secret to all but Hastings. The four men accepted the news without concern. If Hastings decided there would be a fifth member and that member was to remain anonymous, then, that was fine with them.

At night, the rats would come out, and the roaches, on their nocturnal forays, scurrying here and there—rooting about. The boy could hear them, clearly, even above the din of the street noises outside his window. While the boy's two brothers and three cousins—they all shared the same room—snored in sound sleep, he would lie awake, eyes cast upward to the discolored and cracked ceiling, listening—thinking—wondering. There was more to life than this, he knew. The deplorable conditions of his inner city neighborhood were something above which he would rise, he told himself. How he would make the climb was not clear to him, so, night after night, he would lay awake for hours listening to the foraging vermin, the bumps and bangs, the racing engines, the screeching tires, the yelling, the screams, the sirens, and the occasional gun shots. As he lay there, he pondered his future. His name was Norman Thomas Johnson

The morning sun always brought the sameness of squalor and abuse and hunger for Norman. . His aunt, an alcoholic, was an overbearing, violent, abusive woman. Norman could not remember a time that his aunt was ever completely sober. Empty wine bottles were scattered all about the decaying tenement apartment Norman and his adopted family called home.

Norman Johnson did not know who his father was and had never known his real mother. She had died giving birth to him on a threadbare sofa, in her tenement apartment. With no phone to call for assistance and a voice too weak to muster more than a whisper, Norman's mother lay in the darkness, racked by despair. The labor pains hammered her already weakened body as she lay there, hour after hour, alternately sweating and shivering. Her two other sons, three and two years old, toddled about in the apartment seemingly oblivious to their mother's predicament. The newborn baby's cries attracted the attention of a neighbor. The police responded, then an ambulance. Norman's mother was pronounced dead on arrival at the county hospital. After three days in the hospital, Norman was turned over to the custody of his mother's sister.

The next span of years for Norman were anything but easy. Try though he might, Norman never quite fit in with the rest of the children in the family, or those in the neighborhood. An outcast among his own, Norman spent his time alone. Thoughts of suicide began to tread into his thoughts at the age of twelve.

One rainy summer evening, young Norman Johnson wandered into an open assembly gathered in a non-descript building adjoining all the other equally non-descript buildings lining the street. Norman was only seeking temporary shelter from the rain. What he found in the building, however, was to change his life. The building he had happened into was the temporary home of an Islamic mosque. Norman knew nothing of Islam as he found a seat near the back. The many smiles and head nods he received from the others gathered in the room touched him. A feeling of acceptance slowly descended upon him. Perhaps it was this feeling that made him so receptive as the speaker took his place behind the lectern and began talking. Norman listened intently to the rudiments of Islam. He accepted the words as truth. He had never given any thought to religion. He had, of course, heard of God, but that God was of no significance to him. This Allah that the speaker was describing, however, was a different matter altogether. Here was a deity Norman could relate to. Here was something of substance, something that had meaning to him.

Around him, adult black men were nodding their heads affirmatively in agreement with the words of the speaker. A warmth enveloped Norman. When the speaker stated that it was no accident that those assembled in the room had come to be there on that rainy evening, that it was the divine will of Allah, Norman was hooked. He had found a niche in life. Islam had a place for him, and he would gladly fill it.

In the days to follow, any time the mosque was open, Norman was there. He would sit, silently, in the back, soaking up knowledge. During one of the visits, he was given his first copy of the Koran. It was a treasured gift for Norman. Time spent outside of the mosque was quickly filled with time spent studying the truths to be found in the words of the Prophet.

The teasing at home began when his brothers caught Norman reading the Koran. Laughter ensued when Norman informed his family that he had embraced the Islamic faith. Ridicule turned to outright anger when, with the help of some of the older mosque members, Norman changed his name. Norman Johnson was no more. In his place stood Khalied Ibrahim Humari. No amount of persecution could sway him. Khalied had found sanctuary in Islam. He turned his eyes and heart to the Prophet for guidance.

In those early days, despite his family's continued ridicule and belittlement, Khalied was zealous and full of pride in his black heritage. He studied the leaders of his faith and sought to emulate their example. His favorite was a fiery figure who, for Norman, personified power and resolute devotion to the cause. That leader was Malcolm X. For the first time in his short life, he had something to believe in, and he immersed himself totally in the blossoming Civil Rights movement. Had he remained exclusively with the Koran and not been exposed to the politics of the Nation of Islam, his young mind may have remained whole. As it was, events confounded expectations and the first of many doors opened in his formative sub consciousness—doors leading to writhing, screaming madness.

When Malcolm X, Khalied's shining light, returned from the Holy land with a new message—a message of peace—Khalied had been confused. When Malcolm broke with Elijah Mohammed and the established sect and formed a group of his own, Khalied was even more confused, and a little fearful. Khalied remained faithful to Black Islam, but a seed of doubt had been sown in his troubled mind. The assassination of Malcolm X, in 1965, at the hands of the Fruit of Islam, blew an entire wing of doors off their hinges in the corridors of Khalied's mind. An indefinable resentment was born in his deepest marrow.

As the years passed, Khalied's resentment continued to grow in almost direct correlation to his loosening grip on sanity. Painfully, he began to recognize that the world he idealized, the ordered world of Allah, was far removed from the world he was experiencing. Inwardly, he waxed cynical and developed a sincere dislike for the baseness of common man. Gradually, Khalied retreated within the writings of the prophet, relying no more on the hypocritical words of his superiors in the movement. He kept his feelings, and his tottering rationality, buried, however, and continued to climb in the political arena of the established order. His zeal for the Nation of Islam was forever gone. The close proximity to the movement's powerful, ambitious leaders afforded Humari a disconcerting view of the greed and hypocrisy of his fellow man. The behind the scenes power grabbing and hypocrisy sickened him. The Nation of Islam, he saw clearly, bore little resemblance to the teachings of the Prophet. Aesthetics, material goods and lusts, these were the fabric of Islam's leaders. The people followed blindly. There were no faithful.

Lose what he might of zeal and expectations, Khalied clung to hope as the only anchor connecting him with reality—hope that light might dawn on the masses. For, even with his mind failing at an alarming rate, Khalied was a believer. In 1972, he made the Haj, the mandatory perambulation of the holy circuit. Khalied had, like many believers before and after, been moved by the religious experience. Unlike most others, however, Khalied came away from the pilgrimage certain that Allah had spoken exclusively to him—singled him out from among millions.

In a throng of believers, in the revered Meccan shrine, the vision had come to Khalied on the second turn around the huge, black curtained cube. To an overwarm and perforated mind, Allah revealed his will and that will was dark. In the heat and press of humanity, Khalied had watched in enraptured bliss as the Kaaba transformed itself, before his squinting eyes, into a huge ship. The ship hovered above the people who were, by now, no more than a sea of undulating bodies. Khalied watched in silent wonder as a robed figure stood atop the ship's upper deck and looked down upon the masses. The figure was, suddenly, Khalied himself and the people were, just as suddenly, the Nation of Islam writhing in a sea of muddied, troubled water. One by one the many people slipped beneath the filthy surface, screaming and flailing wildly, never to return, drowned in blackest corruption. When the last was gone, Khalied alone remained looking down upon a now becalmed sea. Against the glare of the broiling afternoon sun, a second figure approached. It was a slight person, veiled, a female, clothed in purest white chador. The two silhouettes joined and brilliant light consumed them.

Khalied shuddered from the reality of the vision as he passed out of the shadow of the dark cube. For the remainder of the day, he wandered about, as if entranced, thanking Allah for his infinite mercies and most excellent wisdom. The vision's meaning was clear to Khalied. Allah had been attentive to his frequent and fervent prayers for answers about the future of Black Islam. Now, the all knowing Allah had provided the answer. The only way to purify the believers was to begin anew. The blacks in America, Khalied interpreted, were going to suffer a violent cataclysm. Khalied and others, particularly the woman Allah had chosen for him, would rebuild the following and the following would be faithful—pure and free from corruption.

Exhilarated that Allah had chosen him for such an important work, Khalied spent four days wandering the sand around Mecca telling any and all who would listen of the vision. An ancient, wrinkled man approached the exuberant Khalied on the fifth day and prophesied to him, exhorting Khalied to be silent, lest evil befall him and Allah be forced to choose another, less fluid of tongue, believer. Khalied responded immediately to the, what had to be, certain message from Allah. He closed his mouth, resolved to keep the matter a secret and returned to America, content to carry on as normal until Allah spoke again. Khalied's silence had come too late.

Amongst the flow of believers that had crowded the space surrounding the Kaaba on the day that Khalied received his vision, had been an infidel—a field operative of the U.S. Central Intelligence Agency. The agent's mission was to monitor Khalied Humari's activities. Humari was a known member of the subversive Nation of Islam and bore watching both at home and abroad. The agent had shadowed his subject for a full week noting nothing out of the ordinary. During the trek around the Kaaba, the agent positioned himself close to Humari, in the event that the black subversive might attempt to make contact with someone. On the second pass, a strange look had overcome Humari's face—a far away stare directed towards the huge, black object of Moslem fascination. The agent watched Humari intently, shifting his gaze from Humari to the Kaaba and back to Humari again. Humari seemed lost in his own world. The agent, having to look ahead, every so often, to keep his bearings, marveled that Humari had not had to do the same. Humari kept moving all the time, his eyes pinned to the top of the cloth covered cube. Maybe, the agent had thought, at the time, the heat was getting to Humari. After a short span, the look on Humari's face was replaced by yet another as he passed out of the dark cube's shadow. From that point, Humari's stare was directed centrally on a blazing sun. Humari continued to stare into the sun long enough, the agent decided, to break anyone's stare. The crowd made yet another turn and Humari averted his gaze from the sun. The far away stare remained.

The curious look on Humari's facè remained throughout the final revolutions and throughout the remainder of the afternoon. Feeling a bit at unease, the agent decided to take a chance. Moving quickly through the ever present crowds, he took a circuitous route that brought him directly into the path of Humari. The agent had to move, slightly, to one side to avoid certain collision. Humari looked right through him, oblivious to anything, and passed within inches of the agent.

"Got to be the heat!" the agent told himself, wondering.

When Humari started telling everyone about his divine vision, the CIA agent decided that, heat or no heat, Humari had gone off the deep end. If not, the experienced agent told himself, if Humari were sane, then the whole thing was a very well played ruse. The agent found it difficult to believe that there was any code or hidden message in the incredible story which Humari was expounding to all, but he was obligated to check it out anyway. He searched the crowds until his eye fell on the man he sought. A confederate. He approached the aged informant in an indirect manner, paused near him to bend and adjust his sandals and delivered his orders. The ancient man ran a gnarled hand across his forehead, signifying that he understood the agent's instructions, latched his eyes on Humari, and sliced through the crowd with purpose.

Humari had silenced himself immediately. So much for secret codes. The agent's report would conclude that Humari was mentally imbalanced. The FBI reviewed their sister agency's field agent's report and conducted two additional close contact investigations of their own on Humari. Their conclusion mirrored that of the CIA—the subject was, in layman's terms, harmlessly insane. Surveillance of Khalied Humari dropped off tremendously. Apart from occasional checks, Humari was left to his own designs. His name was deleted from all 'unofficial' priority lists. Had the government continued its surveillance, Black Tuesday and the Revolution which followed may have been thwarted. Hastings approached Humari in the Summer of 1984.

In the back of his mind, Hastings had, on many occasions, toyed with the notion of having an associate on the inside. Such an ally, he deduced, would give him an edge he could not otherwise obtain. To know the black thoughts, to anticipate their movements, to have some form of influence over their actions—these would be very beneficial tools. Search though he did, Hastings could find no such mole. He considered dozens from black political groups across the country, but discarded each name in turn. His list included, perhaps, the most prominent black politician of the day, but, in that particular instance, Hastings quickly decided that the man was not to be trusted in casual matters, let alone with secrets of such magnitude.

Hastings had almost given up all hope of the services of an insider when, in the Spring of 1984, during an industry sponsored picnic, he happened upon an uncanny bit of fortune. It was late in the evening. Most of the guests had departed and only the diehard partiers remained. Hastings was one of the latter. He and Roger Delong had been attacking what was left of the buffet table when the call of nature had hit him suddenly. Hastings sneaked into the hedges to relieve his bladder. There, Hastings overheard the muffled conversation from the opposite side of the hedges. Curious, he side stepped closer to the source of the voices. By the time he was in a position to hear the entire conversation, it was almost over, but what he heard was enough.

From the sound of the voices, there were two men. From the slur in their suppressed voices, it was apparent to Hastings that they were either fairly intoxicated, or putting on a good act. They were talking business. Spook business.

"How many of those guns do you suppose they have buried away?" One man asked.

"Sheesh!" The other answered, "Thousands, there. That I know of. The same at other places, I guess. Who knows?"

"Well, that's no big surprise." the first replied, "They've been squirreling guns away for years, now. God only knows how many weapons those guys have stockpiled. Nation of Islam. Hmmpff. What kind of crap is that?" Hastings ears perked up at the mention of the black organization.

"No shit!" agreed the other, "Kill the white man. Kill the white man. All they need in that group is the right somebody with balls enough to lead 'em and it's Katie bar the door."

"Yeah," echoed the first, "That idiot they've got now has guts. He just doesn't have too much sense. I don't know too much about the number two guy. What's his name?"

"Humari?" responded the other.

"Yeah," answered the first, "That's him. Humari. Is he a threat?"

The other laughed lightly and answered, "Forget about him. He's not leading anyone anywhere. He's a flower child and, what's more, he's gone crackers."

"Really?" asked the first, "I thought he was in line for the throne."

"May be. Who knows?" answered the other, "But, that doesn't change the fact that he is still crazy as a hatter. We've known it for a couple of years, now. Saw him running around like Chicken Little with his head cut off over there in rag head land telling everybody and their goat that all the blacks in the U.S. were toast and only he and a very few, 'chosen', others were going to survive the upcoming death orgy. We're pretty sure that he still believes that he will be establishing a new nation of believers one of these days. Allah has ordained it."

"You're kidding?" said the first, incredulous.

"Nope." came the immediate reply, "Dead serious. The guy's a flake. Twisted. Out there. Bonkers. Harmless."

The conversation switched to another topic and Hastings tiptoed out the way he had come, his mind racing. He was slightly on guard. The conversation struck too close to home. All he had been thinking about for the past three weeks was who to approach for the fifth post on the Planning Group. He had about given up all hope of finding an insider, now, here he was presented with an ultimate insider—the number two man in the Nation of Islam. It was too good to be true. Warning alarms were flickering amber.

Hastings fought the alcohol to compute the new information objectively. The chances that he had been set up to hear the conversation were, albeit entirely possible, remote. The affair had been too spontaneous. Hastings had heard Humari's name before, but did not know more about him than he held a position of authority in the black organization. He was going to make it his business to find out more. First, however, he had to check out the men who were engaged in the conversation. Grabbing Delong by the arm and propelling him alongside, simultaneously motioning for him to be quiet, Hastings skirted the hedges and moved around to where the two men were standing.

"Get a good look at these guys, Roj." Hastings said quietly just before rounding the final corner, "I want to know who they are."

Delong had nodded in agreement, turning suddenly serious.

The two men quit talking as Hastings and Delong turned into the walkway. Delong studied their faces as he passed. His stare was returned. The two men stood still and quiet as Hastings and Delong passed. After the two intruders had moved off a respectable distance, the two men resumed their conversation.

As soon as they were out of earshot, Delong declared in a whispered voice. "The little guy is CIA. Barry Tarrenton or Tarrowen, or something like that. I'm not sure about the other guy, but he had that spook look too. What's up?"

"Not sure, yet, Roj." Hastings answered, smiling, "But, I'll let you know. What do you say we get back to that roast and make us some samiches?"

"You got it, Partner." Delong agreed.

On the following Monday, Hastings began his research on Khalied Humari. With a little effort, he was able to obtain a copy of the FBI file on Humari. Included in the file was a reference to the CIA agent's field report from Mecca. By Wednesday, Hastings knew everything he needed to know about Khalied Ibrahim Humari, f.k.a. Norman Thomas Johnson. All that is except for if the man could be trusted. That was the most important necessity. Hastings would have to trust Humari fully if he was going to fit into the Planning Group the way Hastings had planned.

Hastings watched and waited for three months before deciding to approach Humari. The potential payoff possibilities with an insider like Humari, Hastings concluded, would be worth the gamble of the approach. Recognizing that he was dealing with a troubled man, Hastings planned the approach with an eye towards appealing to Humari's eccentric views and spiced the encounter with lies.

Pete McNair was dispatched on the secretive meeting. His mission was clear. His amazing story line had been rehearsed and re rehearsed. McNair assured a nervous Hastings "I can pull this off, no problem!"

Hastings believed him, but knew that should the plan fail, McNair would, without having to be told, kill Humari and erase the trail.

On a warm, sun-filled morning in late July, Pete McNair strode purposefully up behind a strolling Khalied Humari and his single bodyguard. McNair timed his movements precisely and, when Humari and his guard were immediately adjacent one of the park benches that lined the walkway, launched himself into the Fruit of Islam bodyguard. His movements were fluid, powerful, and precise. The guard was dead, neck cleanly broken, before McNair rested him in a sitting position on the bench. The short maneuver had captured no one's attention other than Humari's, who now looked on McNair with stunned astonishment.

"Do not mourn the passage of this man," McNair instructed in solemn tones, "He's but the first of many which shall perish in a sea of destruction."

The stranger's words struck home in Humari's whirlwind mind.

"We must talk." McNair told the open mouthed Humari, "Your Allah has ordained it."

Humari obediently sat down on the bench adjacent McNair, the dead body of the guard keeping watch at the end of the bench. The conversation which followed was short and to the point, with McNair doing all of the talking.

An unexplainable, irresistible force had, McNair told the bewildered Humari, for weeks been pulling him toward the influential black leader. It was only recently, McNair explained, that it was revealed to him that the mysterious force was none other than Allah. He could not understand why Allah, a god he had heretofore not believed in, selected him to contact a black man. There was just no sense to it, McNair confessed—not in the face of his plans to kill as many blacks as possible. Eventually, McNair said, Allah had told him that Humari would explain it all.

A look of divine peace had settled upon the black man's face. McNair rejoiced, inside. Humari was sold. Silence descended as Khalied basked in the nearness of his god. Allah had spoken. Khalied's years of patience, of waiting and watching, were coming to a close at last. To Khalied, McNair was not so much a messenger of Allah as he was an unwashed infidel being used as one of Allah's tools. McNair was not to worry, Khalied instructed, the most benevolent and all knowing Allah had carefully intertwined their destinies. Khalied would be McNair's faithful servant and McNair would be Khalied's brute executioner. The end had come and Allah's will was about to manifest itself through their worthless bodies.

McNair had feigned overpowering awe and agreed to accept Khalied's assistance and guidance. When he asked what he should do with the dead body of the bodyguard, Khalied told him not to worry, that he would say that the guard had simply not shown up for the morning walk. The police would find his body and make their own conclusions, but no one would know of their meeting. McNair had pretended to be unconvinced and worried, but Khalied had assured him that the plan would work. Allah had ordained it.

McNair departed in excellent spirits, eager to meet with Hastings. The CIA agent had been correct. Humari was quite mad. Functional but mad.

The sailor was making his way back from the vessel's bow. Hastings watched his awkward approach. The crunch of his footfalls seemed to echo in the stillness. As he neared, Hastings saw that he was very young, perhaps still a teenager. The youthful face seemed out of place out here in the middle of an ice covered sea. Hastings thoughts flashed to a collection of other youthful faces—faces he had pitched into a firestorm.

In darkest night, deep in the swamps of eastern Louisiana, far from the nearest road, a military training facility was hacked out of wilderness. The new facility was to be the birthplace and training ground for Martin Hastings' hate-filled brain child, the New Order Army. Prior to this night, the camp had been just another of the many elements comprising the plan that had been forming for over two decades. The site had been carefully chosen from among dozens of potential locations. With secrecy the paramount concern, an area had to be selected that would allow for the creation of a training camp with minimum disturbance of the land and flora. Before the first chain saw was cranked, countless hours were spent determining adequate camouflage and concealment of the camp's facilities. Nothing would be allowed which might catch the eye of passing planes or of those who studied satellite photographs. The efforts were successful. Tents were erected and training facilities constructed in such a manner that only careful scrutiny at very low altitudes offered any hint of the camp's presence.

Within hours of the completion of the camp's construction, recruits began arriving from all over the nation. They arrived, for the most part, bewildered. None had the slightest idea of where they were, or more important, why they were there. The next months would be the hardest that any of the recruits had ever experienced. Completely isolated from the outside world, the camp's 15 drill masters, hand picked by Hastings' Planning Group, were shouldered with the responsibility of molding the 400 plus young men into an elite fighting force. No one would leave, the drill masters had been informed, until each recruit had been transformed into a ruthless fighting machine that would follow orders without question and would rather yield their lives than shrink from an assigned mission. In addition, and more importantly, the drill masters were tasked with thoroughly washing the minds of the recruits, stripping them of their identities and ideologies and embedding, in their place, an intense and irreversible hatred for blacks.

For one full year the recruits were conditioned and drilled from sunrise to late in the night by the tough and unrelenting drill masters. The typical day began at 5:00 a.m. with a five mile run through the humid, insect infested, stagnant swamps. For the purposes of the run, each recruit would carry a twelve pound steel bar in his hands and a hundred and twenty pound pack on his back. Absolute silence was demanded during the early morning runs. Talking or any other unnecessary noise during the run resulted in immediate and severe disciplinary action of such a nature that, during that year, those unfortunate recruits dealt the punishment, never committed a second offense. There was something about being stripped naked and suspended upside down for an entire day, just inches above a stagnant swamp, just out of the reach of alligators and snakes and at the mercy of omnipresent mosquitoes and biting flies that motivated offenders to reform drastically.

Following the morning run, the recruits would be fed a large breakfast, and, then, they would be marched to the training area's grueling three-mile obstacle course for two hours of intense exercise. After this, the recruits would spend two hours in classroom instruction where their brains were further stripped of any latent beliefs and ideologies they had developed in the outside world. The empty spaces in their conscious and sub-conscious minds were effectively filled with the art of warfare and the hate-filled, racist propaganda. By midway through that first year, the recruits, to the last man, were convinced, through hours of half truths and outright lies, that the black race was an evil race, a cancer on the face of the earth which must be removed at any cost.

After the sessions of classroom instruction, the recruits' fatigued minds having been fed with the requisite knowledge, they would be marched to lunch. Following lunch, the recruits were allowed one full hour of free time, during which they engaged in sports activities, swimming, relaxing, or writing letters to their foster parents or girl friends.

Following the afternoon free time, the recruits would take another five mile run, complete with steel bars and packs, and, then, would spend the remainder of the afternoon and the early part of the evening learning and practicing weapons and hand to hand combat skills. After this, the recruits would eat supper and then participate in yet another five mile run. At 10 p.m., the recruits would be allowed to return to their tents, exhausted and ready for bed. At 4:30 the next morning, reveille would sound and the days would repeat themselves. There were no weekends, no holidays, and no contact with the outside world. Only training and more training.

Jeff Kelly was typical of the average recruit in Hastings' New Order Army. Young, 18 years, athletic, letters in football and baseball, quiet, intelligent, and an orphan. Like the other recruits, Kelly despised the earliest weeks at the camp, and with good reason. The first forty days were hell on earth for the recruits as they were pushed to and beyond their physical thresholds by the strict and overbearing drill masters. The effect on the stunned recruits' confused, terrified minds was total and devastating. Beginning about the third month, Jeff and the other recruits underwent a gradual transformation and, one by one, grew to enjoy the rigorous physical training, and to accept the strictly imposed discipline. Their minds, assaulted on every front for those first forty days, had been softened to a very pliable mush. The harshness of the daily training subsided somewhat from the fortieth to around the sixtieth day. By that time, the drill masters recognized, the recruits' eyes had taken on a far away, vacant stare. Another month was allowed to pass before the drill masters decided that the recruits were ready. The hate filled propaganda began along with little gifts of free time and better food. Jeff, like most other recruits, allowed his mind to be consumed by the hatred spawning from the ever present anti-black propaganda to which they were subjected.

Derek Conway was another typical New Order Army recruit. Like the others, Derek had intensely disliked the earliest weeks of training at the camp. Upon arrival, he was 18, and silently sullen, speaking only when spoken to, and, then, only sparingly. His high school life had been great. He had been very popular, owing, probably, to the fact that he was an outstanding athlete. His grades had been excellent and he had been offered football scholarships by the Universities of Colorado, Michigan, Georgia Tech and a number of other smaller, less widely recognized colleges and universities. Betty Conway, Derek's adopted mother had tried to console him when he learned that he would not be allowed to attend college straight out of high school. The arrangement, she explained to her confused, angered son, had been made years ago, when Derek was still a ward of the state. The decision was out of their hands. She and his father had signed an agreement that provided that Derek, upon graduation from high school, or his nineteenth birthday, whichever came first, would take part in a two year, government funded foreign studies program. At the time, she told him, it seemed like a great opportunity, offering their soon to be son an excellent start in life. They had signed the agreement without hesitation. Derek, inconsolable, failed to accept the news. Surely, he pleaded, there was a loophole. There had to be some legal maneuvering that could allow him to go to college instead.

Overcome with frustration he had, finally, demanded that his parents find a way to get out of the contract.

The demand broke through Richard Conway's, Derek's adopted father, silence on the issue. He had listened to the conversation between his wife and son without comment, reading the morning paper. Now, angered at the tone in his son's voice, he dropped the newspaper and looked at Derek. He was not loud. He didn't have to be. The look in his eyes said volumes. Derek had learned, early, respect for his adopted father, and had seen the look many times before. Derek flinched, involuntarily. A fourth generation coal miner, Richard Conway believed in fair and stern discipline and had dealt it copiously to his adopted son over the years. He had not had to strike Derek for greater than five years, but he did so, now, without hesitation. Derek had forgotten just how quick his adopted father was. The reminder was immediate and jarring as the miner's rough palm whacked him in the back of the head. The familiar stars danced before him.

"You show some respect for your parents, boy." Derek's stepfather admonished sternly, "You'll do what you are told and I'll not tolerate your talking back to your mother. You're going on this program and that's all there is to it. You got it?"

Derek bit his slightly trembling lower lip and mumbled, "Yessir."

His stepfather looked at him hard for another instant, then returned his attention to the paper.

The monthly government stipend payments Richard had received over the years for Derek's care had been generous and had supplemented his miner's income handsomely. While others he knew, many times, had gone without, thanks to the monthly government assistance checks, Richard's family had not had to do so. A proud man, Richard did not look on the money as a handout and was quick to tell people so. The checks were payment for a service. He was not about to turn on the hand that fed him and was not going to allow his son to do such either.

Later, the same week, Richard had taken Derek aside to talk further. Derek, still angry and hurt, listened sullenly as his stepfather had explained that football could, and would, wait. Education, he pointed out, was more important. Two years, Richard promised, was not a long time. If Derek stayed in shape, he could play football when he returned. He would still be young. The colleges would still be there. If he couldn't get a scholarship, then he could walk on anywhere he chose. The two years of foreign studies would give Derek a tremendous head start in maturity and education over the other members of his future class and teammates, allowing him to give more focus to the sport. Derek would have to grow up and accept reality. There would be no more discussion. The decision was final. Two weeks after graduation, Derek was on his way 'to Brazil.'

In the first rays of dawn, Derek arrived in the swamp with a group of twenty other 'students', after an all night flight. The camp was far from what Derek had expected. The heat and humidity were draining, the insects fearless, the accommodations Spartan. He and the other nervous young men were herded into a large tent for orientation. A bald, heavily muscled, wind worn and scarred man in camouflage fatigues greeted them there. Something was wrong, Derek thought, suddenly chilled. Gone immediately were any romantic notions Derek may have entertained about adventures in Brazil. He and the others listened in stunned amazement as the camp's superintendent explained that they were now under his care and were expected to follow his every rule without question or hesitation. Failure to conform would result in immediate and severe consequences. They were, the tough authoritarian announced confidently, completely severed from the outside world. There were no means of escape. They would train, they would attend class, and they would grow. When, and only when they had satisfied the requirements for advancement would they be allowed to depart. And, from the looks of them, the gruff character surmised, that would be a long, long way down the road.

Derek was assigned a number, 655, and a cot in a tent with twenty-four other recruits. A box at the end of the cot had the words "Conway 655" stenciled across the top in bold black letters. The twenty-four other cots were empty, their inhabitants, Derek would later learn, gone for a morning run. The remainder of the first day was consumed in getting haircuts, shots, and physicals, and being issued clothing and assorted gear. Accompanying all of this were further unending and comprehensive orientation instructions. It was close to eleven p.m. before Derek was allowed to return to his tent. He collapsed on the wool blanket and fell instantly to sleep. He did not wake as, fifteen minutes later, his tent mates filed tiredly in and collapsed on their respective cots.

The trumpet sounded at 4:30 a.m. causing Derek to bolt upright in the chilly darkness, slapping at the cloud of mosquitoes that had descended upon his sleeping flesh. For several seconds, he was confused, unaware of where he was. Slowly, he remembered, and the fear returned. Around him, the other young men were already climbing out of their cots. They reminded him of zombies. None spoke to him. None seemed to even notice him. Derek dressed quickly in the uniform he had been issued and joined the others, in file, in front of his tent. The hell began.

At Hastings' instructions, the families of the recruits had been told nothing of the Louisiana training camp. A cover story was fabricated for each recruit to account for the time required for training. Some families were told that their sons had entered the U.S. military. Others were told that their sons had joined the Peace Corps. All of the cover stories indicated that the son was out of the country for an extended period. The recruits were instructed that any revelation on their part to the outside world of the existence of the camp or the things that were going on would be dealt with in a most severe manner. The recruits had been drilled in the meaning of severe, and, consequently, kept their messages brief and altogether devoid of details. The drill masters carefully screened all outgoing mail to ensure that the contents of the recruits' letters were consistent with the cover stories given their families. Other members of Hastings' expanding network ensured that correct postmarks were affixed to the letters to make it look as though the letters had originated from whatever section of the globe where the recruits were believed to be.

That the recruits could be so successfully molded into a devoted, highly motivated military unit over such a relatively short period of time was no fluke. The New Order Army had been one of the earliest elements of the Planning Group's plan. Consequently, it had received significantly more attention than many of the other elements. The activities and personnel at the swamp training area were the result of careful and complete planning, right down to the selection of the recruits when they were still infants.

Beginning in the earliest days of the Planning Group's activities, Hastings, again through intermediaries, established a significant charitable trust fund for orphaned children. The monies provided by this fund were designated to assist families that adopted such children. In the years to follow, Hastings had donated millions of dollars to the charity, which to Hastings, was no charity at all, but, rather, an investment. Hastings saw to it that a portion of those families receiving assistance were carefully screened for certain desirable qualities. The ideal family, in Hastings' interpretation, was a couple, either childless, or with, at the most 2 children. They would be from a rural community. They would be white and they would be, preferably, not overly intelligent.

Locating parents matching Hastings ideal description was not at all difficult. There were untold thousands of such families spread across the U.S. From among these families, only the most favorable were selected for further scrutiny. After a period of 2 years of surveillance and experimentation with the potential candidates, 500 such families were selected. Once chosen, the couples were manipulated to accept the child of Hastings' choice. The manipulation would follow these couples. Personnel in Hastings' expanding organization kept watch to ensure that the children were raised in the manner that Hastings desired. The process, for the most part, went flawlessly. None of the adopted parents ever suspected that they were not in complete control.

Hastings needed a means to get the children into the hands of the selected parents. Duncan Fowler provided the means by walking a bill through Congress which provided for the establishment and funding of a Federal adoption placement agency. An agency he agreed to oversee closely, an agency, he argued passionately, for the children. The liberals had lauded him for his compassion. The conservatives, unsure what he was up to, found themselves voting with their adversaries across the aisle. Their constituents demanded it. The adoption agency was formally enacted with little difficulty. It was another coup for Hastings and the Planning Group. The selected families began to be approached by local adoption services at the direction of the newly established Federal agency.

The babies were selected, with likewise planning and careful method, from among the thousands of orphaned children available. From a final list of 1,300 orphans, 600 male, Caucasian children under the age of 2 years were painstakingly examined, tested and finally selected for Hastings' far-fetched scheme. Following selection, the children were painstakingly profiled and their portfolios added to the Planning Group's growing New Order Army file.

The Federal Adoption Agency, established by Congress, was manned by volunteers. The volunteers were, in accordance with Hastings' design, selfless, civic-minded, responsible community servants who had absolutely no idea of the machinations lying beneath the surface in the adoptions. Such volunteers derived a tremendous amount of satisfaction, both personal and moral, in walking the adoptions through to provide a home for the unfortunate orphaned children. Likewise, the chosen families were unaware of the manipulative forces that had suddenly invaded their lives. In addition to ensuring that the selected children were placed into the correct homes, Hastings and the Planning Group went a step further and appointed a select group of confederates to monitor the adopted children as they grew. The individuals entrusted with this most important assignment were very efficient in their work and kept an excellent account of the affairs and activities of the chosen families and their adopted children from the beginning. Hastings' secret organization continued to grow.

Of the original 600 orphans placed in the foster homes, 400 were selected for participation in Hastings' New Order Army. Of these 400, 368 survived the first year in the swampy training area. The other 32, who, for whatever reason, could not adjust to the harsh military life, were allowed to return home, or so it was presented to the other recruits. What actually happened to the 32 young men was they were quietly killed, their bodies run through a meat grinder, and the remains fed to alligators and turtles in the swamp. Martin Hastings was a firm believer in absolute security.

The swamp training camp, as planned, did not attract overly close attention from local authorities, being only one of many such paramilitary type training areas scattered throughout Mississippi and Louisiana. Those officials that did evidence significant curiosity in the activities at the training area were either paid off or met with convenient, life ending accidents. When the last recruit was gone, the swamp camp's training facilities were completely disassembled and the site was sanitized. After a week of the sanitation, no trace of the camp was left, let alone any clue of the activities that had taken place there.

At the conclusion of the harsh and demanding year in the swamp, Hastings had his army. The recruits had been transformed into soldiers, soldiers more highly trained and in better physical condition than any regular soldier or special forces soldier in any other army on Earth. In their hearts and minds they carried an intense hatred of the black race.

The 368 NOA soldiers were broken into ten groups for initiation into the second year of their training—urban operations. The new training areas were situated in Wisconsin, Missouri, New Mexico, Alabama, Colorado, New York, and Oregon. Efforts taken to conceal the activities at the Louisiana swamp camp were repeated at each of these new training areas. During the break between training phases, those soldiers desiring to do so were allowed to return to their homes for a short two week stay. Those that took advantage of the offer were very closely monitored during their brief visits. Hastings had come too far and had invested too much time, money and effort to allow a breach of security to jeopardize his plans. There was no breach. To the man, the 368 man New Order Army was completely and almost irreversibly brainwashed, with each soldier believing himself to be a direct emissary of God with a mission to wipe the devil black man from the face of the planet. No one, apart from a fellow NOA soldier was to be trusted. The drill masters had done their jobs well.

Even with Hastings' vast resources, he recognized the need for a supplemental income source to finance his dark plans. Police investigators had a peculiar knack for following money trails and Hastings had no intention of allowing his schemes to go sour through any such investigative effort. An untraceable source, or, at least, a source that was not directly traceable to him or the Planning Group was necessary. The means to obtain the extra money was settled upon after just one brief meeting of the Planning Group. Delong and Fowler had come up with the idea. It would be a well coordinated scheme that would both secure funds and drive a further wedge between black and white relations. The mechanics of the plan, Hastings left to the Planning Group. In short, the services of a number of black criminals would be secured, through whatever means necessary. These black individuals would perpetrate a number of seemingly unrelated armed robberies, over a span of weeks, across the U.S. The money obtained would be funneled into the overall plan's operations. The blacks used for the robberies would be kept in the dark, each unaware of the entire scheme. When the robberies were over, the blacks would conveniently disappear. Hastings liked the idea.

Kelvin Brown had been in and out of prison for the greater part of his life. He was forty- three, jobless and illiterate. Since his last stay in prison, eight years for aggravated assault, Kelvin had robbed two convenience stores and one liquor store. His home was the street, alleys, parks, anywhere he could find. Hunger gnawed at his guts and the need for a drink plagued his soul. The money had run out two days earlier. Penniless and slouched in the bench, Kelvin was contemplating his next move when the white man approached him.

"Kelvin Brown?" the man asked.

"Who wants to know?" replied Kelvin, instantly suspicious, his hand moving instinctively to the knife in his pocket.

"Well," answered the white man, "I'm not the law, if that's what you mean."

Kelvin studied the white man for a few seconds. Well dressed, clean cut, could be the law, but they weren't supposed to lie about stuff like that. Finally, Kelvin asked, "You ain't got no subpoena or nothing like that do you?"

"No," the man replied, "nothing like that." He lowered his voice significantly and cast a quick glance around him before continuing. "I need somebody for a special job and I was told Kelvin Brown was the man."

Kelvin, curious now, urged the man to continue.

The bus hissed to a stop alongside the curb and the boarding passengers filed past the two men, paying them little attention. After a moment, with another hiss and a black smoke roar, the bus pulled away from the curb leaving Kelvin and the white man behind.

"Let's go get a drink." offered the white man.

"Sure," smiled Kelvin, "We can do that, as long as you're buying."

"You bet." agreed the white man.

In the booth at the bar, the white man explained to Kelvin exactly what he was looking for. Kelvin wolfed down greasy fries and listened with mounting interest as the white man laid out the plans for a major bank job. Kelvin had never robbed a bank before, but he had always wanted to do so. The plan, as described by the white man, seemed fool proof. Kelvin would not even need to carry a gun for the job. The white man would, he told Kelvin, arrange for a particular teller's child to be kidnapped just before the robbery. The teller would hand over the money without any fuss and Kelvin would march out of the bank. He would be sitting, pretty as a picture with, if the white man was right, and Kelvin did not have any reason to suspect otherwise, almost a quarter of a million dollars. That was a lot of money. And half of it would be his. That was more money than Kelvin could make in a thousand liquor store jobs. Kelvin liked the plan, but it seemed too good to be true.

"Why me?" he asked finally, draining is second beer, "Why can't you do it yourself?"

"I won't lie to you," the white man answered, "I've got a wife and three kids, a steady job, a comfortable life. I don't have any desire to go to prison." The white man took a long drink of his Jack and Coke before continuing, "If something goes wrong, and I don't expect anything will, but, if it does, I don't want to be implicated. This is a big job. I could have used anybody for the job, but I chose you because you have a reputation for keeping your mouth shut."

Kelvin considered the man's words for a moment before answering, "Fair enough. When do we do it?"

The white man smiled broadly and extended his right hand across the table, "How does tomorrow sound?"

'Put all the money in the bag, hand it to me with a smile, and say "Thank you Mr. Bevins." No alarms, no paint, no surprises, or little red haired Julie, so cute in her blue jump suit with the little clowns, will die painfully.' The note was simple, direct, and terrifying in the hands of Christy Jennings, teller at the Consolidated Savings Bank. Panic flooded her emotions. Julie was her four year old daughter, her only child, and the product of a failed marriage. Tears formed in her eyes as she remembered dressing Julie in the blue jumpsuit this morning before dropping her off at the day care center. She had no doubts that the threat was real. The note shook in her trembling hands. The black man who had given her the note, still standing at the window, was now glancing nervously about and getting impatient.

"C'mon, woman, give me the money!" he threatened, quietly, "Or, your little girl is road kill!"

Slowly, Christy, lower lip quivering, emptied the contents of her cash drawer into the deposit bag, careful to omit the exploding paint pack. She handed the bag to the black man and with painful smile said, "Thank you, Mr. Bevins."

"No," the man replied, turning with the bag, "Thank you, Christy. Have a nice day."

Christy Jennings watched the black man depart the bank, hating him deeply, fighting the tears on unsteady legs. When the man was out of sight, Christy waited two beats, then snatched the phone from its cradle and frantically punched the number to the day care center. "Come on…Come on," she whispered shakily, as the phone rang for the third and fourth times.

"Valley Child Care," came the answer at the other end, "Could I help you?"

"This is Christy Jennings. Is my daughter Julie O.K.? I need to speak to her right away!"

There was a momentary pause from the day care center employee, "Uh…just a second Mrs. Jennings," and then, muffled, "Eleanor, come here." Another pause, then more muffled conversation which Christy could not discern. Her heart was sinking rapidly and an indescribable feeling of dread was building.

A second voice, a tentative voice, came on the line, "Mrs. Jennings? This is Eleanor Rhodes."

"Yes," Christy answered, "This is Christy Jennings. I need to speak with Julie very badly."

Eleanor Rhodes was confused as she replied, "Mrs. Jennings, your father picked up Julie about 15 minutes ago, just like you instructed. Is there some kind of problem?" Christy's father had been dead for two years.

The color drained from Christy's face, the phone fell lightly from her grasp and clattered to the desk, her eyes rolled slowly upward, and she melted to the carpet in a dead faint. Other tellers rushed to her assistance.

"Mrs. Jennings? Mrs. Jennings?" the tiny voice in the receiver beckoned, "Are you there?…Mrs. Jennings?" When no reply was immediately forthcoming, Eleanor Rhodes turned to her employee and instructed, "Margaret, go across the street and get Chief Nelson, right now."

Kelvin Brown, smiling broadly, entered the back seat of the waiting car two blocks away from the bank.

"How'd it go?" the driver asked, putting the car in gear and merging slowly into traffic.

"Walk in the park!" Kelvin answered enthusiastically. For the first time, he opened the pouch the teller had handed him and peered inside. The sight warmed him all over. His white partner had been correct. There must have been close to half a million dollars in his lap. "Yessir!" he exclaimed as much to himself as to the white man, "I always wanted to rob me a bank!"

"Here's her note, right here, Chief." Mrs. Rhodes said, handing the crumbled bit of paper to Chief of Police William Nelson, "I've seen her handwriting more than once, and that's it! And what about the phone call? I definitely know Mrs. Jennings' voice. She must have gone crazy…or, she's up to something crazy…but, I couldn't imag…"

Chief Nelson interrupted, "Eleanor, did the little girl recognize the man as her grandfather?"

Mrs. Rhodes answered, after a short pause, "Well, Chief, She was asleep, and her grandfather just carried her out without waking her."

Chief Nelson tugged at his chin. "So," he began, "let me make sure that we've got this straight. At about seven a.m., this morning, Mrs. Jennings dropped her little girl…"

"Julie." Mrs. Rhodes interjected."

"Yes," Nelson continued, "Dropped Julie off here. At about ten twenty a.m., this morning, a stranger, an older gentleman, enters and presents you, Eleanor, with a note, supposedly from Mrs. Jennings, which states that he should be allowed to take Julie home for the day."

"I don't like that 'supposedly' business Chief," interjected Mrs. Rhodes, "I'm telling you, I know Mrs. Jennings handwriting."

"Alright, Eleanor," Nelson replied, "Don't get riled. We're just wading through the facts, here." The police chief paused, collecting his thoughts, then, continued, "And this note has a number which you should call if you have any questions. And you called. And Mrs. Jennings answered. And she said that everything was O.K. and you should allow Julie to leave with her grandfather."

"That's right." Mrs. Rhodes confirmed.

"So," continued chief Nelson, "you allow the man to carry sleeping Julie away, and 15 minutes later, Mrs. Jennings phones you, Eleanor, and wants to speak with Julie and then hangs up."

"Well," Eleanor answered, "Betty actually answered the phone when Mrs. Jennings phoned, and I don't think that Mrs. Jennings hung up."

Chief Nelson looked at the crumpled note again. 'Mrs. Rhodes, this is Julie's grandfather, Mr. Casey. He has my permission to pick up Julie early today. Phone me if you have any questions. Christy Jennings. 282-2944' "Eleanor," Nelson asked, a creeping suspicion rising within him, "Do you have Mrs. Jennings work number?"

Eleanor gave Nelson a curious look and stated, pointing to the note, "You're looking at it, right there."

"So," Nelson concluded, "You called the number just as it appears on the note and did not check your files?"

"Well, yes'" admitted Mrs. Rhodes, a bit sheepishly, "but, I've called Mrs. Jennings before, and I'm sure that that is the number."

"Can we just check?" Nelson asked.

"O.K." Mrs. Rhodes answered, "But, I don't see the point." There was a moment's silence as Mrs. Rhodes thumbed through the Rolodex.

"James…Jamison…Jaruth…Jennings. Here it is. Christy Jennings. Place of Work. Residence. And…here we go. Work Phone? 282-2994. There!" Mrs. Rhodes proclaimed as she spun the Rolodex around so that Nelson could see the number.

Chief Nelson nodded his head slowly and held the note before Mrs. Rhodes face, his suspicion now turning to icy fingers of dread. The color was quickly draining from her face as Mrs. Rhodes shifted her gaze from the number on the note to that of the Rolodex. The numbers were not the same. "How?…" she mumbled, lower lip beginning to quiver slightly, "but…how?…How did?…Why did?…"

Chief Nelson did not reply, he was on his way out the door. "Don't you go anywhere, Eleanor," he called before exiting, "I'll be back in a few minutes."

Eight miles outside of town, the car in which Kelvin Brown was traveling pulled to a stop at a rest area.

"What's up?" asked Kelvin as the driver shut off the car.

"Got to pee." answered the driver.

Kelvin watched as the driver disappeared into the rest room, then returned his attention to counting the money on the seat beside him. After a space of three minutes, the driver returned. "Whew!" exclaimed the driver as he reentered the car, "The pause that refreshes. I needed that."

"I heard that." answered Kelvin, still counting.

"How much did we get?" asked the driver, peering over the seat at the money. "I'm up to $328,680 and still counting." Kelvin beamed. "Not bad for a couple of minutes work." He was still slowly thumbing through a stack of twenties and looking down when the driver removed the silenced .380 from its concealed location between the front seats. Kelvin never looked up, never suspected anything, as the driver leveled the pistol at his downturned head and squeezed the trigger three times. Death was instantaneous. The jerks and spasms continued for several seconds. The driver started the car, eased out the rest area and headed west.

Julie Jennings was located at the bus station across town, later that same afternoon, scared but unhurt. Across the country, the other kidnapped children also turned up in public places, all uninjured. Despite intensive questioning, none of the children were able to provide much in the way of assistance towards apprehending their kidnappers. The case had, for all practical purposes, dead ended even before it began.

Kelvin Brown and the other black bank robbers were, although, for the most part, identified by use of the bank films which captured the robberies, never located. Most, but not all, of the men, like Kelvin, died quickly. The bodies were dismembered, ground to pulp and transported to one of four predetermined locations across the U.S.. At these locations the remains were packed for shipment to selected cat and dog food production plants. There the remains were introduced to the process lines, to disappear forever. The money from the robberies was filtered into Hastings' master plan.

The scene was one that was to repeat itself in 81 cities across the continental United States over the following six days. As reports of the bank robberies and kidnappings flooded in, it did not take Federal investigators long to conclude that they were looking at a well planned and well executed conspiracy. In each instance, the suspect, a black man, would enter the bank and present the bank teller with a note which demanded money and contained threats against one or more of the teller's family. Also, in each instance, the robberies were preceded by, in some cases, only seconds before the robbery, the kidnapping of the family members who were threatened. In almost every instance, the family members were abducted without incident. There were four reports of casualties at day care centers where the operators of those facilities had refused to allow the children to depart. In each of those cases, the operators had been assaulted. Three had died. The fourth was hospitalized with serious wounds, but was expected to recover. Pending cases were placed on hold as the Federal Bureau of Investigations and other law enforcement agencies concentrated their efforts on solving this, the largest criminal conspiracy of its type in the nation's history. In all, 118 banks had been targeted and the take was estimated to be in excess of $35,000,000.

It was William T. Sherman, the Union's madman, who is credited with proclaiming that war is hell. Through recorded history, man has gone out of his way to prove the proclamation correct. Who first stated, 'all is fair in love and war' escapes me, but mankind has put forth every effort to justify this proverb also. The things that Martin Hastings and the Planning Group were proposing were tantamount to war—a race war with the objective of completely destroying the black population of the United States. Everyday emotions, moral correctness, humility, and compassion, historically, are not included on the guest list to war parties. Hastings and the Planning Group members knew full well the implications of their plans, and had resigned themselves to the callous mind set that is necessary to kill, without remorse, man, woman, child and dog. The enemy, the black man, became a number. Black faces, black spirits, were replaced, in the minds of Hastings and the Planning Group, with figures, mathematical integers to be subtracted coolly from the grand total by whatever means necessary. War was, after all, hell, and Martin Hastings was not going to allow public opinion to mold his actions.

Lethal chemical and biological agent research and usage is likely as old as civilization. Developed and deployed carefully, such agents have, throughout history, provided quite a useful tool in the hands of murderers. Military minds need not stretch overmuch to find innumerable applications for these deadly substances. What better utility exists to secure the maximum amount of deaths with a minimum of toil and accompanying gore? The extremely small amount of such agents which are required to kill the average human being is amazing. The simplicity of manufacture and relative ease of delivery of the agents has some very scary implications. The fact that mankind is capable of using such agents without remorse is documented historically. Martin Hastings and the other members of the Planning Group recognized, early, that chemical warfare could be a very effective weapon in their armory, a weapon which could go far in aiding their efforts to destroy the black man.

Hastings had financed the experimentation with biological agents, in the eighties in North Carolina, Pennsylvania and New Jersey. Contaminating shipments of canned fruit with a particularly nasty microorganism, Hastings saw to it that the canned goods found their way to shelves in grocery stores frequented primarily by blacks. The effects had not been all that he had hoped, and, ultimately, roughly as many whites as blacks had been killed. The many deaths, 27, had been attributed to a particularly virulent form of Salmonella and were quickly forgotten by the rest of the country. Other experiments in biological contaminants produced limited results. The targeting variable proved to be too uncontrollable. Ultimately, Hastings discounted biological agents as a primary weapon in his arsenal. Chemical agents were much more controllable and equally, if not more, deadly than their biological counterparts.

Hastings turned his resources to the development of chemical agents, but not before ensuring that the remaining stock piles of biologically contaminated food stuffs were distributed to stores offering the greatest likelihood of black consumption. Three cases of contaminated peaches found their way to Golden Food Mart, on the outskirts of Harrisburg, Pennsylvania.

Katrina Lovell, one arm supporting the frail, loose skinned arm, the other firmly around the old woman's narrow stooped shoulders, helped her age-worn, 91 year old grandmother down the walkway and to the waiting car. It was shopping day. Tuesdays had been shopping days for as long as Katrina could remember. As a child, she had always enjoyed the weekly trips to the grocery store with her mother and grandmother. Lately, the routine had become tiresome. With Katrina's mother's death, two years earlier, the responsibility of caring for the grandmother had fallen squarely on her shoulders. It was a responsibility that was already taking its toll on Katrina.

Beatrice Edwards Washington had lived a full life and in its course had seen the world in which she lived undergo both terrible and marvelous changes. The years had treated her kindly, but their sheer numbers were now overwhelming her as her body functions slowly decayed. Always an active, strong-willed woman, Beatrice found it hard to accept the notion that she was old and not long for this earth. Although her mind still functioned, it was not as crisp as in her younger days and, often, Beatrice would become frustrated at her memory loss. She lived alone, refusing to move in with her granddaughter's family, or, God forbid, into a nursing home. Daily, she fought to retain her independence. For, above all, independence was the one thing in life that Beatrice Washington held dearest.

In 1866, Beatrice's grandmother had died independent, after a lifetime of slave labor in the tobacco fields of North Carolina. In 1865, forward elements of Sherman's advancing Union Army had overrun the plantation on which she had been born and had lived for 21 years. Huddled in fear of the dirty, pillaging white soldiers, Beatrice's grandmother, along with the other 11 slaves, had been unceremoniously freed. More soldiers would pass through in the days to follow, destroying all in their path. When the last of the army had passed, nothing remained of the Plantation that had been her entire world. Her husband of two years spent the days scouring the surrounding countryside in search of work to support himself and his pregnant wife, but found none. Times, throughout the south, were harsh in those days, especially on freed negroes who no longer were afforded the care and protection once provided by their owners. Almost overnight, five million slaves were left to fend for themselves in a world of 'haves' and have-nots', where even the 'haves' were struggling to survive. The winter following her emancipation, Beatrice's grandmother, underfed and exposed to the bitter cold, contracted pneumonia and died. In her lifeless arms, bundled up and breathing heavily, Beatrice's infant mother softly cried.

Life for Beatrice's mother turned out to be as hard or harder as that of her slave mother before her. From virtually the time she could walk, Beatrice's mother spent nearly every waking hour laboring in the tobacco fields. Though not a slave, the small recompense she received for her exhausting work was barely enough to provide an existence. At 17, she, like her mother before her, married a field hand. In a one room shack situated among a collection of other such run down shelters, Beatrice's mother and father raised eight children, of whom, Beatrice had been the youngest.

Beatrice's memories of life on the tobacco farm were not fond memories. She had despised the hard life there, and, at 14, had run away from the one-room home, and fled to Pennsylvania. It was there that she had met Robert Washington, a dark, handsome, intelligent, and educated railroad employee. He was the best thing to ever enter Beatrice's life. The two had fallen in love and were married soon thereafter. In the following years, Robert's railroad salary provided Beatrice with a fine home and many niceties which most other black families and many white families of the time did not have. Through the aid of tutors, Beatrice learned reading, writing, mathematics, and history in her new home. Beatrice, denied an education as a child, thoroughly enjoyed the new learning experience, and, for the remainder of her life, was a voracious reader of books.

Robert Washington died of a brain hemorrhage in 1958. The railroad pension and insurance money he left behind had been sufficient to allow Beatrice to live comfortably but heartbroken. Beatrice still missed her husband, and seldom did the day go by that she did not think of their happy times together. Her only daughter had looked after her well-being since Robert's death. Now that she too was gone, her granddaughter had assumed the responsibility. Beatrice was thankful for her granddaughter, as the two made their way slowly to the car.

"I'm sorry to be such a burden to you, Katrina." Beatrice said weakly as Katrina helped her ease into the car's front seat.

"Don't be silly," Katrina replied, "You know that you're no bother to me." She fastened the seatbelt around her grandmother.

"Well," Beatrice continued, "I know that I am. Remind me to get a can of peaches while we're at the store and I'll fix you one of your favorite peach cobblers."

"O.K." Katrina promised and closed the car's door.

Golden Food Mart catered to a primarily black clientele. Beatrice Washington had shopped there for close to half a century. The store had undergone numerous changes over the years trying to keep up with other grocery stores and the larger supermarkets. Aisles had been changed, stock shifted from one end to the other and back again, check out lines had turned into computerized registers, a deli had been added, but, through it all, the store remained a familiar place to Beatrice. Beatrice was most comfortable with familiar things. It had taken much persuasion on the part of Katrina before Beatrice would use one of the new wheel chair shopping carts the store had provided for its disabled patrons. It had only been a few months earlier that Beatrice had finally relented and had tried out one of the carts. Now, each time that she and her granddaughter would enter the store, even though she secretly enjoyed the ease of shopping they provided, Beatrice would still put up a half-hearted resistance to sitting in one of the carts. This day, much to Katrina's surprise, Beatrice headed straight for one of the specialized carts without a fuss, and the two commenced their weekly regimen of traversing the aisles of the Food Mart.

Overhead, in the spaces above the suspended tile ceiling, a tiny timer clicked down to zero and activated an electric gate. The gate triggered the opening of a small valve on a pipe running through what appeared to be a large electrical junction box. From the valve in the pipe, laboratory grade ether began to drip onto the 2-inch layer of solid chlorine pellets lining the junction box's bottom.

Katrina and Beatrice continued to survey the aisles as pressure from the deadly gas emitted by the reaction of the ether and the chlorine began to build rapidly inside the air tight box above. Cart nearly full now, they were on their way to the checkout counter when Beatrice remembered the can of peaches. "Oh, Katrina," she exclaimed, "I told you to remind me to get some peaches for your cobbler, and you didn't."

"I'm sorry, Nanny," Katrina apologized, "I forgot all about them. You wait right here, and I'll run get some."

"No," Beatrice replied firmly, "We'll go get them." and, wheeling the cart around, rolled toward the canned fruits section of the store.

The pressure relief valve affixed to the side of the junction box began to strain under the pressure exerted by the expanding gas inside the box. Beatrice selected two cans of peaches, placed them in her cart with the other groceries and, together with Katrina, headed, once more, for the check-out counter, fumbling in her purse for the right discount coupons.

Katrina and Beatrice were leaving the parking lot when the valve affixed to the side of the junction block broke loose and ricocheted among the girders. Cleo Bennett, the store's assistant manager, heard the metallic pings in the ceiling and gazed upward quizzically. When he heard no more of the strange noise, he shook his head and returned his attention to the produce order forms before him. The deadly gas spewed from the junction box in a misty cloud, rapidly filled the ceiling space, and began to drift downward into the aisles of the store. In less than four minutes, Barnett, two cashiers, and seven customers lay unconscious on the grocery store's tiled floor. Henry Phillips, the store's butcher, was almost overpowered by the gas as he swung wide the meat locker's door and reentered the cutting room. Stumbling backward into the meat locker, Henry slammed the insulated metal door and gasped for air. Quickly, he grabbed the emergency phone and dialed the store manager's number. The phone beside Cleo Barnett's head rang eight times, but he did not answer. The 36 year old assistant store manager was dead. When there was no answer from the manager, Henry phoned the police.

Katrina ensured that her grandmother was comfortable on the couch watching television before she returned to the kitchen to put away the groceries. As she busied herself unloading the plastic sacks and placing the items in their appointed spots, Katrina did not hear the special report interrupting the afternoon soap opera. Nor did she see the live footage of the phalanx of emergency vehicles assembled in front of Golden Food Mart. While busying herself putting the last can of peaches in the cupboard, she did not see the lifeless bodies being lifted into waiting ambulances. She did not see the horrified look that had rested upon Beatrice's face. She did not see her grandmother suddenly clutch her left shoulder and lean hard against the back of the couch. She did hear, however, the pained gasp Beatrice made as her 91 year old heart fluttered violently and stopped.

"Nanny?" Katrina called, instantly. There was no answer. "Nanny?" she called again, louder this time, moving toward the den. "Nanny!!" she cried when she turned the corner and saw the slumped, open eyed form of her grandmother. In panic, Katrina rushed to her grandmother's side, grabbed a frail arm and anxiously felt for a pulse. The tears began.

Martin Hastings' first experiment in killing blacks with the aid of chemical agents had resulted in the deaths of 10. The police had responded to the Golden Food Mart within two minutes of Henry Phillips' call for help. The first policeman to enter the store saw the still bodies of two cashiers and one customer sprawled on the floor. Immediately on guard, he drew his pistol and moved cautiously in their direction. The dizziness hit him suddenly and, unable to stand any longer, he buckled to his knees. His partner, just coming through the store's entrance, ran to his aid, and, alertly, recognizing the danger, pulled the dazed officer out of the store and onto the sidewalk. After a few minutes in the fresh air, the afflicted policeman slowly returned to his senses, shaking his pounding head slightly and rubbing the back of his neck.

The next emergency personnel to enter the store were the respirator equipped firemen. Two of these made their way to the back of the store, found the meat locker, fitted the frightened butcher with a respirator of his own and escorted him out the back of the store via the loading dock. The other firemen rushed to remove the store's victims to fresh air and begin artificial respiration. Their efforts were in vain. The butcher would be the only survivor.

When the store's windows and doors were propped open by the firemen, the gas was already, largely, dissipated. The draft removed any residual amounts and the air within the store was again safe to breath. The Fire Marshall began his investigation. The smell within the store was familiar to him. Over the years, he had been to a number of accident scenes involving incapacitating gases. The majority of those involved gas supply leaks. The others usually involved the inadvertent mixture of household cleaning compounds. This smell was of the latter type. The victims had appeared as if caught in sleep, the first responders had told him. Such a description of their state was also consistent with effects of exposure to the types of deadly gases emitted when common chlorine bleach is mixed with ammonia, turpentine or other such cleaning compound. The Fire Marshall walked quickly along the end of the row of aisles looking for the anticipated stock boy with a mop bucket. When he did not find him, the investigator made his way to the warehouse…Empty. After a cursory search of the warehouse, no chemicals anywhere, he returned to the main section of the store. His curiosity was heightening, now. He walked along the end of the row of aisles again, slower this time. When he reached the aisle containing the home cleaning goods, he stopped. Despite much searching, he found no ruptured containers. Nowhere in the store could he find any evidence of accidental mixing of cleaners or any other chemicals. There was , simply, no obvious explanation for the gas.

The search for the source began in earnest as policemen and firemen alike spread out through the store in a foot by square foot search. Accidental death was ruled out when, finally, the junction box was discovered. After examining the obviously engineered delivery device, the Fire Marshall made a bee line to City Hall while crime scene tape was stretched across the store's entrance. Police homicide detectives began an investigation of their own.

Sergeant Gerard Humphries watched as every inch of the box was dusted for prints. It was a 3 foot by 1.5 foot metal rectangle, about 4 inches deep, suspended between the rafters. Four metal conduit pipes ran to and, presumably, through the box. There was a small hole on one end of the box. The opening was discolored. Humphries could smell it—a faint chemical odor. The gas that had killed all of those people, he deduced, had definitely come from this box. The forensics man shook his head in a silent negative—there were no fingerprints to be found on the box.

"What kind of idiot would go to this kind of trouble to kill somebody?" Sergeant Humphries wondered. So far, nothing interesting or out of the ordinary had turned up on any of the victims. One remained unidentified, but she was an elderly woman, and Humphries was not holding out any hopes on that lead going anywhere. Therefore, he concluded, this was not a hit. So what was it? The gas, most likely, had not been intended for any specific person. Maybe it was a revenge thing against the store's owner, he would check into it, but Humphries had his doubts. The instincts that made him a good detective suggested something more. What? He was not sure. That he was dealing with a whacko seemed obvious. Who beside a deranged lunatic would put together a scheme like this?

In the days to follow, Humphries would chase all possible leads to their dead ends. There was nothing special about the metal of which the box was made, nor was there anything unique about the metal pipe which had contained the ether. Anyone, with practice and the right tools, could have constructed the delivery device. Solid chlorine and ether are reasonably accessible to a large segment of the population. So, neither the box nor its contents offered any substantial clues. Humphries turned to the particulars associated with the installation of the box. According to store accounts, the last maintenance that had been performed which would have allowed a worker access to the area above the ceiling tiles was a sprinkle system repair job a couple of years earlier. Humphries did some checking and found that the plumbing company that had performed that job was still in operation. A visit to the business and a check of their records provided the names of the two men that had actually done the work. Neither of the two men were still employed by the plumbing company, and only one still lived locally. The other had moved to Connecticut.

Humphries ran the plumbing company's former employees' names and social security numbers through the crime net but, apart from a couple of DUIs for one of the men, came up empty. Humphries interrogated both. Neither even remembered the job. "After all," it was explained to Humphries by each in turn, "I did hundreds of jobs in lots of different places. They all run together." It became increasingly clear to the eleven year veteran of the police force that, unless someone came forth and admitted to the crime, it would remain unsolved.

Very early in the investigation, to avoid what city authorities termed unnecessary panic, the police department spokesman attributed the deaths at the store to the accidental mixing of cleaning chemicals. The press, though somewhat dissatisfied with the dearth in sensationalism, appeared satisfied with the plausible explanation. The story was pursued no further. The police files, however, remained open. The case gradually lost its priority, however, as investigation into the gassing failed to reveal suspects or any clues apart from the gas delivery device. More, newer, crimes required attention and the case file was transferred to a seldom opened metal cabinet in the corner.

Realizing that he could never practically assemble an army large enough to accomplish his objectives, Martin Hastings had, through various intermediaries, actively sought out, purchased, manufactured, or otherwise obtained and stockpiled tremendous volumes of the deadliest substances known to man. In this manner, Hastings eliminated the need for a large standing army and paved the way for the inconspicuous development of his compact and highly mobile, New Order Army (NOA). With a minimum amount of research, it was not at all hard for the Planning Group to identify, locate, and target every predominately black school, day care center, church, business, and shopping center in the United States. With equal ease, access to such institutions and facilities, under the guise of routine maintenance, inspection, or the like, was arranged and accomplished. Without incident, inconspicuous packets of death complete with remote triggering devices were successfully deposited in each of the targeted areas. Likewise, utility vehicles in black communities across the nation remained altogether inconspicuous as linemen and public water technicians strategically placed similar packets in those communities.

Apart from Hastings and the Planning Group, no one was aware of the sinister contents of the packets. Some were told that the packets contained surveillance equipment. In many instances, the packets were manufactured to resemble standard replacement parts, and the technicians installing them never suspected differently. In most instances, those installing the packets were told nothing, other than when and where to accomplish the job. Within a space of only three months, Hastings had successfully directed the placement of enough chemical agent to kill, under favorable conditions, a substantial portion of the black population within the United States.

---◆---

PS102 in the Bronx, New York City, was not unlike many schools of its type across the country; old, outdated facilities, unkempt, graffiti-covered walls and lockers, overcrowded, with an enrollment that included close to ninety percent minorities. The teachers, overworked and underpaid, for the most part, did their best to try to educate the youths that gathered in their classrooms daily. There were some success stories, but these were the exception rather than the rule. Most of the students, not unlike students from time immortal, took no interest in an education and saw school as a hindrance to more important things, such as playing, watching television, or any of a number of more, in their estimation, worthwhile things. Despite the metal detectors stationed at the entrances to the school, and the patrolling school guards, the violence, so prevalent on the streets, regularly found its way into the classroom. Teachers not only faced the problem of trying to educate youths who had no desire to learn, they also faced the very real danger of suffering injury, even death, at the hands of those same students. The thankless profession of teaching was not an enviable one in such an environment.

Martha Taylor had been a fifth grade teacher at PS102 for eleven years. In those eleven years, students had assaulted her on eight separate occasions. The prominent scar on her forehead resulted from a gash she sustained in her first year of teaching at the school. It happened early in the year when a particularly troublesome student, a twelve year old black girl in pigtails, who resented being told to sit down, had shoved Martha violently causing the stunned teacher to fall hard against the corner of a large metal desk. The other students had watched in amazement as the unmanageable black child ran from the classroom while their teacher lay dazed on the floor, blood streaming from the open wound on her head. Martha received twenty-seven stitches and cried all night over the incident. Her husband, furious, tried to convince Martha to give up the position at the school, but she would not hear of it. The black girl was expelled and Martha had completed her first year without further incident.

In her second year at the school, unruly children slapped Martha in the face on two separate occasions. Her index finger was broken and both eyes beaten closed during her fourth year while attempting to break up a fight between two black boys on the school's playground. She was nearly strangled to death during her fifth year by a particularly troublesome youth. This youth would go on to be executed for murder in Texas as a young adult. Martha was hit by a flying desk and knocked unconscious in her seventh year, stabbed in the right leg the same year, and had a plug bitten out of her left arm in her ninth year. Teaching proved to be a more danger riddled profession than Martha had realized.

Each year, Martha told herself that 'this' would be her last year—that she could take no more. Yet, each Fall, despite her husband's pleas, she would return to the classroom full of optimism that things would be different. Even in the face of the many assaults against her, Martha Taylor retained her basic, deep seated love for children, and took pleasure in trying her hardest to influence her pupils in some positive way.

It took someone of Martha's character to teach in such a school for so many years. Most teachers gave up after only a short stay, seeing their plight as hopeless. Martha did not fault such teachers for giving up so easily. Sometimes, she even envied them, but in the final analysis, she found purpose and satisfaction in her service to PS102.

Tuesday, September 12, began like any other school day in Martha's fifth grade classroom. The sixty plus students slowly came to order and took their seats under Martha's coercion. School had been in session for just over three weeks. Long enough for the newness to wear off and for routine to set in. Already, one of Martha's students had been expelled for bringing drugs to school, along with a .38 pistol. Martha wondered how many more would be expelled before the year was through. She finally managed to get her students settled, then, called the roll. There were not many empty seats as had been so common during her previous years at the school. Attendance had improved dramatically with the passage of the City's new truancy laws which held parents responsible for their children's absences. Martha had rejoiced at the imposition of the stricter laws, "Now," she had said, "if we can just get a law that makes the parents responsible for the students' progress, too, we'll really get somewhere."

The rain hammered in sheets against the streaked glass of the second floor classroom throughout history and spelling. Midway through science, the rain subsided a bit, and, by the time the lunch bell rang at noon, the rain had faded to a mere drizzle. Martha was thankful for the break, in both the rain, and the schoolwork. She led her class to the large lunchroom and then retreated to the relative quiet of the teacher's lounge for thirty welcome minutes of much needed relaxation.

The lounge was overly warm and stuffy. Martha opened one of the windows and breathed deeply the cool, moist air.

Half a world away, Martin Hastings placed a call to Peter McNair from his offices in Sydney, Australia. "Sell all shares in Consolidated Fibers!", was the only message. From Chicago, the coded order was sent out all over the US.. Within moments of one another, from Maine to California, NOA operatives activated their primary remote detonators and, after a space of two minutes, the back-up detonators.

Responding to the electronic commands, in schools, day care centers, businesses and communities all across the country, tiny valves popped open and lethal pressurized gases spewed and expanded outward.

In the halls of PS102, inside of twelve fluorescent light ballasts, heating coils encased in glass tubes immersed in mercuric cyanide began to glow a brilliant orange. The barely audible hissing sound made by the colorless cyanogen gas as it exited the ballasts went undetected. The halls and rooms of the old school building were rapidly filled with the pungent, lethal expanding gas.

Martha turned suddenly from the open window as she heard the first of the screams. "What now?" she thought as the screams magnified. She rushed to the lounge's door and jerked it open. Immediately, Martha's eyes filled with water and her breath was wrenched from her as the acrid gas seared her throat and nasal passages. Weakly, she fell to her knees and grasped her chest. She was only vaguely aware of the still forms already lying in the hall as her body was seized by spasmodic jerks flinging her face long to the hardwood floor. Martha Taylor's twelfth year of teaching would be her last. In indescribable agony, the thirty-six year old black woman died in the halls of the school to which she had devoted a third of her life. Within five minutes, the cyanogen gas dissipated to be replaced by oxygen, but the damage was done.

The normally cacophonous noise and busy activity was replaced by an eerie, calm silence as, in the rooms and halls of PS102, one thousand nine hundred and fifty eight students, teachers, administrators and school guards lay dead.

Less than four blocks away from PS102, Kendrick Fellows was skulking along the sidewalk, peering into parked cars, and searching for something, anything, to steal. His immediate goal was to obtain money to buy a rock of crack cocaine to see him through the remainder of the day. The strange pop and hissing noise emanating from the transformer on the pole just down the street captured his attention. He watched in amazement as four pigeons resting on the pole's outriggers suddenly folded their wings and fell to the street. A look of confused shock fixed itself upon Kendrick's eyes as the invisible cloud of surplus German World War II nerve gas enveloped him. Almost instantly, his body went numb. He tried desperately to suck in air but could not as the electrochemical signal to expand his diaphragm would not travel the length of his phrenic nerve. Fellows collapsed where he stood and lay quivering, dying, on the filth strewn sidewalk. A passing cab, driver's window down, passed through the deadly cloud and smashed into a row of parked cars lining the street. The cab driver's head rebounded off the steering wheel before finally coming to a final rest on the car's horn. The blaring of the horn attracted the attention of many in the housing complexes and apartments lining the streets. Windows went up, and heads popped out to witness the commotion. The gas instantly reached out and grabbed the onlookers. Without bias, the deadly nerve agent killed all in its path.

In virtually every major city, and in many smaller cities and towns across the U.S., similar scenes were unfolding. Nationwide, television programming was preempted to make room for the special bulletins that were beginning to pile one atop the other. The country, the world, was stunned at the news of the mass deaths. That the lethal gases targeted blacks exclusively was without question. Investigators scrambled to place blame but could identify no substantial links, no suspects, and no clues, other than the detonation devices and the vessels that had been used to contain the poison gases. White extremist groups were quick to distance themselves from the killings, claiming no responsibility or afore-knowledge. Leaders from every nation on earth, without exception, condemned the senseless waste of human life that had occurred within the borders of the US. In what would become the single most devastating mass murder in recorded history, the death toll was at a staggering four-plus million and rising hourly.

From coast to coast, stunned Black leaders were vociferously outraged and demanded immediate justice and retribution. The U.S. government, equally stunned and outraged, was at a loss for explanation and could only offer the weak answer that no terrorist or racial extremist organization had claimed responsibility. Law enforcement officials were clueless and frantically grasping for leads. Americans, black and white alike, watched in shocked disbelief as the terror of September 12 unfolded on their television screens. In shaken silence, Americans watched, in horror, the images displayed on their television screens—images of row upon row of motionless body bags, weeping mothers, enraged fathers, confounded politicians, inert men, women, and children, so many children, faces frozen in agonizing grimaces of death. "What evil ", asked the anchorpersons, "could be behind the tragedy that had beset the nation. What diabolical mind or minds was capable of releasing horror of this magnitude? How could such a thing as this happen in the strongest nation on earth? Where, if anywhere, was safe from a repeated attack?" There were no answers.

Still in his offices in Sydney, Martin Hastings did not watch the news coverage. He was busy overseeing the implementation of the next phase of his campaign.

As reports of the mass killings filled the air waves, prison wardens across the U.S. were quickly instructed to sever all communications between the prisoners and the outside world. Over the days to follow, incoming mail which made reference to the killings and the subsequent unrest would not find its way to the prisoners. It was the Justice Department's intent that prisoners, black and white alike, not be inflamed by the terrible reports. These preventative measures, naturally, triggered violent reactions on the part of the prisoners. Many prisons experienced riots as the enraged prisoners fought to have television and radio contact restored. Such riots, although a significant problem, were much more desirable than the possibility of race wars erupting among the prison populations. Despite the precautions taken to keep the prisoners uninformed of events occurring outside of the barbed wire, news of the magnitude of the killings gradually found its way through the locked gates, and, inevitably the unrest being experienced outside the gates also found its way inside.

David Frazier was a veteran FBI agent and was very good at his job. Throughout his years in the Bureau he had demonstrated an uncanny ability to see through the clues involved in crimes, get into the mind of the criminal, and solve cases that 9 out of 10 other law enforcement officials would give up on out of frustration. It was not that he was psychic or anything nearly so exotic, there were, after all, cases that even he could not solve. It was more that he possessed an exceptionally rational mind which functioned well at sorting through evidence, piecing the various bits together to form a plausible whole. Though certainly no genius, Frazier was of well above average intelligence and had finished first in his class at the FBI Academy. Following graduation from the Academy, he had devoted himself fully to the Bureau. Long hours meant nothing to him. Very quickly, the FBI became his life. While other agents married and started families, Frazier contented himself sifting through case files, examining forensic data, or staking out suspected federal criminals. His devotion to duty earned him various titles among his peers over the years, none of which were very endearing, but he paid no attention to these. The few friends he had, only a handful, tried, in vain, to get Frazier to lighten up a bit, to relax and enjoy life for a change. Frazier would not be persuaded. He did not feel that he was missing out on anything. He had a family, after all, his sister, her husband and their adopted son. He would see them, generally, at least once a month and on holidays such as Christmas and Thanksgiving. Surely that was enough family for anyone. Despite the light hearted ridicule sometimes leveled in his direction, the other agents recognized his abilities and respected him for it. When a case was too tough or evidence too sketchy for a conviction, David Frazier was the man to call and everyone knew it.

Frazier was on the trail of a mass murderer in those first weeks of September. The Crayola Slasher, the murderer had been labeled, was a cold blooded pedophile who had killed at least fourteen children in six states. The children had all been boys between the ages of ten and fifteen. In each case, they had been sexually assaulted and subsequently strangled with a rope, and mutilated with a knife. The name Crayola Slasher came from the fact that, in each death, a single Crayola crayon would be found inserted somewhere in the dead boys' bodies. The Crayola Slasher had been killing for at least three years and, so far, law enforcement officials had been unable to come up with any clues. Frazier had taken over the case three months earlier and had spent endless hours examining and reexamining the evidence. Now, he was getting close and he knew it. From existing evidence and possible witness accounts, Frazier had assembled a profile on the Slasher complete with a sketch of what the killer probably looked like. He was convinced that the killer was a traveling businessman, possibly a salesman, whose duties carried him into a number of states. He was, Frazier deduced, most likely, overweight and white.

On Wednesday, September 13, when Director Victor Williamson called Frazier to his office, Frazier thought that it would be to talk about the serial killer case and how it was progressing. He was wrong. His assignment, the Director informed him, had been changed. He was, Williamson instructed, to drop everything and concentrate exclusively on the Black Tuesday murders. Frazier would, he was also told, head the FBI's task force on bringing the perpetrators of the heinous acts to justice. Frazier balked.

"But, Vick," Frazier argued, almost pleading, "I'm close to this whacko. I know I am!" He peered into his superior's eyes, searching. The look there told the veteran agent that his boss was not going for it. Frazier tried again, harder. "It's not in my report…yet, but…" with an obvious emphasis on the 'but'. There was a small, barely discernible spark in Williamson's eyes. Frazier continued, "I'm convinced that I was in his neighborhood last week." Williamson did not look convinced. "I spooked him, Vick. He ran."

"You were in California last week." Williamson remembered aloud.

"Yeah, That's right." Frazier confirmed. Williamson settled back in his chair and gave Frazier the 'I'm listening' look. "I was checking some leads with the Los Angeles office and the urge just kind of hit me…" The spark flickered again in Williamson's eyes. He was altogether familiar with and had a great respect for Frazier's uncanny urges. They had resulted in the solving of many cases over the years. "…to drive down to Barstow." The spark retreated again.

"Barstow," Williamson questioned, "that's where they found the first boy, isn't it?"

"Yes," Frazier answered, "I see where you are going. The guy is a long distance actor. I was convinced of that also. The whole drive down, I was telling myself I was crazy. I kept racking my brain trying to figure out what to do once I got there. I spent three days walking around the dead kid's former neighborhood. I asked a bunch of nowhere questions to a bunch of people who couldn't remember anything. Still, the urge to stay persisted. The day before yesterday, I saw the morning paper…" He removed the newspaper from his briefcase and held it out for Williamson to See. It was an Arizona publication and the headlines read "Slasher Strikes in Tempe!" Williamson was already familiar with the case. Another boy had met his death at the hands of the Crayola Slasher. "…and I knew. Yes, the guy is a long distance killer—an intelligent, long distance killer, but, above all else, however, he is a paranoid killer. The first murder had been close to his home and it had been easy. It probably had pleased him immensely, but the resultant police invasion into the neighborhood had been terrifying for him. At that point, he figured out the advantages of out of town crimes and had, through time, as is obvious from forty three dead bodies, perfected his skills. When I showed up in his backyard and started asking questions, he got spooked again and ran." Frazier slapped the newspaper with his free hand. "He wasn't due for a kill for another two months. I flew straight back here." He paused for a moment hoping Williamson would say 'alright' and allow him to pursue the case. He did not. Frazier tried one final time. "Two weeks, Vick, a month at most and I'll nail this sick worm. I know it!"

Williamson leaned forward in his chair considering Frazier's argument and shaking his head slowly. "Sorry, Dave." he announced firmly, "The Slasher is going to have to wait. Black Tuesday takes precedence. The whole country is screaming for action. Hell, son, we're looking at better than five million dead bodies here."

The figure registered, for the first time, in Frazier's mind. He had, of course, seen the headlines, and knew something of the Black Tuesday murders, but with his mind so intently set on tracking the Crayola Slasher, he had not, as of yet, considered the number of dead. Frazier was suddenly staggered. Williamson saw the realization dawn across Frazier's face.

Frazier accepted the new assignment without further complaint. In characteristic form, he dove headlong into the case, completely immersing himself in the details. The number of deaths was unbelievable. The effect on the public was replete with both grief and electric intensity. Frazier knew, from experience, that he could not allow the emotions of the case to influence him. He could see that emotion, clearly, in the faces of the other agents assigned to the task force. He tried, in vain, to separate the junior agents from their consciences, to force them to concentrate on the evidence and the evidence alone—to remain objective. In the end, Frazier had to accept the fact that he was asking too much. Just about everyone in the country knew someone who had died on September 12. Such tragedy is not so easy to approach in a purely objective and clinical manner. More than once, Frazier himself felt the tug on his hardened heart strings, as he viewed the many photos of the masses of dead bodies—tiny children frozen in death.

There were over 9,000 different crime scenes to be investigated, 9,264, to be exact. The obvious links were easy to discern for even the greenest investigator. 5,723,634 people were dead, thousands were still in hospitals. Of the dead, slightly more than 1,360,000 were white, Hispanic, or of races other the African-American. The balance, almost four and a half million, were black. Each of the crime scenes were in a predominately black area. All the investigators agreed on one point— the murders had to have been racially motivated. The poisonous gases used, although varying from crime scene to crime scene, were very advanced and very deadly, indicating that much research had to have been devoted to their selection. The gas delivery devices had all been cleverly and professionally concealed so as to escape all but the most thorough examination which, again, indicated that much research and planning had gone into their placement. The triggering devices used to release the gases were, in every instance, remote, radio wave activated devices which, although not state of the art, were very reliable. The presence of secondary triggering devices were a demonstration of the perpetrators' determination that the carefully conceived and executed plot would not fail. Obviously, all, including Frazier, agreed, they were not dealing with any run of the mill racial extremist or terrorist group. The person or persons responsible for the Black Tuesday atrocities were obviously determined, intelligent, technologically sophisticated, and backed well financially. Here, the trail dropped off sharply and splintered in a million different directions.

Frazier, accustomed to working alone on cases, saw immediately that there was not enough time for him to begin to attempt to examine each aspect of the Black Tuesday evidence alone. In a flurry of assignments, he broke from his normal mold and delegated responsibility for chasing down leads to the other members of the task force. A number of the agents were assigned to tracing the origin of the gases used in the murders. Others were given the responsibility of tracking the origin of the triggering devices. A full dozen agents were assigned to investigating the delivery devices themselves, their construction and installation. Frazier would, he decided, try to fit the pieces together as they filtered in from the field. This did not mean, he instructed the other task force members, that he would be confined to the desk. He would try to visit as many of the crime scenes as necessary. "Whoever killed all these people", he told the task force as he hefted the pile of death scene photographs from his desk, "is going to pay. We're going to make sure of that."

The office and field quickly became Frazier's home as increasingly greater amounts of his time became absorbed in sifting through the mounds of evidence associated with the Black Tuesday murders. He phoned his sister to explain the situation so that she wouldn't worry when she could not contact him at home. She had extracted his assurance that he would be at her house for Thanksgiving. Maybe Chris, her son, Frazier's nephew, would be home too, she offered. Frazier hoped that his sister was right and that his nephew would be home for Thanksgiving. It would be good to see him—to forget the madness for a while, and relax. Chris had been in the Orient off and on for two years doing some kind of volunteer work with some national relief agency. The activities, whatever they were, seemed to be making a man out of him.

Frazier's parents had died when he was 17, leaving him to care for his 9 year old sister, Sandy. Their untimely death in an auto accident, not seven miles from their home, had hit Frazier hard. The suddenness dealt him a severe blow, but he had suppressed his emotions and never allowed the pain an escape. Ever the reasoning mind, even at that age, Frazier understood, straight away, that he had become his sister's parent. There was no time for tears on his part, Sandy was devastated. Frazier would have to be strong for her.

The insurance money left behind had been more than substantial to provide for the orphaned children. This money, coupled with the house in Knoxville, the summer cabin in Gatlinburg, the 253 acres in the Smokies, and the formidable number of stocks willed to Frazier and his sister, amounted to a legacy which would allow the children to emerge from the crisis on solid ground. Their parents had gone to great lengths to secure the future of their children.

Sandy had been in the car with their parents, but had escaped being killed, albeit only barely. She had stayed in the hospital for two weeks following the accident. Sandy's doctor told Frazier that, as a result of her injuries, she would never have children. The hurt deepened. The drunk driver who had weaved across the double yellow lines and hit Frazier's parents' car head on walked away from the accident with only a few scratches and bruises. Following the trial, the drunk driver served two years of a thirty year sentence for manslaughter, before being paroled and released into traffic again. The fact that the man was drunk at the time of the accident did not nag at Frazier. After all, Frazier reasoned, there was nothing wrong with drinking, provided it was done in a responsible manner. That the man did not have a driver's license also did not particularly bother Frazier. Again he reasoned, lots of people don't have a driver's license. The fact that the man was black also did not enter into Frazier's contempt for him. There was but one thing that fueled Frazier's anger and that was the simple fact that the man, regardless of the circumstances, was a murderer who had failed to receive justice. Frazier got his first taste of a twisted American Judicial system, and he did not like it. The lesson would not go ignored.

The accident was in April. So was the funeral. Frazier missed only a few days before returning to complete his senior year in high school. Any free hours he had were devoted to caring for Sandy. Frazier found the responsibility not at all burdensome. To the contrary, he enjoyed it immensely. The first weeks were the toughest, as it seemed Sandy cried continuously and could not be consoled. With the end of the school year, however, came a dramatic change in his little sister as if the spirits of their parents had been exorcised from her thoughts. As the years passed, Frazier envied Sandy for the catharsis. The spirits would, it seemed, never leave him.

Following graduation, Frazier was declared exempt from the draft due to his unique situation in having to raise a child. He was offered a job by a friend of his father's in a medium sized law firm, in Knoxville, as a paralegal assistant. It was a fancy term for a catch-all gopher who, sometimes, did a little inconsequential research. Frazier had leapt at the opportunity. But, he told his new employer, it would have to be only part time since he did not like the idea of Sandy being at home by herself all day. Later, Frazier arranged for one of the neighbors to take care of Sandy from 9:00 to 4:00 every weekday, at a fee. Frazier had insisted on paying. Sandy would be no trouble, the neighbor had explained, in attempts to refuse the money Frazier was offering. Sandy and Jenny, the neighbor's daughter, also 9, would keep one another busy. "I should pay you" the neighbor had kidded Frazier, "for keeping Jenny out from under my feet!" Frazier would not be dissuaded, and, in the end, the neighbor was forced to accept remuneration. Sandy was more than happy with the arrangement. She was getting tired of big brother bossing her around all the time.

The break from parenting was good for Frazier. He threw himself into his duties at the law firm with youthful enthusiasm. He enjoyed the quiet, subdued atmosphere of the handsome law offices with their glass covered oak tables and desks, the leather covered chairs, and the sharply dressed employees. The offices had an aura of 'correctness' that appealed to him. After only a few days Frazier made up his mind to become a lawyer. With the passage of time, his mind would change.

Truman Kelso, Frazier's new employer and former friend to Frazier's father, took an obvious interest in his late friend's orphaned son from the very first. Kelso and Frazier's father had been close friends since long before Frazier had been born. The news of the deaths of Frazier's parents had shaken Kelso up also. He was a prominent attorney in the State of Tennessee and was, through a combination of money earned and money inherited, filthy rich. He had grown up with Frazier's father in Knoxville. The two had been inseparable during their childhood, establishing ties that led to a life long friendship. Both had received scholarships to the University of Tennessee. Kelso for academics. Frazier's father for football. Kelso had been best man at Frazier's parents' wedding and, likewise, Frazier's father had been best man at Kelso's. When Frazier's father's car had failed to start the night his mother went into labor with Dave, it was Kelso who had driven them to the hospital.

As the years passed and their families grew, the two saw one another less and less, but, up until the fatal crash, they had still made a point of doing something together a couple of times a year. When Kelso heard the news of his friend's death, it was as if a piece of himself had died. He had cried for close to an hour, then his thoughts had turned to the children. He determined to keep an eye on Dave and Sandy out of love for their parents. The siblings could have done worse for a benefactor.

When the school year began again, Sandy was in the fourth grade and more of Frazier's time became available for himself. Kelso talked him into, after much deliberation, enrolling in college. Frazier could take classes, Kelso told him, at the same time that Sandy was in school, so the experience would not interfere with his responsibilities at home. And, as for his job, his hours at the firm could be manipulated in any manner necessary. Education, Frazier was finally persuaded, was the most important thing he needed to enable him to continue to care for Sandy by the best means possible. If Frazier would not consent to allowing the firm to foot the bill, and he would not, then certain of his parent's stocks could be repositioned and the profits gained thereby would be more than sufficient to cover the cost of tuition. Frazier agreed, applied, and was accepted into the University of Tennessee.

It was during the first semester of his freshman year that he met Victor Williamson. Frazier had finished his Calculus test quickly and had taken advantage of the free time before his next class to walk to the law firm, it was only eight blocks away. It was the lunch hour and Frazier knew there would not be many people hanging around the offices. He would be able to catch up on some of his duties without much undue interference. When he arrived the offices were, indeed, almost completely empty, with the exception of the receptionist and whoever was present with Mr. Kelso in his office. The door to that office was, as usual, closed. Frazier busied himself taking care of the outstanding projects.

Frazier was busily filing the 'R's when Mr. Kelso's door opened and the stranger walked out followed by Mr. Kelso. The two were laughing and Mr. Kelso was slapping the large stranger on the back familiarly. They were obviously friends. Kelso noticed Frazier standing by the row of filing cabinets and called him over. "David. I didn't expect you this morning. Come on over here and meet an old friend of your father's." Frazier returned the remaining folders to the 'to be filed' box and made his way across the office to the two men. "David's been doing excellent work here since he joined us." Kelso was saying to the stranger as Frazier approached. "He's knocking down the 'A's over at the University these days and we don't get to see him as much as we would like. He shouldn't even be here, now, actually." He shot a forced stern glare at Frazier.

Frazier smiled and replied, "I just got out of class early and had a couple of hours to kill is all. Figured I'd kill them here." He extended his right hand to the tall, smiling stranger. "Hello. I'm Dave Frazier."

"Hello, David," the man greeted, applying firm pressure to his hand, "I'm Vick Williamson. Pleased to meet you at last." What did he mean 'at last'? Frazier wondered. "Looks a lot like his daddy, doesn't he Truman?" Asked Williamson. "Not quite as ugly."

"Not quite." answered Frazier lightly.

There was an awkward silence for the space of an instant, before Kelso chimed in. "Vick's a G-man, Dave. A regular big shot for J. Edgar. He's even ornerier than he looks, so, you better watch your step around him."

The stranger smiled broadly and slapped Frazier's shoulder lightly. "That's right, David. We've got eyes everywhere."

Frazier returned the smile. He had never met a government agent before, a government law enforcement agent, anyway. The stranger looked quickly at his watch, noted the time, said his good-byes and departed the office. Frazier's eyes followed him out. An unexplainable admiration had developed within him.

Kelso saw the look in Frazier's eyes and interpreted it correctly. "Damn, that's a sharp kid!" he observed, silently. Kelso had known about Frazier's good grades in high school, but it was not until Dave began working at the firm that he got a true picture of just how intelligent the young man was. Developed correctly, Kelso had decided, Frazier had a mind which could go far. That was the principal reason he had been so insistent upon Frazier going to college. "Your father and I," he said to Frazier, breaking the silence, "took a couple of classes from Vick at the University. We had quite a few lively discussions among ourselves back in those days. Knocked down quite a few bottles of sour mash whiskey too. After Vick entered the FBI, he still dropped in to see us every now and then, whenever he was in town. And, as you can see, he still does."

"What does he do in the FBI, Mr. Kelso?" Frazier asked.

Kelso had smiled broadly and answered, "Anything he wants, Dave. Anything he wants." Kelso returned to his office and Frazier returned to his filing.

Over the next four years, Frazier would see Williamson a number of times at the firm and would, in the process, develop a type of friendship with the Federal agent. Ultimately, it was Williamson's influence that convinced Frazier to enroll in the FBI Academy. It was also Wiliamson's influence that paved the way for Dave's acceptance at the exclusive school. Kelso had volunteered to take care of Sandy, who was now a growing young lady, mature for an eighth grader, but Frazier would not allow it. Sandy was his responsibility exclusively. Sandy accompanied him to Alexandria. There, Frazier enrolled her in a private school for girls, despite her pleadings for him not to do so. She was, although certainly not for the first time, angry with him, but he had accepted the anger, sure that she would get over it soon. She did. By the second week of school, she had forgotten her anger with her older brother and was back to her normal difficult, albeit happy, self.

Frazier's classes at Quantico were arranged such that Sandy never had to come home to an empty apartment. Frazier managed, with only a little inconvenience, to always be there for his little sister. He excelled in his studies at the Academy. Williamson tracked his accomplishments with obvious pride. Kelso also monitored Frazier's progress closely and often made otherwise unnecessary business trips to Maryland, Virginia or D.C. just for an opportunity to visit Dave and Sandy. It was during those days that Frazier finally acquiesced to calling Kelso, Uncle Truman. Sandy had called him that from the very beginning. After all that his father's friend had done for him and his sister, Frazier decided, the title of respect was the very least he deserved.

When Frazier graduated at the top of his class at the Academy, Williamson gave everyone who would look his way the 'I told you so' look. He congratulated Frazier exuberantly. Kelso and his wife also attended the graduation ceremony and Uncle Truman had beamed, with a father's pride, throughout the entire event. Dave and Sandy Frazier had become, to him, the children he never had. Tears were in Kelso's eyes as Frazier accepted the diploma.

Through more maneuvering on Williamson's part, Frazier's first assignment was in Washington D.C., just a short drive from the Alexandria apartment. With this arrangement, Sandy was able to continue to attend the private school, now a sophomore, and Frazier was still free, though not as free, to be with her evenings. In her junior year, Sandy moved on campus, as was the tradition at the prestigious school and Frazier was able to devote more time to his duties. The time began to soar by.

Sandy met a young man in her senior year and fell madly in love. Frazier did not like him at first, for some indefinable reason. As time passed, however, his feelings changed and he grew to like and, finally, love the young man. His name was Brian Hunter, and he was the product of a lower middle-class family from Richmond, Virginia. He was two years older than Sandy and also a student at the University of Virginia. The two dated for two years and were, with Frazier's blessing, married, following Brian's graduation from college. Brian took a position with a Tennessee engineering firm and the two moved away. Sandy cried a lot at the airport, but Frazier assured her that everything would be O.K. She finally managed a tiny smile before boarding, arm in arm with Brian, the southbound plane. It was a long, hot summer . In the Fall, Brian and Sandy adopted a son—Christopher David Hunter. Frazier became an uncle.

Chris Hunter grew up idolizing his FBI uncle. His fondest memories of childhood were those which included his uncle Dave. Likewise, Frazier cared deeply for Chris and often went out of his way to lavish praise or gifts upon his young nephew. Sandy and Brian would half-heartedly chide Frazier for spoiling their son. Frazier's only reply on such occasions was "Somebody needs to. It might as well be me!"

The revelation that he had been adopted had not diminished Chris's love for his adopted parents or uncle and, obviously, had not affected his uncle's love for him. Chris was fourteen when his parents hit him with the truth. They loved him as their own, they assured him, and he could feel that love, but they felt, they explained, that Chris should know the truth. The news shook him initially, but he recovered quickly. As the years passed, he did not see why he should have known the truth.

Sure, he did not look much like his parents, but, then, there were lots of children who did not resemble their natural parents. Ultimately, he wished that he had never been told. Uncle Dave appeared disappointed the first time Chris mentioned that his parents had let him in on the news of the adoption. Frazier, too, thought that the revelation was not a good idea. Later, Uncle Dave would tell him about the wreck that killed his adopted mother's parents and the injuries sustained by his mother, then only a child—Injuries which had taken away her ability to conceive and carry a child. In the final analysis, his uncle told him, commonly shared blood and genes were not absolutely necessary ingredients for a loving family. Adopted, or not, Chris was his nephew and that was that. Chris felt the same way.

Mid way through his senior year in high school, Chris received the notification that he had been especially selected for a unique position in an overseas educational program. The news filled his head with adventurous notions. His parents shared his enthusiasm, agreeing that such an opportunity could not be passed up. Uncle Dave had reservations, but when he saw the immediate disappointment in his nephew's eyes, he quickly hid all such reservations and congratulated Chris fervently.

Towards the final days of that senior year, Chris developed some reservations of his own. A year was a long time. A year spent several thousand miles away from home might be even longer. His feelings, his parents explained, were natural and understandable. They would not enjoy the separation any more than he, but, in the great scheme of things, the experience would be worth any temporary hardship or inconveniences. Chris would, they promised, learn independence, responsibility, and self reliance. There were millions of people, they pointed out, much older than he that had still not learned such vital lessons.

Despite the rationale of his parents, the reservations continued to linger in the back of Chris's mind even as he waited to board the plane one week after graduation. He successfully fought back the tears as he said his farewells to his parents. Sandy was not able to contain her emotions and her tears flowed freely. Uncle Dave was not at the airport. He was on an yet another important case somewhere. Chris understood. Brian gripped Chris's hand firmly, the first time the two had ever shook hands, before embracing him in a bear hug. Chris, boarding pass in hand, joined the disappearing line of passengers. Two days later, he stepped off another plane into the humid hell of a Louisiana swamp.

Lee Wallace quit school in the first weeks of the ninth grade and went to work at a garage repairing automobiles. He showed a natural inclination towards the trade, and, before long, had established himself as an accomplished auto mechanic with an uncanny sixth sense for diagnosing engine problems. Marvin King, the owner of the garage where Lee was employed, recognized the young man's talent early and paid him well for his services. Quiet, industrious, never idle or lazy, like the other mechanics, Lee was King's model employee. What King did not realize, what he could not see beneath Lee's calm surface, was the hatred the young man felt for him simply for the color of his white skin. King could not see the hurt behind the soft brown eyes, had no inkling of the pain and hostility that coursed through the young man's veins. King would likely have been chilled to the bone had he been able to peer beneath the surface and view the bottled rage and disgust broiling there.

Lee Wallace hated the white man, all white men. It was white men that had taken his father away and, finally, killed him like some common animal in a stinkhole prison. It was white man that had driven Lee's mother over the edge to a world where no one could reach her. And, now, it was white men that would offer no assistance for a broken old woman gone stark raving mad. Lee's entire life, since the ninth grade, had consisted of the garage and home. Home was where his mother waited, locked away in an empty room in a dilapidated public housing complex, her only contact with the outside world-Lee. But Lee knew that there was no real contact. He could tell by the vacant look in his mother's once proud eyes that the woman he once knew and loved was dead. All she had in the entire world, was Lee, and he was determined to care for her until the end. He often prayed that God speed up that end. The woman he tended constantly bore little resemblance to the woman he had known as his mother. Her skin, stretched tight across her large bony frame, was waxy and did not look completely human. Day by day, she slipped further into herself. The toll on Lee was incalculable.

Lee found solace in his work at the garage—found escape among the many oily, disassembled engine parts. Working with the tools, taking something that was completely torn down and reassembling it to a working condition, was a catharsis to Lee's tormented soul. The creeper was the psychiatrist's couch, the oil and grease the therapeutic lotion. In the engines, Lee found escape. Completely involved in his work, Lee would shut out the rest of the world and work the mechanical puzzles, wind through the maze of nuts, washers and gaskets. When the work day was over, Lee would collect his lunchbox, he always ate at the garage, and go directly home. Time and time again, Lee declined offers to accompany the other mechanics for drinks and socializing. After many such failed attempts, the others gave up on trying to lighten up the life of their quiet co-worker and left him to himself in his tortured, confused world.

Lee's father, Jerome Booker Wallace had seen combat as a marine in Vietnam. The first tour, in 1967, had been terrifying, but, upon return to the States, he found life too tame and, after six months, reenlisted for another tour. In 1969, a third of the way through his second tour, a land mine returned him to the land of the cheeseburger early. The wounds he sustained led to an early discharge from the military and a permanent limp. Following his return from Vietnam, Jerome, an uneducated man, had bounced from job to job never establishing himself. Although unsuccessful in the workplace, Jerome Wallace was a good father to Lee and a faithful husband to Lee's mother.

In 1978, circumstantial evidence linked Lee's father to the robbery and murder of an out of town business man. The twelve man jury, all white, had deliberated only 15 minutes before finding the unemployed black man guilty of capital murder. The judge, also white, sentenced Lee's father to life imprisonment plus 5 years. Tears streamed down the cheeks of 8 year old Lee Wallace as his father was led, hand-cuffed, out of the courtroom. It would be the last time Lee ever saw his father. Jerome Wallace died in prison four months later when he was stabbed to death during a fight with another inmate. Shortly thereafter, Lee's mother receded within herself, and for all practical purposes, Lee was left an orphan in a white man's world. His hatred for the white man had been mounting steadily ever since.

The news of the Black Tuesday deaths of greater than one million blacks melded with Lee Wallace's already intense hatred of the white man. On that fateful September evening, as he viewed, with mounting unrest, the horrible images displayed on the television's screen, Lee was irreversibly galvanized to action. An idea began to take shape and build upon itself in his hate-filled mind. 'How long?' he wondered. 'How long would the whites continue to walk all over blacks? How much more could blacks take before they struck back?' The whites had killed his father and God knows how many more just like his father. Now they were killing the children too. Lee had taken all that he could.

Rising suddenly and switching the television set off, Lee entered the room that his parents had once occupied—a room that now stood empty. From the top of the room's small closet, Lee retrieved a time-worn cardboard box. Gingerly, Lee placed it on the dust covered bed. With new found purpose, Lee rifled through the box's contents, the only possessions left behind by his father. The clothes packed into the top of the box, Lee threw on the chair beside the bed. Beneath the clothes lay Jerome Wallace's marine uniform. Carefully, Lee spread the dress blue uniform with its single stripes and two rows of multicolored ribbons upon the bed. Still deeper in the box was a collection of papers; old ticket stubs, some Playboy magazines, several letters and his father's military personnel records. These Lee laid on top of the clothes in the chair. Deeper in the box, wrapped in a dirty Holiday Inn towel, Lee found Jerome Wallace's service .45, complete with several discolored brass jacketed .45 cartridges and an extra clip, already loaded. Out processing from the military in the late sixties had been a confusing affair and Jerome Wallace had taken advantage of that confusion by walking away with the military handgun. Lee turned the heavy pistol over and over in his hand, liking the feel of power it possessed. Lee's mother had always hated the gun and had begged Jerome Wallace, more than once, to dispose of it. Finally, Lee's father had hidden the .45 in the Holiday Inn towel and told his wife that he had sold it. He let Lee in on the secret a few weeks before he was arrested for murder. Lee was, his father warned, forbidden to ever touch it. That rule was meaningless now.

Lee leveled the pistol at the closet mirror and studied the reflection there. He looked hard and long, but despite his efforts, he could find no resemblance to his father in the face or body that confronted him. The .45 trembled in his grip and Lee tossed it on the bed next to the uniform. In the bottom of the box, wrapped in newspapers packed inside more crumbled newspapers, Lee found the item he had most sought after—a single claymore mine. It was a live souvenir of the hell Jerome Wallace had experienced in the strange land so far away. Jerome had smuggled the claymore out of Vietnam via the U.S. postal service. Lee fingered the raised lettering on the front of the small, green plastic weapon, "FRONT TOWARDS ENEMY". He carefully laid the mine on the bed alongside his father's .45 and rummaged deeper in the crumpled newspaper until he found the detonator. A strange smile weaved its way along Lee's face as he inserted the blasting cap into the slot on the claymore.

Marvin King looked at the grime covered clock situated on the wall of the garage right next to the tattered fold out of Miss December . 9:43. "Where is that boy?" It wasn't like Lee to be late, he thought, and hoped that nothing was wrong with his most industrious employee. The phone rang and King entered his office. He was surprised to find Lee waiting there. He was even more surprised, bewildered actually, to see Lee in a military uniform, his hair shaved close to the scalp. A sudden chill ran along the base of King's neck. It was not the uniform, or Lee's sudden appearance that gripped him with unease. It was more the strange look on Lee's face which did so much to unnerve him. The phone continued to ring.

"What in the cat hair are you doing, boy?" King asked immediately, shaking off the irrational fear that had momentarily raced through him, and trying to take control of the moment. "What's the idea of showin' up here nearly two hours late?…And what's with the GI Joe look?" There was no reply from Lee. "Well?'" King continued, "Don't you have anything to say? I've a good mind to…"

King stopped in mid-sentence as Lee removed the .45 from the jacket pocket of the uniform and leveled it squarely at him. "Now, hold on son," King said rather weakly, raising his hands and moving slowly backward, "Let's don't do nothing stupid. I don't know what's eatin' you, but if y…"

Lee's finger tightened on the trigger and the pistol spit flame and leapt in his hand. The force of the .45 slug's impact tore Marvin King's back away and propelled him, already dead, into and through the garage office's smudge covered plate glass window. Lee's ears rang with the pistol's loud report. The glass was still falling from the large window's frame as Lee bolted through the office door and into the garage.

The other three mechanics were in a nervous group by the grime covered parts washer, open-mouthed gazes fixed upon the body of their former boss lying face-up in broken glass, shocked eyes open, fingers of ever expanding crimson stretching along the floor beneath him. As one, they panicked when Lee burst into the garage, gun in hand. All three bolted, as one, towards the garage's open bay door. The .45 bucked in Lee's hand again and again as the deadly projectiles reached violently out and snatched the lives of the three terrified mechanics.

Lee returned the pistol to the pocket of his father's dress blue jacket and, stepping over the crumpled, bleeding bodies of the three dead men, climbed into the driver's seat of the Chevrolet Lumina parked in the service bay. He felt above the sun visor for the key, and, finding it, started the engine, backed into the alley and sped away. Exhilaration pumped through him. For the first time in his life, he felt a sense of satisfaction. It was as though a tremendous weight had been removed from his shoulders.

The floor of the New York Stock Exchange, when in session, is, arguably, one of the most seemingly chaotic and busy places on the face of the earth. As brokers in the pits yell and shove, maniacally buying and selling, the scene is, to the uninitiated, quite maddening. It is a scene which repeats itself every business day as capitalists engage in the most lucrative form of gambling known to man.

From the visitors' gallery, Lee Wallace watched the jumbled mass of activity on the Exchange's floor. How he despised what he saw. "This" he said to himself, as he watched the traders darting here and there, pausing only to shout some incomprehensible jargon and hastily scribble something on the collection of papers carried in their hands, "is what the white man is all about. Buy. Sell. Greed. No concern for others. Unwilling to share the wealth with any but those of their own skin color." The presence of other blacks among the traders did not appear to be noticed by Lee. Or, perhaps, he simply saw them as traitorous blacks wanting to be whites. Lee patted his chest to ensure that the claymore he had taped there was still firmly in place. It was. Lee made his way to the trading floor.

"Excuse me, Soldier…" the graying security guard said to Lee as he approached the trading floor's entrance, "…but, visitors are not allowed on the floor during trading sessions. You'll have to watch from the visitors' gallery."

"Oh," replied Lee, smiling absently, "My Bad!" With lightning quickness, Lee struck out at the guard, crushing the old man's windpipe with the heel of his hand. A brief look of hurt surprise crossed the guard's face before his eyes rolled upward in their sockets and he collapsed with a quiet thud to the floor. Lee was through the door and in the midst of the traders in an instant.

There was a look of curiosity on the faces of some as Lee waded into the crowd, but most did not notice the intrusion of the young marine. Lee faced his body toward what he felt to be the densest mass of bodies. Then, feeling in his trousers pocket for the detonator's trigger, Lee clenched his teeth and, just as warning was being raised at the entrance, with a simple click, triggered the mine. Lee Wallace was killed instantly as 1.5 pounds of C4 detonated and 700 steel balls leapt from where his chest had been and ripped into the crowd of traders. The effect was devastating.

---◆---

The appearance of the blue lights' flash and the siren's shrill wail were not unanticipated. The NOA had been thoroughly trained for every possible contingency, and knew, by rote, what actions to take. With finely tuned precision, Derek Conway, the team driver, pulled the van alongside the road, cut the engine, released his seatbelt, and exited the van. He met the State Trooper midway between the two vehicles. Derek was encouraged to see that the Trooper was alone. "What's the problem, corporal?" he asked, noting the Trooper's rank by the insignia on the law enforcement official's collar, "Did I do something wrong?"

"No," answered the Trooper, "There's no problem. I just need to see your license and registration and take a look in your van."

Derek's heart quickened its pace, but only slightly. He touched the brim of his cap with his left thumb, the prearranged signal, and replied, "Sure. No sweat, man…" Lee led the Trooper around to the passenger side of the van, "…Let's take a look."

"You know" stated the Trooper as he followed Derek to the van's side door, "the windows are too darkly tinted on this thing. Don't you?"

"You're kidding me!" Derek feigned surprise, reaching for the door's handle.

"No," stated the Trooper, "I'm not kidding. These things are way too dark. A man could hide just about anything in there without fear of it being seen. So, naturally, us cops just get curious when we see 'em this darkly tinted."

"Well," replied Derek, stepping to one side and opening the sliding door, "I guess you've got your job to do, just like everybody else."

The look of surprise that crossed the Trooper's face as he saw the five commandos in the van was permanently etched there as the accelerating 9mm projectile ripped into the space between his eyes and out of the back of his head. With practiced precision, a plastic garbage bag filled with absorbent cloth was fastened about the dead man's head and shoulders and he was deposited on the van's floor atop more absorbent material. One of the team members quickly exited the van, entered the Trooper's vehicle and pulled away. Derek returned to the wheel of the van and followed at a short distance.

Greater than twenty years of planning on the part of Martin Hastings and the Planning Group had been dedicated to the success of the NOA squads. Once the terrorist force was activated, the intricate attention to detail was very evident. September 15, three days after the merciless gassing of the black schools and communities, the NOA squads were given the 'go' signal. Their mission, to seek out and destroy as many blacks as possible, to cause as much chaos as possible, and to escape detection at all costs.

The first night, the squads had been cautioned, would be critical. They must ensure they inflicted the maximum amount of damage in the shortest amount of time possible. The first night, they would be unexpected—not so, thereafter. The first night would be easy. The difficult operations were still to come. That the NOA squads had been unexpected by the black communities was, indeed, an advantage. The fact that those same communities were still, for the most part, reeling from the blow delivered on September 12 was yet another advantage.

Across the nation, determined and highly motivated NOA squads deployed from their safe houses and made their way to their respective areas of operation. Nothing had been left to chance. The orders were clear and concise. Each phase of the various operations had been rehearsed and rerehearsed, covering every conceivable contingency. As the night of September 15 fell across the U.S., the NOA squads moved into the streets of America's metropolitan areas and began their deadly patrols.

In the darkness, the night vision goggles worn by the NOA squad members provided another element of advantage as they slipped in and out of the shadows of the urban jungles, stalking their prey. Advanced silencers and flash suppressers allowed the squads to target and eliminate their black enemy with minimum attention being drawn to their locations. Bags affixed to the ejection ports of the specialized rifles the squads carried collected each spent cartridge leaving no potential evidence behind for the authorities. With rapid, deadly ease, the six man NOA squads made their way, street by street, block by block, through the bowels of the inner cities of America. A scattering of dead blacks marked their passage. Dawn's light would find the majority of the NOA squads quietly returned to their safe houses. It would also find cities paralyzed with fear as the deadly results of the squads' mission became evident.

LaShara Powell, a 36 year old, unwed mother, had been watching the three black youths from her third story window. Having turned out the lights, she closed her curtains partially and peered out into the darkness. The youths, occupying a vacant lot directly across from LaShara's building, were unaware of her gaze. At first, she had watched the youths to ensure that her son was not among them. In the darkness, it had taken several minutes before she was able to determine that he was not. Afterward, she had continued watching out of curiosity. Every few minutes a car would pull alongside the curb where the three youths were stationed. One or more of the youths would approach the car, exchange something—drugs for money, LaShara was sure—then return to the vacant lot. It was useless to phone the police, LaShara knew from experience. Nothing would be done.

LaShara watched in silent disgust as the youths plied their illegal trade. After more than an hour of watching, she had grown tired of the activity and was about to close the curtains completely when one of the youths spun violently and fell to the ground. With renewed curiosity, LaShara moved closer to the window, straining her eyes against the darkness, unsure what she had seen. The other two youths, still facing the street, were unaware that their friend was inert behind them. 'What in the world?' LaShara thought, as yet another of the youths was slammed to the ground. The third youth, seeing his companion go down, turned to flee, but took no more than two steps before he too was propelled face first to the gravel. An uneasy fear crept beneath LaShara's bathrobe. That the youths had been shot was unmistakable, yet she had heard no shot and, had seen no passing car. She altered her position at the window so as to look down one side of the street and then the other. For better than a minute she continued to scan the street in both directions. Nothing...Wait. Just up the street was a movement, or was it? She narrowed her gaze and continued to scan the darkened street. Yes. Yes, there was a movement. A man was down there moving up the street like a cat in the darkness. The man's quick movements reminded LaShara of television shows she had watched over the years. She watched curiously as the figure stealthily darted from cover to cover, rifle at ready.

LaShara watched the lone figure with frightened amazement as he made his way closer and closer to the three motionless forms lying on the ground opposite her apartment. The shadowed man looked to her like a soldier out of place in a run down community. A new sense of terror erected the hairs along the base of her neck as LaShara detected a second, and then a third man moving along the street behind the first. As the strange men moved closer, LaShara could see that each of the men were wearing strange looking goggles over their eyes. They were dressed in all black uniforms, carried, what appeared to LaShara, military rifles, and seemed to be searching every corner of the street. With panicked suddenness, LaShara moved back from the curtains as one of the men glanced towards her building. Quickly and shakily she jerked the phone from its cradle and dialed 911.

"Emergency Response Center" came the answer at the other end of the line.

"This is LaShara Powell," she announced excitedly, "I live at 5114 East Jefferson…The Peter's Towers. There's three men down there on the street with guns and they just killed some boys right in front of my apartment. They looks like soldiers!"

"Alright, Ms. Powell," replied the man's voice at the Emergency Response Center," Just slow down and we'll get help on the way. How many men did you say?"

"Three!" answered LaShara, still panicked, "There's three of them and they're carrying rifles and dressed like soldiers or commandos or something. They just shot three boys right down on the street in front of my apartment!"

"Alright, Ms. Powell," the man soothed, "just relax. Help's on the way. Can you see the men right now?"

"Hell No!" LaShara answered quickly, "I closed my curtains and I ain't going near that window again. Those guys got some strange lookin' eye goggles on and I bet they can see in the dark, and I ain't about to make my black ass one of their targets!"

While the man at the Emergency Response Center talked with LaShara, another dispatched patrol units to the area. "Just stay on the line, Ms. Powell. We'll be there any second." LaShara could hear sirens approaching in the distance.

As the sounds grew louder and louder still, LaShara's curiosity overcame her fear and she moved toward the window and drew the curtain back slightly, phone still cradled to her ear. A single police car, lights flashing, was coming up the street in the same direction the three men had come from. Two more police cars were arriving from the opposite direction.

"O.K.", LaShara spoke into the phone, "The police are here, now. I see them in the street."

"Alright, Ms. Powell. We thank you for your call. If you don't mind, we'd like for you to go down and speak with one of the police officers."

"Forget that!" LaShara exclaimed, "I ain't goin' down on that street. You tell them to come up to me if they wants to talk!"

"Now, Ms. Powell," reassured the Emergency Response operator, "With the police on the scene, you couldn't possibly be in any danger. All we want you to do is go down and tell the officers what you know."

"No way, white boy!" LaShara said with a tone of finality, "I'm on the third floor, apartment 4C. If ya'll wants me, that's where I'll be!" LaShara hung up the phone, and returned her attention to the window.

The point NOA soldier saw the curtains in the third floor window move slightly and, quickly, signaled the other two team members. The three had then quickened their pace and moved rapidly up the street. When the first sirens were audible in the distance, the three cut into an alley, sprinted across four blocks and entered the prearranged rally point. The other three members of the six man squad were already there awaiting their arrival. Two of the members took up defensive positions and the remaining four settled into sleep waiting for dawn.

Officer Mike Levesque had been watching a group of black teenagers assembled in the parking lot of a convenience store when the call concerning the three men with guns crackled across the police net. Jefferson Street was less than a half mile away from his present position. "Central, 510…rolling on your last." He spoke into the radio's microphone.

"Roger, copy 510." came the reply.

Levesque flipped the toggle switches activating his patrol car's emergency lights and sirens and peeled out of his place in the shadows. Across the street, in the convenience store's parking lot, the group of teenagers bolted in all directions. Levesque smiled, "Not tonight, boys…Maybe next time." The patrol car roared towards

Jefferson Street with a deep throated moan accompanied by the pulsating wail of the siren.

Levesque, the first patrolman on the scene, squealed to a stop in front of the Peter's Towers apartment complex. Down the street, he could see two more units arriving. He deactivated the siren and trained his patrol car's spotlight on the motionless bodies of the three black males lying in the abandoned lot opposite the apartment building. Grabbing his 12-gauge riot gun, he exited the patrol car and cautiously approached the dead youths.

By the time Levesque had reached the first of the dead black youths, the other units were arriving at the scene. Turning his back to the street, Levesque quickly knelt down, pried the roll of bills from the claw-like hand of one of the dead youths and surreptitiously pocketed it. Then, rising, Levesque called to the arriving policemen. "Hey, Joey. Looks like we got three cold ones here. Why don't you go upstairs and try to locate our caller and Frank and I will check out things on this end."

"Sure, Mike." One of the other officers answered and quickly disappeared into the apartment building. The second policeman joined Levesque alongside the body of the dead youth. "What we got, Mike?" he questioned.

"Beats me." Levesque answered, "Looks like some dead indians. Probably crack heads who were caught selling on somebody else's corner. Who knows? We'll let the suits figure it out."

The two officers wondered around the abandoned lot cursorily examining each of the dead bodies in turn. "All of 'em took it in the head, it looks like." Levesque offered to the other officer, who agreed. "And my guess is that they were high caliber rounds, too." Again, the other officer agreed. Other units were arriving on the scene. Levesque made way for the police photographer and ambled over to an unmarked green sedan that was just coming to a stop. A crowd of curious onlookers had begun to assemble. "Hey, Bobby." Levesque greeted the detective as the latter stepped from the unmarked vehicle. "They got you slummin' these days, don't they?"

"Yeah. Yeah." the other man replied removing a pack of cigarettes from his jacket pocket, "But, it's a living. Somebody's got to hold you street weenies' hands." He paused, faced into the wind, cupped his hands and lit a cigarette. "What have we got here, Mike?" The two men walked towards the formerly abandoned lot now overrun with law enforcement officials.

"I'm waiting on you to tell me." Levesque answered, "Three dead, crack dealing indians, all head shot from long range with a large caliber weapon is my guess."

"That's some pretty heavy guessing, there, big guy," the detective jested, "you trying to take my job, or something."

"No way, Bobby," Levesque responded, "you can keep it. Just leave me dumb, fat and happy."

The detective knelt down on the trash strewn lot and examined the first of the dead bodies. The detective's name was Joshua Dorn and, despite his eighteen years on the force, examining dead young people still unnerved him. He would, he had long since resigned himself, never get used to this part of his job. Death, encountered often enough through his years, seemed out of place, unnatural, when it visited the young. For Dorn, such deaths represented an inequity in the eternal mesh of life. It was an indefinable dread that descended upon him as looked over the sprawled, lifeless body before him. The boy could not have been much older than Dorn's own son. What future had this one been cheated out of, he thought as he examined the bullet's entry and exit routes. Probably a life of unemployment, drugs, and conflict with society, he answered as he noted that the projectile, probably an expanding, high caliber round, had entered the youth's right temple near the top of the ear. The youth's eyes and entire left side of his head were missing, blown away by the force of the impact as the heated metal made its exit. It was a gruesome sight, head shots often were, but, it was, certainly, not the worst the detective had encountered in his career. With a pair of tweezers, Dorn gingerly removed a plastic bag from the shirt pocket of the dead youth. Holding the bag in the light, he examined the contents…crack cocaine.

"Well, Mike," Dorn stated holding the baggy of drugs up for the other officer to see, "Looks like you were right. With this much crack, they had to be selling."

"Big surprise, huh?" remarked Levesque.

Dorn turned the drugs over to another officer and returned to the task of examining each of the dead bodies in the lot. One of the youths had been shot directly in the forehead, the other in roughly the same spot as the first youth. It appeared that all three had been killed instantly. On the basis of his cursory examination of the bodies and nature of the wounds, the detective deduced, as Levesque had, that the shots were delivered from long range and had caught at least two of the youths by surprise.

"Not the standard M.O. for a turf dispute, is it, Dorn?" asked Levesque.

The detective looked down the street into the darkness. "No," Dorn answered after a short pause, "not unless we've got some new Rambo drug gang who are deadly proficient with military weapons." He removed another cigarette from the half-empty pack, lit it, and asked, "What about the report of the three men? Have we got anything on that, yet?"

Levesque shook his head, "No. I was the first on scene, here, so, I figured I better stick around before toolin' around the neighborhood looking for bad guys. Joey Sparks is upstairs talking to the witness. You might want to check them out."

"Yeah," Dorn agreed, "that's as good a place to start as any, I guess. Why don't you hit the streets and see what shakes loose, and I'll go talk to the witness."

"Sure thing, Boss." Levesque agreed, "Don't get none on you!"

"Right," Dorn acknowledged, half smiling and turning towards the apartment building, "Get out of here, you reprobate!"

Levesque laughed and returned to his patrol car. The engine roared to life, the rotating lights sent waves vibrating through the night, and Levesque weaved the car through the maze of other emergency vehicles, easing slowly down Jefferson Street. He waited until he was several blocks away from the crime scene before pulling slowly to the curb. There, he removed the roll of bills from his pocket and quickly thumbed through them. "$1100 some odd dollars!" he said silently, smiling, "Not too shabby, Mike. Not too shabby at all!" He put the car in gear again, and eased out into the street, unaware of the NOA soldier's eyes following him from the abandoned warehouse across the garbage strewn lot.

The police radio crackled with reports of more dead bodies.

---------------◆---------------

Whoever first labeled the ghetto a concrete jungle hit upon a metaphor of profound application. The inner cities, the government sponsored housing projects, the confined masses of disenfranchised inhabitants had, over the years, developed into filthy, crime-infested dens of inhumanity, in which no one, not even the fittest, was safe from potential harm. In most such areas, as in some far away rain forest, the morning's sun would find, beneath a canopy of glass, concrete, and steel, the jungle undulating and shifting among dozens of familiar patterns. The air is alive with the noisome cacophony of the jungle floor's inhabitants, in this instance, man and his machinations, as they forage. Cautious eyes dart, tentatively, here and there, alert to the possibility of a predator's vicious attack. The light offers some, but not much, refuge and the jungle's occupants work quickly to harvest the days work before night, and its accompanying terrors, brings terrible, albeit equally familiar, patterns to the jungle—disjointed, violent patterns—a mosaic of uncertainty, fear, rage, and death. Street lamps, the few remaining, unbroken ones, strain futilely to throw light upon the darkened trash covered sidewalk and graffiti covered walls. In the distance garbage cans rattle and a cat cries in agony as it fails to outmaneuver the pursuing dog and forfeits its right to live in the jungle. But these were not the only sounds of the living night. There were also muffled shouts, here and there— shouts of laughter, and of pain, of anger, and of frustration. There were baby cries mingled with blaring stereos, mechanical noises, and the occasional wail of sirens. The sounds took shape of their own and melded with the senses to create an evil, intoxicating opiate. Night had descended upon the jungle, and the wise were now barricaded behind locked doors. The predators, well rested, ventured into the shadows of the jungle to begin anew their prowl of bloodlust.

"S'up?", Rodenel Griffis greeted as he approached the group of youths gathered about the porch of the decrepit house. A portable stereo positioned on the stairs leading up to the porch boomed its message of violence and despair in sing-song rhyme meshed with a primordial beat. There was an exchange of hand shakes and slaps as several of the youths engaged in the street gang's ritual greeting with the newly arrived member.

"Ain't nothin' to it, Home."

"Just chillin' and waitin' on the thrillin'."

"You the man, G-dog. Slam it on in!."

"Yo, word!", said another, rising from his seat on the porch. He was older than the others, perhaps in his mid to late twenties, and bore not a few scars. The dark badges of raised flesh on his face and arms proclaimed his experience with life in the jungle. He was not very large, did not appear physically threatening, yet he had the crazed look of one not to be trifled with. He was obviously the gang's leader. "You holdin' rock, G-dog?" he asked, rhetorically, extending his hand, palm raised to the newcomer.

Rodenel smiled at his gang's self proclaimed leader, hating him deeply, fearing him even more deeply, and answered, "Am I your man, Steel? Or what?", Rodenel reached down the front of his Georgetown Hoyas sweat pants and retrieved a ziploc plastic bag. The bag was approximately one quarter full of pellets of crack cocaine and Rodenel held the bag high, allowing all to see, before pitching it to the leader and announcing, "And my boy says that this is some kickass fine cheese, Home."

The other youths voiced their approval of Rodenel's rating of the drug's potency, and eyed the bag hungrily. The leader allowed a smile to pause temporarily upon his face as he surveyed the contents of the bag, kneading it between his fingers and smooth palm. He pulled one of the small nodules from the bag, sniffed it and held it to the light. After a moment, he returned the crack rock to the bag and retrieved another which he subjected to the same crude analysis. "Hey, Ho!", he called over his shoulder into the dimly lit house, "Bring the setup ahead on. Me and my boys got some serious bizness."

"I heard dat!" exclaimed one of the youths.

"Word!" echoed others as the youths formed a semi-circle around their leader and waited on turns inhaling the fuming, torch-fired cocaine through a coiled glass tube.

During this activity, a police squad car, windows closed, driver's eyes straight ahead, eased by, not 30 feet away, in the street in front of the house. There was no panic on the part of the gang at the sight of the patrol car. The youths did not pause from openly smoking the crack. Those not actively involved with the actual act of inhaling yelled obscenities and threats at the patrol car, taunting the white policeman within. The gang's members were secure in the knowledge that no policeman in his right mind would venture out of the relative sanctuary of his car, alone, in the jungle, especially at night. The clamor continued until the car was out of sight.

In the bushes at the corner of the abandoned house across the street, the NOA sniper watched the gang through his weapon's scope. He watched the crack pipe being passed from member to member. One of the other two NOA soldiers with him tapped him on his left shoulder. It was the signal to fire at will. The sniper flipped a switch at the base of the high tech scope and there was a barely audible whine as the laser targeting system warmed up. After a few seconds, a small red dot appeared on the back of the head of Rodenel Griffis. The NOA sniper took a deep breath and slowly squeezed the rifle's trigger.

On the porch , Rodenel inhaled deeply on the glass tube as the others looked on. Suddenly, his head exploded, showering the other gang members with blood and brain matter. The crack pipe slipped from his hands and shattered at his feet.

"What the hell!" exclaimed Steel, instantly bounding to his feet, only to have the sniper's second bullet rip into his chest and propel him through the plate glass window behind. The NOA sniper quickly squeezed off two more rounds, and two more gang members went down spurting blood.

The remaining gang members, in confused panic, scrambled in every direction. All three NOA soldiers rushed from their positions and ran directly at the porch where the gang had been gathered. With deadly speed and accuracy the NOA squad poured round after round into the bodies of the frightened youths. In less than twenty seconds, the firing was over and twelve black gang members lay dead on the porch and in the yard in front of the decrepit house. Two of the NOA soldiers then entered the house while the third remained outside. There was a single scream from the house's interior as the NOA soldiers dispensed with the occupants. As quickly and silently as they had appeared, the NOA squad disappeared into the darkness to identify and neutralize other targets. Minutes later, the police patrol car again cruised by in the street, windows closed, driver's eyes straight ahead, oblivious to the dead youths. It would be several hours before the carnage would be reported.

The September night was still and warm and the heat was magnified among the crowd gathered at the First Street A.M.E. Church in Los Angeles, California. Hand held fans beat incessantly throughout the buzzing crowds in efforts to drive back the heat and accompanying sweat, a nervous sweat born of heat, anger and unease. The crowds had gathered to hear the words of the visiting dignitary, the recognized leader of the Nation of Islam movement, the Reverend Mustafa Ahmet. The bright lights directed towards the stage for the benefit of the closed circuit cameras only added to the heat. The speech would be simulcast to like assemblies all over the country. The audience was anticipated to be in the millions. The projections were underestimated. Crowds overflowed every area where the broadcast was to air.

The Reverend Mustafa Ahmet, replete in flowing silk robes and gold jewelry, took his place behind the heavy pulpit and studied the faces of the crowd that had gathered in the sanctuary. The anger and frustration he saw there pleased him. He was equally pleased to see the pews overflowing and was emboldened by the fact that the streets outside the church were equally packed with angry blacks. Reverend Ahmet's bodyguard contingent flanked him on each side of the podium and in a menacing row along the front of the altar. Behind him stood Khalied Humari, his closest associate.

Humari smiled, years of careful planning were coming to a head. Humari had been in contact with the white man, Allah's tool, on and off over the years since their first meeting so long ago. Those meetings, for the most part, led to now, to this podium, and the message Ahmet was preparing to give. Early in those meetings, Allah, through the white man, had revealed to Khalied his purpose. To initiate the flood of his vision, Khalied must convince Ahmet of the necessity of taking up arms against the whites. Only then could Allah's will be made manifest. Only then would the impure blacks be purged from the face of the earth.

Humari set about on his divine mission with singleness of purpose. Slowly at first, a bit here and a bit there, Humari urged his superior to take the necessary steps to promote a confrontation with whites. As weeks turned to months and months to years, Humari's urgings began to gain purchase in Ahmet's reasoning. McNair had phoned Humari on September 14. His message was urgent. Allah had proclaimed that now was the accepted time. Yes, Humari had agreed, Allah was speaking. Humari, immediately ,set about convincing Ahmet. The years of urging compounded with the events of Black Tuesday and the subsequent inner city attacks worked together to bring Ahmet around to Humari's reasoning. Ahmet would take a stand and call for the black community to stand with him against the whites. Naturally, he would give Humari none of the credit for his decision.

Ahmet stood and peered out over the assembled masses and basked in the feeling of importance. Behind him, Humari basked in the realization that the hand of Allah was about to be revealed. From off-stage, the producer gave Ahmet the thumbs up sign and the cameras began rolling. The crowd grew quiet in anticipation.

"Brothers and sisters, I stand before you, tonight, with a heavy heart." Ahmet began, in soft tones, "The thing we have feared is upon us." The 's' seemed to go on forever. "The pale horse of death has been released in our midst and gallops, unhindered, upon a road paved with the blood of innocent black brothers and sisters." Again, the 's' lingered. "It races through our communities and through our homes. It takes from us our security, our hope, our chirrens." The 's', once more, followed by a short pause, then, raising the voice slightly, "Who among us has not seen the destruction of its passage? Who among us has not lost a loved one beneath its thundering, murderous hooves?"

All was quiet. Ahmet waited. The crowd had no reply. Ahmet leaned close to the microphones and spoke again. "The wake up call has sounded, brothers! The alarm is ringing, sisters! From where comes this horse?" He paused again. "There can be no doubt, but, that it is a horse bred and nurtured by the white man—a horse molded by the white man and protected by the white man. That the hope of the white man, who is unwilling to share this planet with any other race, is to see each black man dead in the street is, now, clearly undeniable."

An apprehensive stillness continued among the crowds as Ahmet shifted position behind the pulpit. "There is no need," he continued, "for my explaining the purpose of this gathering. We all know the purpose. Our grief is terrible. The blood of our loved ones cries to us all. Tuesday last saw Satan's scourge fall upon millions of our innocent chirrens. Murders occurring nightly since Tuesday signal an evil force at work against our race. There can be no denying this, despite the white man's claim to the contrary. That so many of you are gathered here, and elsewhere across this stricken Nation is an indicator of the desire which you and I share. The desire to bring justice."

A small murmur danced through the assembled congregations. "I aks those of you who, through the years have placed your faith in the white man's government, what say ye now? What say ye, as our people are murdered and the white man's government cowers and stands idly by in the background? They tell us they are doing all that can be done to locate the assassins. They tell us that justice will be served. They tell us not to fear—that we are safe. They lie and we believe. They call and we answer…They kill and we do nothing! And now, brothers and sisters,"

Ahmet continued, voice now raised loudly for dramatic effect, "how much more will we endure?"

The crowd, uneasy, was no longer quiet.

"How long," Ahmet asked, "will we stand in the shadows allowing the white man's pale death horse to run unhindered through the bloody streets of our communities? How long will we remain blinded to the truth as the white man so callously destroys our race, so callously murders our families, so coolly lies in our faces?"

Ahmet paused again, allowing the unsettled masses to ruminate. After a moment, he raised his smooth hand and waved it across the congregation, calling for silence. "I say unto you, my brothers and sisters, the time to act is now. The white man has made his goals uncompromisingly clear, and the black man is not included in his plans for the future. No longer can we allow our chirrens, our defenseless, to be murdered by the white dogs as we stand idly by and let it happen…Are we to be like the Jews and march, silent as lambs, to the ovens? Are we to wait, inactive, for death to visit each of us in turn?"

A scattering of 'nos' rippled through the crowd of angry listeners.

"Are we to trust the white man's government to bring the murderers to a white man's justice? Are we to continue to offer our race as a sacrifice to further the objectives of these same white men?"

More and louder 'nos'.

"Then what, brothers? What are we to do if it is not to take up arms in defense of our own?"

A murmur of agreement rippled through the emotional congregations—those assembled before Ahmet, and those viewing or hearing the speech across the country.

Reverend Ahmet, well practiced in manipulating a crowd, recognized the growing murmurs of agreement as the timely opportunity to provide a well directed shove to drive the assembled masses into a frenzy—a frenzy which, if properly channeled, could convert them into an army—an army bent on extracting revenge. "Yes, brothers," he boomed, hammering the pulpit with clenched fist, "Yes, sisters. The answer is clear. Our course is plainly mapped and unalterable. There are only two roads before us. The one, the white man's road, the road we have traveled for three centuries, leads to certain destruction. It is a road without security for our people, without hope for our people, without provisions for a future for our people. It is a road of subservience, a road of dishonor and shame. A road we have traveled for much too long now. A road we must abandon." Again, he hammered the pulpit, causing the microphones to squeal. "Yes, brothers! Yes, sisters! It is time to detour. It is time to take the alternate road. Our very survival dictates that we must take the alternate road. The road which leads to freedom. A road which leads to a freedom apart from the white man, far removed from his oppression, far removed from his greed and his guile. Yes, brothers! Yes, sisters! The time to detour is now!"

The noise among the congregations grew by orders of magnitude.

Reverend Ahmet basked in the unrest momentarily before, again, stretching his hand across the congregation, and continuing, "But, I tell you, brothers and sisters, the white man will not allow us to pursue our own road without a fight. I tell you, brothers and sisters, I warn you brothers and sisters, I admonish you, brothers and sisters, we MUST take up arms to pursue the alternate road!"

A hushed quiet fell on the listeners as the meanings in his words filtered through to understanding.

For years, members of the black community had contemplated armed revolt. Occasionally, black fringe groups had worked hard to bring about that revolt, but, never before had a leader of the stature and political importance of the Reverend Mustafa Ahmet called for blacks to arm themselves. Ahmet's message was clear to even the most obtuse of those listening to the speech. Government agents who had tuned into the broadcast, monitoring its content, were stunned at the words of the black leader. Instantly, they went to the phones. Ahmet was advocating revolution and from the sound of the black followers, it appeared there was about to be some major trouble.

At the pulpit, Ahmet continued with renewed fervor. "Yes, brothers and sisters, there are no easy solutions. I say unto you that there is a battle ahead—a war—a war where our very existence hangs in the balance. In the past, we have been weak, but, I say unto you that the time for weakness is gone. Never again will the black man turn the other cheek to the continued abuse of the white devils. I say unto you that, if we value our lives, if we desire freedom on this earth, if we would have our chirren be secure, then, we must take up arms now, in this instant, without hesitation, without thought of reprisal, without regard for any and withstand the white scourge to its face. The pale horse must die. We must take up arms and ensure a place of security for our families! Take up arms and break the chains of the white man's oppression! Take up arms and, with the help of our vengeful and mighty Allah, wrestle independence from the evil, twisted, satanic grasp of the white man!"

The crowds erupted in deafening cries of support and agreement. Reverend Ahmet's dramatic rhetoric had achieved his desired results. With a contented gaze, Ahmet watched the crowd. Behind a mask of solemnity, Reverend Ahmet rejoiced. Deep within, he could feel the spirit of the Revolution he had fathered. Now the white man would know the fury of the black masses. Finally, the white man's yoke of oppression would be broken and a new, powerful black nation would be born. A nation in need of dynamic leadership. And who else would be more worthy or deserving of such a glorious and demanding honor as leading so powerful a nation than himself? The wheels of ambitious greed spun unhindered in his mind as he watched the crowd roar in defiance to the white man's control. Some among the congregation held weapons aloft. The other crowds across the nation picked up the cries, and the Revolution was born. Still silent, behind Ahmet, Humari stood with eyes closed, giving thanks to Allah.

Ahmet's speech, though brief, was perfectly timed, catching the black population at a point when they were most terrified, most uncertain of what the future held. His carefully chosen words had struck the right notes in the unsettled masses of bewildered and frightened black citizens. Before the closed circuit screens went black, Reverend Ahmet raised a clinched black fist in salute before him. Humari, smiling broadly, now, also raised a fist. To the man, Ahmet's bodyguard contingent mimicked the gesture.

In the streets outside the church, the Los Angeles policemen assigned to monitor the assembly, suddenly recognizing the danger, quietly slipped into their patrol cars and eased away from the area. The police net crackled with warnings of an imminent riot.

---◆---

Sundays were supposed to be days of rest. Lazy days of peace on earth and good will towards man—not so Sunday, September 17. It was a beautiful, sun filled morning. Richard and Marsha Howell, cruising along in the rental car, sitting practically atop one another, married less than 24 hours, were on their honeymoon. They had come to Los Angeles from their home in Lawrence, Kansas, to see the ocean, California, Hollywood, and maybe, if they got lucky, a movie star or two. On this morning, the two had decided to take an unguided tour of the city and surrounding countryside. Richard had been driving for over an hour and was, after so many turns, one way streets, and counter turns, completely clueless as to his location. That they were lost did not seem to concern either of the two young lovers. They were already happily lost in one another's closeness, oblivious to the world outside the rental car.

Had they known anything about the results of Reverend Ahmet's speech of the preceding night , or had they taken the time to glance at one of the many newspapers in the Hilton's lobby, or had they simply turned on the car's radio, Richard and Marsha would have, no doubt, been alerted to the very real threat of extreme civil unrest in the Los Angeles area. Had they known anything about Los Angeles, they would have turned the car around when they passed the sign that said 'Now Entering Compton'. Had this been any other day, or had they been black, Richard and Marsha Howell may have lived to enjoy their marriage. But this was not any other day and they were white. With violent suddenness, the young couples' carefree happiness was about to dissolve.

Jerome Lanning had been among those present at the fiery speech of Reverend Ahmet the night before. He had not required the urging of the Reverend to take up arms against the white man. Jerome had taken up his arms a full 19 years earlier. The product of a fatherless home, Jerome had taken to the streets early in life mostly to get out of the house and away from his violent, sometimes drugged, always drunken, mother.

On the street, Jerome quickly learned that the secret to survival was strength—cold, heartless strength. At 15, Jerome killed for the first time. It happened during a gang fight with rivals from a few blocks away. The other boy had been older and taller than Jerome, but not fast enough to escape the wide arc of the knife's blade held in the angered Jerome's hand. The sharpened steel had cut a wide gash across the unfortunate youth's abdomen and his intestines had expanded outward through the hole. The fight had broken up to the screams of the dying youth. Jerome stood his ground watching his adversary die before him. He had felt no remorse at the act. Rather, he was filled with a certain dark satisfaction. Later, Jerome would brag about the act, and boast of his ability with a blade.

By stealing, selling drugs, and pimping, Jerome managed to eke out an existence on his wits. Apart from the occasional run-ins with the police, Jerome managed to elude justice and escaped the penalties of spending tremendous amounts of time behind bars. In the course of his criminal, street wise life, Jerome had, quite literally, gotten away with murder on more than one occasion. His elusiveness and cunning, combined with his cool ruthlessness had made him the leader of his street gang by the time he was 17. Over the years, that leadership had been challenged countless times. In each instance, Jerome had emerged, though in many cases wounded to varying degrees, with his command intact. The pretenders, or the majority of them at any rate, had emerged as corpses in garbage dumps, sewer lines, gutters or other such out of the way places. Due to his reputation, Jerome had been the subject of many drive-by shootings also. His uncanny ability to escape from each of such attempts upon his life only added to his reputation of fearlessness, cunning, and luck.

For the majority of Jerome's life, apart from the occasional white store clerk or stranded motorist, it had been other blacks who bore the brunt of Jerome's violence filled attacks. That had changed, however, shortly after the famed Rodney King affair in the early 1990s. Watching the tape of the white officers mercilessly pounding King with their batons had awakened in Jerome a previously untapped hatred. With newly found reason for living, Jerome turned his murderous sights on the white man. No longer did Jerome commit crimes exclusively for profit. He began to find an indescribable satisfaction in casually shooting white drivers on the highway, or shooting into crowds of whites wherever they might gather. These were activities that Jerome accomplished alone, possessing the aforethought that his continued leadership of the gang would be severely jeopardized, had his gang been aware of his killing for reasons other than profit or revenge. Even among street gangs, Jerome recognized, there were codes of conduct, and his unnatural desire to kill whites did not fit the code.

The Reverend Ahmet's speech had changed the code, however, and Jerome had had no difficulties convincing his gang that it was their duty to 'take up arms' as the Reverend had instructed and "'witstan' the face of the white man." Now, Jerome explained to his gang members, being outnumbered as they were, it was the responsibility of all blacks to kill as many whites as possible. If profit could be gained in the killing, so much the better, but it was not to be the single motive for carrying out their natural duty. Just as Reverend Ahmet had manipulated the crowds, Jerome, too, manipulated his gang, transforming them from a gang of ordinary ruffians to a band of fervent zealots bent on the total destruction of the white race.

Richard and Marsha Howell were on a collision course with Jerome and did not have an inkling of the danger. Jerome saw the shiny new car when it turned onto the street four blocks down. He recognized, instantly, that the car was out of place as it turned slowly, hesitantly, and came in his direction. At slightly greater than two blocks distant, Jerome could tell for sure—the car's occupants were white—a couple, man and woman, nestled close together. Jerome compressed his lips into a tight line. He turned the junker's ignition key and the engine coughed to life.

"Strap Tight, Homes!" he ordered the others in the car as he continued to closely watch the approaching white coupler coming steadily in their direction.

"Yo!" questioned one of the gang members in the back seat, "S'up wi' dat? You trippin' or sump?"

"We fixin' to bust some white ass!" Jerome replied, now leaning slightly over the steering wheel and gunning the engine, "Tha's wha's up wi dat, and you best be holdin' tight, Home, or your ass may be floatin' in the wind. You dig?"

The youth in the back seat, now noticing the oncoming car, quickly fastened his seat belt and held his legs high in front of him, feet planted firmly against the front seat. Jerome allowed the oncoming car to get within twenty feet of the front of the stolen car and then threw the transmission into drive and stomped hard on the accelerator.

The impact came without warning. One instant, the couple was cruising contentedly along. The next instant, their world exploded with crunching metal and splintering glass. The rental car was knocked backward by the force of the collision and the engine sputtered momentarily before going dead. Richard, dazed from the impact, though not injured, instinctively fumbled with the door handle, trying to get out of the car. Through the spider-webbed windshield, he could see the angry face of the other car's driver. He could almost feel the hatred there. Black men began filing out of the other car. Richard pulled out on the door's handle and shoved. The door would not move. Richard, even though seriously addled, wondered why the other driver, who was now getting out of the car, looked so mad.

"Surely," Richard thought aloud, "he doesn't believe this is my fault." He shoved again against the door, but it was jammed tight from the collision and refused to open. "Marsha," he said finally, "move over here, honey, and let me crawl out your side. My door's stuck."

There was no reply. For the first time since the impact with the other car, Richard looked in Marsha's direction. The sight chilled him, cut through some of the fuzziness in his reasoning, and snatched him partway out of the haze and into reality. Marsha was slumped over in the passenger seat, unconscious. Her hair a mat of blood and glass fragments. "Oh God!," he cried, wrestling with his seat belt and leaning towards her, "Oh God!" He shook the shoulder of his limp wife, willing her to wake up. "Marsha?…Marsha?!!!" Crying now, his hand went to her wrist, fingers probed for a pulse. To his relief, he found one.

The car's back door opened violently. Richard, all but helpless with fear over his wife's condition, half-turned at the sound. There was a black man in the opening between car and street.

"My wife is hurt!" Richard announced to the man, "Call an ambu…"

Brilliant fireworks exploded in Richard's head as the black man crashed a short length of steel pipe above and just behind Richard's right ear. Numbed, Richard cried out and fell heavily against the dashboard, hands cradling his head. He struggled to retain consciousness against a cloud of dripping darkness. In dreamlike horror, he watched as Marsha's door was wrenched open. Frozen, he saw the black hands reach in, clasp hold of his newlywed wife's still form and yank her to the street. Gathering all the resolve he could muster, his fear now compounded by helpless, frustrated anger, Richard drunkenly lunged towards the passenger doorway. The black man in the back seat hit him again, harder this time.

Head swimming and barely conscious, Richard watched through agonized, tear filled eyes as, only inches away, Marsha's clothes were torn away revealing the naked pink skin beneath. The black hands explored, roughly, her private places. One of the large black men began lowering his sweat pants. It was the last thing that Richard Howell would ever see. Another blow from the back seat and the cloud descended upon him. He fell face down on the floorboard. Behind him, the black man leaned far forward, and brought the steel pipe down upon the back of Richard's head over and over, with a primitive fury, until, finally, with a sickening crunch, Richard's skull gave way.

Satisfied that he had killed the white man, Jerome tossed the bloody length of pipe into the floorboard beside his victim and, smiling, crawled out of the rental car to join the others in their bacchanalian fest.

Mercifully, Marsha Howell never regained consciousness. The 20 year old newlywed died in the street with, as the county coroner's report would reveal, 116 stab wounds in her chest, stomach and legs.

Elsewhere in the city, other whites were also witnessing, first-hand, the rage of the black community. Angry blacks, still in the grips of the Reverend Ahmet's fiery speech from the preceding night, converged on white churches all over Los Angeles and the surrounding communities. With unrestrained violence, whites from all denominations were dragged from sanctuaries and were beaten and spat upon by over-whelming numbers of angry, vengeance seeking blacks. Like scenes from some incredible, dark fiction, a century of black anger and help-lessness was being vented with volcanic passion. Many among the vic-tims died that first Sunday. Some died from gunshot or knife trauma. Most, however, were simply beaten without mercy.

The police forces were overwhelmed with calls for assistance. Their presence at some of the scenes did precious little to halt the violence, at any rate. Most units responding to the calls immediately came under attack by the enraged mobs. Policemen quickly became so immersed in the difficulties of protecting their own lives that they were of little or no help to the citizens being attacked. Twenty six California policemen were counted among the four hundred and sixteen other people killed in and around Los Angeles that Sunday.

And, that was only Los Angeles. Elsewhere, as word of the violence in California hit the wires, confrontation sparked and the scenes of terror were duplicated in virtually every other major metropolitan area in the United States. Blacks, by the thousands, joined in spirit of sanguine solidarity, lashed out against their own, local white populations. Whites, also by their thousands, upon hearing news of the attacks, began the inevitable retaliation. By nightfall, warnings had been issued, nationwide, for citizens to remain in their homes. Millions of confused citizens watched the unbelievable scenes of chaos unfold on their television screens. Blow led to blow, the flames were fanned, and the revolution advocated by Reverend Ahmet was underway.

All across the nation, the Revolution sparked. Violence spawned violence and gaping wounds were cut into communities from the coasts to the heartland, as years of frustrated bigotry metamorphosed into destructive fury.

Ahmet woke early that Sunday morning to monitor news reports. He was not forced to wait long for the first hint of a smile to rest upon his smooth face. As the day progressed and the reports of violence intensified in both scope and regularity, he was pleased to detect hints of mounting panic among the 'establishment'. His ears inside the beltway assured him that the very foundations of the Republic were rattled. In the hours following his speech, Ahmet had feared that the blacks, should they take up arms as he prompted, would only wither in the face of determined police intervention. Watching the scenes as they played on his large screen television—the flailing mobs, the overturned, blackened police vehicles, the dead patrolmen—Ahmet breathed a sigh of relief. His fears were unfounded. His optimism soared.

Khalied Humari, Ahmet's almost constant companion was beside himself with joy. Allah was moving in a powerful way. It was a movement that would not have been possible without his own, direct intervention. Surely, a great award awaited him.

Less than one hundred miles away, Martin Hastings, in a cabin overlooking the Shenandoah Valley, was also watching the reports of the violence that was sweeping the country. He wore no smile upon his face, but was pleased, nonetheless. Reverend Ahmet's speech of the previous evening was not unanticipated. Indeed, the rhetoric emanating from behind the lectern was only another part of Hastings' well conceived plan. His investment in a fifth Planning Group member had paid off handsomely. Humari had pulled it off. The blacks had taken up arms. Things were proceeding smoothly, on schedule, and as anticipated. Black Tuesday had been more successful than even he had dared hope. The NOA squads had become invisible, nocturnal terrors which were inflicting terrible casualties. Now, finally, the blacks were retaliating. The stage was set for the final acts. His thoughts turned to Kelly. Soon, he told her memory, you will be avenged.

---◆---

Watching the clouds of his own breath disappear into the sea air, Hastings felt no remorse, nor regret for his actions along the course leading up to Black Tuesday. He was as convinced, now, as he had been from the inception of the idea. Blacks were a cancer in the democratic system that had to be excised. The cost to the United States, however, had been much greater than Hastings and the Planning Group could have imagined. The thoughts of that damage, perhaps irreparable damage, troubled him deeply. Try though he might, he could not reconcile himself to the fact that it was a price that had to be paid. Certainly, the participants had been willing to pay.

From the earliest days of his decision to take the course of revenge, Hastings understood that any chances for the success of any such revenge depended on the active support of the white population. He also realized, early, that such support would only come if the whites were prodded into action. Hastings could think of no better motivation to mobilize the white majority than a violent uprising on the part of the blacks. Although the small army he had amassed would, if successful in its various operations, eliminate a substantial bulk of the black population within the United States, Hastings knew that, ultimately, without the support of the white population, his quest was in vain. Hastings' understanding of human nature provided him with nothing but optimism that, once the blacks retaliated in any fashion, the whites would, in earnest, join the fight to eliminate the blacks. Hastings' optimism proved well founded. The retaliation that, now, was being broadcast to the entire world created the magnet Hastings desired to pull all whites, by their noses, into the cause.

By the end of the day following Reverend Ahmet's speech, thousands of whites had been killed and countless more wounded in the attacks that marked the beginning of the Revolution of blacks in North America. Across the nation, in every state, gunfights raged between police forces and black mobs. In only few areas, were the conflicts suppressed by strong police intervention. In such areas, the black mobs, content with their small display of solidarity and force, when faced with significant numbers of police, retreated. Most areas, however, only saw small conflicts metamorphose into violent racial storms as the confrontations rapidly escalated into small scale battles as the blacks refused to disperse in the face of concentrated police confrontation. Streets were barricaded. Communities became instant war zones and casualties began to mount rapidly on both sides. By the morning of September 18, white citizens in those cities most thoroughly engulfed in the violence, despite police warnings, took up arms of their own and joined the battles in the streets.

The 1st Platoon of Charlie Company of the 1-94th Infantry Battalion, a National Guard unit from Fayetteville, N.C., unloaded from the three deuce-and-a-half transports in Chicago's south side during the pre-dawn hours of September 20. The 37 men hastily took up positions along both sides of the street and in the buildings lining the street. Portable generator units barked and emitted their distinct diesel aroma and, instantly, bright light illuminated the otherwise darkened streets. In the distance, the sound of sporadic gunfire was clearly audible as small battles continued throughout the city. Captain Russell Shirley, Charlie Company's commander, busily moved from position to position issuing orders to his unsettled troops. The company's RTO followed closely behind.

Captain Shirley, a real estate salesman in his civilian life, had been a member of the National Guard for eight years. Apart from a short tour of two days' duty guarding businesses in Cape Hatteras, North Carolina, against looters, following Hurricane Julia, this was the only real action he had ever experienced. On the exterior he was calm and all business, inside, his guts churned as adrenaline raced through him as he realized how truly unprepared he actually was. Every few seconds he would survey the deserted street, in both directions, searching for any hint of movement, any possible threat to his Company. Twice he saw bands of people, black or white he could not tell, crossing the street in the distance, but, so far, none had ventured near 1st platoon's position. He hoped that none would. At present strength, Captain Shirley's Company was greater than 50% black. He was very unsure as to how the blacks in his command would react to an order to fire on other blacks. He could sense the unease among the other members of his command, as they too pondered the question.

The skyline to the east began to lighten gradually. The Company's 2nd and 3rd Platoons were patrolling the same street three miles further south where they had been dropped off earlier. The six two and a half ton trucks that had been used to transport those platoons from the airport were now parked alongside the other three from which 1st platoon had unloaded. The 2nd and 3rd platoon's line of march would bring them to the defensive perimeter, if nothing went wrong, within the hour. Captain Shirley maintained constant radio contact with the other two platoons. His orders, though brief, were clear. Charlie Company was responsible for the entire area of 63rd Street west to the Airport and east to Jackson Beach. Civilians encountered in the area were to be ordered off the streets. Those that would not conform to orders were to be apprehended and held pending pick up by civilian law enforcement officials. Looters, vandals and those civilians offering armed resistance were to be eliminated with extreme prejudice. Captain Shirley was very much aware that no more than a handful of his 114 man company had ever fired live rounds at another human being. He hoped that none would have to do so during this present mission. His hopes were soon shattered.

The sky began to lose its shadow to be slowly replaced by a cloudless blue as the newly arrived sun chased the darkness from the streets. The smell of smoke from distant fires filled the chilly morning air. Captain Shirley ordered the power generators silenced and the flood lights extinguished. The abrupt cessation of the diesel generators' rumbling created a vacuum of silence inside the defensive perimeter. Shirley contacted his company's patrolling squads for a status check. They were, now, less than a mile and a half away and had encountered no hostile activity. Shirley was beginning to feel a bit more at ease when the police siren north of his company's perimeter snatched his attention. The single patrol car had turned onto the street less than 100 yards from the perimeter's edge. The car slid to stop, sideways, in the middle of the street and two policemen, shotguns in hand, got out and took positions on the near side of the vehicle, facing up the street. From that direction, other sirens could be heard closing in. Captain Shirley searched the vacant street beyond the police car with his binoculars. It was not long before he saw them—two other police cars were in pursuit of another vehicle. The three cars were speeding in the direction of the perimeter, directly for the police car blocking the street. All eyes within the perimeter turned toward the sound of the approaching sirens. The policemen standing behind the parked patrol car leveled their shotguns across the roof of their vehicle and trained them on the approaching car, which was not showing any sign of decreasing its speed. Captain Shirley ordered his men to standby in case the car broke through the roadblock and attempted to penetrate the perimeter. A wave of metallic clicks coursed through the perimeter's interior as rounds were jacked into well oiled chambers and selector levers were switched to semi-automatic. With nervous anticipation, the weekend warriors watched as the approaching cars bore down on their position.

It very quickly became obvious that the fleeing car was not going to stop for the police roadblock. Captain Shirley wondered, as did others, if the car was going to swerve to avoid hitting the parked patrol car. He jumped, involuntarily, as the officers behind the parked police car opened fire on the approaching vehicle. Still, the car came forward. One of the policemen, seeing that the oncoming car was not going to stop or attempt to avoid impact, quickly ran in the direction of the National Guard Unit's perimeter. The second officer remained stretched across the trunk of the patrol car firing into the oncoming vehicle. It cost him his life. With an earsplitting crash, the fleeing car struck the parked patrol car just behind the rear wheel and careened sharply to the right, swapped ends, struck the burned out frame of another car alongside the street and rolled to stop just 30 yards in front of Captain Shirley.

On impact, the policeman that had remained behind was flung a dozen yards or more and now looked like a broken rag doll lying in the street. The second policeman was bending over him as the other two patrol cars arrived and squealed to a halt. The Guardsmen looked on as, slowly and shakily, the black passengers of the other car began exiting the mangled vehicle. The car's driver, unconscious from the impact, did not move. Four policemen closed on them, guns leveled. The three black men, trapped, nowhere to run, glanced nervously about. The policemen ordered them to place their hands over their heads and moved in slowly. The policeman that had been leaning over his dead partner, now approached the fugitive's wrecked car. He reached the driver's door and violently yanked it open. Before the other policemen could intervene, the enraged officer pulled the unconscious driver to the street.

"You son of a bitch!" The angry patrolman snarled at the inert black man before kicking him forcefully in the ribs.

"Hey!" interjected another of the policemen, "What are you doing Barnes?!"

"You stay out of this!" the maddened policeman answered, "This punk killed Kent." He kicked the motionless black man again.

One of the other black men moved towards the angry policeman. Immediately, he was struck over the back of the head by yet another policemen and knocked to the ground.

"Hey!" came a voice from inside the perimeter, "Cut that shit out!"

Captain Shirley whirled to see who had made the comment. His men, out of their positions, were now bunched in splintered groups watching the events unfold. "Get back to your posts." he ordered angrily.

Some, but not all, of the soldiers responded to the command and slowly ambled back to their assigned positions. A group of eleven black soldiers failed to move and stood defiantly staring at the police.

"I told you men to get back to your posts!" Shirley repeated, red faced, "Now, Move!"

None of the soldiers did so. The other members of the squad looked on nervously at the open insubordination of the black soldiers. Nervous glances, black and white, flitted back and forth, fingers tapped trigger guards.

In the street beyond the perimeter, only vaguely aware of the National Guard spectators, the angry policeman kicked the driver again. Another policeman quickly moved in and grabbed the out of control officer. There was a scuffle. The noise of the affair caused Captain Shirley to return his attention to the street and away from his mutinous soldiers. The car's driver, doubled over on the pavement, began to stir as the two policemen wrestled over him. Another police-man moved in to assist the second officer in controlling the third.

Corporal Demetrius Galen was among the eleven soldiers who had failed to return to their posts at Captain Shirley's command. Anger had been steadily building in the young man for days. Seeing the white policeman kick the unconscious black driver had catapulted his anger to the forefront. Fingers gripped tightly about the handle of his M-16,

Galen watched the three policemen scuffle. Captain Shirley, nervously watched the scuffle and was not sure what to do. The police had not requested assistance, but it appeared clear that they needed some. He was contemplating sending a fire team out of the perimeter to help, when, to his amazement the unruly officer broke free from the grasp of the other two, leveled his shotgun at the now semi-awake black driver and pulled the trigger. The buckshot ripped into the head and upper body of the black man, killing him instantly.

Captain Shirley was in momentary shock.

Unable to stand still an instant longer, one of the other black captives bolted, only to be shot in the back, out of reflex, by another of the policemen.

Inside the National Guard perimeter, Corporal Galen's rage overcame him. "Bastards!" he shouted, raised his M-16 to his shoulder, and took deliberate aim at the policeman that had shot the driver. "Die, you white piece of shit!" Galen spat as he squeezed the trigger.

In the street, the policeman's knees buckled and his eyes rolled inward as the flaming round spiraled through his head. Another black soldier, standing alongside Galen, raised his weapon and leveled it at the policeman that had shot the fleeing black man and fired off a four round burst, killing him also.

Instantly, pandemonium broke loose with an unbridled fury inside the Nation Guard's perimeter.

At Corporal Galen's shout, Captain Shirley had snapped out of his stupor and whirled to face the group of mutinous black soldiers. Before he could react, Corporals Galen and Williams had fired upon the policemen outside the perimeter. Captain Shirley dropped to one knee and clumsily unholstered his 9mm service automatic and pointed it at the group of blacks. "Drop your weapons, now!" he ordered loudly.

There was no response from the group of soldiers.

In the street, the three remaining policemen had scrambled for cover and were now calling urgently in their portable radio for back-up. The remaining two captive black men continued to stand, confused, arms held overhead, in the street, in front of their mangled car.

"I am ordering you," Captain Shirley yelled at the group of black soldiers, even louder this time, "to drop your weapons!"

With a defiant yell, Galen squared off with his Company commander, leveling his M-16 at the same time. Panicked, Captain Shirley jerked the 9mm's trigger and the pistol leapt in his hand. Corporal Galen was knocked off his feet by the impact of the slug in his chest.

"Eat this!" screamed one of the other black soldiers from his position further within the perimeter. Angered at the shooting of his friend, the weekend warrior focused his rifle's sights on the base of the Company commander's skull and squeezed the trigger. Searing pain swept through Captain Shirley and the breath was choked from him as the .223 caliber round tore out his throat.

As if on cue, gunfire erupted from every position within the perimeter in a free for all that pitted white soldier against black. One of the black machine gunners trained his M-60 on the remaining policemen. The policemen's choice of cover had been sufficient to shield them from most conventional small arms fire, but offered no protection against the onslaught of the hundreds of screaming steel core, brass jacketed rounds that assailed them. Within seconds they were dead. The two black men that had been standing in front of their car through it all, now, ran up the street and escaped. Inside the perimeter, one of the white guardsmen took careful aim from his position on the rooftop and dropped the black machine gunner that had killed the remaining policemen. Sweeping the interior of the perimeter with his sights he shot several more blacks before a 40mm grenade detonated behind him, silencing him forever, and raining debris on the street below. The fuel tank of one of the transport trucks ignited when stitched by the gunfire of a dying soldier and the entire truck left the ground as its tank exploded with an earth shaking thump.

The sanctity of the perimeter had given way to the fury of a battle ground. Half a mile further down the street, the approaching Platoons heard the gunfire. There could be no mistaking the sound of the military weapons. First Platoon was under attack. Lieutenant Jason Castle, a real estate salesman in real life, the patrol commander, tried desperately to reach Captain Shirley on the radio. Static was the only reply. At Lieutenant Castle's direction, the seventy plus soldiers increased their pace and headed towards the sound of the action at a brisk, noisome trot.

The firefight inside the perimeter lasted less than a minute. When it was over, eight black men remained alive. Twenty-nine other soldiers lay dead or dying. Corporal Galen, gingerly rubbing his bruised ribs beneath the flak vest, was among the living. The other black soldiers were gathered about him.

"Well, Brothers," Galen said through teeth clenched against the pain, "we're in some deep shit, now." He pointed at the inert, blood soaked body of Captain Shirley. "What do you think Castle is gonna say 'bout that?"

The others did not answer.

"I'll tell you what he's gonna say." Galen answered his own question. "We're responsible! That's what! We're responsible and we're goin' to jail!." He waited for a reply. There was none, as the seven other blacks, still in a state of shock, merely shrugged their shoulders and stared at the dead bodies, or into the distance. "Well," Galen continued, "I don't plan on going to jail for this shit!"

One of the others finally spoke up. "Well, whatcha gonna do, D? We can't hold off two platoons."

With a grimace, Galen reached inside his tee shirt and removed his ID tags. "I don't plan on bein' here when they show up." He answered. "Anybody goin' with me, give me your dog tags."

The others, all the others, curious, complied. Galen directed a few of the remaining soldiers to load the bodies of several of the dead black soldiers into one of the remaining transports. When this was finished, Galen removed his camouflage jacket and pitched it in the truck with the dead soldiers. The others followed suit.

"O.K." Galen said, when all was as he had directed, "Let's get the hell out of here." Turning, Galen pitched a hand grenade into the back of the transport truck and, accompanied by the others, ran up the deserted street. The blast's hot air buffeted them when they were less than thirty yards away. Bits of shrapnel whistled in their midst, but no one was seriously hurt.

"Congratulations, Bros." Galen said half-heartedly as he continued to run along the sidewalk, "You're all dead niggers now!" Eight new soldiers joined the black Revolution.

In Washington D.C., the White House was reeling. The attacks by the black mobs, feared since the news of the September 12 murders, had rocked the government. Each violent action on the part of the blacks was being met with an equally violent reaction on the part of the whites. To say the situation was out of control was, clearly, an understatement. Like a great tidal wave gaining strength with each city it coursed through, the terror flooded the country. The failure of local and state law enforcement forces to contain, let alone stop, the violence, had forced President Blount to impose martial law by the third week of September. Under Executive Order, the National Guard was mobilized and deployed in numbers as never before in American history. But, even that had not been enough to stem the tide.

Confusion had rapidly became the mood of the day. Distrust, fear and uncertainty prevailed in every area where whites and black were in contact. The same distrust, fear and uncertainty was conspicuously present in both houses of Congress. National Guard units deployed to control the riots were suddenly faced with situations for which they were neither trained nor equipped to handle. It was not a question of military superiority. The National Guard clearly held the upper hand with regard to firepower. The question—the problem—was much more basic. Young black and white soldiers who had trained and lived together for months, in some instances, years, trained to locate, contain and destroy the enemy, were suddenly unsure who the enemy was. Since every military unit deployed was completely integrated, this basic problem quickly assumed immense proportions. It became obvious, in the earliest stages of the deployments, that the effectiveness of the National Guard to control the rapidly escalating violence was non-existent. Predictably, almost immediately, incidents involving guard units fighting among themselves erupted as racial mistrust overbalanced military discipline. The mutinous reports from the field shook the officers at the Pentagon. The implications were terrifying.

Although placed on full alert, no regular military units were activated. The Joint Chiefs of Staff, also integrated with the presence of General Wilkins, the U.S. Air Force's first black Commanding General, were well aware that the nation's regular troops, regardless of training, were equally susceptible to the type of chaos that was being demonstrated among many of the National Guard units. The military career generals were determined not to put the regular forces to the test, or, if unsuccessful in keeping regular units out of the fighting, were determined to, at least, delay their deployment as long as possible. Their report to the President was straight-forward, the National Guard would have to deal with its problems and stop the rioting as well, without the aid of regular forces.

By the middle of October, the Country was completely engulfed in civil war. Blacks and whites attacked one another with vengeance. Daily, intense battles raged on both coasts, in the heartland, and from border to border. Leaders of the large North American Latin-American community were faced with a dilemma. The white man's system against which the blacks revolted was also a system which appeared biased against them. Change to the system could only be beneficial. However, deep seated feelings of distrust which had existed between themselves and blacks for generations prevented the majority of Latin-Americans from embracing the black cause. It became evident, early on, that neutrality was not an option. The nature of the conflict precluded such a luxury. Other ethnic groups, for the most part, had already sided with the established government. By the first week of October, Asians, Indians, and those of European origin had joined forces with the whites. Only certain immigrants from African and middle eastern countries sided with the blacks. The numbers that did so were not significant.

Another group of Hispanic origin, those that preferred to call themselves Chicanos, those that had little respect for 'vendido Latin-Americans' and even less for 'niggers' and 'gabachos', saw the Revolution as a perfect opportunity to liberate Aztlan, their conceptual homeland, from the control of the United States. Theirs' became a campaign of killing everyone, white and black alike, who crossed their path. They vented their frustrations, which had been building their entire lives, with fury. An already undermanned and over worked California law enforcement network bore the brunt of this radical groups first assaults. To don a police uniform in those earliest days of the Revolution was to sign one's own death warrant.

The remaining Latin-Americans had the presence of mind not to stand in the radical group's, the Batos Locos, ex-cons, and generally disgruntled Chicano citizens', way, but they were still not clear on what sort of stand to take for themselves in the Revolution. That is until, on October 21, a group of black youths, not a faction of the newly established Revolutionary Army, went on a killing rampage in a barrio of southern California. 163 people, mostly women and children, were killed in the senseless massacre. News of the murders spread rapidly and all debates ended as the choice was made—Mexican-Americans took up arms and fell in alongside whites. Blacks had created yet another enemy for themselves.

Dr. Norris Benjamin cast a wearied look at the wall clock, 2:24 a.m., and leaned over so that the nurse could wipe his sweating brow. His arms were red to above the elbow with the blood of the dying man on the table before him. It was Benjamin's thirteenth straight hour in the operating room. It had been 27 hours since he had last slept. A line of patients were backed up in preparation and more were arriving by the minute. There was no time to curse the madness. Lives were fading.

The emergency room's floor was slick with blood and cries of pain and despair filled the halls. Benjamin was reminded of the year he had spent in a field hospital in Bosnia/Herzegovina. At least, there, he had gotten a break from time to time, casualties arriving only in random spurts. Here, now, there was no break. The wounded continued to arrive in seemingly endless numbers. The hospital was already overflowing with violence victims in need of immediate and intensive care. Supplies were almost completely depleted. Blood was getting scarce. It had been that way since the last week of September. All of the staff doctors were on continuous duty and had been since the first of October. They, like Benjamin, snatched sleep in bits, whenever and wherever they could. There was not a lot of sleep for any of them. Something, they all agreed, would have to be done soon. Their abilities, all recognized, were being greatly impaired by the stress and exhaustion. Careless mistakes were being made and lives were being lost needlessly. There was no place to turn for help. The madness was everywhere.

Benjamin shook his head from side to side, trying to fight off the fog of mind numbing tiredness, and busily tried to salvage the life of the rapidly fading gunshot victim on the operating table. The sound of the gunfire seemed dreamlike to the exhausted surgeon and failed to set off any alarms in his fight or flight response mechanism. His attention, what little remained, was centered exclusively on the tangle of organs in the open wound before him. He snapped back to full consciousness when the operating room's double doors burst open. He turned in time to see a handful of armed black men filling the open doorway. The truth registered only an instant before the rain of lead tore through him and the other occupants of the room.

The revolutionaries fired into the still bodies several more times, ensuring that their task was accomplished completely, before moving on to other rooms. Dr. Benjamin finally received his rest, eternal rest, sprawled across the inert, bullet riddled body of one of the black nurses. In the hall outside the operating room, black and white wounded alike were silenced forever—more victims of frustrated hatred.

The Black Tuesday murders had sent massive shock waves through-out the world. The proponents of the New World Order, the Council on Foreign relations, the Trilateral Commission, and other such would-be world controlling groups were taken completely by sur-prise. These political groups found themselves standing helplessly on the sidelines as the Revolution erupted days later. As events contin-ued to unfold, several all night sessions were held at various points on the globe as members of the various organizations met to con-sider all the options. The consensus opinion arising from such meet-ings was very disturbing. Despite the cost in human suffering and death, it was concluded that the Revolution was a necessary thing. The members of these elitist groups, worldwide, had long since rec-ognized that the largest obstacle in their common goal of one world government, currency, and order, was the American people. For years these groups, the Trilateral Commission, and Council on Foreign Relations especially, had sought to gain control of the population of the United States through executive and legislative manipulation. They had moved subtly in the early years, but, of late, they had been open in their support of radical constitutional change. With the latest in assaults on militia groups, and strict gun control measures recently becoming law, the groups were well on their way towards disarming the American public, an agreed necessity, when the Revolution erupted.

Another group, a darker, more powerful group, was watching events in America closely also. This group was an anonymous collection of would-be controllers, the existence of which was unknown to all but the most influential persons on Earth. Like the other, more widely known groups, this group's goal was also single world government—a government of absolute domination. The Revolution was only three days old when the most prominent members of this group pronounced that the Revolution would serve to occupy the American public sufficiently to allow for the acceleration of the established timetable for the introduction of their proposed New Order. A meeting of their own was called.

On November 11, a very secret, ultra high level meeting was convened on the top floor of a business tower in Brussels, Belgium. The hour was late, the halls were darkened, and an army of guards were positioned before the conference room's doors. The floor had been cleared twenty-four hours prior to the meeting. More guards had been stationed in and around all stairwells and elevators. No one who did not belong would be allowed near the floor. The twelve men assembled for the meeting comprised the entire group and represented the most powerful people on the face of the Earth. One was American, the remainder from Europe and the Far East. Each of the twelve wore the look of power. The mood was electric. Each knew the purpose of the meeting. All had looked forward to such a meeting for the greater part of their lives. The twelve men had never before assembled together, most had never met. To do so may have caused undue scrutiny by any of the world's intelligence agencies—scrutiny that was unwanted and avoided with the most extreme prejudice. It was, after all, in their secrecy that these men possessed their power. History had given them a healthy respect for the common masses.

For nearly a century, the group and its predecessors had manipulated world events from behind the scenes, taking extreme care to conceal their involvement in world events from the eyes and ears of ordinary citizens. At best, they were a ruthless bunch, able to look beyond their betrayals and deceit, beyond their periodic advocacy of mass slaughter of innocents, to the ultimate gain of wealth and absolute power. Nothing was nonexpendable. Nothing was impossible to them. They had demonstrated that, more than once, through the years, on every continent. When the invading German had swung wide right instead of directly into France in the first years of the twentieth century it was at the direction of the group. It had been the same group which ordered and oversaw the destruction of humanity in the ovens close to 30 years later on the same continent. There was no continent, no nation, which had not felt the influence of the powerful group. Assassinations of world leaders, elections of world leaders, transportation accidents, wars—the group had ordered countless through the years. When the wall came down in the '80s ending the Cold War, it had been at their order.

The group had watched the activities of Martin Hastings for years, and had allowed him the freedom to execute his designs. They had even, on occasion, assisted him, without detection, along the way. The Revolution had not come as a surprise to them. It had been inevitable for greater than a century. Now that it had actually occurred, their long awaited moment had arrived. The events in the United States provided a unique opportunity to put into motion plans made in the previous century, plans which had been enlarged and refined through the years, plans which paved the way to a single world government united by a single currency and a single language.

The Brussels meeting had been awaited for decades. Now, that it was actually taking place, the group's members eagerly discussed their relative parts and steps necessary to ensure that the proper steps were taken to fully capitalize on the terror which now gripped the strongest nation on the planet. Contingency plans were reviewed, alterations made, and logistics worked through. In less than an hour, the meeting was over and, one by one, the group disbanded. Calls would be made. Orders would be issued. The world would be subdued. With stoic optimism, each man left the meeting full of purpose.

With the passage of time, Julie Darnell became accustomed to the disapproving stares she often received when out in public with her black husband and their mixed race children. The disgust filled looks no longer made her uneasy like they had in the early years. She had met Abe, her husband, in the college years. Julie welcomed him to her bed after only the second date. Two months later, Julie was pregnant and the two were engaged. She had seen nothing wrong with falling in love with and ultimately marrying a black man. Her parents had opposed the marriage and, even now, treated Abe with contempt. Her two daughters received the same treatment during the infrequent visits to their grandparents' home. The welcome at Abe's parents' home was no better. Harassment from the neighbors began the day Julie and Abe moved into their new house in Doraville, Georgia. In the three years they lived there, their car tires were slashed twice, windows broken with rocks numerous times, obscene and threatening phone calls were an almost everyday occurrence. The message that they were hated and unwanted in the neighborhood was crystal clear, but they refused to be intimidated and tried their best to ignore the harassment. Abe was away on business the night the molotov cocktail was hurled through the living room window. Julie, a sound sleeper, had not awoken at the sound of breaking glass. The flames spread quickly and smoke filled the house.

Julie and her two daughters, mercifully, succumbed to the smoke long before the first flames licked at their flesh.

Abe returned from his trip to find a blackened frame where his house once stood. The yellow barrier tape surrounding the house filled him with dread. He tried to prepare himself for the worst, but was unsuccessful as, when he learned that Julie and the children were dead, he broke into uncontrollable sobbing. The Fire Marshall suspected arson. Abe had no doubts. He could see the proof in the knowing looks of his neighbors.

That was a year earlier. Abe left Georgia and moved west, taking a job in Kansas. When the Revolution broke out. Abe, still keenly feeling the loss of his family, bought a Chinese SKS rifle out of the trunk of an acquaintance's car for $120.00. The case of 7.62 rounds came from the army surplus store across town. Abe quit his job and, packing the weapon and ammunition in his car, headed south.

The Revolution had not yet reached the sleeping Doraville community when Abe pulled to a stop along the street where he and Julie had once made their home. He cut the engine and sat in the silence, breathing deeply. The fear was gone. He had made up his mind to go through with it and there was no turning back now. Mental images of his beloved wife and children's charred bodies fueled the drive for revenge within him. Hate radiated from his eyes as he exited the car, quietly, rifle in hand. Opening the car's back door, he retrieved the heavy bandoleer of extra magazines for the SKS and looped them over his neck. He took a short look at the neat rows of houses lining both sides of the empty street. Another house, he noted, had been built where his had once stood. The pain of his loss surged. With determined purpose, he stalked across the freshly watered lawn of the first house at the end of the block.

Entry was easy. The back door was unlocked. Abe crept through the darkness, rifle at ready. The padded carpeting softened his foot falls as he eased along the darkened hallway leading to the ranch home's bedrooms. He reached the first of these and peered inside. It was the child's room. Abe passed it up, continuing down the hallway. The next door opened to the sleeping couple, a wide space on the bed separated them. Abe eased through the opening. The soft moonlight issuing through the bedroom window glistened on the narrow bayonet affixed to the Chinese rifle in his hands. He gained bedside access without disturbing the room's sleeping occupants. Without a moment's hesitation, he drove the slender bayonet into and through the body of the sleeping man, piercing his heart. Death was almost instant. The man jerked once, violently, shaking the bed. The man's wife's eyes fluttered open. Instantly, Abe's left hand shot out and covered the startled woman's mouth. With his right arm, he yanked the bayonet from the limp body of the woman's dead husband and rested its dripping tip at the hollow just above her heaving breasts. Wild eyed, the woman struggled beneath his hand. Abe looked deep into the terrified, pleading eyes and smiled. The bayonet went in easily. Abe had to release his hold over the woman's mouth and used that arm, along with his right, to maintain hold on the rifle, pinning the helpless woman's violently gyrating, dying body to the bed. After a few frantic seconds, it was over. Abe removed the bayonet from the woman's throat, wiped the blood on the bedspread, and made his way back to the child's room.

The second house was securely locked. No door or window would yield to his efforts and Abe was forced to move on to the next house. He found the doors to this house also locked securely, but an open window in the utility room made for quiet, if not easy, access. The family cat, disturbed by the late night intrusion bounded to the floor from its resting place atop the clothes dryer. As Abe's feet met the floor, the cat rubbed against his pants leg and purred. Abe reached down and patted its furry head. He had always liked cats. An airplane roared by close overhead piercing the silence. Abe entered the kitchen and moved to the hallway. He heard voices and froze in the darkness. After a minute of listening Abe recognized the voices as coming from a television set. He continued down the hall.

The first bedroom was empty. The bed was neat and unrumpled. Abe remembered that this family had a teenage son and younger daughter when he had lived in the neighborhood. This was probably, Abe concluded, the son's bedroom and he had probably moved out for college, or other such. Abe moved on. The second bedroom contained the daughter. She was not the youngster Abe remembered. Looking at her, in the darkness, it was obvious that she had grown substantially. She lay atop the bed's covers, naked, her tanned body bathed in the soft moon glow. Abe stared for a moment, before moving further down the hall.

The next door opened to a bathroom. The last door along the hall was the parent's bedroom. Abe turned the handle slowly and leaned against the door as it opened with a creak. Abe paused for a second, then, gritted his teeth and pushed the noisome door open wide enough to allow him to pass through. A small television set flickered in the corner of the room. Jack Lord stood on the rooftop of a building and stared off into a rerun of Hawaii Five-0. The room danced in the cathode ray tube's flickering light. Against the wall, opposite the television, stood the bed. Upon it were the two sleeping forms of the room's occupants. Abe tiptoed to the bed's side.

"Hey! What the hell are you doing!"

The voice came from behind him, in the hall. Startled, Abe whirled and fired wildly. The bullets struck the door frame and the couple's son, just coming in for the night, dove to cover.

Awakened by the sudden violent noise, the couple in the bed sat upright in disoriented confusion. The black stranger had his back to them facing the doorway, in his hands was a rifle. They rolled, as one, from the bed and to the floor. Abe, paying them no attention, moved towards the hall, weapon ready.

"Mark!" yelled the father from his kneeling position behind the bed, "Get your sister and get away!"

Abe, wild eyed, whirled around at the sound of the father's voice and yanked the trigger a number of times. Again, the bullets went wild and thudded harmlessly into the bed and wall creating a mist of fabric and sheet rock. In the hall, Mark, the son, had been sweating nervously and tried to muster the courage to reenter his parent's bedroom. In his hand he held a 9mm pistol. The weapon was a secret he had managed to conceal from his parents for over two years. He had bought it from the friend of a friend who needed cash. Up until this point, it had just been something cool that he possessed. He had only fired it on two previous occasions and, then, only at cans and bottles. Now, faced with the realization that he would have to fire it at a living human, the pistol was not so cool anymore.

The bark of the black man's weapon coming from his parent's bedroom erased his fears and provided the necessary motivation to propel Mark into the doorway. He dove into the room, prone on the carpet like he had seen in some movie, sometime, and leveled his pistol at the black man. The semi automatic jumped in his hands and the first two shots went high, but the terrified youth kept pulling the trigger rapidly.

At the report of the first shot, Abe pivoted to face the new threat. A second shot whistled close by above and ripped through the acoustical tile ceiling. Abe yanked the trigger of his own weapon and the SKS spat flame. A third shot came from the teenager on the floor and a 9mm slug brought with it blinding, burning light as it creased Abe's temple. Abe staggered from the blow and continued to pull the SKS trigger. An irregular pattern of holes were punched through the sheet rock on the bedroom's wall well above his prone adversary. The parents, frozen in the unreality of the moment, stared in open-mouthed fear. As their son and the intruder fired at one another.

The next 9mm slug caught Abe squarely in the chest and was followed in immediate succession by four more. The 7.62 projectiles from the SKS crawled up the wall and into the ceiling as Abe's eyes turned upward in their sockets and his body tilted backward. The SKS went silent as the clip's last round burst from the barrel and Abe's body fell with a muffled thud, lifeless, to the carpet.

In the corner of the room, Mark's mother began sobbing hysterically. Mark's father cradled her in his arms and rocked back and forth looking at the still form of the intruder. Mark remained prone on the carpet, trembling uncontrollably, the smoking, empty gun still trained on the dead black man. In the hall behind him, draped in a sheet, his confused, frightened sister stared into the room in disbelief. The family had survived its first brush with the Revolution. Abe, bathed in the flickering, bright light of a commercial, had not.

David Farley was 23, unmarried, unemployed, and content collecting his unemployment pennies. He loved football, fighting, women, and Budweiser. The order was variable. He pledged his allegiance to nothing. He had dropped out of school mid-way through the tenth grade and had spent the years to follow in random cycles of employment and unemployment. Farley had tried many jobs over the years. The first had been a position at a local dairy farm feeding cows and cleaning up after cows. The early and long hours at the dairy farm got to him in less than two months and he quit. Sacking, stocking, and cleaning at the grocery store was not so bad, but the pay was not good enough, so Farley had given up on that job after six months. The years to follow included less than enthusiastic attempts at carpet installation, building framing, drywall installation, and service station attendant. None of the jobs had appealed to his wants and he quit each, with the exception of the gas station, where he was fired under suspicion, rightful, of pilfering at the till. David Farley had no goals, no plans, and no plans to develop any goals. His was a non-structured, by the day, hand to mouth existence. Cable television, cigarettes, and beer were his touchstones.

With a destructive passion, David Farley hated Negroes. It was a hatred that came naturally to him, passed down from his father and his father's father before him. Despite his own lack of intelligence and his demonstrated propensity towards ignorance, Farley knew, in his deepest being, that all blacks, 'monkeys' he called them, were inferior. The news of the Black Tuesday deaths did not disturb him in the slightest. The small lifeless bodies arranged in row upon row did not prompt any sympathetic conscience within him, no sadness or concern. To the contrary, he had openly rejoiced at the reports of the deaths of so many blacks, gleefully trekking to the State store and splurging on a fifth of Jack Daniels. He spent the remainder of that night watching the special reports, sipping whiskey and grinning broadly.

When the Revolution erupted, Farley was ready. As he saw it, it was the perfect opportunity to vent hatred on the black man without fear of reprisal. With little effort expended, Farley located and secured the assistance of four of his friends—friends that shared his prejudiced and warped views—friends that were willing to drop everything and join battle with the black race. On September 19, one week to the day following Black Tuesday, the five self proclaimed crusaders packed their suitcases, shotguns, deer rifles, plinking pistols, coolers, and potato chips into Farley's pick-up truck, and, leaving their homes in Missouri, roared northeast. Their quest—kill blacks.

George Tucker owned and operated the Double Shot Package Store on the outskirts of Springfield, Illinois. Even in the face of the dangers due to the unrest and in disregard for the endless pleadings of his wife, the middle-aged black man continued to open the liquor store for business, daily. So far, there had been no trouble in the immediate area of his store, a predominantly white section of the city. If there was going to be trouble, George wanted to be at his business to protect his property instead of huddling in fear at home. Besides, he explained to his wife, men will always be men, and men like their alcohol. If he weren't there to sell it to them, especially in the face of the Revolution, they would just break in and steal it. His argument fell on deaf, concerned ears and, this morning, his wife had wept openly as he left the house. Her tears had disturbed him, but George was not a man who could be so easily dissuaded from a decision.

The morning had been quiet, only a couple of customers. George was watching one of the network morning programs that had sprung up about the time of the Revolution. The commentator was speaking about the Reverend Ahmet's latest visit to the front lines in some major city and introducing the 'exclusive' coverage of the event. George scowled as Ahmet's face filled the small screen. "Asshole!" he said lowly, even though he was alone in the store. He despised the ambitious reverend, seeing through his facade, and blamed all the chaos directly on him. George did not share Ahmet's views, did not subscribe to the black majority's present desire to kill white men. George depended on the white men, the bulk of his clientele, to stay in business. He did not, in any way, feel threatened by white men. In the twenty years that he had owned the liquor store, George had been robbed twice. In both instances, it had been blacks, not whites, who robbed him. A third robbery attempt had been made, again by a black man. This one, however, had been foiled by the muzzle flash and flaming lead of the .357 revolver that George kept beneath the cash register ever since the day after the second robbery. The would be robber's back was torn half away by the force of the expanding hollow-point projectile ripping through him. The look of surprise slowly glazed over upon the man's dead eyes as Police congratulated a satisfied George, telling him that he had done the right thing, that he had sent a clear message to the other punks on the street.

Apart from the occasional bounced check over the years, George had had no trouble with whites. It was this personal experience that convinced George that he had nothing to fear from white men. Twenty years of successful business demonstrated to him that he could coexist with the white race and, regardless of the violence raging around him, he had no desire to jeopardize that arrangement. He would not actively seek a confrontation in the present struggle, but he would not back down should he be threatened. His, George decided, would be a position of conditional neutrality.

David Farley and his four companions had been traveling all night and were running low on beer. Their expedition, so far, had been fruitless. The group had seen no blacks. The highways, for the most part, had been deserted. They had bypassed St. Louis, despite the urge to participate in the battles raging there, and plunged headlong into Illinois. Just west of Springfield, Farley saw the large "Double Shot Package Store" sign and wheeled into the store's parking lot. Farley and two of his friends entered the liquor store to find, much to their delight, that the cashier was black.

At the sound of the bell, George Tucker looked up to see the three white men enter the store. He watched as they made their way to the beer cooler and extracted four cases of Budweiser. One of the men had a nervousness about him that put George on guard—he had seen the look before. When the men placed the beer on the counter, George announced, "I'll have to see some ID gentlemen.

The tallest of the three white men smiled broadly and answered, "Sure thing." Farley pulled out his wallet and produced the Missouri driver's license. George studied the license, compared the picture with Farley's face and, satisfied, returned it. "Very good, Mr. Farley," he said, "will there be anything else?"

"Yeah," replied Farley, "We need a carton of regular Marlboros and a couple of packs of Salem Lights." George laid the cigarettes on the counter alongside the beer and rung up the merchandise. "That'll be $79.38." he announced.

Before George could react, the nervous looking one pulled a pistol from its place of concealment inside his camouflage jacket and pointed it squarely in George's face.

"No," said Farley, standing beside the gun holding man and smiling broadly, "I think this'll be on the house today, Monkey." Fear leapt in George's throat. "And," continued Farley, "I reckon we'll be taking whatever you've got in the register as well." George visibly shaken, began laying the money on the counter.

The store door's bell jingled again and the three men turned their attentions, momentarily to the door, to see an elderly white woman entering the store. George, seeing an opportunity, quickly reached for the .357.

The gun in George's shaking hand had barely cleared the counter when the nervous man, turning back towards him, and seeing George's intentions, squeezed the trigger of his own weapon. The sound of the blast was amplified by the smallness of the store. George was thrown backward against the rows of miniatures, blood pumping in bright spurts from the blackened hole in the front of his shirt. The elderly woman looked on, in frightened amazement as Farley leapt over the counter and began stuffing bills into his pockets. The shooter kept his pistol trained on the dying body of the man behind the counter while the third man watched the old woman intently.

After a few seconds of strained silence, the woman casually walked to one of the whiskey racks and retrieved two bottles of Evan Williams and, then, having second thoughts, replaced the fifths of Evan Williams and chose two bottles of Wild Turkey instead. The third man continued to watch her as she made her way to the counter. Farley, continuing to collect the money in the cash register also watched her as she approached.

The nervous shooter glanced rapidly back and forth between the dead man and the old lady, unsure how to react to this unplanned occurrence.

"Could you hand me a pack of Vantages from back there?" the blue haired woman asked of Farley as she reached the counter.

Farley thought about it for a second, then smiled at the woman. "Sure thing, ma'am." he answered, reaching for the cigarettes, "Here. Take three packs."

"Thank you, young man." she said, accepting the cigarettes, and returning Farley's smile. "Could I get a paper sack, too?" Farley reached beneath the counter, snapped open a brown paper bag and placed the old woman's whiskey bottles and cigarettes into it. He noted the woman casting cautious glances at the shaking gun in the hand beside her, "Put that gun away, Joey." Farley instructed the shooter, "It's gettin' on my nerves." Slowly, the nervous man returned the pistol to his shoulder holster.

The woman smiled. "Well, how much do I owe you?" she asked Farley.

He smiled broadly and shook his head slightly, "Not a thing, ma'am. Everything's on the house today."

The old woman returned his smile and said, "Well, O.K., I guess, but you boys be careful, now. There's a whole bunch of people in this neighborhood who might not take to the killing of niggers like we do."

"Yes ma'am." Farley answered. "We'll be careful."

The old woman collected the sack from the counter and, without looking behind her, exited the store.

Farley still smiling, watched her leave, then, leaping over the counter, slapped the nervous one on the shoulder and exclaimed, "How 'bout Grandma, there, huh? I just knew that we were gonna have to smoke her too." He grabbed a Snickers bar off the rack beside the counter and stuck it in his shirt pocket. Then he grabbed another and slapped it into the nervous man's hand. "Damn fine shootin' there, Joey. If you hadn't smoked that nigger, he'd of got one of us for sure with that hog leg of his." Farley surveyed the crumpled form of George's dead body for a moment, then, grabbing two of the cases of beer, prompted, "Let's get, boys. There's more where he came from." The third man collected the remaining two cases of beer and the cigarettes and the three left the liquor store.

George Tucker's murder would go uninvestigated. The turmoil caused by the Revolution dictated that police forces suspend normal operations and concentrate exclusively on combating black rebels. George's murder was not the only one not to be investigated. Throughout the duration of the conflict, countless thousands of deaths would receive the same inattention. David Farley's lawless group of killers was also not the only group of its kind. Small groups of whites, blacks, and Chicanos, across the country, were finding pleasure in the anarchy, traveling wherever they pleased, doing what they pleased, killing who they pleased. Atrocities condemned by Americans for years now found their way to the United States. After the incident at the liquor store, David Farley and his friends had continued east leaving a trail of empty beer cans.

50 miles west of Danville, Illinois, they overtook a car occupied by two black teenagers. Farley pulled his truck alongside the other vehicle and stared into the scared faces of the two blacks. In the pick-up bed, one of Farley's companions leveled his 12-gauge at the car's driver and squeezed the trigger. The 00 buckshot tore into the black youth, killing him instantly. The passenger was also hit, in the legs, by the ball bearing like projectiles. Farley howled with laughter as the blacks' car careened off the road and rolled lazily over and over down the embankment. The truck came to a slow halt and pulled to the road's shoulder. Farley slammed the transmission into reverse and backed up quickly. When they reached the area where the car had left the road, Farley and his companions jumped from the truck and bounded down the hill to the mangled car.

The car's driver, hanging half in, half out of the overturned car, was dead. The passenger, dazed and bleeding was trying to crawl out the car's broken windshield. The five whites watched, in amusement, the black youth's painful attempts at exiting the vehicle. Intent on his efforts to get out of the car, the injured black teenager was oblivious to their presence. Fighting the wrenching pain, the 17 year old grunted and clenched his teeth pulling his body through the small opening. It was not until he finally rolled clear of the car that he saw them. With broad, evil smiles they stared at him. Terror filled his body. He raised his bloody hands towards the five white men, tear filled eyes pleading for mercy. He would find none. Farley removed the .357 from it's holster at his side and leveled it at the helpless youth. "Yeah!" He taunted, "Go ahead and whine, you little shit! Where's your civil rights now?" The others laughed loudly. The youth lowered his hands and attempted to rise. Farley pulled the trigger and sent the hollow pointed, expanding round screaming into the unfortunate youth's head. Farley kept the pistol trained on the black youth for another few seconds, then returned it to the holster announcing, "Boys, It don't get no better than this!" All laughed heartily.

After rifling the dead youths' bodies and car for any valuables and finding nothing, the five whites returned to their truck and headed east once more, their blood lust unsatisfied. Empty beer cans continued to be expelled from the truck as the five got steadily drunker. The sun rode high in the sky making the day uncharacteristically warm for the season. It seemed the five murderers had the entire interstate to themselves.

Thirty-two miles from the spot where Farley and his buddies left the black youths lying dead in the ravine, the truck's right front tire blew. "Shit!" Farley exclaimed as he fought to retain control of the steering wheel. He managed to keep the truck between the lines and, finally, pulled to a grinding halt alongside the highway's shoulder. None of the truck's occupants had heard the shot that had resulted in the blow out.

In the line of trees, 300 feet away and above the five white men, lay three black men, watching their prey through rifle scopes. They kept the crosshairs passing from white man to white man as Farley and his friends piled out of the truck and stretched lazily, looking at the flat. One of the white man leaned across the side of the truck and reached for the spare tire. In the woods, a finger tightened on a trigger and flame leapt from the end of the high powered rifle.

The speeding projectile slammed the white man into the truck and the spare tire rolled, wobbling, away. The other four white men, hearing the gun's report, dove to the high grass. "Jesus!" One cried, "Where'd that come from?" All four searched the horizon, frightened, weapons ready.

"Bill?" called another.

"Forget Bill!" Farley answered quickly. He could see Bill's open, non seeing eyes and the gaping hole in his upper chest, "The sons of bitches killed him!"

Another shot rang out from the woods. Farley saw the smoke. "They're up there!" he shouted, pointing in the direction of the trees beyond the road. The three remaining white men, the fourth had been silenced with a bullet in his lungs, turned their weapons towards the tree line and began firing wildly.

The three black men hunkered down a bit, but the move was unnecessary. The incoming fire was striking harmlessly in the trees above them. All three returned the fire. From their vantage point, silencing the white guns was easy. The fire fight was over as quickly as it began.

The bullet slammed into Farley's hip and rolled him over violently. The pain was a white hot fire. Nearby, one of his friends moaned weakly. The other was already dead. "Joey?" Farley called to his moaning friend.

"I'm hit, Dave." Joey answered weakly. "I'm hit bad."

"Alright," Farley assured him, "just take it easy. We'll get out of this shit, yet." Slowly, painfully, Farley inched towards his wounded friend.

"I'm cold, Dave." Joey announced, weaker now. "I feel funny."

"Hang on, Joey," Farley encouraged, "I'm comin'."

In the wood line above, the three black men watched the wounded white man crawl towards the other. Evil grins were set upon their brown faces. "I'm gonna smoke 'im!" announced one.

"No you ain't!" disagreed another, "You got da las' one!"

"Easy!" interjected the third, "We'll do this the fair way." He pulled a quarter from his pocket, flipped it end over end into the air, caught it, and slammed it down on his forearm. "Call it." he directed the first black man.

"Heads." was the answer. The third black man lifted his hand and looked at the quarter and announced. "Heads it is!"

"Alright!" exclaimed the first.

"Sheeit!" cursed the second.

The pain in his hip was blinding, but Farley continued to pull himself towards his dying friend casting occasional fearful glances in the direction from which the gunfire had come. Joey, already gone, watched his approach with vacant eyes.

Above, the black man rested his rifle in the crook of a dogwood tree and carefully centered the scope's crosshairs on the base of David Farley's skull. Ever so slightly, he applied pressure to the trigger. The rifle jumped in his hands. He looked through the scope for a final instant, then turned to the other two men, smiling broadly. "Heads it ain't!" All three laughed.

---◆---

The couple had left Trenton on the Tuesday following the outbreak of the Revolution. They loaded the car and headed into Pennsylvania. Fleeing the violence that prevailed everywhere, he had taken her to the park where his parents had taken him as a child—way up in the hills, a world away from the hassles of the city. The Revolution could not last long, he had told her. The Government would handle things, arrest the bad guys, and things would be normal again. They would simply wait it out in the woods.

The couple found a good camping spot alongside a clear mountain stream, not too far from the road, and pitched their tent. They had brought enough food, beer and drugs to 'rough it' for quite some while. They would vacation peacefully while the rest of the country got over its growing pains. At least, that had been their plan. For three entire, uneventful days, the world had been theirs and they were alone in it. Intruders arrived in the early morning hours of the fourth day.

The two black men had stolen the car in Winchester, Virginia, and headed north. The car's owner and his wife were left, dead, on the blood soaked kitchen floor of their suburban home—only two of a greater number of persons in the neighborhood who had died at the hands of the same two black men. The men were from New York and had been on a killing spree since day one of the Revolution. Along their violent path, they had left scores of victims in New Jersey, Delaware, Maryland

and Virginia. When they pulled onto the Parkway in the early hours of Saturday, September 23, their taste for killing and blood was nowhere close to satisfied.

The two black men passed the time in silence, windows open to the crisp mountain air, easing along the asphalt at 30 miles per hour, depositing a broken trail of beer cans, heater fan working overtime. It may have been coincidence, or simply, fate that caused the one black man to call for the other to stop the car along the nondescript, lonely stretch of roadway. Both men exited the vehicle to relieve their bladders in the woods' edge. The night was cool and their breath came in mists. The quiet was almost total.

The smell of smoke caught their attention. After a moment, as their eyes adjusted to the darkness, they could see its thin trail reaching heavenward. As their night vision continued to improve, they spied the source of the tell tale odor, a glowing camp fire's bed. Below them in the quiet, tree filled valley, they could just make out the outlines of the station wagon and the small tent at the stream's edge. Mischievous smiles developed instantly on both brown faces.

"Stay here." instructed the first black man, "I'll be back in a minute." With that, he returned to the car, started it and drove away, leaving the second man standing in the wood line. After going a short distance, the man in the car saw what he was looking for—an opening in the woods—and steered the car off the paved surface and onto the grass. Weaving among the trees, he pulled the car into the woods several dozen yards. Far enough, the man determined, that it would not be noticed from the road. Once satisfied, he left the car and trotted back to the place where he had left his companion. Very quietly, the two descended upon the still camp site.

The larger raccoon stopped ripping through the cellophane for an instant and chattered menacingly at the younger male that had wandered into the camp. This loaf of bread was his meal and he was not about to share it with any young upstart. The smaller raccoon took the hint and ambled softly, back arched high, away. The older bandit watched the retreating youngster with intent before returning its full attention to the torn loaf of bread. Seconds later, he stopped abruptly and raised his nose in the darkness, sniffing. Gripping the cellophane quickly in his teeth, he turned and bounded away in the darkness.

"What was that?" came the whispered question in the woods above. The two black men stopped in their tracks and kneeled to the leaf covered ground. The noise made by the raccoon as it dragged the loaf of bread away had made its way to the men. They paused and waited several minutes, absolutely quiet, before continuing slowly downward.

"It's nothing." Answered the second man after a space of moments. "Let's go."

In the camp, the two could hear the faint snores issuing from the small tent. Peering, ever so carefully, through the small window at the rear of the tent, the two could see the young white couple snuggled in one another's arms. The dark smiles broadened as the two made their way around to the tent's zippered door. Slowly and quietly the tent's door was unzipped. The faint snoring continued. In the bushes not far away, the inquisitive, shiny eyes of the juvenile raccoon looked on with curiosity. After several quiet, painstaking moments, the tent's flap was open. The secondary, netting flap was also zippered. Bored with the stealth, the two had looked at one another, exchanged an unspoken agreement, then ripped the flimsy net wide, simultaneously gripping the base of the now waking couple's single sleeping bag and yanking hard. The small raccoon, startled by the sudden activity, bounded off into the misty darkness.

Disoriented and confused, the two naked young lovers were dumped, unceremoniously, on the cold ground before their tent. Fear gripped them both as they looked up to find the two black men, guns in hand, howling with laughter. The woman attempted to cover herself with her hands. She could tell by the black men's stares that she was not doing a very good job.

"What do you guys want?" asked her boyfriend shakily after a few seconds.

The smile disappeared from the first black man's face and he kicked the naked white man viciously. "Shut up, white boy!" he ordered angrily. The kicked man doubled over in pain, breath driven from his lungs by the force of the blow. The woman, terrified, reached out for him. The second black man intercepted her before she had moved more than a few inches. Grabbing her under the arms, he snatched the frightened woman to her feet and held her erect.

"Let me go!" she squealed, struggling weakly. The black men laughed again. The first black man lifted a flashlight from beside the tent and shone its light upon the naked body of the woman, nodding approvingly. The fear in her face only served to arouse him more.

The boyfriend, still huddled on the cold ground, could see the intentions in the black man's eyes and the fear jelled in his spine. He struggled to get to his hands and knees.

"Hey, Babe." The first black man said enticingly to the trembling woman. "What say you and me crawl back in that sleeping bag and wrestle a little bit?" The second black man smiled an evil smile. The helpless white woman in his grip whimpered softly.

On the ground, the boyfriend mustered his courage and pleaded. "I've got some money and some coke…Lots of coke. You can have it. Just let us go. We haven't done anyth…"

The first black man did not allow the boyfriend to finish. Lashing out violently, he brought the flashlight down hard on the side of the white man's head. The light went out and the boyfriend collapsed to the earth with a painful groan. Teeth bared in anger, the black man kicked the unconscious camper in the ribs, violently. "I told you to keep your cracker mouth shut, boy!" Slinging the broken flashlight into the darkness, the black man pulled a knife from his belt and knelt beside the prone white body. "White boys never do listen!"

The panicked woman squirmed feverishly in the second black man's hold. Her struggles were fruitless. Eyes wide in terror she watched as the knife was raised high in the crisp night air. In mute horror she watched the blade as it hung there, suspended by the brown arm above the unconscious form of her boyfriend in dream-like animation. The quiet echoed in her throbbing head. The knife fell swiftly. Then, just as swiftly, raised again. Her eyes shifted to her boyfriend's back. Dark, thick blood was oozing just between the shoulder blades. In trance-like resignation, she continued to watch as the knife plunged again. This time slightly lower and to the left. The blood, lighter, spurted immediately and forcibly from the hole made by the cold blade. Her body went limp in the black man's grasp.

The early morning mists creeping from the floor of the valleys seem to, at once, magnify and obscure the players in nature, enveloping them all with a certain otherworldly magic. Time stands still and sounds take on a tangible presence in the noisome quiet. Surely, earliest man experienced like feelings in the timeless mist—stood silent in its presence and only listened, sniffing the air, enraptured by the uniqueness of the moment—stood there, pondering his existence, in that brief moment before the all powerful sun breaks the horizon, and light, and, eventually, heat drive the mist away. The solitary park ranger resting against the hood of his dark green Bronco along the crest's overlook continued to ponder his existence long after the mist was gone. The parkway was silent. Few cars had been up there since the turmoil began. All the Rangers were on call though…just in case.

Robert Evans had been a U.S. Park Service Ranger for six years. He liked the unsupervised activities that being a park ranger entailed—no hassles, no desk to be stuck behind, no boss constantly looking over his shoulder, and pretty good pay. Evans had been fortunate to land the job at a time when many of his acquaintances were unemployed and having no success finding work. He had been in the right place at the right time with the right qualifications. The veteran's points he had earned for his five years in the U.S. Navy, coupled with his stellar performance on the placement examination, afforded Evans a rapid interview for the government position. Soon thereafter, Evans was hired. Six years later, his performance appraisal ratings were without blemish, he had survived the Service's recent cutbacks, and Evans had his focus on retirement in nineteen years.

The years, Evans had thought, until recently, would pass easily. Now, as he stood in the warming bath of the morning sun's rays, he was unsure about the future. He was unsure if there would be a job and, more disturbingly, unsure whether he should keep it if it did remain. The world was igniting around him and Evans was sure that he could not remain detached for much longer. The present was tearing him between conflicting emotions.

The disturbing news reports that began on the twelfth had continued and had amplified as time progressed. Following the unfolding coverage of the reported violent events of the past few days had caused Evans to engage in some deep introspection. Answers were not immediately forthcoming.

Evans' possessed an above average intelligence. At the age of 28, he was mature beyond his years. He had been a star high school student excelling in every subject in his small county public school. He had been eligible for an academic scholarship through the United Negro College Trust Fund, but lost the slot to another black student. Evans' father, a laborer was unable to afford a college education, so at 17, Evans had joined the navy and was subsequently exposed to an almost complete spectrum of the diverse cultures offered by the world. During the years in the navy and the years as a park ranger, Evans had considered college more than once, but always managed to fabricate a plausible reason for not pursuing a degree. He was a husband of five years and father of two children—the head of a house that was strongly rooted in the community church and active in the practice of the Christian values taught there. He was comfortable, Evans told himself. He did not need a formal education. Things were going nicely—nicely, that is, until this madness broke out.

Evans still could not accept the cold reality of the Revolution. After the television's Special Reports on the Sunday following Black Tuesday, Evans had plugged in the VCR, turned on Loony Tunes tapes, and had sternly instructed the children not to switch the channels. There would be no more watching of regular television. From that point, Evans watched the broadcasts of the increasing violence from the 13 inch set in his tiny workshop, or listened to them on the radio. The children grew tired of watching the same tapes over and over, but no amount of pleading would convince Evans to change his mind about television.

Evans had not allowed his wife to take the children to school all week, hoping against hope that the madness would end. It had not. There would be no school the next week either. A thought passed through Evans' busy mind and he shuddered. The thought bore visions of tiny, still body bags containing children that would never attend school again.

Evans continued to wrestle with the moral questions. Which side was in the right? His church was divided over the questions. Two-thirds of the congregation had not been there for Wednesday night's service. To the uneasy handful of faithful, Pastor Victor Danielson repeated his heartfelt advocacy of peace and the offering of the other cheek. God was in control. The absent, dissenting majority believed otherwise. Many of these, Evans knew to be devout, ardent Christians, yet they condemned Brother Danielson's stance as that of a coward. It is the time, these brothers and sisters were proclaiming, for God's nation of kings and priests, his peculiar people, his chosen few, to break the bonds that held them and stand up to the satanic treachery of the government and the white men who supported it. The words that Reverend Ahmet had spoken had been true words, inspired words, prophetic words from the throne of God. That Ahmet did not embrace Christianity did not seem to bother them. The truth, to them, was obvious, regardless of the messenger. It was time to possess the promised land as Reverend Ahmet had instructed. Evans was altogether unsure.

Reverend Ahmet's call to revolution tugged deep on Evans' innermost being and battled fiercely with the opposite forces of reasonableness and security. All that Evans had on earth in the form of material things he had obtained through his position in the white man's establishment. Why should he now turn against his earthly providers? This argument did not stand up well against such prominent biblical passages as "take no thought for the morrow", "lay not up for yourselves treasures on earth", and "set your affection on things above, not on things of the earth."

Evans did not hate white men. He held, he firmly believed, no malice towards any man on the basis of skin color. He was, however, acutely aware that he need not look far to see the evidence of the evil of the white man. Evans believed Reverend Ahmet's portrait of the whites to be, for the most part, true. He realized that the white man would never accept the black man. He knew enough history and human psychology to understand that whites, with but few exceptions, would always look down on him for the color of his skin. Despite knowing these things, Evans could still not reconcile the act of killing or of participating in the killing of another human being except it be for his country in a time of war. Which posed yet another enigma. Many were calling the present unrest war, now. And why not? It certainly resembled one. It had all the elements, down to the debris littered streets complete with dead innocents. Armies of lawless marauders roamed free, killing at will. If the Revolution was not war, what was it?

Early on, Evans turned to his Bible for answers. Jesus preached peace and walked the walk. As the Son of God, he could have called down tens of thousands of anxious, ready angels to wipe the Scribes and Pharisees, Herod, Pontious Pilate, and any that dare mock and revile him, off the face of the earth, but he did not. Silent as the lamb to slaughter he was tried and found faultless. Regardless, he was condemned, spat upon, beaten, ridiculed, had his back ripped to hamburger, and, finally, was nailed to a beam and suspended in the air to die. Still, Jesus did not lash out at his tormentors. Still, he loved them. Still, he died for them. God is love…is Christ. That was the one side. But, there was another. Had not God instructed the Israelites to kill every man, woman and child west of the Jordan. Kill them all, God said, leave none alive or a curse would follow. They left some alive. They were cursed. The curse followed the Jews through history to the present. Could the present disorder be a call from God, Evans wondered, a divine order to rid the world, or at least this country, of the white man? The emotions battling within him made it impossible to tell.

The sky to the east began to lighten gradually as Nathan Gurley rolled up his sleeping bag and affixed it to the frame of his backpack. He kicked dirt over the remaining embers of the fire that had burned out sometime during the night and stirred the dirt and blackened coals with the toe of his hiking boot. Nathan had been on the Appalachian Trail for almost three full weeks, now. Every year, since his college days, Nathan had taken time off from work a day existence to disappear into the mountains. He loved the solitude and the peace offered by the great outdoors during his excursions. This was his twentieth such trip in as many years. In those years, he had hiked the Grand Canyon twice, the length of the Rockies twice, trekked through Canada once, Alaska twice, the Yucatan Peninsula once, with the balance of the trips taking place along Nathan's favorite trails in the Appalachian Mountain chain. With no radio, newspaper, or other such connection to civilization, Nathan was completely cut off from the outside world during his yearly expeditions. Nathan liked it that way, his purpose being, after all, to get away from the rat race. Nathan did keep up with the days, however, and was aware that this dawning day was September 23.

Only twelve days remained until Nathan had to return to the grind of his lucrative carpet distributorship. He had planned the trip so that the final week would be spent exclusively in the Blue Ridge Mountains. That left him just four days in which to reach Virginia. Nathan estimated that he was now at least two thirds of the way through Pennsylvania. The next four days would be long days in which he would have to cover many miles. The thought of the distance to be traveled brought with it no stress for Nathan. He had gone further, faster before. Any deadlines were self-imposed, at any rate. His plans were not etched in stone and were subject to change at the slightest inclination.

Nathan leisurely completed packing his gear and took a circular walk around the area to insure the camp site was clean and undisturbed. Satisfied that things were as he had found them the afternoon before, Nathan hoisted his pack onto his back and rejoined the southward trail. The slight morning chill signified Summer's end and offered hints of the winter to come.

As always, Nathan had planned and timed his trip well. The mountains were alive with the colors of Autumn as the trees' leaves filled the valleys and hilltops with brilliant hues and subdued pastels. To Nathan, the beautiful landscapes provided a type of catharsis from the stress and strain of everyday existence in the twenty-first century. He did not miss the company of his fellow man. Solitude was a refuge for him. Nathan had tried, twice before, to bring someone along on one of his month-long getaways, but, both times, the trips had grown old after just a few days, his partners not relishing the seclusion with the same zeal as Nathan. After the second such attempt, Nathan resolved to make all future excursions solo flights. He had never regretted his decision.

In the morning mist, Nathan paused alongside the trail to watch a mother bear and her two, jet-black, almost purple cubs playfully splash about in a mountain stream several hundred feet below. Nathan had been watching the wild creatures for several minutes, taking occasional photographs, and trying to remain inconspicuous, when the she bear raised her head suddenly, alarmed, and sniffed the air. The cubs, sensing their mother's sudden concern were instantly motionless. With a grunt, the she bear bolted from the water and disappeared into the thick brush at the streams edge, the cubs following closely behind. Nathan watched the trio disappear into the thicket and wondered what had spooked the bears. He thought, for an instant that it might have been he who had caused their flight, but the wind was blowing briskly in his face. There was no way that the bear had detected his scent. "Must be another hiker." Nathan thought. "Oh, well." He told himself, "it was fun while it lasted." He re-shouldered the heavy pack, moving his shoulders to settle the weight in place, and set off down the trail once more.

Nathan had not taken more than a dozen steps when he heard the faint sound, an out of place sound. He stopped and strained his ears. Around him, all was quiet. Other ears had heard the faint sound also and momentary silence had filled the woods. Nathan listened intently for a moment, but heard only the wind as it rustled among the soon to be falling leaves. He was about to move on when he heard the sound again, closer this time. It was a scream—a woman's scream. Someone was in trouble and they did not sound too far away. Nathan's heart quickened a beat. On impulse, his arm went to his side and his hand rested on the bone hilt of the omnipresent bowie knife. Nathan headed down the path at a trot, adrenaline suddenly pumping and ears trained ahead.

Nathan had traveled about 40 yards when he heard the scream again. It was, definitely, he decided, a woman's cry for help and it was much closer this time. Nathan increased his pace to a full sprint. Branches whipped at his face and tried to wrestle his pack away as he ran along the narrow trail. When the scream came again, it was no more than 100 yards away. Nathan slowed, dropped his backpack to the ground, and unsheathed the bowie knife. He crouched low behind a large oak, and peered into the woods slightly below and to the left of the trail. He saw her instantly.

She was young, in her twenties, and naked, running wild eyed through the brush, arms flailing wildly before her. The terror on her face was clearly evident. Less than thirty feet behind her followed the apparent source of her torment—two laughing black men, taunting and calling obscenely, chased her. The woman passed just below Nathan's place of concealment. He allowed her to pass, and kept his attention focused on her pursuers. Seconds later, the first black man passed, alternately grunting and laughing. Nathan, remaining motionless, was close enough to smell the man as he passed. He waited for the second man. He did not have to wait long. As the second man reached a point parallel to and below his concealed position, Nathan launched his body through the air and tackled the unsuspecting black man with his best open-field form—Nathan had played linebacker for his university's football team. The force of the blow propelled both Nathan and the black man into the base of a large poplar tree. The impact drove the wind from the black man. Nathan brought the heavy base of the bowie knife's hilt down on the base of the black man's skull. With the adrenaline pumping as it was, Nathan hit the black man far harder than he had planned. The sudden crack, corresponding quiver, and, then, limpness could only mean one thing. Nathan had severed the black man's spinal cord. The man was dead. With no time for regret, or reflection, Nathan turned his attention to the other black pursuer.

Unaware of the commotion behind him, the second black man had continued his pursuit of the fleeing white woman. "Slow down, honey!" he called, "You can't get away!"

The woman had come to sudden life when the black man had touched her back at the campsite. One instant, she had been laying there, huddled upon the ground, sobbing. The next, she had been up like a shot and running away at full speed, screaming like a banshee. The sudden movement had caught both black men by surprise. The first black man was caught with his pants down, literally. The second had taken up pursuit, immediately. The frightened woman ran with cat-like speed. It was all the men could do just to keep sight of her. As the sun began to rise and the forest's floor began to lighten, seeing her became easier. The pursuit quickly turned into a game for the pursuers. The reward, both men had known, would be sweet. After several minutes of chasing, however, the fun was wearing off. The remaining black man, unaware of his accomplice's fate chugged onward, but was growing tired of the chase.

Nathan ascended the hill, once more, and ran along the trail above and behind the black man and the frightened woman. The terrified woman broke through a thick line of brush and entered a clearing in the forest. She stumbled, momentarily. The pause was enough to allow the gasping black man to close the distance. With a grunt, the black man stretched out, grasped his prey just below the knees and tackled her.

"Gotcha, bitch!" The black man announced, gleefully.

The woman, terrified, let out an ear splitting scream that quieted the forest once more.

Robert Evans, cruising slowly along the parkway, heard the scream echoing up from the valley to his left. Quickly, he cut the truck's engine and glided to a crunching rest along the road's side. He snatched the seatbelt off, bolted from the seat, ran a few yards into the woods and listened. He heard the screams again. His heart took up a staccato rhythm. Drawing his revolver, Evans sprinted down the mountainside in the direction of the sound.

Nathan, no longer able to see the black man through the dense undergrowth, could tell from the screams that the man had caught up with her. Nathan crashed through the brush and headed off the trail, down the hillside. In an instant, he was at the edge of the clearing and could see the black man atop the screaming girl, one arm pinning her, the other pawing at her naked body. Nathan, heart beating rapidly, sprinted in their direction, launching his body, once again, through the air and onto the black man's back.

Robert Evans reached the clearing in time to see the two men wrestling violently. The naked white woman was on the ground, still screaming. Evans saw the flash of the large knife in the white man's hand as the two men rolled on the floor of leaves in the clearing. Then , Evans saw the black man struggling to remove a gun from his trousers.

"Halt!" Evans boomed.

The two men did not respond. Evans pointed the .357 revolver in the air and fired a single shot. The weapon's booming report echoed along the mountainside, splitting the morning and stilling the moment. The two men stopped fighting and separated.

Nathan, chest heaving, sucking air, slowly backed away from the black man, knife at ready. The black man remained sitting, gun in one hand, the other hand tenderly probing his bleeding lip, his eyes fixed on the black park ranger.

"Drop the gun!" Evans ordered.

The black man looked back and forth between his foe and the park ranger for a moment before tossing the pistol, reluctantly, towards the wood line. Evans turned his attention to the white man.

"You," he commanded, "Drop the knife!"

Hesitantly, Nathan complied, allowing the bowie knife to slip to the ground.

"Now," continued Evans, "both of you down on your bellies!"

Both men did as instructed. Slowly, gun trained in the direction of the men, Evans made his way to the sobbing white woman.

The sweat and many scratches that covered the young woman's trembling body told Evans the story. She had been chased through the woods by one or both of these men—her naked body the prize. Evans removed his service jacket and, helping the terrified woman to sit upright, wrapped it around her. That accomplished, he returned his attention to the two men. The black man was inching to his knees, looking towards the gun he had pitched away.

"Don't even think about it!" Evans cautioned, discerning the man's intentions.

The black man paid no heed to the warning, and, suddenly rolling to one side, leapt to his feet and sprinted towards the wood line and the waiting gun. Nathan, motionless, watched.

"Halt!" Evans yelled.

The black man did not slow down. Evans raised the .357 above his head and fired another round in the air. The black man did not stop, but dove for the gun, grabbing it and bringing it up in the direction of the park ranger.

Without further hesitation, Evans took quick, deliberate aim and fired his revolver once again. The black man was blown backward and collapsed in a heap on the leaf strewn ground…dead. Nathan watched the fallen black man, searching for signs of life. When he saw none, he took a relieved breath and began to roll over.

"Don't you get stupid too!" Evans warned, pointing the pistol at Nathan.

Nathan froze. His eyes turned to the hysterical woman. She would explain everything to the ranger. Or, so he hoped.

As things stood, however, no help would be immediately forthcoming from that quarter. The events of the morning had supplanted the terrified woman's capacity for rational thought. With a blank stare she looked in the direction of her dead black assailant and whimpered.

"Here," Evans instructed, removing the handcuffs from their leather pouch on his belt and pitching them to Nathan, "Put these on."

Nathan retrieved the handcuffs and complied with the ranger's wishes, confident that everything would be O.K., eventually.

"Base Control?" Evans spoke into his radio, weapon still pointed at the white man, "This is Seven. Come in, over."

Marco "Mad Max" Colletti watched the live footage of the black unrest on his 52" television screen. An underworld boss since the days of the Gotti shake-up, Colletti, as his nickname suggested, was no stranger to violence. The son of Sicilian immigrants, Colletti had grown up on the mean streets, learning early the necessity for proficiency with fists, clubs, and, later, guns. Violent death was nothing new for him, yet, the scenes unfolding on the Special Report were, nonetheless, unnerving. He watched in mounting dismay as white citizens were abused and killed at the hands of the black mobs.

"Jesus Holy Christ!" Colletti exclaimed as the live mini cam zoomed in on a black man emptying a 9mm clip into an elderly white man's jerking body, "Can you believe this fockin' circus, Frankie? Look at these jungle bunnies! Where's the fockin' law?" Colletti positioned the bottle of scotch over the tumbler's opening and poured, eyes fixed on the screen. "I can't believe this shit! That's fockin' 42nd street, Frankie! Forty-fockin'-Second street! Next thing you know those black sons of bitches will be beating on my fockin' door." Colletti took a deep gulp from the tumbler. "This situation is way out of control Frankie! Way out of fockin' control!" He took yet another deep gulp from the tumbler, wiped the excess from his sweating lip and issued an order. "Get on the horn and get us some more soldiers up here, right now!"

Colletti set the drink on the coffee table and hurried over to the bar. Once there, he felt beneath the bar's counter, found the hidden release switch and flipped it. With a click and a mechanical whir, the wall opposite the bar swung open, revealing a steel shrouded compartment. In the compartment were weapons of every imaginable sort. Colletti selected a well oiled AK-47 from the racks of weapons, slammed a 30-round clip into the receiver and placed three more clips in his pockets.

Frank Mancuno, Colletti's trusted, lifelong friend and underboss was at the phone in the corner of the room hastily issuing coded orders. Also present in the room were five more made men. These were Colletti's closest confederates. They already held weapons. Two had M-16s. One held an Uzi, and the remaining two nervously gripped 12-gauge riot guns. Their eyes were pinioned to the television's huge screen. Outside the house, twenty other men, soldiers in Colletti's "business thing", patrolled the grounds, alert for any sign of danger. A fifteen foot wall separated Colletti's residence from the street and surrounding residences. The wall, made of steel reinforced concrete was over four feet thick and designed to withstand an artillery barrage. The wall's gate, the only entrance or exit from the grounds was a double walled steel affair that was also engineered to take the type of abuse dealt out on a battle field. "Mad Max" Colletti did not believe in leaving anything to chance.

That Colletti's home was a virtually impregnable fortress was not a mistake. He had personally overseen its construction and took careful steps to ensure that no corners were cut when it came to security measures. Over the years, Colletti had made more than his share of enemies. There were more than a handful of angry men who would take extreme pleasure in Colletti's death. On the streets, he was a target. Here in his compound was the only place where he felt reasonably safe. Colletti retrieved his glass of scotch as Mancuno was rising from the telephone.

"Help's on the way, Max." Colletti's underboss announced, "We got ten boys comin' in from Fat Jerry" Jerry Batiggliosi was another underboss in Colletti's organization, "and twelve more or so of Amati's bunch from the docks. All should be here inside the hour. But..."

"But what?" Colletti interjected.

"But," Mancuno continued, "the boys from the dock have to come right through that soup!" He pointed at the television screen, "And that ain't gonna be no cake walk."

"Fock that!" Colletti replied, "You tell them not to take no shit off any fockin' moolie." He raised the AK-47 and peered down the iron sights toward the television's screen. "It's obvious that New York's finest ain't gonna be around to say nothin'. You tell them to blast holes through that fockin' crowd, and to get here pronto! Capeesh?!!"

"I hear you, Max.", Mancuno assured his boss, "I told 'em to bring the armored car and to load for war. They'll be alright."

"Your fockin' A right they'll be alright!" Colletti echoed, "Those are my boys. And ain't no fockin', ignorant, greasy ass nigger been born that can deal with my boys!" Colletti smiled a nervous smile. He hoped he was right.

Frank Amati returned the phone to its cradle and turned to face the others gathered in the warehouse. "Well," he began, "It's official. That was Frankie. The boss is getting nervous. He wants more heat on the hill and we're it."

One of the others spoke up, pointing to the television screen. "You mean we got to go out in that?"

"That's right!", Amati answered, "We got to go out in that. You got a problem with that?"

There was no answer. At six feet five and two hundred and forty pounds, Frank Amati was not a man to argue with. He had been a soldier in the Colletti Family for eight years -more than long enough to know that when "Mad Max" called, you better jump. Hastily, he issued instructions. "Alright. Gino, you and Willie stay here with Jerry and Haney and watch this place. And I mean watch it. If there's any grab-assin' going on, you'll answer to me! You see any niggers pokin' around here…you smoke 'em. Got it?"

"No problem, Frank." answered one of the others.

"The rest of you" Amati continued, "are going with me. Load the heavy truck with everything we got and put a move on it. I'll take seven in it and the rest of you follow in the armored car. We're going to have to cut our way to the compound." The compound is what everybody called Colletti's fortress.

The men scrambled in different directions, hastening to comply with Amati's instructions.

Back at Colletti's fortress, one of Colletti's underlings was calling attention to another, smaller television screen in the corner. "Boss! Take a look at this!"

On the small screen, a police patrol car was being surrounded by a black mob. The patrol car was attempting to back up, but the blacks were pushing another car into the street and turning it sideways to block the patrol car's retreat. The faces of the policemen inside the car were clearly visible through the camera's eye. The fear etched there was unmistakable.

"Look at those crazy niggers, Frankie!" Colletti exclaimed, watching the humanity swarm around the beleaguered police car. "Un-fockin'-believable!"

The policemen within the car were equally incredulous. The situation was well out of control.

"407. Central." Officer Mike Bevins, twelve year veteran of the police force, called excitedly into the microphone. No answer. Bevins called again. "Central this is 407, come in, over!"

The patrol car was, now, completely surrounded by the mob. He could move neither forward nor backward. His partner, a rookie, stared wide eyed out the windshield at the angry, taunting faces, his white knuckled hands gripped tightly about the service pistol on his belt.

"Don't even think about pulling that hog leg, Daniel!" Bevins warned through clenched teeth, forcing a smile, "We'd be dead before you cleared leather."

Bevins returned his attention to the radio microphone, "407. Central? Come in, over."

There was a crackle on the set and then the reply, "Go ahead 407."

"Roger, Central." Bevins acknowledged, "I'm at the 2600 block of 42nd and I've got a situation here. I got citizens all over the car, and they don't look happy. Request immediate assistance, over."

"Roger, 407." came the reply, "We copy, but, be advised that all, repeat, all units are tied up at the moment. The duty officer advises that reserves and additional regular units from upstate are on the way, but the first of these won't be on the street for at least another 45 minutes to an hour. Copy?"

Mike Bevins' heart sank with the news. In twelve years he had never been refused backup. The seasoned veteran paused before replying, unsure what to say, even less sure what to do. "Roger that, Central. We copy."

"Sorry, 407," the radio crackled again, "Hang in there, big guy."

"Roger, Central." Bevins returned, "Thanks."

Bevins recradled the microphone as the radio erupted with other calls of semi-panicked patrolmen, across the city, calling for backup. For most, there would be no help. Hell was unleashed on the city and the thin blue line had been swept to the side.

"Well, kid," Bevins stated, head swiveling among the angry faces outside the car's windows. "I guess its just you and me against all these indians. Got any suggestions? What do they say to do about things like this in the Academy these days?"

The rookie, rigid and pale, too sacred to answer, did not. The patrol car was now being rocked violently from side to side as the mob screamed obscenities at the two white policemen inside, taunting, daring them to exit.

Aggravated now, Bevins switched from radio to PA and spoke into the microphone, "Disperse." He commanded. "You are ordered to disperse! Stand away from the car!"

The words only served to further enrage the mob. They pressed in upon the car, shaking it with renewed fury. Inside, Bevins and his partner were being tossed roughly side to side in the front seat as, now, the patrol car's tires were leaving the ground.

"Jesus! Kid," Bevins exclaimed, "this is gettin' hairy!"

Suddenly, with a final, mighty shove, the patrol car was on its side.

"GET IN THE FLOORBOARD, KID!" Bevins shouted, simultaneously pushing, almost bench-pressing, his partner in that direction. The mob surged again and the patrol car lazily flipped completely over. There were screams as the press of the crowds made it impossible for those nearest the car to get out of the way in time. Several of the rioters were smashed beneath the overturned vehicle. Those unfortunate rioters not killed instantly by the car's weight called out in agony. There would be no help for them, either.

The mob quickly shifted and, in splinter groups, dissolved, continuing down 42nd Street, rage unassuaged, looking for more targets. The gas poured in rivulets from the overturned vehicle as the two trapped police officers struggled, in vain, to escape. One of the gasoline streams meandered across the asphalt and found its way to the gutter, and, in the gutter, a smoldering cigarette. The resulting flame backtracked with purpose to the gasoline's source. The patrol car exploded with a resounding thump, leaving the pavement, completely, for a split instant. Bevins and the rookie, as well as those of the mob that had been injured by the overturning of the car, were, instantly, engulfed in searing flames. The screams died quickly.

The camera captured the entire scene. At Colletti's fortress, a dozen eyes watched in stunned silence. "Jesus." Mancuno whispered.

Across the city, the group at the warehouse was ready to go. It had been less than ten minutes since Amati had issued his instructions.

Eight men piled into the converted beer truck. The remaining five loaded into the armored car. Twelve minutes after the phone call from Mancuno, reinforcements from Amati's group were on the way to Colletti's compound. Amati rode in the beer truck and maintained constant radio contact with the trailing armored car. Two more radios sparked in the beer truck. These monitored the police and emergency networks. Panic filled voices rode the airwaves.

Amati's instructions to all members of the expedition had been explicit. If any blacks along the route so much as looked at the trucks in the wrong way, they were to be shot. Business as usual was out the window. The rules had changed. New York was a war zone. Police were not going to be a problem, today. With a dull roar, the two vehicles pulled out of the warehouse. The remaining men closed the heavy sliding doors behind them, waving their good-byes.

Less than a block from the warehouse, the two trucks encountered the first mob—about forty blacks armed with baseball bats, steel pipes, and the occasional rifle or handgun were spread out along the street walking in the direction of the docks. The mob parted and Amati's vehicles passed through without incident. Amati watched the blacks through the side mirror and radioed the warehouse. "Gino?" He spoke into the microphone. "Come in, Gino. This is Frank."

There was a short pause before Gino answered, "Yeah, Frank. We're here. What's up?"

"Gino," Amati spoke into the microphone, again, "we just passed a whole bunch of niggers coming your way. Some of them are packing, and they look serious, so youse guys be ready!"

"Gotcha, Frank. No problem." Gino assured his boss.

"Don't be playin' no games with these guys, now, Gino." cautioned Amati, "You best make believers out of them if they show up. They better not mess with any of Max's stuff or it'll be your butt, Gino! You know how Max gets when somebody messes with 'his' property."

"No problem, Frank." Gino answered, "We got it."

The radio went silent.

A brick rebounded off the passenger door of the beer truck. Amati jumped at the sudden, metallic thump. Scanning the street, Amati saw the black teenager that had hurled the brick. The youth stood in the doorway of one of the gutted buildings lining the street, staring at Amati with telegraphed disdain. Amati slid back the partition between the cab and the truck's converted cargo bay.

"Wax that little zit, Mikey!" Amati ordered.

One of the men, stationed at a portal on one side of the truck, took careful aim at the black kid in the doorway and squeezed off three silenced rounds. The empty casings rattled to the floor of the truck at the gunman's feet. On the sidewalk, the youth was hurled, violently, against the blackened door casing, just a millisecond behind the mush-roomed bullets that splintered the charred wooden facing. A vacant stare followed the passing trucks as he slumped, lifeless, to the sidewalk.

"There you go, Mikey!" Amati cheered, watching the black teenager fall to the ground and smiling broadly. "That'll teach that punk some respect for his betters."

Five streets further along, the two truck convoy encountered its first real obstacle. Three burned out frames of cars had been stationed in the street. They were arranged in such a fashion as to completely block pas-sage. A group of about fifty armed blacks were milling around the crude roadblock and were eyeing the approaching trucks with mischievous intent.

"Oh shit!" Amati exclaimed, as he spotted the roadblock, "Here we go!"

Joey Bosco, the beer truck's driver, narrowed his gaze looking for a possible opening in the roadblock. "You want that we should turn around, Frank?" Bosco asked, not anxious to challenge the obstacle.

"Hell no!" Amati answered enthusiastically, "We ain't turning around for no jungle bunnies. We're goin' over 'em!"

Bosco looked at his boss with disbelief.

Years earlier, Mad Max had taken a personal interest in the peculiar customization of this particular beer truck. One of the extra touches was the steel reinforcement of the truck's front end and frame. The reinforcement was engineered to provide extra strength and ramming power to the truck. It was a customization specially designed for conditions such as this makeshift roadblock. Amati had not been present for the truck's refit, but Colletti had assured him that the truck could break through any roadblock. Looking, now, at the three burned out shells before him, Amati took Colletti at his word. He only wished that he had asked for a demonstration.

Amati spoke into the microphone alerting the armored car, behind him. "O.K. boys, we're bustin' through. Hang close." Through the partition between the cab and the cargo area of the beer truck, Amati warned, "Youse guys better grab onto something back there. It's about to get real bumpy."

Grasping the restraint bar and turning to the beer truck's driver, Amati instructed, "Alright, Joey. Let's make some noise."

Bosco, still reluctant, but unwilling to challenge an Amati order, gritted his teeth hard and nodded his head affirmatively. Not at all sure of himself, Bosco dropped the transmission back two gears and pressed downward on the accelerator,.

The beer truck's modified diesel engine roared. At the roadblock, the blacks, sensing that the oncoming trucks were not going to stop, hastily moved behind the make shift barricade. When the trucks continued to gain speed, the more anxious among them opened fire upon the approaching vehicles.

Lead flattened against the beer truck's reinforced cab and splattered on the bulletproof glass.

"Son of a bitch!" Amati exclaimed, "Are these bucks crazy or what?" Tiny web-like cracks began to form in the outer layers of the specialized windscreen. No glass, bullet-proof or not, could withstand, for long, the assault of hundreds of rounds. The roadblock was growing larger and larger as the distance between the truck and the obstacle closed. At twenty feet from the cars, Amati braced himself against the truck's dash. Bosco shifted up another gear. The truck lurched forward.

The converted beer truck hit the roadblock at fifty miles an hour. An explosion of discordant sound reverberated along the street and echoed among the building faces as metal savagely ripped into and through metal. Those blacks who had been foolish enough to remain behind the roadblock were crushed, instantly, as the force of the oncoming beer truck shattered, almost vaporized, one of the burned out cars, riding into, up and over it, while sending the other two cars spinning erratically along the street. Mere flesh did little to stop the violently spinning metal projectiles. Several blacks, unable to escape the paths of the vehicles were injured. Some were killed.

The beer truck did not lose any appreciable speed. Amati, realizing that they were through the roadblock, safely, smiled broadly and patted the truck's dash, "Way to go, baby! Way to go!" He playfully slapped Bosco in the chest, "How 'bout that, Joey? Is this a machine or what?"

Bosco forced a smile, his guts churning, his knuckles white on the steering wheel. He shifted up yet another gear, backed off the accelerator and slowed to about 40 mph. Disbelief was etched upon his pale face.

In the side mirror, Amati watched as the trailing armored car eased through the debris strewn breach. Puffs of blue smoke hovered above the protected vehicle as the men inside busily shot at any remaining blacks. Amati returned his attention forward. There were still eight miles to cover. They were not out of the woods yet, not by a long shot.

Back at the waterfront warehouse, Gino Henderson listened to the radio traffic. He delighted in the armored car's account of how Amati had smashed through the roadblock. Gino wished he had gone along. He wanted to be where the action was, not baby sitting the warehouse. He always managed to miss out on the fun assignments. What a thrill it must have been, he thought, to burst through a roadblock and shoot blacks at will. It was the promise of excitement that had lured him into organized crime.

The son of a hard drinking steel worker. Gino had dropped out of school and left home at the age of sixteen. He took to life in the streets, easily. Money was no problem. New York City was full of easy marks. Tourists, businessmen, pedestrians with pockets full of spending cash. It was the easiest thing in the world to stick a knife or gun in their frightened faces and take it all. Stealing parked cars was also comically simple. Sure, he had the occasional, inevitable run in with the law and had spent several periods behind bars, but the money was good and any attempts at reforming his character fell on deaf ears. Gino Henderson enjoyed life as a criminal.

Fortune smiled on Gino during one overnight stay in a precincts' lock-up. He had been picked up on suspicion of burglary early in the evening. For once, Gino was innocent of the charge. But, he did not argue. It was a rainy night and he was happy to be inside out of the weather with the promise of a hot meal and warm place to sleep. There were eleven other men, besides Gino crammed into the small cell. Two of these, long-haired, tattooed biker types were hassling a third man, a smaller man, in expensive clothes. Apparently, they wanted the small man to give up his place on the bench bolted to the wall. Equally apparent was the fact that the smaller man was not willing to give up his place. Gino watched the building conflict with interest. The smaller man was not backing down to the threats of the two larger men. Gino was mildly impressed with his courage.

"You punks don't have a stinkin' clue," the man was saying to the two bikers, "who you're messin' with, do you?"

"Like we give a rat's ass, wop!" answered one of the two, "We don't care if you're the pope! Get your ass out of that seat."

Being of Italian ancestry, himself, Gino took offense at the use of the word 'wop'. He edged closer to the argument.

"Bite me, punk!" answered the smaller man.

"You stupid puke!" the second of the two men said, simultaneously lashing out and punching the smaller man squarely between the eyes. The first of the two, then, grabbed the smaller man by the shirt and yanked him from the bench, slinging him to the floor.

The smaller man, dazed from the blow, struggled to regain his feet, but the one that had punched him delivered a powerful kick to the smaller man's stomach, doubling him up in pain.

Gino moved before even thinking. He closed the distance between himself and the biker in a flash. With lightening quickness, he reached out and grabbed a handful of hair and snatched downward while bringing his knee up forcefully. The biker's nose shattered under the impact of face to knee and blood spurted as the biker slumped to the floor, unconscious. The second biker reacted too slowly to Gino's unexpected attack. The heel of Gino's flattened hand caught him directly in the adam's apple, cutting off his air supply. The biker swung wildly at the space where Gino's head been only an instant before, but Gino easily ducked the blow, grabbed a handful of the remaining biker's hair and propelled his head into the concrete wall.

Gino was still driving the biker's head against the wall when the guards burst into the cell and laid hold on him. The biker slumped to the floor alongside his partner as Gino was being man-handled out of the packed containment cell.

The smaller man shakily got to his feet, brushing off his expensive clothes, and straightening his tie. "What's your name, kid?" He called to Gino from across the bars.

"Gino." Gino answered, no longer struggling. "Gino Henderson. You?"

"You can just call me, Frankie." The smaller man answered moving closer to the bars. "I appreciate what you done for me, Gino. I won't be forgetting it."

"Sure," Gino answered, "no problem. Glad to help out."

The brief exchange ended as Gino was propelled through the door, down the hall, and was thrown, roughly into the drunk tank. The fight in the cell would cost Gino another week in jail. The bikers also got another week tacked on to their stays. The smaller man was released that night after a visit from his lawyer.

Alone with his thoughts in the drunk tank. Gino paid little attention to the smaller man's promise that he would not forget what Gino had done for him. Gino was not even sure why he had helped the man, other than he had always had a dislike for long-haired types. He cursed himself for getting involved. If he had just minded his own business he would have been a free man in the morning. As it stood, however, he doubted he would be on the street anytime soon. He leaned back against the cold, gray blocks, cradled his head in his arms and wished he had a cigarette.

Five days later, as Gino steeped out of the Precinct house into the blinding sunlight, the smaller man in the expensive clothes was there, waiting for him. He stood in front of a parked, black Crown Victoria, a huge smile on his face. He was flanked on either side by two, imposing, hard looking men. It took Gino a few seconds to recognize the man. Finally, the face clicked, and Gino returned the smile.

"Frankie, right?" Gino asked, stopping directly in front of the man.

"You remembered." The smaller man answered. "That's great, Gino. I told you I wouldn't forget what you' done for me, pounding that biker trash. And Frank Mancuno is man of his word."

Mancuno extended his hand. Gino accepted it in his own and pumped hard. "Hey, Frankie," He said, still smiling. "It was nothing. I mean it. You don't owe me nothin'."

"Yeah." Mancuno answered, "Maybe not. But, what say we take a ride and get away from this stinkhole?"

"Sure." Gino answered, "Why not."

Gino climbed into the back seat of the Crown Victoria behind his new acquaintance. The other two men took places in the front seat and the car pulled away from the curb and into the stream of yellow cabs.

"How 'bout a beer?" Mancuno asked as they flowed along stopping and starting with the traffic.

"You read my mind." Gino answered, accepting.

Mancuno nodded towards the front seat and a Heineken was passed back to Gino.

"Thanks." Gino replied, accepting the ice cold beer. He settled back in the seat and turned up the bottle half in a single drink.

Mancuno smiled. "Thirsty, huh?"

"You bet." Gino answered. "It gets mighty dry behind those bars. Say, you don't got any smokes, do ya?"

"Sure." Mancuno affirmed, "What kind you want?"

"Marlboro." Gino answered. "Reds."

"Yeah," Mancuno replied, "that figures" He nodded towards the front seat again. "I'm a cigar guy, myself."

"Thanks, again." Gino said, as a pack of Marlboros were handed across the front seat.

Mancuno watched as Gino drained his beer and tore into the package of cigarettes. "You don't know who I am, do you, Gino?" He asked.

"Sure." Gino answered, "You're Frankie." Gino pushed the lighter in and placed the cigarette between his lips.

"No," Mancuno replied, "I mean, who I really am."

Gino lit the cigarette and took a deep draw, before facing the man beside him and shrugging his shoulders. "No, I guess not. Who are you?"

"Do you know who Marco Colletti is?" Mancuno asked.

Gino coughed, midway through the second draw on his cigarette. Everyone knew who Mad Max Colletti was. "You're not Marco Colletti?"

Mancuno laughed. "No, Gino, I'm not Marco. But, I do work for him."

Gino turned, suddenly, serious. Realization began to dawn. "You mean you're…" the words trailed off.

"That's right." Mancuno answered. "I'm what you think I am. and, now, you must see that when I say I don't forget what you done for me, it really means something."

"Uh huh." Gino stuttered. "I mean…uh…wow!" Gino had often dreamed of getting in with one of New York's major crime families, but had never entertained any hope of actually doing so. Now, here he was in the car with one of the heavies in the biggest of those families and the guy was talking about owing him a favor. Gino could scarcely believe his good fortune. He was, suddenly, very glad he had jumped on the bikers.

Mancuno laughed again. "How'd you like to work for me, Gino?"

Gino felt like a child at Christmas. "Are you kiddin'?" He exclaimed. "I'd love to work for you, Frank…I mean, uh, Mr. Mancuno."

Mancuno slapped Gino on the shoulder. "You knock out that 'Mr.' crap. I'm Frankie to you, got it?"

"Yeah." answered Gino, "I got it. Thanks, Mr. Ma…I mean, thanks, Frankie."

That had been five years earlier and Gino had worked for the Colletti family ever since. In time, Gino hoped to become a made man—one of the privileged few. With a sponsor like Frank Mancuno, it was only a question of time.

The sound of glass breaking somewhere in the warehouse snatched Gino back into the reality of the moment. "Willie. Haney." Gino called, pulling a revolver from his shoulder holster, "Go check that out."

The two men grabbed shotguns and disappeared into the shadows. The other soldier in the room, Jerry, moved close to Gino and nervously fingered the Mini-14 in his hands. Both men stood in silence staring in the direction Willie and Haney had gone. Gino wished Amati had left more soldiers behind.

There was what seemed an eternity of silence. Then, shouts, curses and, finally, gun blasts. The deep throated booms of the shotguns were joined with bangs and pops of other weapons. Then came the sound of automatic weapons fire. The booming of the shotguns ceased.

"Shit!" exclaimed Gino. "Shut that fuggin' door!" He turned to the radio and keyed the mike as Jerry headed for the door.

"Frankie!" Gino called, urgently. "Come in Frankie!"

Amati's reply was almost instant. "Yo! Gino, what's up?"

The sudden gunfire behind him caused Gino to turn. Jerry was slumping lazily to the floor, his back a confetti mess, the wall behind him covered with spattered blood. Gino raised his pistol and fired off several rounds in the direction of the black forms flooding into the room. The returning fire nearly decapitated him.

"Gino?" the radio crackled, "GINO!!?" Amati cursed. He had heard the gun blasts over the receiver. He could only imagine what happened next. It was not a pleasant thought. Gino had been a good friend. The past tense was almost certain. There could be no doubt. The radio's silence was telling. The blacks had taken the warehouse. Anger coursed the length of his body. Colletti would not be happy when he got the news. Someone would pay. Amati had to put the thoughts out his mind. he had troubles of his own for the moment.

Two miles from Colletti's fortress, the road was blocked again. This time, a semi truck and trailer, two garbage trucks, and a cement truck were stationed with a number of smaller obstacles to block passage. No amount of reinforcement, Amati knew, would allow the beer truck to break through this mass of vehicles. He instructed Bosco to turn right and the converted truck took a side road, skirting the roadblock. The armored car followed, less than 50 yards behind. Blacks along both sides of the street fired on the passing vehicles. Their shots proved ineffective against the two trucks' armor. Bullets, simply, flattened against the trucks' armored sides and glass. The trucks' foam filled, reinforced tires were immune to all but the most concentrated fire. Gunmen inside the trucks were well protected and had relatively unobstructed fields of fire from which to engage the blacks. Those black gunmen that foolishly exposed their positions paid dearly. The trucks' gunmen were enjoying the ease with which they were disposing of their adversaries.

It took the two trucks almost twenty minutes to cover the final distance to Colletti's city fortress. As the days of the Revolution progressed, it would only be such vehicles, armored vehicles, that would dare venture into the streets. By the fourth month of the fighting, no vehicle at all, regardless of type, was safe.

Colletti was hopping mad when he got the news over the radio from Amati. His waterfront warehouse was in the hands of the blacks. The reinforcements he had called for had taken the better part of three hours to complete what was, normally, a twenty minute drive. Blacks were gathering forces outside his fortress and, on top of it all, the television's cable had been severed. Colletti cursed himself for not running an alternate underground line, or at least installing a satellite dish. His anger built to a rage. He considered venting his fury on Amati, but, wisely, decided against it when he saw the look on Amati's face as he dismounted the converted beer truck. The anger present in those eyes clearly matched his own. Amati was a trusted subordinate. He was also big as a house. Colletti picked another subordinate to chastise.

The others turned away from the scene as Colletti flew into one of his characteristic rages. Pounding the selected lieutenant with fierce and repeated blows, Colletti hurled obscenities and cursed the world for his present misfortunes. All knew that it was best to leave Mad Max alone at times like this. The lieutenant would not be seriously injured. In a day or two, Colletti would see to it that the unfortunate man was presented with a handsome cash roll and, with time, the incident would, as much as possible, be forgotten. It had happened before. It would happen again. Such was the prerogative of an underworld capo.

Outside the high walls of the manor, another man was seething with rage. Yet, he had no scapegoat to throttle. His name was Luther

Jennings, and he had followed the two truck convoy for almost the entire route, starting at the first road block. It was there that Luther had lost his only brother.

Luther had watched, helplessly, from further down the street as the beer truck had slammed into the makeshift roadblock behind which his brother defiantly stood. Luther had yelled as loudly as he could to his brother, warning him to get out of the way. But, even as Luther yelled the words, he knew that he was too late. His brother never had a chance. In a flash, he was caught in the explosion of flying, twisted metal. For Luther, there had been no time for tears. That would have to come later. Revenge was the priority.

Luther had followed the two trucks, on foot, from the roadblock, careful to stay out of the sights of the gunmen contained in them. He had no plan, no idea of how to stop the trucks, he just knew that he could not allow his brother's killers to escape. He was not overly surprised when the trucks pulled into the compound of the biggest mob boss east of the Mississippi. In the days before the Revolution, the wise thing to have done was to cut his losses and leave. No one in their right mind dare mess around with the underworld boys. It just was not healthy. But, that was before. Now, there were a new set of rules and rather than leave the mob compound alone, Luther was working on a plan to get inside.

---◆---

In the hills, above the violence, Nathan Gurly waited patiently in the eight by twelve steel cage at the rear of the Ranger Station. Two Park Rangers had remained in the woods, with the Ranger that had detained him, to check out Nathan's story. The woman he had saved had been carried to a hospital in the valley by another ranger. Nathan hoped she would open her mouth soon. He had no desire to spend the remainder of his vacation in confinement. He still had no idea of the terror which was rocking the Country.

Twenty-three miles away, Robert Evans and the other two Rangers investigated the camp site. They found the second dead black man about 150 yards from the first. His neck was broken just like Evans' prisoner had told them. The camp site by the stream's edge about a mile further down the trail was not in the prisoner's account. It added a telling dimension to the case. The dead white man they found there had, apparently, been stabbed to death. There was no murder weapon laying around, but from the small size of the wounds on the naked man's body, they did not appear to have been caused by the prisoner's large blade. The dead man's name, taken from his driver's license, which they found in the tent along with his wallet, $126.00 in cash and about a half ounce of cocaine, matched the name on the car's registration. The third Ranger found the black men's car, or what was assumed to be the black men's car, another mile or so further down the parkway. The keys were still in the vehicle which had, according to that Ranger, been well hidden. Nathan's story appeared to check out. The two white rangers and one black discussed the matter.

Ranger Bryan Calloway, the shift supervisor, pinched a lip full of Copenhagen and, placing his thumbs behind the front of his gunbelt, in familiar manner, addressed Evans. "Well, Rob, it all hinges on what the girl has to say, I guess." He spat lightly and brushed the residue tobacco from his mustache. "But, it looks to me like what your boy says is pretty straight." Evans did not reply. Calloway continued. "I'm not a homicide detective by a long shot, but my guess is that the camping couple got caught with their pants down. One or both of our dead guys came along," he pointed through the trees in the reported direction of the black men's car, "killed Mr. Vincent here," he changed the direction of his pointing, his finger slightly bent in towards the dead man's body, "and then turned their amorous attentions towards our young basket case." The third Ranger nodded his head in agreement with his superior's appraisal of the situation.

Evans picked up where Calloway had left off. "The girl panics, screams bloody murder and takes off like a scared rabbit into the woods. The killer, or killers, takes up the chase. Our unknowing back-packer, Mr. Gurley, hears the commotion, investigates, decides to take action, jumps on the trailing man, kills him, and takes off after number two. I get there just in time to keep the two wrestlers from killing one another."

"Yep." Calloway agreed. "That's how I see it." Evans and the third Ranger saw it the same way.

Naturally, the State Police would have to conduct their own investigation before Mr. Gurley could be cut loose, but the Rangers had decided that Nathan was guilty of nothing more than trying to assist a fellow human being. He was to be commended, not condemned.

The State Police told the Rangers not to hold their breath waiting for the arrival of investigators. As for any dead bodies, the Rangers were told to take a lot of pictures and get them to the morgue. There was not enough time for a full blown investigation. The Rangers could, they were also told, consider themselves extremely fortunate if more than one investigator showed up.

"Damn!" Calloway replied to the dispatcher at the end of the conversation, "Things must be really going crazy down there, huh?"

"You don't know the half of it!" came the instant reply.

As the afternoon progressed and the sun rode high in the clear sky above the forest's broken canopy, the flies found the dead bodies.

"Where are those damn ambulances?" Calloway questioned angrily, looking at his watch. "They should have been here two hours ago!" He had tried a dozen times, already, to contact the hospital from his cell phone with no luck. The radio was of no assistance either.

It would be another six hours before the single ambulance arrived. There were bullet holes in its side panels.

"It's about time!" Calloway quipped, "We've only been waiting all day!"

The ambulance attendants, visibly shaken, but not from the Park Ranger's biting tone, ambled over to where the three Rangers stood.

The driver broke the silence and announced, matter of factly, "We're not going back to the hospital without armed escort!" He shoved his hands in his pockets and rocked back on his heels. "You're lucky we made it here at all. All hell is breaking loose down there!"

At the ambulance driver's words, Evans thoughts turned immediately to his family. He looked at his watch. There were still two hours until shift change. The uncertainty returned. He tried, six times, to contact his wife during the remainder of the afternoon, with no result. Death had already visited her and the children. It would find Robert Evans also, when he returned home that evening. The ambulance's driver was correct—hell was breaking loose.

The magnitude of the black uprising caught the white population completely unprepared. Disillusioned citizens quickly found that the shot gun and deer rifle were poor matches for weapons designed for combat. The two century old belief that any black insurrection could be instantly quelled by unified resistance vaporized in the first weeks of fighting. Blacks, despite being vastly outnumbered on the whole, quickly consolidated their own forces and took to the offensive. With a rage born of generations of discrimination against them, the combatant blacks attacked whites, wherever they were to be found, with maniacal fury. By the end of the Revolution's first month, America had become a battle ground for dozens of loosely organized armies. The objective, not unlike the objective of so many armed conflicts, was simple—kill the enemy. Achieving the objective, however, soon met the same problems as those other conflicts—logistical problems were cropping up on every front.

The U.S. government, unable to control the rapidly deteriorating situation, had finally been forced to formally recognize the white militia's right to exist. But, recognition alone was not sufficient. Beginning early in December, the government began to quietly supply certain of the larger white groups with arms, ammunition, and other necessary supplies. For these groups, a certain order began to arise from chaos. Other groups of white combatants, indeed, the majority of the bands of whites, however, were not the benefactors of any government support. These groups, like the blacks, were forced to improvise and to provide for themselves. The distinct disadvantage for the white groups lay in the fact that the blacks had an inside track to obtaining necessary war making supplies. Along virtually every border, arms and associated supply shipments were streaming into the U.S. The material, for the most part, originated from areas whose interests were inimical to those of the status quo in the U.S. As a direct consequence, the supplies were targeted, almost exclusively, for use by the blacks.

For the duration of the conflict, the average white combatants received no foreign support of any consequence. These groups, out of necessity, became little more than armed raiders—opportunists who took what they could where they could find it. The greater majority of such groups were fighting out of necessity—fighting to preserve home, family, and tradition. Other white groups, however, existed that cared precious little or not at all about restoring order. The motivation among these ran a broad spectrum ranging from bacchanalian blood lust to a racist desire to annihilate the black man. These groups reveled in the conflict, finding absolute finding absolute delight in the imposed anarchy. Ultimately, groups such as these only served to confound the efforts of other whites. Regardless of their individual motivation, by February, most of the smaller white groups found themselves dangerously low on ammunition at a time when the blacks, with the ever increasing foreign assistance, enjoyed a surplus.

As early as the last week of November, Hastings was perplexed. The years of careful planning provided by the Planning Group were, now, useless. Things were way out of control. He, like countless others, had underestimated the strength and resolve of the blacks. Before the Revolution, those whites which had pondered a race war had, for the most part, Hastings included, assumed that such a conflict would last, at the longest, a month. Blacks, they expected, would offer significant resistance at first, but would soon crumble in the face of overwhelming odds. The casualties, all agreed, would be high on both sides, but the supposed outcome was never in question. Now, nothing was for sure. Hastings had become a spectator in his own war. Instead of saving the nation, it was more likely that he had destroyed it.

At the end of the Revolution's first month, it became obvious to Hastings and others that expectations and reality were at opposite ends of the spectrum. The blacks were proving themselves to be daring and efficient warriors and were showing no signs of weakening. Whites were reeling and were on the defensive virtually everywhere. Victory was not only not on the horizon, but had become frightfully questionable. Hastings had opened a Pandora's box and he quickly found himself no longer in control. Apart from the continued activities of the NOA, 112 soldiers remained alive, Hastings participation in the conflict was, for all practical purposes, over. He had accomplished his objective of igniting the whites against their black neighbors, but the keg had not exploded properly, and had started a fire that threatened to consume the entire nation.

--- ◆ ---

Eddie Hart liked the feel of the heavy Russian made AK-47 rifle in his hands. He liked the sense of power it provided him. He liked the deep throated burping noise it made when he fired it. Most of all Eddie was amazed at its bullets' effects upon the human body. He had witnessed those effects many times. At first, Eddie was reluctant to join in the fight against the whites. That seemed like a lifetime ago to him, now. With little enthusiasm he had accepted the AK-47 that was handed him, in October, as he stood among the crowd of other black youths at the street's edge alongside the weapon filled van. The van's guards, black clad, black bereted Fruit of Islam soldiers, strictly supervised the distribution of the weapons and cast alert gazes, constantly, in all directions. The weapons which they were distributing had been collected and stockpiled for years for just such an occasion as this. The distribution began the day after Reverend Ahmet's call to revolution. By the time Eddie Hart received his, over four hundred thousand semi automatic rifles and pistols had already been handed out across the U.S. Tens of thousands more waited to be distributed. Most had gone immediately to front line service in the hands of zealous black youths. The success of the weapons distribution campaign was being felt keenly by the whites.

Eddie Hart was born in a white man's world in a grimy, roach infested brick tenement building in Harlem, New York. The youngest of seven children, Eddie had learned, early, what it was like to live in poverty in one of the richest nations on earth. He grew up watching his single mother work two, sometimes more, jobs to support her family. Her efforts, though substantial, were nowhere near enough to keep Eddie and his brothers and sisters properly fed or clothed. Eddie never knew his father. Indeed, the only black men he ever saw were those on the streets of his neighborhood—Men who did not have time to spend with a runny-nosed kid. Even with a mother, Eddie was, for the most part, on his own. Between jobs and sleep, Eddie's mother had little time to spend with her children. To Eddie, she was just another of many faces in the overcrowded tenement building.

Eddie had watched with only half interest as the imposing Fruit of Islam soldier patiently explained how to load and operate the AK-47. In other groups, other Fruit of Islam soldiers demonstrated the operations of various other weapons which were being handed out. Eddie could almost feel the anticipation in those gathered around him. He could see it in the smiling faces of his neighborhood friends. Eddie was intelligent enough to recognize that this was no game—that war was not romantic. He also possessed sufficient character to realize that hatred based on racial lines was lunacy. Above all, he had the common sense not to voice his feelings to his friends. The Revolution had begun, there was no doubt about that, nor was there any turning back. The mood of the black community was clear enough to Eddie. He knew that an outward display of his reluctance to participate in the Revolution would most likely result in his own death. Eddie was not ready to die. Out of necessity, he decided to join his friends on their raids into the white communities. Such activities averted any unwanted suspicions against his loyalty. He went voluntarily, but resolved, to himself, not to kill.

The resolution dissolved, and the reluctance to kill passed the first time a white man fired at Eddie in anger. It was during the third raid in which Eddie participated. The first two raids had been nothing more than drive by shootings consisting of hundreds of rounds being poured into white peoples' houses. As far as Eddie knew, no one had been hurt during those raids, but his friends had been temporarily satisfied with a feeling of accomplishment. The youths would pile into cars with their weapons loaded and ready and drive to a white community, fire wildly into the homes, and then speed off into the darkness for a night of drugs and drinking, celebrating their 'conquest'. No more than dangerous mischief, Eddie told himself.

Eddie fired his gun, along with the others, on the first two raids. He took special care, however, to ensure that his bullets impacted harmlessly in trees or other such inanimate objects. The third raid in which he participated had started out the same as the previous two excursions, but rapidly got out of hand when the would be soldiers found themselves in armed confrontation with angry whites.

The first shot came without warning. The youths were easing along the predominantly white neighborhood's street, in two cars, looking for targets when the shot rang out. The windshield of the lead car shattered as the incoming bullet struck the car's driver in the shoulder. The car swerved violently against and over the curb and slammed into a tree, coming to an abrupt halt. Eddie, in the trailing car heard the shot and, instantly, turned his attention to the area from which the shot came. He saw three white men with rifles gathered behind a pile of concrete blocks in an alley between two houses. He saw other armed white men further down the alley running towards the three men. Eddie watched, scared, as the three white men opened fire on the lead car. The four youths in the car, Eddie's friends, never had a chance as the onslaught of bullets ripped through the car and filled their bodies with lead and shrapnel. The driver of the car in which Eddie was riding slammed on the brakes, threw the transmission into reverse and squalled backwards out of the street, across a yard, and into a space between two houses. The five terrified black youths, Eddie included, bounded from the car and hit the ground. The five then low crawled to the corner of one of the houses and peered, cautiously, down the street.

Eddie saw that there were now eight white men gathered near the concrete blocks. Two others were near the lead car looking at Eddie's dead friends. A hollow thud, followed by a grunt, captured his attention. The report from the shots came a split instant later. One of the white men by the concrete blocks was firing in their direction. Grass began to leap in front of Eddie as the other white men took up firing in his direction also. Intense fear gripped Eddie. Directly to his left, his best friend lay wide-eyed and motionless, dead, a dark hole just below his neck, along his shoulder. Like frightened animals, Eddie and the other three youths quickly scrambled behind the cover of the house. The ground from which they retreated continued to churn. Eddie's dead friend's body jerked as dozens of rounds ripped through his lifeless form.

As Eddie watched these events, his fear slowly turned to anger. His reluctance to participate disappeared with every new bullet slamming into the earth and his friend's body.

"Let's get out of here!" demanded one of the frightened youths.

Eddie, back firmly against the house, hands gripped tightly around the AK-47, replied instantly, "No way! We're gonna wax these crackers!"

"C'mon Eddie!" One of the others exclaimed, "Let's go. There's too many of them!"

Eddie, now enraged, lashed out and struck, with clenched fist, the one who spoke. "Shut your mouth!"

The stricken youth repelled from the blow and looked at Eddie with a confusion. The other two youths also looked on with confusion. Eddie slowly stood to his feet. "I told you assholes that this shit wasn't gonna be no game, and I meant it. Now, the first time you really step in it, you're ready to run? That's whacked!" Eddie spat, yanked the AK-47's bolt back and slammed a round into the chamber, "Well, I'm not runnin'. I'm stayin' and gonna kill these sons of bitches!"

The firing from across the street had ceased.

"Gerald," Eddie instructed the one which he had hit, "You want to leave so bad. Get in the car and haul ass back down the street."

Gerald did not move. Eddie leveled the gun at his frightened friend's head.

"I said," he repeated, "GET IN THE CAR AND GO THAT WAY!" Eddie pointed in the direction from which they had come. "And you best keep your head down if you don't want it blown off."

Gerald sheepishly climbed in the car, eyes fixed on the end of Eddie's gun.

"You two," Eddie turned his attention to the other nervous youths, "grow some balls and work your way behind this house and see if you can get up the street across from the crackers. When Gerald pulls out, I figure every one of them white rubes will open up with everything they got thinking we're all trying to get away. If they come out in the street shooting at Gerald, we should be able to wax their asses."

The two young blacks bounded away to comply with Eddie's directions. Gerald, petrified with fear, looked at Eddie, his eyes pleading.

"Move your butt." Eddie spat.

Gerald started the car, squealed onto the street and roared away. As Eddie had guessed, the ten white men immediately opened fire and migrated slowly towards the street's center focusing their efforts on hitting the fleeing car. At least one of the bullets found it's mark and the retreating car careened into another, parked car with an ear splitting metallic crash and came to a stop. With an angry roar, Eddie leveled his AK-47 at the group of white men standing less than fifty feet away and squeezed the trigger. The terrible burping began. Four houses down, Eddie's two friends also opened fire. The white men, unsuspecting, were effectively caught in the ambush with nowhere to hide from the screaming death that leapt among them. In less than 30 seconds, it was over.

Clip spent, rifle barrel smoking. Eddie viewed, with unnerving satisfaction, the crumbled bodies of his white adversaries in the street. A whoop of triumph sounded from his friends a hundred feet away. A child was crying loudly in one of the houses.

"Daddy?!!" The child cried, "DADDY?!!!"

War was not romantic. It was no game. Eddie was now a part of it. Suddenly, he felt very dirty. A wave of revulsion swept across him. He put his hands on his knees, bent over and vomited twice before joining his two friends in running away.

That had been months earlier, when the Revolution was less than two weeks old. Where the youth had once stood, now stood a man, a battle wearied soldier with premature lines upon his brow. Since that third raid, Eddie had participated in dozens more. The killing had come easier with each successive raid. Day faded to night and to day again in an endless cycle of kaleidoscopic violence. Eddie lost count of the numbers of dead—white and black alike. None of his original group remained alive, apart from him. He discovered that he was a natural leader. When the fighting began, the fear would leave and in its place would come calm assurance.

A grenade ended Eddie Hart's life in the first week of May. He died screaming. There were many like Eddie, black and white, all over the country. In time, death would find them all.

---◆---

Frank Todd had said the Pledge of Allegiance to the Flag hundreds of times in his 37 years. From his later school years onward, as he would, for whatever reason, recite the pledge, he would listen to the words, conscious of their meaning. Each time, he felt that he earnestly believed and supported each word. Now, he was not so sure. The United States was still, in his estimation, the greatest country on earth. Or, at least, was the greatest the last time he had joined others in reciting the citizen's creed. That had been at a high school football game just before the madness began. It was his son's first start in a high school game. Not bad, Frank would boast, for a tenth grader. The crime rate had been high, as was unemployment, interest rates and inflation, but these were things which were familiar to an American public which had grown up with them. The rest of the world was its normal insane self. The former Soviet Union was still writhing in disconcerted stages of development and 'progress'. Bombings had become a daily affair as England and Ireland, Catholic and Protestant, waged increasingly nasty attacks upon one another in continuation of their ancient feuds. A dozen other nations broiled in unrest. All was normal.

Frank stood mid way up in the stands, hat in hand over his left breast, facing the limp flag. "I pledge allegiance", he recited with four hundred other voices, "...to the flag...", it was faded and tattered, 'Needs replacing.', he decided, "...of the United States of America, and to the republic for which it stands..", Frank noticed that there were others in the stands who were not saying the pledge and he assigned his own reasons to each,"…One nation, under God…", the 'God' part, he recognized, was a stretch anymore, "…indivisible…", ununiteable was more like it, "…with liberty and justice…", my how terms lose their meanings over the years, "…for all." The Star Spangled Banner had followed, reminding Frank how poorly he could sing. He was not alone as he struggled through Key's words, he knew them all, along the difficult musical scale. Things were not so bad. The average man could cope. Frank was an average man.

That was then. Now, he was full of uncertainty. The Revolution was two weeks old. The magnitude of the unrest was painfully obvious. Franks' neighbor and friend of twelve years had died in New Orleans during the first days of the Revolution. He had been in Louisiana on a sales assignment and had been found, hacked to death, alongside his burned out rental car. 'Hacked to death? What was that?' Frank questioned silently. 'This was the United States, not some third world sweat hole.' People were not supposed to be hacked to death in the U.S. The family had been, understandably, devastated. Frank felt a deep and long lasting sorrow for his neighbor's widow and two daughters. Their father had been a good man and his passage had created an irreplaceable void. It was all so pointless.

Pointless though it may have been, the death of his neighbor drove home, in Frank's consciousness, the seriousness of the conflict. The term 'Race War' had been around all of Frank's life. Almost everyone admitted that it could happen, but very few had actually believed it would. Now that it was happening, Frank, like countless others, was caught off-guard. He was not a soldier—not a policeman. He had no weapons training. How could he be expected to join in a war? But what else could he do? He saw the news reports. He could tell that government forces were having little or no effect on the revolutionary blacks. Communities all across the country were being leveled, their populations massacred. Men, women, and children were being gunned down, knifed, beaten to death in their own homes. There seemed to be little question of it for Frank—he would have to fight. The real question was when? Would it not be better, others counseled, to go now and confront the blacks wherever they may be found, than it would be to wait for the alternative, for the time the blacks came to them, came to their community, their homes, bringing destruction. The debate was, at times, heated. In the end, the majority opted to stay in the neighborhood. They could not go charging off on a campaign and leave families behind to fend for themselves. The best course would be to fortify a strong position from which they all might band together to withstand and drive away the blacks, should they show up at all. Surely, they argued, the Revolution would end soon. Frank was altogether undecided.

The Mormons, in their Utah stronghold, had subscribed to the bunker style philosophy. Look where it got them. The very stockpiles of food and ammunition that the Mormons had relied on to sustain them through 'the end' had proved to be the magnet which attracted black and white marauders alike. The zealous latter day saints turned the first attacks with relative ease, but, as time passed and the Revolution expanded, the numbers and tenacity of the attackers eventually broke through the Mormon barricade. Defenders were killed, their women and daughters violated, and their food, arms, and ammunition stores looted. Mormon cities were leveled and had become, now, only charred memories. Frank wondered, if the Mormons, who had anticipated the unrest, who had planned for its advent and taken steps for their personal protection, could be so easily defeated, what chance did his community have? Then again, any chance at all would be greater than the one offered by the alternative of leaving his family behind while he went off to fight elsewhere. Frank silently cursed the government for putting him in such a position. Why did they not call out the army and crush the rebellion? Why should citizens be left to defend themselves?

Ultimately, Frank sided with the majority and decided to make his stand at home. His only weapon was a single .357 revolver. When the evil visited his neighborhood, the revolver's six rounds were not enough. Two found their targets, four went wild. Still, the dark bodies filed into the house. Frank's wife and his children were screaming in terror. Frantically, Frank tried to reload the shaking revolver. The .223 projectiles stitched his chest with staccato thumps. Frank fell to the blood soaked Persian carpet, dead eyes fixed on the open front door. The screams behind his lifeless body ended abruptly. A fire was tendered, the evil moved on, searching out fresh prey.

When the Revolution erupted, those Americans who had, over the years, clung to their Second Amendment rights and who had the foresight to purchase assault type weapons prior to the ban in the early 1990s were in a decidedly better position to defend their homes and families than those Americans who had not done so. There were a surprisingly large number of Americans who had complied with the Government's wishes and had rid their homes of all firearms. This group of Americans came to regret that decision. The Revolution was scarcely one week old when it became evident, nationwide, that security would have to be provided at the grass roots level. The Government was simply, for whatever reason, not prepared for violence of such magnitude. Those who had turned in their firearms at the Government's request, black and white alike, now saw the folly of their actions. The revelation came too late for most of these as they fell easy prey to the rising number of roving bands of murderers that seemingly came out of the woodwork as the violence escalated. Misconceptions and preconceived notions of the Government's ability to provide security rapidly dissipated as entire families were brutally murdered with no hope of resistance. Parents were forced to watch, in helpless horror, as their children were killed before them. Defenseless fathers were forced at gun point to watch as their wives and daughters were unmercifully raped and otherwise violated. Many cursed the Government that had taken away their weapons, but, ultimately, these Americans had no one to blame but themselves.

There was another large group of Americans scattered from coast to coast who, prior to the Revolution, had relinquished their semi-automatic rifles and pistols, again at the Government's urging, but had kept their shotguns for personal security. These Americans soon found that their reasoning had been disastrously flawed. Those who had relied on shotguns to provide security found themselves to be at a distinct disadvantage when the terror found its way to their doorstep. Like Frank Todd, many died in the act of frantically trying to reload. Shotguns proved to be no match for a determined foe armed with semi-automatic weapons equipped with multiple round magazines. On the other hand, in the earliest days of the conflict, the roving bands of revolutionaries and vigilante groups often skirted and avoided, other than in situations like those encountered by the Mormons, those residences defended by weapons which the Government had so blatantly frowned upon and had declared illegal. The bands were content to seek easier targets elsewhere. After all, easy targets abounded.

The situation worsened when the electricity went. Power outages had occurred intermittently since the onset of the conflict in September. But, in almost every instance, the service had been rapidly restored. As black revolutionaries established lines of communication and began to act in coordination in the, what they now called, Revolution, strategies were agreed upon and established. The black leaders clearly recognized that their only opportunity for success against overwhelming odds was to perpetuate and intensify the chaos across the country. Disruption of public utilities, it was determined, would be a most effective means of contributing to the unrest.

Early in November, a coordinated campaign was launched against electrical, natural gas, and water supplies in every major city in the Continental United States. Utility line repairmen dispatched to repair the problems began to come under attack from black revolutionaries. Scores of the repairmen and their police escorts died. Unwilling to place their lives on the line without adequate protection, utilities workers called a national strike. President Blount, acutely aware of the consequences of failing to restore utility service to hundreds of millions of panicked citizens, quickly intervened, and commanded the unions representing the utility employees to suspend the strike and to order the repairmen back to work. National Guard soldiers, he promised would be detailed to accompany repair crews. The unions, aware of the

National Guard incidents in Chicago, Detroit, Philadelphia, New York, and other areas, refused to comply with the Presidential Order. Frustrated, Blount angrily commanded that alternate repairmen be conscripted from wherever and everywhere possible and be put in service immediately.

2,500 such substitutes reported for duty within one week of the President's directive. Escort for each repair crew consisted of at least a Platoon-sized National Guard force. The efforts were not enough.

The nation's roadways were killing fields. No transfer trucks were able to travel their lengths unmolested. Communities that depended on the highways as a lifeline shriveled and died. Gas supply pipelines stretched for hundreds of miles and remained vulnerable despite constant security patrols by the government forces. Water mains and power lines also made easy targets for determined black revolutionaries who saw the crippling effect which their destructive activities had upon the white man. The blacks destroyed supply lines and transfer stations at will and, with such repetition, repair crews could not combat the problem. Though thousands more emergency repairmen were put into service over the following weeks, it very quickly became apparent to all parties, President Blount included, that defending, let alone repairing downed lines was not possible.

Three fourths of the United States was without utility service when winter's first storm rolled across the plains and headed east. In normal times, the unseasonably bitter cold that accompanied the season's first punch would have been expected to take but a small toll in human life. Even in the absence of utilities, the toll would not be expected to be overly large owing to community action groups, relief shelters, and the world renowned American resilience and charity when it came to providing aid for the suffering. At a time of revolution, however, a time of distrust, fear and hate, man quickly looses much of his humanity and seeks survival for self and family above all else. Historically, the weak and the helpless suffer during such times.

In the United States, the suffering began as the freezing air mass descended during the late evening hours of November 24. On Thanksgiving day, the winter storm headed out to sea south of Buzzards Bay, Massachusetts. In its wake, greater than 5,800 were dead of exposure in eight states, and the tally was rising. That close to eighty percent of those killed from lack of heat, food and water were black did not sway the revolutionaries from their campaign of denying utility services to the masses. Casualties were acceptable, after all, for the greater cause, and it was certain, to them at least, that it was the white man and not the black man that would ultimately suffer the most.

The campaign to deny utilities had another effect—an unplanned, unforeseen, profound effect upon the Revolution. The loss of utilities proved to be the final impetus to action for a great many whites that had, until that time, refrained from participation in the raging conflict. The loss of basic essentials hit these ordinarily peaceful white citizens close to home and signaled, blaringly, to them that the Revolution was real. The blacks' refusal to allow services to be restored only reinforced, in their minds, the hate filled rhetoric spouting from those whites which were actively fighting to destroy the Negro race.

When reports of the numbers of dead killed by the cold reached these previously non-committal citizens, the numbers the revolutionary blacks would have to face in combat more than quadrupled, virtually overnight. It was a statistic that would go unnoticed by those blacks who continued to dictate strategy, until it was too late. For the first time, the black revolutionaries were enjoying a real advantage, and were seeing the effects of their campaigns on the system. The government was on its knees. The Revolution was going strong and millions more blacks had rallied to the banner. Rays of hope dawned in heretofore skeptical minds. Perhaps the cause was not hopeless. Maybe, there was a chance that the white man could be defeated. The blacks turned their attention to the next logical target, 'government protected' convoys on the nation's highways. The food began to disappear.

The three black men eyed the weapons with a school boy's delight. From the safety of the small basement, viewing the video of row upon row of artillery pieces contained in the barbed wire containment area of the Army National Guard Armory, the small military guard contingent assigned to safeguard the weapons did not appear at all threatening. The number of guards was of little significance anyway. The government could place an entire regiment around the area and an attempt would still be made. The weapons had to be taken. The success of the Revolution dictated such. The plans were already made.

Houston Carter was a slight figure of a man. At five foot eight inches tall, he weighed no more than one hundred and ten pounds, soaking wet. Carter was a private in the Army National Guard. After completing basic training and technical school, Carter had opened a small printing business in Little Rock, Arkansas. His National Guard duties every other weekend had not overtly interfered with his lifestyle. The soldiering duty was easy and the money was a nice supplement to his far from blossoming printing shop income. Things were fine for him. He was not married. His parents were both dead. He had no brothers and sisters, no familial ties to Arkansas, but he was content.

Carter's contentment vanished when the Revolution descended and he found himself and the other members of his detachment assigned to guard the assorted weapons and ordinance at the Little

Rock National Guard Armory. Carter had only left the compound twice since September. The first time was to take part in a convoy of weapons to Baton Rouge. The second time was as emergency leave to check on his home and business. Both were blackened shells, as was much of Little Rock.

Carter zipped his over-sized fatigue jacket against the cold night breeze and watched the stars. Thoughts of his home and printing shop no longer haunted him as they had over the last couple of months. Their meaning had become, suddenly, temporal to him. People were dying. Lots of people—in lots of places—were dying. So far, Carter had seen no combat action. But, he had heard plenty—every day and every night distant explosions and gunfire pierced the silence. In the barracks. there were rumors of military installations being overrun.

Houston Carter had no intentions of being a hero. He vowed to stay alive. Embraced in the brisk air, he felt alive. He had grown to enjoy the quiet guard duty—just him and his thoughts alone in the sand bag bunker on the perimeter He crouched down behind those bags, now, and cupped a cigarette in his hands. It would not do for the Duty Sergeant to catch him smoking while on post. Despite the current conditions, the Army was still the Army and breeches of discipline were things to be avoided. Yet, Carter's need for nicotine won out, as it often did, over military regulations. He cast occasional, paranoid, stolen glances to the perimeter's interior. Carter could have spared himself of the worry. Both the duty sergeant and the tower guard were already dead—victims of a long range sniper's accurate fire.

In the black distance, unseen eyes studied Carter's position through night vision binoculars. Behind the man with the binoculars 120 black-clad revolutionaries waited for the signal to attack. 600 yards away, opposite their position, an additional 80 revolutionaries awaited the same signal. A dozen miles away, on the deserted ribbon of Interstate 30, a convoy of flatbed and cargo trailer semi trucks snaked towards the armory. Around the trucks and for miles, in every direction, were spaced other vehicles loaded with black revolutionaries. Front end load-ers were present on some of the flatbeds, but most of the trucks were empty. Their cargo was waiting inside Houston Carter's perimeter. It was the first coordinated campaign of the Revolution.

Houston Carter finished his cigarette, field stripped it, and put the butt in his jacket pocket. He looked at his watch. 0343. Still another two plus hours before relief. Carter hated twelve hour shifts. He stood and stretched in the chill night air, stomping his boots against the cold.

40 yards away, a black clad revolutionary took careful aim with his crossbow and squeezed the trigger. The dart spit from the bow with a muffled, thumping noise and spiraled through the darkness. The razor sharp tip sliced through Carter's field jacket, flak jacket, camouflage blouse, and non-regulation undershirt with no difficulty, burying itself and the dart into his chest. Carter dropped his M-16 with a clatter upon the cold, concrete floor of the bunker and stared dumbly at the colorful fletching protruding from beneath his sternum. Slowly, he buckled to his knees and grasped at the dart with both hands. He tried to call out, but his breath was gone, and the sound he made was pitifully weak, car-rying but a few yards before dying against the other sounds of the night. A second dart whistled by in the blackness, missing Carter's kneeling body. A third did not miss, hitting and passing through Carter's right biceps. Carter spun with the impact and fell prone on the cold floor, his life rapidly fading. The revolutionary soldier keyed his microphone three times.

In the distance, the assault leader heard the radio's signal. One bunker was taken. Two more to go. The second signal came moments later with the death of the second perimeter guard. The assault leader issued the order to stand by. 200 anxious black warriors fidgeted in the darkness.

Near the entrance to the weapons compound, the guard in the third bunker fell into firing position and scanned the field ahead with the sights of his M-60. He had heard something. His heart pounded within his chest as he removed the radio from his web belt and whispered into the microphone.

"Foxtrot 3, Tower." Inside the tower at the other end of the containment area, the radio call fell on dead ears.

"Foxtrot 3, Tower." Again, the call went unanswered.

"Shit, Gardner!" the bunker guard cursed through clenched teeth, "Wake your butt up!" He tried a different route.

"Foxtrot 3, Control." There was a short pause before the reply came from the National Guard command post.

"Go ahead, Foxtrot 3."

"Roger, Control. Be advised that I've got negative radio contact with Tower."

"Roger, Foxtrot 3. Copy negative contact. We'll try to raise him by land line."

There was a moment's pause. The guard continued to scan the open ground before his position, machine gun trained straight ahead. The radio crackled again.

"Control, Foxtrot 4." They were calling another of the perimeter bunker guards.

There was no answer. "Control, Foxtrot 5?"

The hairs stood on the guard's neck. The third bunker guard also failed to answer the call.

"Control, Foxtrot 3," the voice on the radio was noticeably excited now, "Maintain your position. The mobile reserve force has been activated and will be enroute. Copy?"

"Roger that." answered the nervous sentinel, relieved that help was on the way.

"Damn!" the assault leader cursed angrily. He had hoped that the tower and all the bunkers could be taken without alarm before the assault. As he monitored the National Guard's radio transmissions, he realized that the need for stealth was over. He raised his own radio to his lips and gave the single order, "Go."

From two sides of the compound, 200 revolutionaries jumped to their feet and rushed towards the barbed wire. The single remaining perimeter guard heard them before he saw them.

"HALT!!!" the terrified guardsman screamed into the darkness. Immediately, bullets peppered the ground and sand bags around him. He buried his head and squeezed the M-60's trigger sweeping the barrel back and forth in a grazing fire. 100 yards away, tracers cut through the onslaught and dozens of black attackers fell headlong into death as their legs were cut out from beneath by the hail of 7.62 mm projectiles. Several among the attackers immediately fired their 40 mm grenades in the direction of the bunker. The M-60 continued to bark as the grenades made their slow arcing flights. In a tumbling succession of ear splitting booms, the machine gun and its operator were silenced for eternity.

The National Guard's mobile reserve force never made it out of the building. The revolutionaries quickly cut and blasted their way through the fence and closed in on the group of buildings housing the artillery compound's contingent of guards. Any soldier foolish enough to venture outside or show himself at a window or doorway was met with an immediate and intensive hail of fire. The grenades began to arc towards the buildings just as the first of the transfer trucks began arriving at the compound. After a few moments of noise, fire, and screams the battle was over. The loading began, uncontested.

Less than twenty minutes later, the convoy, straining under the weight of field ready artillery pieces and ammunition, departed the armory and split in two directions. As the miles passed, the convoy continued to divide and redivide until it was a scattering of individuals, pairs, and groupings of trucks surrounded by car loads of armed revolutionaries heading to forty separate locations. Sixty four pieces had been taken. It was a start, but not nearly enough. There were many more armories spread across the country. Others would be visited.

The Revolution suddenly increased several notches in intensity. The heavy weaponry was put into immediate service. For three long months, the defenses of a great number of whites and their allies had proved impregnable despite, in some cases, extreme efforts on the revolutionaries' part to gain access. Fire bombs, hand grenades and dynamite had exhibited little effect on a significant number of enemy strongholds. Assaults were consistently repelled with unacceptable losses. The large bore artillery rounds changed the situation, in the revolutionaries' eyes, most favorably. Wheeling the large guns into favorable positions relatively safe, albeit short, distances from the objective and firing directly into the enemies' positions had very immediate and desirable results. The almost point blank impact of the heavy shells obliterated defensive perimeters. Blacks would pour through the breech before the dust had settled and the gunfire would begin.

As time progressed and the flow of fresh ammunition continued to increase, many of the revolutionary forces altered their strategies and practiced bracketing their target from long distance. When they found the range, the barrage would commence. The hail of screaming fire destroyed the enemy within its own fortifications without the loss of a single black. Revolutionary leaders liked that very much.

It was a cold, gray winter and, across the country, the whirlwind raged. The scale of the violence was unlike any experienced in recorded history. Those speaking out against the violence, the more vociferous among them, were systematically eliminated regardless of color. The armed struggle that pulsed in the country's interior was a tacticians nightmare and an opportunists dream. On the government's part, the situation was grim. There were no clear physical boundaries separating the combatants. There were no advantageous staging areas or jumping off points from which to launch offensives or make defensive stands. The battlefield was everywhere and dynamic—fluid and uncontrollable. Conventional warfare theory had little application. The Revolution was less comparable to a conventional war than is was to an expansive bar room free-for-all in which bullets took the place of fists.

The American Civil War had stood for years as the bloodiest period in American history. That conflict had lasted four long, taxing years and had pitted brother against brother in an emotion filled contest. The number of American casualties in that struggle were more than the combined totals of all American casualties for all other wars in which the United States participated in the 19th and 20th centuries. By the middle of October, those long standing statistics had changed. By a significant margin, the Revolution had surpassed the Civil War's casualty figures, and, having taken the title, stood alone as the bloodiest period in American history. Violence and disease claimed the lives of greater than eight million Americans and the Revolution was showing no signs of weakening. The killing was on the rise. The entire world watched in horror and disbelief as the most powerful nation on earth was power-less to stop the violence that raged within its boundaries—a violence that threatened the nation's very fabric of existence.

President Blount sat alone in the underground chamber, far below the turmoil raging at ground level. In troubled silence, he stared into the dim shadows. It was the 28th day of December. Christmas had not been so merry this year. New Years Eve was only three nights away. The briefing had ended twenty minutes earlier. Blount's mind was still numb from the information delivered so technically precise and clinically sterile over the thick, coffin shaped table. The numbers, of course, could never be completely accurate—not in war. Modern statistical method, however, provided for the rational acceptance of the official estimate as a reasonably close representation for the num-bers of actual dead.

Official is, and always has been, a relative term. In most wars, official estimates generally tend to inflate when calculating the number of enemy dead and evidence a blind eye when tallying friendly losses. As Blount had sat erect, emotionless, hands resting on the heavy table before him, intently listening to the current 'official estimate', the num-bers rocked him to the core of his being. The dread intensified as he pondered the nagging probability that he was hearing the blind eye fig-ures. Despite his every effort to prevent them, tears flooded his eyes, and his nasal passages filled. Silence filled the room. The Country was fin-ished. How could it possibly survive?

After a span of only seconds, the President insisted that the briefing continue. It was the third briefing of its type. The first had come in the early days of October. It was obvious from the daily reports that a lot of killing had taken place since Black Tuesday, but none of the men gath-ered in the room for that first official briefing were, in any way, prepared for the numbers that issued from the subordinate manning the lectern. Naturally, isolated data on estimated body counts had surfaced, periodically, in the course of the daily reports—bits and pieces of a larger whole. The numbers had, from the start, been alarmingly high. Each official, using his or her own calculator, had worked out their own best guesstimate, more than once. By the conclusion of the first comprehensive briefing, it was glaringly obvious that the estimates were nowhere close to the actual situation.

The big picture was far too much to comprehend at a single viewing. Unlike conventional wars, there were no major battles in the classical sense—no engagements that might, in one stroke, effectively cripple an enemy. The fires burned from coast to coast and border to border. The fighting was continuous, the battle lines dynamic. The official body count for numbers lost, given during the first official briefing, was a staggering 8,628,944 dead Americans. Not a single soul in the room had been prepared for that. Color drained from faces, audible gasps were emitted, and, in a few instances, sobs were stifled as the number registered.

The second official briefing came a little over a month later, in November, just before Thanksgiving. The mood in the room was somber and reserved. A funeral pallor rested upon the room's occupants. President Blount fought hard to maintain a leader's stone visage, as did most others. Subconsciously, each prepared themselves for the recitation of the—what they knew to be high—latest official body count. In virtually every community in the United States, dead, bloated corpses lay rotting in the streets and fields. Not all had died from wounds suffered in battle. There was a new enemy that had begun taking a very heavy toll on the population. With the shortage of medical facilities, sickness and disease were on a pace to strip combat deaths of its title as the lead killer in the Revolution. The updated estimate reflected the new enemy's impact. The mental preparation these elected leaders had made towards facing the truth was not sufficient. Again, stunned silence had followed the report. 12,388,531 Americans were dead.

The December report was looked forward to with increasing dread as the Nation shivered under record cold. As they had anticipated, the number was, again, staggeringly high. 29, 102,437. The population of the U.S. was decimated. The reality was unfathomable to any but the most defeatist. Two, sometimes, three generations of Americans brought up on television logic battled in the streets with a wild abandon supplemented with a savvy know how. The hours spent before the set, especially after the advent of satellite and cable broadcasts, soaking in the violence, safely viewing the gore, had prepared the American public for the blood soaked violence manifested by the Revolution. For the combatants, the armchair training provided substantial benefit when the time for application arrived. For the Nation, the training was producing horrifying results.

Blount sat in the silence of his darkened sanctuary and pondered the future. Was there a future? By now, he should have been well along on the preparation of his new year's State of the Union Address. He had not even begun. Although no headlines had proclaimed it, Blount, like everyone else, could plainly see that the Union was dissolved. The losses were too great. If the Revolution had been a war with a foreign enemy, Blount would have, he told himself, surrendered by now. The price would have not been too high to secure life for the population, regardless of the terms. Surrender was not an available option. There was no one to whom he could surrender. The revolutionaries did not have any demands and no clear objective other than the total destruction of whites. There was no central black command. Reverend Ahmet may have believed himself to be the Revolution's leader, but if he did, he was woefully mistaken. After three months of violence, it was evident to all that it was going to be a fight to the finish. Peace was not a viable goal.

President Blount was not the only one wrestling with the implications of the turmoil in which the nation was embroiled. On the west coast, deep in another specially prepared bunker, Martin Hastings sat gazing at a wall. Any solace Hastings had expected to gain from striking out against blacks did not materialize. The pain of Kelly's death was as real as ever. Roger Delong and Peter McNair stayed close by his side.

"Things will turn around, Martin." Delong assured him. "Don't be so hard on yourself."

"Yes." agreed McNair. "Roger's right, Martin. We all knew there'd be snags. I mean, hell, you didn't expect the negroes to just roll over and take it, did you?"

"I don't know what I expected." Hastings answered. "But, I certainly didn't expect to destroy the country!"

"Oh, cut it out, Martin." Delong admonished. "We all knew the risks we were taking. We also all knew that the risks had to be taken. Something had to be done. We all recognized it. So, it's not going quite as easy as we thought. But, what the hell, it's being done. The country will rebound and it'll be stronger for the experience."

Hastings shook his head slowly. "I'm not so sure, Roj. I don't think history's ever seen a mess like this one. Certainly not one that any nation has been able to rebound from."

"Well," interjected McNair, "there's no sense in us sitting around and worrying about it. What's done is done. We've just got to ride it out as best as we can. The outcome is certainly out of your hands, now, Martin."

Hastings was forced to accept the counsel. No amount of worrying was going to impact the situation, apart from driving him to a nervous breakdown. He had to content himself that Rebecca and Laura were safe from harm.

In the days to follow, Hastings contacted the other Planning Group members, with the exception of Humari, one by one. Hastings was, he told them, grateful for their assistance. He apologized that things had gone so dreadfully awry. To the man, his associates had assured him that everything would work out, that they had been proud to assist him and that they would gladly render such assistance again, should it be necessary. Essentially, each said the same things Delong and McNair had—that the steps they had taken were necessary and that the country would survive, somehow. Their words were slightly soothing to the troubled billionaire and he was thankful that he had chosen such a faithful group of associates. The group was disbanded as easily as it was formed. Its identity would not be discovered for another six months.

Elsewhere, on a secure, coded line between Washington D.C. and Brussels, Belgium another conversation was taking place.

"How are things progressing?" The voice from Belgium asked.

"Splendidly." Came the reply from the Washington end of the connection. "The government is at the end of its rope. Any hint of infrastructure is gone. Command and control exists in name only."

"Then," queried the Belgian end, "you think it is time to play our northern card?"

"Yes." answered the Washington entity. "I think the time is right. Any opposition is not probable."

"Very well." The Belgium end agreed. "We will make the call."

The line went dead without a further word. The secretive group was about to take a giant step towards its goal of global domination.

When the Revolution erupted, Clinton Farrell was a retired Marine living a modest life at his home in the hills above Bakersfield, California . Farrell was still a soldier, through and through, and, at 64, was still full of vigor—piss and vinegar, according to him. The six foot two inch, shaved head retiree was still physically fit, robust and energetic. He still frequented gymnasiums, could still bench press 300 pounds, and could still beat eight out of ten men in arm wrestling. Mornings would, invariably, find him jogging his traditional four miles before breakfast. He appeared far younger than his years, having maintained a fit physique and still sporting the classic 'jarhead' haircut—shaved sides and back with stiff bristles meeting at an apex along his broad forehead. Farrell had retired from the Marine Corps as a Bird Colonel and lived a calm, undemanding life thereafter. Until, that is, the Revolution broke. Now, the field was Farrell's home and he was a productive leader for the black cause.

Second lieutenant Clinton S. Farrell, his 'S.' stood for the same thing Harry Truman's had, saw his first combat action as a young Marine on a humid day in August of 1965 in the ICTZ near Van Tuong, South Vietnam. The operation was code named Starlight and had been designed to completely encircle and destroy a Vietcong base. A VC deserter had provided vital intel and all the pieces were in place for a grand victory over the upstart communist forces. Friendly force was available in significant numbers. The element of surprise was theirs. It was going to be a cake walk. Farrell had met the early morning hours absent of fear and full of zeal and determination. The optimism present at the tactical operations briefing telegraphed itself through his eyes. By the end of the day, however, his eyes had glazed somewhat under tremendous blows which had been dealt his confidence. Operation Starlight, like many operations of the Vietnam conflict, proved to be a complete fiasco. American units, Farrell's included, spent the majority of the day lost or misdirected, hacking left and right, encountering opposition from everywhere and nowhere, confounded by frustration. There was no precision encirclement—no containment. The enemy disappeared—trickled into the mist. Apart from an occasional blood trail, there were no enemy bodies—nothing to show for the effort. 45 Americans lay dead.

Things were no better during Farrell's second tour in-country. The year was 1968. Farrell had reentered Vietnam two days after celebrating New Year's Eve with his wife and four month old son at their home in North Carolina. He stepped off the C-130 troop transport into the oven that is Southeast Asia -a battle hardened veteran, now a captain, absent the zeal of his butter-bar days and intent on keeping himself and the men assigned to him alive. On January 11, Farrell arrived at his assigned duty station just south of the Demilitarized Zone, a clearing amongst the ridges called Khe Sanh.. The base, in some form or another had existed since the time of the French occupation of Indochina, but was, now, little more than a patrol base. Farrell spent the early days reaccustoming himself to the country, the climate, and the responsibilities. On January 21, Farrell was gearing up for his first recon patrol when the ground shook beneath him and cries of incoming filled the perimeter. Even in the relative security of his bunker, Farrell had instinctively thrown himself to the ground, arms beneath him, white-knuckled hands gripping the straps of his steel helmet. The explosion that had rocked the earth beneath him had been a large one. Instinctively, he knew, the VC had hit an ammo dump. Things are not good, Farrell had thought as the sting from his busted lower lip found its way into his mind.

The VC rocket and mortar attacks on Khe Sanh were but the prelude to the Tet Offensive. Farrell was correct, one of the first rounds had landed directly on a sizeable ammunition dump. Secondary explosions from that blast alone went on for hours. Long after the VC's Chinese New Year operation was over in the rest of South Vietnam, the bombardment of Khe Sanh would continue. The screaming explosions would erupt, on and off, with varying intensity, for almost three months as the VC lobbed better than two thousand rounds a week into Khe Sanh's perimeter. Farrell's patrol was cancelled that day. Khe Sanh was under siege. The hills were crawling with combatants—none of them friendlies.

A mind numbing routine soon established itself among the beleaguered soldiers defending Khe Sahn. No one was ever more than a few steps from a hole into which they could dive for cover. Sometimes, the incoming rounds were grouped together and continued for substantial durations, but, more often than not, they were isolated, random blasts. Patrols were quickly reinstituted, for, despite the frequency and magnitude of the enemy fire, the mission must go forward. Farrell was never sure where he felt safer—in his bunker, or beyond the perimeter, out where the indians ruled. In his bunker, at least, he did not need to fear friendly fire. Outside the perimeter of Khe Sanh, however, it was a very real concern. Farrell had been around enough, by then, to recognize the very real application of Murphy's Law when it came to the military. With artillery, mortar, and small arms fire, both enemy and friendly filling the air, and with the 'fast burners' and the 'heavies' dropping load after load into the trees, Murphy's Law had ample opportunity to operate in and around Khe Sanh. Farrell did not like Murphy, or his law.

When Operation Pegasus lifted the siege on Khe Sanh in early April, 1965, Farrell had lost 9 of the men assigned to him. Two had been killed in action during patrol operations, seven inside the perimeter. In all, over 200 Americans died during the Khe Sanh siege, most of them as a result of shrapnel or other blast related wounds sustained as a result of bombardment. The statistics suggested Farrell had been, indeed, safer while on patrol than while inside the security of the base. Once again, the enemy faded away without a trace.

Two months after the siege on Khe Sanh had been lifted, the Marines, Farrell included, packed their gear and abandoned Khe Sanh. The move did not surprise Farrell. He was, by now, used to the U.S.'s peculiar habit of fighting for ground only to relinquish it after is taken. He had learned not to question, only to obey. Farrell finished out the remaining months of his second tour in relative security, near the beach, at Da Nang. His next significant combat duty would come, over twenty years later, as a full colonel, when he participated in the planning for both the early landings in Kuwait and later excursions into Iraq in Operation Desert Shield and, later, Desert Storm.

Farrell's record during his thirty-four years of military service had been exemplary. Many other officers with less years and less impressive records had received stars to attach to their shoulder boards, but not Farrell. That he was never promoted to the rank of general, Farrell blamed on the white man's system. In the early years, as a junior black officer, he had seen, all too clearly, the racially biased inequities that were inherent in the disparate system. Consistently, throughout his career, he had seen less deserving white officers obtain rank faster and with more frequency than their black peers. It rubbed Farrell the wrong way to see that the country was willing to ask, or demand, sacrifices from its black soldiers without offering them respect or recognition in return. His military training, however, dictated that his anger be suppressed. Outwardly, Farrell was all spit and polish and 'by the book', making the right contacts, attending the right functions, aligning his political orientations in established tracks. Inwardly, he was afire with rage and conflicting options.

More than once in his career, Farrell had been haunted by self inflicted accusations of 'Uncle Tommery' or 'Iscariot-like' behavior. He spent untold hours questioning whether or not he had sold out to the system. In the final, uneasy analysis, he decided that he had done, had always done, what was necessary to secure a comfortable living for himself and his family. There was no dishonor in this. Turning a blind eye to the inequities was only a small part of the paradigm of surviving in a white man's system.

Since his retirement, old wounds had begun to surface, however, and the question began to plague Farrell again. This time, without the restrictions which had formerly been imposed by the mission, the anger was allowed to grow unchecked and to nurture itself. Years of frustration took their toll and Clinton Farrell developed into a very resentful man. Farrell despised the injustices his race suffered at the hands of the white man's system. Further, he deeply resented the superior aire displayed by well-to-do whites. Very few of whom, he imagined, had the courage to wear their country's uniform, let alone make the kind of sacrifices he had for country, cause, and leader. But, even in the face of his resentment, Farrell was no bigot. He did not hate all white men. There were many white men Farrell had met over the years, men he had led in combat, men he had followed in combat, chance acquaintances in the civilian community, countless white men and women, all of which he held in very high regard—some he even loved. No, Farrell's problem was not with the white man, it was with the white man's system and that system's proclivity towards exploiting the less fortunate.

When the Revolution erupted, the retired Marine had answered Reverend Ahmet's call to arms early and enthusiastically—but, certainly, not out of obedience or respect for the Nation of Islam's proclaimed leader. Farrell disliked Ahmet, the man, and cared little for his teachings. Farrell read the ambitious overtones in Ahmet's speeches, and saw clearly the connivance and power-lust behind the fiery reverend's eyes. Ahmet was, Farrell knew, a power hungry megalomaniac and, definitely, a man not to be trusted. As for the Nation of Islam's teachings—Farrell certainly did not join the Revolution of religious principles. He held nothing but contempt for Islam. Some of the men in his command had been among the dead when fanatic extremists of the Prophet had bombed the Marine barracks in Lebanon. The contempt for Islam was imbedded deeply within Farrell and, despite the significant differences in the beliefs held by the Nation of Islam and the rest of the Islamic world, Farrell grouped them all in the same category—that being, a bunch of rag-headed lunatics. As for his own personal religion, Farrell leaned towards more traditional Judeo-Christian morals and guidelines. His was not a jihad. It was a struggle against inequity.

Farrell did not support the Revolution out of reverence for his roots or 'African heritage' either. He was one hundred percent, true to God, died in the wool American. How his ancestors came to be in the country was of little concern to him. His parents had been born in the U.S. and their parents before them. That was enough roots for Farrell. Whenever he would encounter the popular and trendy manifestation of name changing and the wearing of 'authentic' African apparel by blacks, he would become annoyed. To him, all of that was nothing more than ignorant nonsense. He saw no point in tracing his roots, let alone getting back to them. He was frequently embarrassed by the claims spouted by misinformed blacks proclaiming black racial supremacy in man's earliest civilizations, when the blacks were, supposedly, in control. Any first year student in world history would not venture such an asinine claim. Farrell knew, as countless others knew, that one need only look to the homeland of these boastful blacks, Africa, to see how black men have handled and continue to handle absolute authority. To Farrell, the Revolution was not a matter of supremacy. It was not a matter of hatred. It was a question of fairness.

The system, white man's system, had the proper frame to be the fairest, most effective form of government on the planet. What it desperately needed, in Farrell's estimation, was an overhaul. The old guard had to be replaced with new blood—with representatives which were truly 'representative' of the population and not bent on greed. The system had to be fitted with checks and balances ensuring executive, legislative, and judicial governance on a level playing field. It was obvious to him that the present voting system was not going to afford such representation. If the current government could be pulled to its knees, then, Farrell surmised, concession would be forthcoming and meaningful change not far behind. A concerted, bloody revolution could produce the desired effects. With such a mindset, Clinton Farrell volunteered his services to the Revolution's cause, immediately. He recognized that the time, if ever there was a time, was ripe for revolution. The staggering and unbelievable death toll arising from Black Tuesday—greater than 4 million blacks—had provided a universal rallying cry for all Afro-Americans. Virtually every black family had a loved one or knew someone who had a loved one who had perished in the horrifying poisonings or gassings. Two of Farrell's grandsons, his daughter's only two children, had died on that terrible September day. Emotions were charged to critical mass. Wailing sobs gave way to violent vows of swift revenge. This visible outcry for reprisal was strong and nationwide. Farrell recognized, clearly and correctly, the powerful driving force behind the cries. He also correctly deduced that, when the motivation for revenge is one's loved ones, one's children as was the case, most often, here, the magnitude of the force would fuel a revolution nicely.

In the days following Black Tuesday, Farrell had waited and watched. The fuse had been lit, of this, he was certain. He waited for the detonation. After the Reverend Ahmet's September speech—Farrell had listened to it on the radio—Farrell jogged to a near-by telephone booth and began making calls. The third call produced results.

"Colonel Farrell?" the voice queried across the receiver. Farrell had been on hold for the better part of five minutes.

"Yes." was Farrell's short reply.

"Colonel Farrell," the voice repeated, "How good it is to speak with you. My name is Ahkeem Sahid. This is unimportant. What is important is the fact that your name is before me, now, on a list of persons I am to contact over the next few days. This circumstance, where you have contacted me, first, can only be interpreted as the divine intervention of Allah."

"Yeah," Farrell thought, but did not state, "Whatever!"

The conversation continued and, in the process, the retired colonel was offered and accepted a position with the black revolutionary army. A sense of purpose engulfed him. He was a soldier again, this time a general, commissioned by the Fruit of Islam. He dove into his duties with a righteous fervor.

Throughout the Revolution, Farrell spent much of his waking days and nights developing and implementing battle plans for revolutionary groups along the entire west coast. Calls would come in from all over the country seeking advice. The black revolutionary army had quite an asset in this energetic retired Marine. Knowledge and experience gained through years of faithful service to the United States' military was, now, applied to the conflict at hand. Order formed out of chaos and the black forces were slowly transformed into a formidable force.

Even with the Revolution in full swing, Farrell, despite the obvious dangers, still insisted upon his early morning runs. The morning of January 11, Farrell was midway through one such run when the cellular phone—carried by an aide running alongside the retired colonel— rang. The aide, not slowing his pace, answered the call and spoke lowly. The conversation was brief and encoded. The message was quickly relayed to the jogging revolutionary general. The shipment of Russian made SA-16s had arrived. Farrell's troops would now have at their disposal shoulder-fired surface to air missiles.

Air National Guard flights, unchallenged by the black revolutionaries, proved very successful in locating and engaging ground units. For the first few weeks of the Revolution, the black armies could only hope to evade air attacks by hiding from the seemingly ever present aircraft, or, if detected, by scurrying for cover. Small arms fire proved to be of little or no value to the ground forces in stopping air attacks. Black leaders quickly recognized the need for a solution to this nagging, debilitating problem. An air force of their own was out of the question. The logistics were, simply, not in place for such a venture. The next logical option, therefore, was the acquisition of surface to air missiles and other such anti-aircraft weapons. Feelers were outstretched to the international community seeking a seller.

The inquiries quickly fell on sympathetic ears in certain countries of the middle east and the former Soviet Union. A supply line was opened. Money flowed out and weapons flowed in. Beginning in January, clandestine shipments of anti-aircraft armament began arriving at U.S. ports. The majority of the incoming weaponry bore markings linking it to the new republic of Soviet states. Black leaders, suspicious of the Soviet goals in offering such assistance, had to lay their suspicions aside and use the weapons as they got them. Their options were limited. Success depended on adequate arms to defeat the whites. The SA-16 was the Russian's answer to the U.S. Stinger—a highly effective shoulder-fired surface to air missile. The Russians had learned, the hard way, the effectiveness of the Stinger during its operations in Afghanistan. It had not taken them long to turn out a reasonable copy in the SA-16. Now, the SA-16 was to see actions in the U.S. Colonel Farrell was glad to have them in his arsenal. Without the SAMs, he knew, success was doubtful, if not impossible. Ulterior communist motives were, in the short term, secondary considerations. Such motives, Farrell knew, would have to be dealt with later.

Upon their arrival in the States, the first anti-aircraft weapons were immediately dispatched to the front lines. Clinton Farrell had been clamoring for the weapons since October. Now, finally, 150 of the state of the art missiles had arrived for use by his forces. More, he as told, were on the way. Standing in the run down warehouse which contained the weapons, the retired Colonel smiled broadly. "Now, we'll smoke some white butt!" he proclaimed, hoisting one of the launchers to his shoulder and sighting along the tube. "Our days of watching the sky and cowering like dogs are over!" His aides, surrounding him, reflected their leader's smile, sharing his satisfaction. "Let's get these to the troops ASAP." he ordered. "Next time those weekend warriors buzz our boys and get some fire sent up their butts, they're going to be in for a hell of a surprise!" He handed the SAM to an aide and departed the warehouse with a newfound spring in his step. Things were looking up.

The Revolution had already lasted much longer than even Farrell had imagined possible. Time was an ally of the blacks. The longer the Revolution lasted, he believed, the greater the chances for its ultimate success. If weapons like the SAMs continued to fall into his hands, the Revolution would last a long, long time and the white man would be begging for peace talks. Though thoughts of victory were not prominent in the retired Marine's practical mind, the hopes of victory certainly were. With such hopes, Farrell returned to his mobile command post and began drawing up fresh battle plans for his scattered forces.

Other black leaders across the nation were also receiving their supplies of anti-aircraft weapons. The optimism fostered by the newest additions to the Revolution's arsenals was contagious, trickling down from the highest levels of leadership to the foot soldiers in the streets. The high tech weaponry seemed to add a sense of legitimacy to the infant black armies. Black forces that had, heretofore, moved cautiously in the open, sticking to cover, now, with the addition of the SAMs, made no efforts to conceal their movements. National Guard aircraft found out, too late, the reasons for this new, bold behavior.

Major David Sterling had flown A-10s—'war pigs' he called them—for twelve years. Since the outbreak of the Revolution, the Air National Guardsman had flown over fifty missions in the low level ground support aircraft. His success had been phenomenal. With absolute air supremacy, he and the other members of his unit, like other units across the nation, had been able to prosecute the enemy with a free hand. The small arms carried by the revolutionaries offered but little threat to the tough A-10s. Many of the aircraft had been hit in the thousands of missions, but, so far, none had been shot down. The hardest part of the Revolution for Major Sterling had been locating the enemy. Once that was accomplished, however, the engagement was like shooting fish in a barrel. The black revolutionaries were defenseless against the A-10s firepower. Major Sterling was not sure how many blacks he had killed, but he was certain that the number had to be somewhere in the hundreds. Other fighter aircraft and helicopters had experienced similar success. Such aircraft traversed the skies across the U.S. like roving bands of predators fearlessly seeking their prey. Any gathering of blacks was a potential target.

On the afternoon of January 13, Major Sterling was on a solo patrol in the sky above southern Los Angeles. The situation was such—absolute air supremacy—that wingmen were not being used, so as to allow more missions to be flown, covering more ground with the same number of aircraft. That strategy would end, soon. Sterling had been airborne for about ten minutes when he saw the group of approximately fifty blacks moving through the city streets 2000 feet below him. It had been greater than a month since Major Sterling had seen such a large gathering of blacks on the streets during daylight hours. He began a slow turn in the A-10, and lined the aircraft for a pass over the group of men. When he had made his pass and was satisfied as to their identity as hostiles, Sterling radioed a call to the base's control tower.

"Eagle Control. This is Avenger One. Come in, over."

"Go Avenger One." came the immediate reply.

"Roger, Eagle Control. I've got a group of suspect targets moving north on what looks like 26th Street just south of San Vicente Boulevard. Targets appear armed. Request permission to engage."

There was a short pause before the affirmative reply crackled in the pilot's headphones. "Roger that, Avenger One. Copy armed hostiles. You may engage at will. Be advised, two Black Hawks are enroute from the Naval Weapons Station. ETA is eleven minutes."

"Roger, Eagle. Stand-by." The 35 year old Air National Guard Major put his aircraft into a slow banking turn and dropped to less than 300 feet above the concrete. He would stir things up a bit and wait on the two army helicopters to arrive for mop-up operations.

On the ground, Demetrius Kent saw the National Guard airplane when it was but a small speck in the sky. Demetrius was the leader of a forty eight man band of black revolutionaries that was now roaming through the streets looking for victims. The arrival of the four, hand held anti-aircraft missile launchers the day before had allowed him to finally plan operations in the daytime. Daylight raids were something he had been unable to try since early in November. It felt good to move in the light again.

Immediately upon seeing the approaching aircraft, Kent had ordered the men carrying the SAMs to take cover in the doorways of a burned out buildings. The other members of his group he ordered into the street to attract the plane's attention. The aircraft passed by, low over-head. The I.D. pass. They had been spotted. Kent watched the single A-10 streak away before slowly banking to the right and preparing for another pass. It was coming back.

"Scatter!" Kent yelled to the other blacks. Immediately, the nervous black men under Kent's command sprinted to cover. Over the weeks, they had learned respect for the National Guard aircraft, especially the A-10. In the doorway of a charred shop, one of the black revolutionaries raised the launcher to his shoulder and aimed it at the now approaching A-10.

When Major Sterling completed his turning maneuver and aligned the nose of his aircraft with the street for a strafing run, he cursed beneath his breath. The street was empty. He should have strafed them on his first pass, but operation orders called for an identification pass first. There were no targets in sight when he squeezed off a few hundred 7.62 mm rounds from the plane's mini-Gatling guns. He could only hope to flush some hiders into the open. The blacks, veterans by now, stayed concealed. It did not matter, Sterling decided. The Cavalry was on the way. All he had to do was stay around to keep the blacks in one place and the troops in the approaching helicopters could search them out at their leisure. Sterling soared over the street at a speed just above stall, head turning from left to right, searching.

When the bullets from the plane's Gatling guns began ripping into the concrete, the revolutionary soldier holding the missile launcher had kneeled low against the charred door frame and continued to train the launcher on the approaching aircraft. Just as the A-10 passed, the black soldier squeezed the trigger on the launchers handle. There was a slight jar and a distinct whooshing noise as the missile leapt from the launcher and reached out for the close support combat craft. The missile closed on the A-10 with lightning swiftness. In the cockpit, Major Sterling never knew what hit him. The explosion was terrific as the missile impacted with the aircraft's right wing. The A-10 was instantly transformed into a writhing, spinning fireball.

The black revolutionaries let out a roar of approval as the A-10 was spit from the sky in a dozen flaming pieces slamming into buildings and disintegrating in a mass of twisted, burning metal and composite fibers. The celebration was short-lived, however, as the ordinance that had been carried on the A-10 began to cook off in the resultant heat of the burning wreckage. One of the revolutionaries was hit in the side by one exploding 20mm round's casing and was sent sprawling to the street, dying in burning agony. The other blacks scattered in every direction.

In the distance, the approaching National Guard helicopters could see the mushroom-like cloud on the horizon. Over the tactical net, the air base's control tower was trying to contact the Air Guard pilot.

"Avenger One...Avenger One. Come in, over." There would be no response. The helicopters increased their air speed. In the helicopters' cargo bays, the special forces soldiers, weapon barrels resting downward between their jump boots, nervously awaited drop off. They, like the blacks, were also accustomed to night operations.

On the ground, two blocks from the smoldering A-10 wreckage, Kent yelled for the other two SAM carriers to accompany him and broke into a trot towards the tallest building in the area. He knew the standard operating procedures of his enemy and was well aware that a team of army soldiers would be on the way to back up the fallen aircraft. He was going to be ready for them. He ordered another soldier to locate the rest of the revolutionaries and to assemble them in an abandoned grocery store three blocks to the west. Having issued his orders, Kent and the two soldiers equipped with SAMs raced into the building they had selected and snaked their way to the roof.

When the two Black Hawk helicopters were less than a mile from the crash site, it became apparent to both of the crafts' pilots that the Air Guard plane had gone in. Both helicopters slowed considerably and began a slow reconnoiter of the area. Dozens of eyes scanned the streets below. The A-10 wreckage was scattered over several hundred yards. Here and there, armed blacks could be seen darting in and out of buildings, individuals of the group that had been reported by the A-10 pilot—no chance of isolating any substantial number. One of the helicopter pilots contacted the air base and relayed the situation status.

Kent and the other two revolutionaries watched the helicopters from their semi-concealed position on the roof top. The flight path remained unaltered. The two aircraft continued to circle the area..

"Next time they pass," Demetrius instructed the two launcher carriers, "light 'em up!"

The two SAM holders smiled and continued to train their sights on the circling enemy.

The co-pilot on the lead helicopter saw a glint of sunlight from a building to his left, about four hundred yards away. He narrowed his gaze and concentrated his attention there. At a little over three hundred yards, he was sure. He spoke into the microphone. "Port!," he alerted the pilot, "We got indians on the tall building at 9 o'clock."

The pilot whipped his head around to the left and scanned the building tops. After a few seconds, he saw them. "Yeah! I got 'em!" "Linebacker,' he called the second helicopter pilot, "we got targets on the roof of tallest building at your eleven."

There was a short pause before the reply, "Roger, Junkyard. I've got visual."

"Uh oh!" exclaimed Kent, "They've seen us!" The two helicopters began a slow turn away from the building.

"What are you talking about, Man?" asked one of the anxious men by his side. "They're going the other way."

Kent did not answer, but kept his eyes trained on the helicopters. He knew he was right. The other two revolutionaries knew he was right when the helicopters' noses turned, slowly, in their direction. Suddenly, both helicopters gained speed and fire leapt from beneath them as 7.62 rounds spewed from the guns at their bellies and cut through the morning and onto the roof on which the blacks had positioned themselves. Dust leapt from the rooftop as hundreds of flaming rounds from the Black Hawks raked across its surface. One of the SAM holders, gripped in panic, dropped his missile launcher and bolted towards the stairway door.

"Get back here, you chicken shit!" Kent boomed after the frightened man. It was no use. The words were still scrambled among the clatter of the impacting rounds as the running man was caught as if by wind and perforated with a dozen or more jacketed slugs. Kent returned his attention to the rapidly approaching helicopters.

Aboard the lead helicopter, the pilot and co-pilot both saw the black man drop the missile launcher and run across the roof. "Jesus!" exclaimed the pilot, "Was that what I think it was?" referring to the SAM launcher. The co-pilot, ashen faced, eyes trained on the second black man who continued to aim his launcher, did not answer.

"Cook that son of…" Kent began, but never finished, as the incoming bullets found him. His brain barely had time to register that he had been hit. It was like being hit in the shoulder by a baseball bat. The second round caught him in the head, killing him instantly. Behind him, the second soldier squeezed the trigger on the SAM launcher only an instant before he, too, was caught and ripped to shreds in the fiery onslaught of projectiles. The anti-aircraft missile had barely cleared the outer rim of the building before it, too, disintegrated under the hail of both helicopters' fire.

The first helicopter banked hard left when it became obvious to the pilot that the SAM had fired. The move was purely reflex. Had the missile not been downed by the rain of 7.62s, no evasive maneuver would have saved him. The second helicopter maintained its path and passed directly over the building before climbing slightly and circling. The first helicopter made a quick turn, returned, and hovered directly above the splintered roof. Eight lines snaked the fifteen feet to the bullet riddled surface and the special forces team deployed and formed a perimeter.

Seconds later, the second Black Hawk took the first's place and unloaded its own contingent of the 16 man search and destroy patrol.

Specialist First Class David Cooper lifted the SAM launcher from among the shredded flesh and affixed it to one of the ropes for retrieval by the helicopter…intelligence information. The 16 man force then descended to the street to begin their mission.

The operations intel was flashed across the net. The revolutionaries had SAMs. Eyebrows raised, then lowered. Most had anticipated the news. The blacks had not been expected to go forever without challenging the Government's absolute air superiority. The event had been anticipated. Such weapons were expected in a war zone. The SAMs would present an obstacle, true, but the mission remain unchanged. The enemy had to be broken. Black forces would continue to be located and neutralized. Flights would simply have to exercise greater caution.

Where the SAMs had come from was open to speculation. The launcher recovered from the building in Los Angeles was of Soviet manufacture, but it could have been supplied by any number of a dozen different nations. Already, more than a dozen shipments of arms had been intercepted prior to delivery to the black armies—cargoes of everything from small arms ammunition to tanks and large field artillery pieces had been seized. So far, only one of the seized shipments had been traced to its country of origin…Iran. No surprise there. Naturally, Iran denied that it was providing assistance to the revolutionaries. No surprise there, either. Apart from a stiff warning from the State Department, nothing more could be done. That a significant number of arm shipments were getting through to the revolutionaries was obvious from combat encounters across the nation. The going had, suddenly, gotten a lot tougher.

Nick Stefano ran a bar, 'Reubens', beneath the street, in an inconspicuous location on the fringes of New York City's Upper West Side. He had inherited proprietorship of the establishment from his father, who had, likewise, inherited the bar from his father. The income Reubens provided, though not exorbitant, paid the bills and kept the doors open. Little had changed about the bar over the years. The floors were, as always, the same peanut hull littered, unpolished hardwood. The imported, heavy brass foot rail which ran the length of the bar, though loose, dinged up and badly tarnished, was the same which Nick's grandfather had installed nearly 70 years earlier. The radio had been replaced by the juke box, then another juke box, and, finally, by a big screen television. Newspaper clippings, pictures, and other memorabilia covered virtually every square inch of Reubens' walls. The beer and liquor, glassware, napkins, toilet paper, cigarettes, insurance, and cleaning service were provided, not without a little persuasion, by concerns under the direct control of Vincent Dials, a lieutenant in Marco Colletti's, also inherited, age old 'business thing'. Organized crime had been and would always remain an integral part of the day to day existence of New York and other major metropolitan areas.

Nick liked to think of his bar as an upscale lounge, but it was really no more than a smoke-filled dive, grandfathered into, through convenience of location, an area heavily populated by upscale lounges. The few regulars that frequented Reubens were, certainly, far from upscale. A more appropriate description would be downtrodden, or depressed, lower-middle class, heavy drinkers that looked to alcohol as a universal salve to the ailments of existence. Since the second week of the Revolution, business had been booming. Many of the other bars in the area had closed. Some had been looted and burned. Reubens was only one of few in the entire city that remained open. The fact that his bar was located below ground gave Nick a sense of security—out of sight, out of mind. Hopefully, Nick prayed, the bar would continue to go unnoticed by all but potential customers.

In early November, Nick moved his wife from their mid-town home to a room in the back of Reubens. She would be safer there, Nick concluded, than in the old neighborhood. Things had gotten crazy. By January, things had gotten much crazier. Fearing for his family, Nick dug into his savings account and arranged for his wife, son, daughter-in-law and granddaughter to be carried safely out of the country and to South America for an extended vacation. Since then, he had kept Reubens' doors open 24 hours a day. More than once, over the weeks, battles had raged in the street above the bar, but, even as late as February, blacks had not noticed, or had simply ignored Nick's bar. Nick kept a loaded Uzi, purchased from Colletti's lieutenant, Dials, next to the cash register—just in case. His customers also, for the most part, were always armed. Since the start of the Revolution, being without a gun was not a very wise or safe thing.

By the end of February, the street above Reubens resembled a third world urban battleground. Burned out shells of cars lined the street. Blackened buildings stood silent watch over litter strewn concrete. Reubens, still untouched, had become the only operating bar for a little over twelve blocks. Even with the violence raging everywhere, customers filled the bar at all hours of the day and night. Nick was making more money than he had ever dared dreamed, so much money that he had finally approached Vincent Dials for more specialized protection.

Dials had immediately forwarded the request to Colletti. That very afternoon, four of Colletti's foot soldiers were assigned to around the clock security of the bar. The service cost Nick handsomely, but he did not mind. He was making profits like never before and, despite the cost, some insurance was indispensable. Sooner or later, the blacks were going to target Reubens and Nick wanted to be ready.

The measure proved to be a lucrative venture for Colletti. With the unrest, many of his concerns' normal activities had been indefinitely suspended. To maintain cash flow, he had found that he must diversify and adapt. The extra protection service he provided for businesses still operating in the city was beginning to add up in terms of income. Before long, Colletti had dozens of his foot soldiers subbed out all over New York City. It was easy money, and almost legal too. Colletti did not stand to lose much in the deal either. He had given specific orders that the soldiers not stay around if the heat got too high. If a display of force was not enough to thwart any would be black attackers, his soldiers were to, they were instructed, get the hell out and leave the associated businessmen to fend for themselves. Money for nothing. Colletti liked that.

In the second week of February, the terror swept into Ruebens from the ice covered streets above. The event was inevitable, yet unexpected. All eyes had turned to the single black man as he fearlessly strode into the bar. Silence had descended on the crowd. Nick watched the man, nervously. The two muscle providers sent over by Colletti made their way towards the man, but stopped when he yelled something unintelligible and pitched an aerosol can onto the floor. The black man then turned and bolted for the door.

"GRENADE!" someone yelled.

Reubens' patrons dove for cover. One of Colletti's men pulled a revolver from his shoulder holster, leveled it at the black man, squeezed the trigger twice and dropped the black man before he could clear the door. The aerosol can did not explode, but, rather, after an instant, started hissing. All over the bar, men scrambled to their feet. Just as quickly, men, those closest to the hissing can, began falling to the floor in disjointed spasms of coughing.

"Gas!" someone else yelled.

There was a mad rush for the door. The lethal gas filled the smoky room quickly. In the streets above the bar, gunfire erupted as those attempting to escape the slow death of the deadly fumes below met with instantaneous fiery ambush above.

Nick Stefano died hugging his grandfather's brass foot rail. In the doorway, the two Colletti guards lay equally dead. They had not been able to slip away when the heat got too hot, like Colletti had ordered. They would not be the only soldiers Colletti would lose.

Across the city, Marco Colletti was experiencing some heat of his own. His impregnable wall had been breached. Blacks had penetrated his compound and the combat had joined. Colletti's soldiers, battered and bloody, fought with a primordial intensity to repel the invaders. From the relative safety of his subterranean bunker, Colletti could hear the muffled roar of the battle raging in the fortress above. He clenched and relaxed his fists and whispered obscenities at the black race in general.

Luther Jennings had not forgotten his brother, or the violent death his brother suffered at the hands of Colletti's men. Luther had not lost his desire for revenge. Not a minute had passed since his brother's death that Luther had not been scheming and contemplating revenge. All attempts to gain entrance into the Colletti compound had met with decisive failure and Luther was forced to stew in his frustrated anger. Then, Luther had heard a rumor of a captured artillery cannon, stolen from a National Guard unit, being used in Trenton, New Jersey to hammer at white strongholds. Green lights flickered in his mind. Luther decided that he had to have that weapon.

Luther and twelve others set off for New Jersey to track the artillery piece. Finding it was not so difficult. Acquiring it was a different matter.

The black group that possessed it was, Luther was informed in no uncertain terms, not about to let it go. But, Luther was not to be denied. In a foolhardy maneuver, he and his companions waited until nightfall, then attacked and killed the blacks guarding the heavy artillery piece. A back hoe, acquired earlier in the day, roared to life and eased off the flatbed transfer truck, also acquired earlier in the day. The loading of the big gun onto the truck took only ten minutes. Loading the ammunition took much longer. The process went unchallenged. Luther left the back hoe behind and headed back into the city with a 105mm in tow.

As dawn broke over the smoke filled Big Apple, Luther and his group were back in the city with their newly acquired weapon positioned to bear on the walls of the Colletti fortress. It would be several hours before the first round was fired. It took that long to find someone who knew how to operate it. Inside the fortress, Colletti and his men were oblivious to the activity.

The siege had taken its toll on Mad Max. He had never been able to stand being cooped up in one place for long periods. He had been cursing himself, since December, for not getting out of the country when he had a chance. Other big bosses across the country had skipped out early. Colletti had been stubborn and realistic. The other bosses, he conjectured, would return to find out that they were no longer in control of squat. Colletti was determined to hold onto his empire. As the Revolution continued to rage, he began to see that his empire was not so great as he had believed.

In December, Colletti attempted a breakout in the converted beer truck. He did not go more than three hundred yards. If it had not been for the trailing armored car and the unselfish heroics of some of his men, Colletti would have died in the escape attempt. Since then, Colletti had been like a caged animal, a prisoner in his own fortress.

The artillery fire had begun shortly after noon. Round after round slammed into the wall and exterior of Colletti's fortress. It had become immediately apparent, that the structure was not all that it had been touted to be. The wall held up fairly well through the first few direct hits, but the house was a different story. Within an hour, the relentless shelling had reduced the house to rubble. Colletti had moved to the underground chamber soon after the barrage had commenced, to wait it out. The secret chamber was well stocked with food, water, liquor and other essentials. He could wait a long time. He was still waiting when the gaping hole was finally blown in the fortress's perimeter wall and the triumphant blacks flooded through the breach.

After a few minutes, the muffled firing ceased. The silence was ominous. Mad Max cringed. His empire was at an end. He buried his face in his hands and leaned back against the cement wall. When the gunfire resumed above, Colletti had strained his ears and experienced a small glimmer of hope.

The firing ceased after a few minutes to be followed by still silence. Colletti settled back again. Luther Jennings and many of his group lay dead in the streets outside the rubble that had been Marco Colletti's fortress. The artillery piece's owners had reclaimed their property.

Mad Max Colletti went truly mad several hours after discovering that the only exit from his underground chamber was jammed securely and would not budge despite his efforts. Something was wrong with the ventilation system as well. The food and water would last long after the last of the air was gone.

It was a rainy Ides of March morning and Chris Hunter sat huddled in the charred housing of the overturned central heating unit in the basement of the burned out residence. Cold, hungry, exhausted, he shivered in the darkness, white knuckled hands gripping the rifle before him. Chinks in the armor had been developing over the previous two weeks. Questions, troubling questions, began arising as Chris had slipped in and out among the shadows, avoiding humans. As the lonely evenings passed, the formidable wall of racial hatred built by the instructors in the swamp, so long ago, began to chip away. Light pierced the darkness. Realization had come in the early hours of the morning. He sat, now, awake to the reality, cursing himself for his stupidity. How could he have been so ignorant…so weak, to be brainwashed so thoroughly…so easily? His mind carried him to September.

The first raids had been, like they had been told, easy. His squad was well trained and highly motivated. In and out, with surgical precision. Inflicting maximum casualties. That first weekend, the blacks had been easy targets. It was the fourth raid before any member of his squad had even been fired upon. The zealous NOA soldiers, Chris included, performed their mission with a religious fervor. The killing came without effort. On his first night, Chris had killed 46. He had been disappointed with the low number. Most of the other squad members had done better. The hate filled propaganda which had been so effectively and completely hammered into their sub conscious minds provided an intense personal satisfaction in the soldiers each time another black was neutralized. Theirs' was a righteous cause.

When the Revolution started, the situation changed substantially. The blacks were no longer such easy targets. For Chris's squad, just as with every other NOA squad spread across the Nation, the mission became increasingly difficult. Patrols shifted, of necessity, from search and destroy missions to purely combat missions. It took all of the skills they had learned in their two years of training just to survive. Chris's squad fared much better than most of the other NOA squads. It was December, before they had lost their first man.

It was a stupid error. The NOA squad had been on their way back to the safe house from a night of successful raiding when they walked into the ambush. The sun was not far away and they still had a way to go. They were together, all six. Their interval was too tight. They knew better, had been trained better. The firing had begun just as they had entered the alley. Had the ambushers waited another instant, or had their fire been more accurate, the entire squad may have perished on the garbage strewn concrete. As it was, two soldiers went down immediately under the fire, the remaining four turned, as they had been trained, into the storm of bullets and charged, firing. The tactic worked. The novice ambushers panicked. The squad members gained access to the building and the firing continued. They killed six of the ambushers. At least three got away.

In the alley, two NOA soldiers lay dead. A third lay prone, bleeding heavily from both legs and arms. The three walking soldiers immediately set about binding the downed man's wounds, then turned their attention to their own wounds. Chris's shoulder burned in searing pain from the bullet lodged there. He was not bleeding heavily and was able to staunch the majority of the flow. The pain, he simply had to deal with. One of the other soldiers had been hit in the calf and forearm. The wounds did not appear serious, the bullets passing cleanly through. The third soldier had only a single graze on his cheek. The kiss of a round that could have decapitated him. All had been hit, at least once, in their body armor, but suffered no more than painful bruises there.

They shifted their attention to their dead comrades. They could not leave them there. Their orders had been specific. No evidence which could identify a NOA soldier was to be left behind. In their present condition, banged up and pressed for time, the sky was already beginning to lighten perceptibly, with a wounded man to transport, there was no way they could pack two additional bodies. The compromise was immediate, also a part of their training. With machine-like efficiency, the hands, feet and heads of their former squad members were removed and distributed among the three backpacks of the walking soldiers. A timed white phosphorus charge was positioned between the two dismembered bodies. It would effectively and instantly take care of their bodies in seven minutes and counting. A hollow core door from inside the building made a suitable stretcher and the four crusaders had shuffled towards the rising sun.

The least wounded soldier left his three companions in the safe house and had ventured back into the dangerous brightness of daylight. After disposing of the incriminating fragments of the dead squad members, he had gone in search of a doctor. The search had not been easy. It was late in the morning before he finally located his 'doctor'. The young man, in his early twenties, had been a third year medical student when the Revolution broke out. Such students had been pressed into service in the middle of November. The measure was of little help. Hundreds of thousands of citizens were dying daily from lack of medical assistance. Doctors were also dying. The Revolution, the world discovered early, did not respect the red cross flag.

The soldier had been very fortunate to locate the practicing, would be physician. It had taken persuasion at gun point to convince the young doctor to make a house call. By the time the two had returned to the safe house, almost noon, it was too late for the stretcher bound soldier. The doctor closed the glazed, staring eyes with his thumb. The young soldier had not cried out, even once, throughout the morning. He had given up his soul silently, knowing that any weakness on his part might bring unwanted attention to their location. The swamp training had been total. Weakness was not tolerated.

The doctor turned his attention to the other two men in the room. One had bandages about his right arm and left leg. They appeared clean. The man refused inspection by the doctor. He had attended to his own wounds using the medical skills that had been drilled into him during the weeks of specialized training. Under the circumstances, the young doctor could have done no more.

The doctor moved to where Chris rested, against the wall. The bandage on Chris's shoulder was not clean. Despite his attempts at cauterization, the wound had continued to bleed. He was still losing blood and, from the look of his clothes, the doctor decided, had lost a lot already. The pain telegraphed itself. The doctor dropped to one knee and placed the bag on the floor in front of him. He fumbled through the implements and medications he had grabbed before leaving his apartment. After a second, he retrieved a syringe and an ampule of Demerol. Chris, eyes set on the doctor, saw the young man's intent and, unable to speak, shook his head back and forth, reaching slowly out with his good arm and grasping the doctor's hand. The doctor looked into Chris's eyes. The message was clear.

"Alright," replied the doctor, "It's your pain. But I really think you could use this."

Chris shook his head again. The pain killer would numb his senses, cloud his judgment and endanger his squad. It would not be allowed. He would deal with the pain alone. Finally, the young doctor shrugged his shoulders and returned the syringe and Demerol to the bag.

The doctor pulled on a pair of examination gloves and moved closer to Chris. Gingerly, he removed the blood soaked bandage and viewed the wound. Three months earlier, the sight of the raw and mangled flesh may have caused the young doctor to pale. Now, after only three weeks of actual practice he did not flinch. He had seen worse, much worse. He poised his right hand over the wound and looked into Chris's tortured eyes.

"This is probably gonna hurt a good bit." The doctor announced.

Chris nodded his head, understanding. The white stars filled his field of view as the doctor began probing.

The bullet was still there, the young doctor's practiced fingers told him, at least its larger fragments. The bone did not appear shattered, but he could not know that for sure without X-rays. The bleeding could be stopped. He stood up slowly, leaned against the table and began speaking to no one and everyone.

"Well. The bullet's got to come out. There's no question about that. I'd like to do it in more sanitary conditions, but there's little chance of that happening, is there?" There was no answer. The Doctor had not expected one. The question had been rhetorical. He continued, without pause. "It's a pretty straight forward procedure. Cut him open, dig out the metal, wash him up and stitch up the hole. Piece of cake! I've done dozens. But, and I think you guys better hear this good, without blood, I don't give him one chance in five of walking out of here." The soldiers did not appear to register any emotion.

The doctor began pulling off the blood stained gloves. "Look, guys. This man has lost a whole heap of blood…and, furthermore," he continued, as if anticipating a reply, "it's not like you can just send Rambo here," he nodded towards the squad member who had retrieved him from the apartment, "out to get some. In case you've missed it, there's a war going on out there. There's been a blood shortage since the first of October. The chances of finding any blood, let alone his type, are about as good as finding a McDonalds open." The two standing soldiers held out their arms, palm up, towards the doctor.

The young practitioner smiled at what he perceived to be camaraderie. He was right, but only partially so. "Sorry, fellas." he stated,

"That's not the way it works. You've got to have his blood type." He shook his head several times. "Didn't they teach that to you in survival camp, or military school, or wherever you've been?"

"We do have his blood type!" both answered in tandem. And they did. It was only another part of the intensive planning that went into the development of the New Order Army. All squads were likewise configured with shared blood types. It was contingency for situations just like this one. The doctor, amazed, did not question the apparent coincidence, instead went immediately to work. Mercifully, Chris passed out early in the operation.

The procedure took a little over twenty minutes. When the young practitioner had finished applying the final bandage, he stood up, stretching. The two soldiers stood also. "Well," the doctor announced, "That's that. He'll probably never pitch in the big leagues, but he should have full use of his arm in a few weeks. I think the bleeding will stop, but you'll need to keep a close eye on it." He dug in his bag again and tossed one of the soldiers a bottle of antibiotics. "For infection." he announced, "It won't affect his reasoning abilities, but it might keep infection from setting in. Make sure he takes them." The soldier nodded affirmatively. "Now," the doctor asked, finally, "Do I get an escort back to my apartment, or am I on my own?" The soldier that had retrieved the doctor earlier smiled and answered. "I'll walk you home, Doc."

When Chris awoke, it was night. The doctor was gone, as was the body of the dead squad member. The two remaining soldiers, sitting in the shadows, saw Chris's eyes open.

"How is it?" asked one, after a moment. Chris shifted his weight a bit. The stabbing pain was gone, replaced by a pounding throb. Weakly, he stood to his feet.

"I can go." Chris announced. Instantly, the other two were on their feet. They distributed the contents of Chris's pack between them and all three men faded into the darkness.

Over the days to follow, Chris's shoulder had healed well and, after about a month, he had full use of his arm again. Just like the doctor had promised.

The fourth squad member died at the end of January in a running firefight. The screeching round had torn his head off his shoulders. His weapon had fallen to the asphalt with a metallic clatter and his body had gone forward, of its own, for several steps before folding onto the street. Chris and the remaining soldier had been unable to retrieve the body, barely escaping with their own lives.

Chris had been on his own since the end of February. The final squad member, Jeff Kelly, Chris's best friend since the days in the swamps, had died in Chris's arms in the dark maze of a storm sewer. At that time, Chris was one of only twenty seven NOA soldiers still remaining alive. The number continued to dwindle. The soldiers had been good, perhaps the best the world has known, but the campaign had been too long. Attrition took its toll. Sneaking along in the shadows, cut off from humanity, Chris's mind began to do battle with the thoughts that had been implanted in the NOA training. The winter, the loneliness, the exhaustion, the hunger, all combined to break through the brain washing. The rain outside continued to fall in icy sheets as Chris sat in the darkened basement crying and contemplating suicide.

---— ◆ ——---

Frazier sat in the worn chair and sipped at the scalding coffee. He had spent the night at his desk, again, and he looked it. His bloodshot eyes were sunken deep in his head. His clothes were a wrinkled mess. He could not remember when he last had changed them. The investigation continued to frazzle his nerves. His waste basket overflowed with styrofoam cups.

The days since September had been frustrating and filled with dead ends and empty leads. The FBI was no closer now, after six months, to finding any answers than they had been at the beginning. The cover up was unbelievable. Whoever they were dealing with, Frazier was convinced, was powerful and had some equally powerful contacts. That narrowed the field, but not so much as to offer optimism.

Over the weeks, Frazier had compiled a list of possible suspects. It read like a who's who of the rich and powerful. The common link among the names, apart from money or political position, was the fact that each had been close to someone who had been killed or seriously injured by black men. The list was up to thirty-three names and growing.

The phone rang, crashing through his fog shrouded mind. "Frazier here." he answered, on the second ring.

"Uncle Dave?" came the voice from the receiver.

It was a blow from out of nowhere. "Chris?!!" Frazier questioned, hoping. The voice on the line was like one from another lifetime. "Chris? Is that you?"

Chris crouched alongside the underground telephone line junction alongside the Kentucky roadside and spoke into the lineman's phone, his eyes moving constantly, searching all directions. "Uncle Dave, I need your help."

"Sure! Sure, Chris." Frazier promised immediately, "Anything. Just tell me where you are."

"Meet me tomorrow…at home." Instructed Chris.

"Home?" Frazier questioned, "You mean Tennessee? Are you in the states?"

"Yeah." Chris answered. "Tennessee…about 10. O.K.?"

"Alright," Frazier agreed, "10 a.m. I'll be there. Chris, you…" Chris did not allow his uncle to finish. The phone went dead.

Frazier stared at the phone in his hand for a long moment before returning it to its cradle. A thousand questions flooded his mind. Did he know, Frazier asked himself, wondering if Chris had found out about his parents, yet. Telling him would not be easy. The pain resurfaced.

It was the second week of the Revolution. Frazier was in New York City when he received the news. Sandy and Brian were dead. They had been killed, Frazier learned, in their home, during a random raid by revolutionaries. The couple had been found in their bedroom, still in bed, their throats pierced. An FBI team had been dispatched to do an investigation of their own, at the direct order of Williamson. Based on all the evidence, the position of the bodies, the nature of the wounds, chances were, Williamson told Frazier, that Sandy and Brian had never known what hit them. It was small consolation. Frazier felt a bit of himself die with the tragic news. Emotions felt so many years earlier, when he had received the news of his parents' deaths, rose to the surface. This time the tears came in abundance. His thoughts had, naturally, migrated to Christopher.

Frazier had received four postcards from his nephew since Chris's departure from the states. The one year's service had, by choice of Chris, expanded to two. He was having a great time, the cards read. He was in the South Pacific, hopping from country to country, helping natives with crops, sanitary services, commerce and a handful of other projects. Frazier had been happy for his nephew, realizing that the experience would benefit the young man greatly. Still, Frazier had wished for his nephew's early return. That is, until the Revolution broke out. After that, Frazier had hoped Chris would remain abroad until the smoke cleared.

The last postcard had arrived two weeks before Black Tuesday. Frazier had heard nothing from his nephew since then. Following, Brian and Sandy's deaths, there was, he had learned, no way of contacting Chris with the news. The Revolution had disrupted any hope of such communication. The U.S. relief agency which was sponsoring Chris assured Frazier that everything was O.K. and that they would make every effort to contact his nephew. Frazier was not satisfied, but there was nothing more he could do. The Revolution had disrupted everything.

The phone rang again, pulling him from his thoughts. Frazier rubbed his eyes and answered it. In the distance, the sound of gunfire echoed through the deserted streets of the nation's capital.

Arranging the helicopter for the flight to Tennessee was easy enough. To the Bureau, Frazier was simply tracking another lead and for such excursions, all of the Bureau's facilities were open to Frazier and the task force. Frazier spent the flight down in silence, immersed in thought. The notion of having to tell Chris about Sandy and Brian's deaths weighed heavily upon him. He watched the landscape flow by beneath the helicopter. The route was not straight. The helicopter's pilot took careful pains not to pass within shooting distance of towns and cities. Bullet holes in the helicopter's frame attested to the danger of flying too close to concentrated areas and every pilot was, by now, aware of the very real SAM threat. The pilot tried not to think about missiles. Even in the rural areas, the countryside bore the mark of a disaster. The scattered houses were no more than burned out shells, cars were overturned, burned out, or askew in the streets and fields. There were no people. They were, if they were wise, hidden out. Anyone in the open was, as hundreds of thousands had discovered, an easy target.

Upon arrival at their destination, the helicopter made two passes, just to be on the safe side, then landed in the small park two blocks from Frazier's sister's house. Frazier instructed the pilot that he would arrange for pick up later. The pilot need not wait around on the ground. "Just circle for while," Frazier had instructed through the headset, "If I don't give you a call within thirty minutes, return to Virginia. I'll arrange alternate transport." It was welcome news to the nervous pilot. He took a look at his fuel gauge—more than enough to do a little flying around. He could handle thirty minutes, no problem. He gave Frazier the thumbs up sign and nodded. Frazier exited the craft and jogged to the tree line. The helicopter rose lazily and nosed northwards. Frazier watched it depart, growing small on the horizon. He checked his watch. 9:48. Right on time. He chambered a round in the mini-14 and stalked away towards his sister's house.

The neighborhood reminded Frazier of pictures he had seen of Germany in the days following World War II. Many houses had been completely destroyed, others were burned out shells. Frazier covered the distance sprinting from cover to cover, pausing only to listen and plan his next move. It took him five minutes to reach Sandy and Brian's old back yard. He had not seen the house since the day after their deaths. It had been untouched then, apart from the blood stained bedroom. Now, the house was a wreck. The roof was gone, the windows all broken and the exterior bricks scorched. Frazier eased across the back yard and slipped into the rubble.

Chris was already there. Frazier was not prepared for the sight that awaited him as Chris came out of the shadows and smiled uneasily. In the place of the boy Frazier had said his farewells to nearly two years earlier, stood a man. His eyes were hollow and worn, sunken and…What? Frazier wondered. Furtive? Wary? It was something else, something indefinable. The slight beard on his nephew's face added years. He was dressed in stained and shredded military type clothing. In his rough, dirty hands, he held a rifle…an HK. The questions ricocheted in Frazier's mind, but they would have to wait. There would be time for answers later. The two embraced.

It was Chris who broke the silence. "Mom and Dad are dead, huh?" The tears were already in Frazier's eyes.

"Yes, Son." Frazier answered quietly. "They're gone. Since September." He pushed away from Chris a bit, hands gripping his nephew's broad shoulders, and looked him in the eyes. There was no definable emotion there. Good…and bad, Frazier thought.

"I sort of figured they were." Chris announced, "I had hoped that I was wrong, that everything was O.K., but, when I got here, when I saw the house, it was pretty obvious. The burned out car in the garage sewed it all up."

"If it is any relief at all, Chris," Frazier began, "I saw the report and the photos of the crime scene. It was an FBI team that investigated. No locals." Chris was listening, but his eyes were not registering. "They went easy." his uncle continued. "They probably never even knew what was happening."

A dog barked in the distance. Chris was instantly on guard, backing away from Frazier, crouching, weapon ready. For an instant, his eyes came to life with a strange sparkle. The look unnerved Frazier, who could vividly imagine himself gazing into the predatory eyes of some jungle carnivore rather than into the eyes of a human. The unease quickly traveled the length of Frazier's spine. The look passed quickly. One of the familiar hunches leapt to the forefront of Frazier's computer brain. Chris had been in the country for a long time.

The silence returned. Chris returned to his feet, smiling sheepishly. "What say you and I go someplace safe and talk?" Frazier asked.

Chris's smile changed, somewhat. "Safe? Is there such a place?" he asked.

It was Frazier's turn to smile. He removed the radio from his vest and spoke into the microphone.

During the return flight, Chris had told Frazier everything. Frazier had packed some food before the trip. He handed it over to Chris. His nephew voraciously attacked the offering. "How long has it been," Frazier asked his nephew, "since you've eaten?"

Chris answered between mouthfuls, "I don't know. A week? Ten days?"

When the food was gone, Chris settled back in the well insulated cabin and told his story, like a repentant sinner in the confessor's booth. Frazier had not even had to ask any questions. Chris gave the complete account, from the time he arrived in the swamp until the phone call from Kentucky. The flight took three and a half hours. Chris was still talking as the helicopter sat down in the FBI compound. Frazier still had a great number of questions, but his nephew needed sleep, not interrogation. Frazier felt a sense of irony with his decision. In the past he had, unofficially, of course, used the technique of sleep deprivation, more than once, to wrestle information from criminals. He had found the technique very effective. Now, his nephew walked beside him, perhaps holding answers to questions that would pave the way to the solution of the most important case to which Frazier had ever been assigned and the questions would wait until Chris was well rested.

Frazier took Chris directly to his apartment within the protective cordon of the four month old FBI Compound. The Compound consisted of a group of buildings and apartment complexes just south of the Potomac in Virginia. The perimeter had been established in late November and the area declared secure and open to essential Bureau and other U.S. Government personnel and their immediate families.

Regular force Marines had been detailed to provide security. The Marines came well trained and very well armed. So far, there had been nothing more than half hearted attempts on the part of revolutionaries to breach the perimeter. All of the attempts had been repulsed with extreme prejudice. Frazier was not so foolish to believe the Compound completely safe, but he did believe that it was the best place for Chris to get some much needed rest. And rest he did, not waking until the afternoon of the third day.

———————————— ◆ ————————————

The boat waited for Frazier, rolling on the swells, about a mile off Rhode Island's coast. His transport to the boat was a 18 foot Boston Whaler launched from the rocky beach just before midnight. The ride out to the boat in the darkest night, in heavy seas, against the stiff, wet and biting wind had been a little scary, even more so than had been his trip around New York City. Frazier had wondered how the Whaler's pilot could possibly locate the larger boat in such absolute darkness. The pilot had seemed confident, smiling broadly, when Frazier had voiced his concerns. After what seemed to Frazier, an eternity, the pilot had backed off the single outboard and spoken into his radio. A light appeared about a hundred yards ahead and to the left of the climbing and falling bow of the small craft. The pilot had applied the throttle and the distance closed.

Getting on board the waiting, larger boat was an adventure in and of itself. The sea beat against the two boats with a disconcerted fury. Finally Frazier managed to snatch a grasp on the larger vessel's ladder and held on. The Whaler backed away a bit to prevent from crushing Frazier between the hulls of the two boats. With a little help from deck hands, Frazier managed to pull himself on board the rocking boat. The Whaler roared to life and disappeared into the blackness. All went dark as the boat's lights were extinguished once more. Nowhere was safe in the United States, not even a mile off the coast. Frazier changed into some dry clothes and drank about a pot of coffee. His stomach was telling him not to do so, but the rest of his body had overruled the objection. Later as he had stood on the heaving deck, a death grip fastened to its lee railing, doing a bit of his own heaving, Frazier wished he had listened to his stomach. He had gone to his cabin, no more than an enlarged closet, and attempted to get some sleep. It would be a long, bumpy ride.

The trip to Martha's Vineyard was expected to take five to six hours. In the rough seas the interval would grow considerably. Frazier reclined in the small bunk and tried to put the rolling cabin and the rapidly narrowing investigation out of his thoughts. He needed rest. He had brought with him the omnipresent mini-14 and a briefcase. He had a nonarranged, unannounced meeting with one of the Nation's most powerful Congressmen. Frazier was, he was convinced, about to break the Black Tuesday case wide open.

Frazier had questioned Chris exhaustively when the latter had rested sufficiently. Frazier had been disappointed to learn that Chris knew absolutely nothing about any of the backers of Black Tuesday or the NOA squads, that he had only been exposed to the handful of trainers at the training camp. What Chris had known, however, was enough to give Frazier a foot up on the case. He knew names, dozens of names of his fellow NOA squad members. It was a start, more of a start than Frazier had had since September.

With a strong suspicion, Frazier conducted a preliminary scan on the list of names. The results of the scan were just as he had suspected. Each of the young men on Chris's list had been, like Chris, adopted. It was a finding, but still no great help. Frazier looked further. After two days of endless record searching and counter searching, he found it. The link reached out and grabbed him. The Men, babies at the time, had all been adopted within a specific time period. Further, although the babies had been placed in their respective foster homes by a number of various localized adoption agencies, another agency appeared prominently in the individual records. The federally funded agency had existed for only a handful of years, and, during its short life, had handled the placement of slightly better than 12,000 orphaned children. A very small number compared to the numbers of adoptions nationwide over the same period. The chances of the apparent link between the agency and the names on Chris's list being coincidence were not likely. Like a seasoned hound on a fresh trail, Frazier nosed in further. The agency, the National Adoption Agency as it was called, was headquartered in Nashville, Tennessee and had a single branch office in Sacramento, California. Frazier poured over the names and available files of the agency's former employees. No one had stuck out. He tried another angle. Lights went on. The Adoption Agency was authorized by Congress as a result of legislation introduced by the esteemed Senator from Massachusetts, Duncan Fowler.

That name leapt out and gripped Frazier's investigative instincts. He had, naturally, seen Senator Fowler's name before. He was a veteran Congressman, a leader in the Senate, and Chairman of the Foreign Affairs Committee. Frazier had seen his name somewhere else, though, somewhere more telling. Senator Fowler's name was among those listed in Frazier's 'possible' file.

The Senator's name had made the list because of several factors. He was powerful, carrying a surplus of political clout. He was rich, inheriting multiple millions of old money. And, the key reason, he had suffered the loss of a loved one at the hands of blacks. That the Senator could be involved, though unthinkable, was definitely plausible, and, in Frazier's reasoning, probable.

The significance of the possible finding was both telling and chilling. If the suspicions rebounding in Frazier's head proved correct, the Black Tuesday conspiracy, and conspiracy it was, had been in the planning and implementation for over two decades. If someone as prominent as Senator Fowler could be involved, then, the possibilities were limitless as to how many others could be.

There was no time for caution. It was a lead, no matter how weak it may have been, and it had to be pursued. Frazier made a quick, inconspicuous inquiry and discovered the location of the Massachusetts Senator. Frazier still had not revealed any of his present suspicions to Williamson. He would not do so, he had decided, until he was completely sure that he was right. He had felt relatively sure when he arranged the trip to Martha's Vineyard and Senator Fowler's summer home.

Armed guards met Frazier's boat at the dock in Oak Bluffs. Frazier handed over his FBI ID. The credentials did not carry the same weight that they had before the Revolution. The three guards eyed him suspiciously before, finally, allowing him to exit the boat. One had asked Frazier, gruffly, what his business on the island might be. His tone had been one of 'you better give the right answer, or your butt is back on the boat!' Frazier had liked neither the tone nor the question. He had turned slowly, deliberately, squared off with the inquisitive guard and replied, "You don't look anywhere near intelligent enough to possess the level of clearance that would be required before I could tell you why I'm here. Am I right?" The guard had scowled. The other two guards had laughed heartily. Frazier walked away.

The Senator's house was only a couple of miles up the beach. Frazier decided to walk. The relative safety of the island was a welcome change from the hell of the mainland. Although things were not altogether placid, armed guards were everywhere, there had been attacks, the situation was orders of magnitude greater than those just a few miles away. Frazier strolled along in no particular hurry, enjoying the relative peace. He could not remember the last time he had taken a safe stroll.

Senator Fowler's summer home, like so many others located on the semi exclusive vacation island, was a three story, weathered gray, cedar shingled and sided affair with white trim and ample porch. Frazier counted three guards in the yard and two more on the front porch. One of those on the front porch had the Secret Service look. The others looked like locals or maybe hire-a-cops from the mainland. All turned their attention Frazier's way when he mounted the first step leading from the sidewalk to the home's stone walkway.

Frazier held his FBI ID high in the air over his head, his mini-14 was slung across his back, barrel pointing downward. He stopped about ten yards from the porch and waited for the guards to reach him. One of the men on the porch, the one that did not look like Secret Service, cautiously descended the stairs and approached Frazier.

"Hi." Frazier greeted the wary guard. "How's it going?"

The guard did not answer, but held out his left hand with a prompting gesture. Frazier handed the credentials over. The guard looked at them for an instant, then ordered, "Wait here." Frazier complied and watched the guard as he reascended the steps and presented Frazier's ID to the other guard. "Yep!" thought Frazier, "He's Secret Service alright." The Secret Service agent took a long look at the badge's photo and another long look at Frazier. He then exchanged some quiet words with the other guard and walked over to a phone near the front door. Frazier continued to stand in the walkway as the phone conversation took place.

"Agent Frazier," the Secret Service agent called when he had returned the phone to its place. "You may come up now."

"How nice!" Frazier answered. He was getting tired of not being shown the respect which his position demanded. He climbed the stairs to the porch.

The second guard kept his weapon trained on him.

"Ease up there, John Wayne." Frazier directed the overly restrictive guard as he mounted the porch. "I'm one of the good guys. You're not supposed to shoot the good guys."

The guard shot a quick glance at the Secret Service agent, seeking advice. The latter nodded his head slightly and the guard lowered his weapon.

"What can we do for you, Agent Frazier?" the Secret Service agent asked dryly, returning Frazier's ID.

"I'm here to see Senator Fowler, actually," Frazier answered, "but I hope that you have already figured that out."

The expression on the Secret Service agent's face did not change. "I'm sorry, Agent Frazier," he announced, "but, the Senator is not seeing anyone today. His schedule is quite full."

The anger began to build slowly.

"Is that right?" Frazier asked with forced congeniality, "Well, well...hmmmm." He reached into his pocket and pulled the ID out again, gazing at it. He shook his head and exclaimed, "Just as I thought."

The two other men on the porch watched Frazier closely, wondering what he was doing.

"It's the same as always." Frazier continued "Federal Bureau of Investigation. It says it right there, just as plain as day." Frazier was pointing at the badge, making sure the men could clearly see. "And there's me...and there—that's my name...Hmmmm."

Impatient, the Secret Service agent interjected. "What is your point, Agent Frazier?"

The anger was reaching critical mass.

"My point?" Frazier echoed quietly, and, then, louder, "My point..." With speed and strength he had long since forgotten he possessed, Frazier lashed out, gripped the rifle in the second guard's hand, twisted violently and simultaneously sent his right elbow crashing into the guard's throat while leveling the captured rifle squarely on the Secret Service agent.

The guard rolled on the porch's floor gasping for air.

"My point," Frazier hissed, breathing hard, "is that I am an FBI agent, by God, on official FBI duty and I don't need an appointment. My presence is appointment enough. Now, you get your ass on that line, right now, and tell the Senator I'm coming in! You got it?!!"

The sweat was beginning to bead on the Secret Service Agent's fore-head. In the yard, the remaining three guards, almost as nervous, unsure what was expected, trained their rifles on Frazier. A tense silence enveloped the porch and yard. Frazier's finger tightened perceptibly on the rifle's trigger. The Secret Service agent noted the pressure. Frazier had intended for him to do so.

"O.K." announced the Secret Service agent, "O.K., I'll call. Just cool down."

"Oh," answered Frazier, "this is about as cool as I get under the cir-cumstances." He kept the rifle's barrel pointed at the agent's head.

Senator Fowler was waiting for him in the dimly lit study. "Well," he greeted as Frazier entered the room, "Agent Frazier. I understand you were quite determined to gain an audience?"

Frazier answered, the anger still fresh, "That's correct, sir. I'm not used to being denied access."

"Oh," replied the Senator quickly, "I wouldn't go so far as to call it denying you access. It's just that these are trying times, as you must surely understand. Things are terribly hectic. If you had only called ahead, everything would have gone smoothly, I assure you."

Frazier moved closer, "With all due respect, sir, I don't make appoint-ments to conduct investigations."

Senator Fowler flinched as if stung. When the first call came, announcing the FBI agent's arrival, Fowler had had no idea of why the FBI would be contacting him at his house. He had instructed agent Jackson, the Secret Service agent, to tell the FBI agent that the Senator did not have time, right now, to be disturbed. When the second call came, it was obvious that the FBI agent was not going to be dissuaded so easily. More angered than concerned, the Senator had granted the FBI agent an interview. The word 'investigation' had hit him from the blind side with a chilling force. Alarms went off in Fowler's brain, buzzers sang and lights flashed. What else Could the FBI want?

The veteran Senator tried not to telegraph the momentary panic, further. He was not successful.

"Investigation?" he questioned Frazier, feigning ignorance and concern.

Frazier searched the Senator's eyes. The look he found there seemed to lift the weight of the world from off the tired agent's shoulders.

"Gotcha!" Frazier thought, a flood of relief washing over him. Frazier had seen the same look in the eyes of countless criminals he had cornered in his years with the bureau. It was the look of panicked fear—the naked fear of having been discovered.

Fowler was definitely guilty…of something. Frazier did not, he realized, have anything but a circumstantial case, yet. He decided to unload with both barrels.

"I'm not going to play around, here, Senator." He announced, plopping the worn briefcase on one of the room's many tables. Frazier reached into the briefcase and pulled out a handful of papers. The apprehensive fear was mounting within Fowler and he had to muster every available ounce of courage he possessed just to remain standing.

"This," continued Frazier, patting the papers , "is all the evidence we need to indict you for a whole bunch of ruthlessly planned and executed murders committed by your New Order Army."

The accusation knifed into the crumbling Senator. They knew! His knees trembled slightly, wanted to buckle beneath him. Until now, he had believed himself to be tough, able to take the heat. He had demonstrated an ability to do just that over the years. He had never shrank from a fight, had always met the opposition openly and with resolve. Situations have a way of changing things. Things were changing now, and had been changing for weeks.

As early as the middle of October, the Revolution had taken on a fury that none of the Planning Group members had anticipated. The NOA soldiers, his boys, the Senator had called them, were doing well. They were coming under increasing threat, but they were accomplishing the mission. There was no problem there. The problem lay with the uncontrolled fury of the black revolutionaries. The terror, the deaths, had become all too much to bear for the Senator. His unease had increased in January, when Hastings had called and announced that the Planning Group was being disbanded, that his part was over. It was obvious, then, that things were out of hand.

"What about my boys?" Fowler had asked Hastings. "What will they do?"

The reply had been instant and devoid of compassion. "They will fight and they will die!" Hastings declared, "They will do as they were trained."

The words had cut deeply, but Fowler saw the unchangeable truth underlying them. He had put on an optimistic face for Hastings' benefit, saying that everything would turn out O.K. Fowler did not believe his own words and, from the sound of Hastings' voice saying its goodbyes, Hastings did not either. Fowler had retreated to the family's vacation home on Martha's Vineyard in attempts to get away from the guilt, but it had followed him.

Now, in the face of the accusations, the guilt was taking a severe toll. Frazier's words continued to bite into him.

"We know all about your racist army, Senator. All the way back to the adoption service. We know about the recruits, the placements, the screening, the training, and the missions."

Fowler continued to shrink. Frazier could plainly see the effects of his allegations on the Senator.

"And with this…" Frazier announced with an almost triumphant tone, gambling. He reached into the briefcase again and pulled out another collection of papers. "…the signed affidavit of the big guy himself, we have all we need to nail you as the primary conspirator in the Black Tuesday murders."

Through it all, the Senator's face had gone ashen, his heart had taken on an erratic beat. Now, with Frazier's presentation of the new evidence, anger had, very quickly, taken the place of fear. The fight response gained the ascendancy, bringing with it pride and self assurance. The Senator's shoulders straightened a bit. He had been betrayed. Hastings had sold him out.

'That two faced S.O.B.!' Fowler cursed silently, taking Frazier's hook and running with it. It all made sense, only if Hastings had really broken. How else could the FBI agent know so much? It was simultaneously unbelievable and cutting, but it was not totally unexpected. A veteran politician, Fowler was well versed in the art of covering his backside. Political history is replete with the discarded corpses of those who had failed to perfect the art. On the odd chance that he should ever be betrayed or otherwise discovered, Fowler had, unknown to and against the orders of Hastings, kept a file of his own, from the very first days. In his file, Fowler had, accurately and in fine detail, documented his activities within the Planning Group. The thick file was resting, this moment, in the safe behind him. It was the last bit of leverage the Senator had. Now, as the FBI agent stood before him speaking the unspeakable, he was glad to have it. He would fight back.

"Lies!" the Senator spat, "Whatever you have there is lies." He pointed his finger stiffly at the papers in the FBI agent's grasp. "I had absolutely nothing to do with Black Tuesday and Hastings knows it."

The name of Hastings registered immediately in Frazier's analytical mind. More light dawned. And euphoria began to settle over him. Frazier could scarcely believe his good fortune. His ploy had worked far beyond his own expectations. The Senator was handing him the mastermind. Martin Hastings. His name was on Frazier's 'possible' list.

The Senator continued his denial. "I knew about it, sure. We all did. But it was Hastings and Delong and that damned shadow member who handled Black Tuesday. I didn't have anything to do with it. Nothing at all." The Senator's face was red, his fists clenched tightly. Frazier believed him, but did not allow his face to show it.

Silence had filled the room. The Senator, chest rising and falling, studied the FBI agent's face, waiting. Frazier returned all of the papers to the briefcase. The pieces of the puzzle were falling, quickly, into place for him now. The scope of the conspiracy was mind boggling, but almost crystal clear. Frazier sat the briefcase on the floor and unslung the mini-14 from his back. Holding the rifle casually before him, he took another gamble.

"Senator, from here we have few options." Frazier announced, "If it were business as usual, I would be reading you your rights and you would be placed under arrest." He allowed the words to hang on the air for a moment. "But, business as usual went out the window with the start of the Revolution. I think you realize the amount of trouble that you're in."

The Senator nodded affirmatively, eyes closed.

Frazier continued, "With the right amount of cooperation, you could take a lot of the heat off."

The Senator's eyes opened, questioning.

"I've got Hastings' story," Frazier lied, "if what you say is true, then what I have is a bunch of lies." He allowed the unspoken proposal to sink in. It was classic wheeling and dealing with the bad guy in hopes of nailing the badder guy. Sometimes it worked, other times not. Frazier hoped desperately that it would work, here. Otherwise, he had nothing but unsupported conjecture and he knew it. He could see the wheels turning behind Fowler's troubled eyes.

"You want an affidavit." The Senator spoke, defeat in his voice.

"Yes, Sir." Frazier answered quietly.

"What does it buy me?" The Senator asked.

Frazier thought about it for an instant, then replied. "A little dignity on your way down."

The Senator shrugged his drooping shoulders. His mind was numb. As if in a dream state, he walked to the large portrait of his grandfather, slid it to one side and rotated the wall safe's dial.

Frazier watched the Senator's movements closely, shifting the rifle slightly, ready.

The safe's door opened wide and the Senator removed a rubber band bound collection of papers. Frazier eyed the stack. It was close to three inches thick. The Senator held them for an instant, like a beloved child, or some priceless treasure, before placing them in Frazier's outstretched hand.

It was late on the night of March 28, when Frazier returned to his apartment in the protected compound. Chris was on the couch, snoring deeply. Frazier crept by his sleeping nephew and entered the bedroom. His head was still light with the euphoria of his good fortune. The file that Senator Fowler had handed over was an investigator's dream. The information was replete with names, dates and details stretching all the way back to the 70's. Hastings' entire plan was contained in the file. Frazier had shaken his head in silent dismay as he pondered the hatred that must drive Martin Hastings. Apart from the names of Hastings and three of the Planning Group's members, the files contained dozens of other names, lesser players in the great whole.

The enormity of the conspiracy boggled Frazier's rational mind. Its fingers were virtually everywhere. Its arrangement was meticulously orchestrated. Frazier could, clearly, see how the conspiracy's dozens of lesser participants could easily be kept ignorant of the overall plan. He could also see, after a small bit of further investigation, that such participants were quietly eliminated when their services were no longer required. Many had, of course, died as a result of the Revolution, but, certainly, Frazier suspected, not all. The inordinate number of early deaths by accident or untimely heart attacks were too high to fit population statistics. The unknowing confederates had been executed. Hastings had kept the plots' ends tightly bound, but not tightly enough. Duncan Fowler had weaved the cord capable of unraveling the entire plot and Frazier now held that cord in his grasp. He still marveled at his good fortune. Had Chris not resurfaced, had he died on one of the NOA raids, Frazier suspected that the truth might have never been discovered. As it was , he had more than he needed of dates, details and names—a wealth of information.

Of the many names, there was one which was conspicuously missing. Its absence troubled the FBI detective significantly. It was that of the fifth member of Hastings' Planning Group. Frazier had looked over his 'possible' list again. It was no help. The unnamed member could have been any of the people, not all were men, whose names appeared there, or none of them. Neither Roger Delong's nor Lee Moore's names had, after all, been on Frazier's list. The mystery, the need to know more, remained and fueled his investigative drive with fresh inquiries. On the return trip to Virginia, Frazier had gone through the Senator's file over and over, searching for a possible clue, something he had overlooked, which would reveal the mystery member. There were no clues, only evidence that the secret member's identity was meant to remain a secret. Frazier comforted himself with the thought that Hastings knew the secret. He would talk.

Exhausted, Frazier fell into silent and, for the first time in ages, almost content sleep. The news of the Senator's death would reach him in the morning.

Senator Fowler had watched from the study's window as the FBI agent walked past the guards on the front lawn and disappeared down the walk towards the beach. He had continued to stare, long after the agent was gone, lost in a maelstrom of thought. After a space of several minutes, the Senator, head weak and pounding, had walked over to the small bar, retrieved a glass from the available stack and filled it with thirty year old scotch. He drained the amber liquid quickly. The heat of the whiskey's passage seared his throat and eased his throbbing head somewhat. He poured another. This one he placed carefully on the bar and walked over to one of the bookshelves lining the study's walls. He pulled one of the books half way out of its space. There was a clicking noise from along the sides of the bookshelf. Fowler pulled outward slightly, then, exerted lateral pressure on the bookshelf. The entire unit slid effortlessly out and by the adjacent set of shelves revealing a large screen television. Beneath the screen was a VCR and several rows of taped movies. From these, the Senator selected one, inserted it in the VCR, and turned the power on.

The Senator returned to his waiting drink and drained it as quickly as he had the first. He grabbed the bottle and the glass, flipped the room's light off and shuffled to the recliner situated directly before the television. He plopped heavily into the rich leather chair, raised the foot rest and settled back comfortably. On the screen, the FBI's warning against unauthorized duplication of tapes was flashing conspicuously. The Senator had smiled faintly at that and poured another drink.

The movie played and ended. The Senator selected another. His call for lunch came, but he declined. The afternoon passed. Supper time came and he declined again. During the break between the fourth and fifth movies, he staggered across the study to another bookshelf. There he selected a particular book. Opening it, he revealed the concealed compartment. Reaching inside, he removed the heavy revolver. He leaned heavily against the bookshelf for a moment, staring at the pistol in his hand, studying it. When the movie started, the Senator weaved his way back to the recliner, pistol held loosely at his side. For the next hour and few minutes, the Senator watched the flickering black and white movie, grinning strangely. It was one of his favorites. Near the end, he raised the .44 caliber pistol to his temple and yanked the trigger. On the blood spattered screen, Slim Pickens whooped, hollered and beat his hat against the bomb as it fell slowly away from the open bay doors and towards the Russian landscape below.

The news of Fowler's suicide did not surprise Frazier. He had expected as much when he decided to allow the Senator to remain on the island. He felt no remorse for the man, no compassion. Fowler was, after all, a criminal. Frazier did not feel that justice had been cheated. These were not normal times. The Senator had imposed his own, more severe, justice. It was enough for Frazier.

With the packet of papers that the Senator had handed over, Frazier had more than enough to prosecute. The right thing to do, he knew, was to turn it all over to Williamson. Still, he could not bring himself to do so. The anonymity of the fifth Planning Group member nagged at him. If Frazier divulged what he knew, now, he stood the good chance, he reasoned, of scaring the mystery member away. He did not want that. He wanted everyone who was even remotely associated with the conspiracy to go down. He decided to keep the information to himself. He would not even tell Chris of his discovery. He packed all of the incriminating documents and memos into a large manila envelope and sealed it with duct tape. As an afterthought, he scrawled a quick note, placed it in a regular envelope and taped it on the front of the duct taped envelope.

Frazier turned his attention towards Hastings. Lee Moore was dead. He had died in February, not of the Revolution's violence, but, rather, in a traffic accident in Australia. 'He got off easy!' Frazier observed to himself. Roger Delong, the final, known member of the Planning Group was Martin Hastings' business aide. He could be assumed to be close to wherever Hastings could be found. Perhaps, he could take them both at once, Frazier silently theorized as he began his search.

Frazier spent the last weeks of March and the first week of April trying to locate the elusive Martin Hastings. The trail was unbelievingly cold and getting colder. The man had, seemingly, disappeared from the face of the earth. Frazier pursued every possible lead, no matter how insignificant, yet, had nothing to show for his efforts. Chris spent the days trying to reacclimate himself to life in society. He still had much to unlearn. He met Alice in the cafeteria at the end of March. She was his age, the daughter of a Pentagon Civil Service employee, pretty and, like Chris, somewhat lonely. The two had fallen in love easily. Each passing day found them spending increasing amounts of time together. Frazier thought it a healthy thing, as did Alice's parents. Anything that took one's mind off the conflict raging outside the protective perimeter had to be a good thing.

Frazier found the lead and cursed himself for not seeing it sooner. It was during his seventh review of phone records of various of Hastings' business concerns. Frazier had checked the locations of all the numbers at least twice, sometimes more, searching for any clue to Hastings' whereabouts and had come up empty. During this, the latest search, the number, foreign in origin, appeared only a few times. It was very close to the number for Hastings' extension office in Belgium. The difference was only one digit. Frazier had overlooked the digit six times. Although it did not seem to be such an all important find, the strange voice in the recesses of his detective mind called for immediate follow-up. He ran the search.

The number was to a phone on a private floor of a Brussels high rise. The voice in his head shouted confirmation. Hastings was in Belgium.

Getting out of the country was not going to be as easy going as the rest of the case had been. Williamson was going to want some rock hard answers before he approved anything like that. Frazier could see no way around it. He needed Williamson's help to have any hope of getting to Europe. He decided to take his chances.

Frazier had been correct. Williamson wanted answers. "I can look the other way on a bunch of stuff, Dave." He told Frazier, "I do it all the time. You know that! But, this is pushing it just a tad, don't you think?" Frazier only smiled. "You're damn straight it's pushing it!" Williamson answered his own question. "Picking up and zipping off to Europe on one of your hunches isn't going to cut it! You're going to have to throw some meat my way before I'll bite on this one. The White House knows that it was you who was at the Senator's House the day before he clocked out. They also know that you're heading up the Black Tuesday case. It didn't take even those guys too long to put two and two together. They know something's up and they're breathing hard and heavy down my neck for some answers. I can't stall them forever." Frazier had expected nothing less. He hefted the briefcase and laid it on Williamson's desk. "What's this?" Williamson asked, suddenly curious. Frazier told him.

Williamson did not like it. Frazier told him that everything, almost everything, that was needed to prosecute the Black Tuesday case was contained in the briefcase, but there was a catch It was the catch that Williamson did not like. It sounded very much like Frazier did not trust him. Why could he not open it now? He had every right. He was the Director, by God!

Frazier had pleaded with his superior and friend and, in the end, won out. He could go to Belgium and do what he had to do. But, when he returned, regardless of what he found there, Williamson was opening the briefcase. Frazier agreed. Williamson, still not happy with the deal, felt he had been short changed. He locked the briefcase in his office safe.

Frazier said his good-byes to Chris, leaving him, Alice and WIlliamson standing at the edge of the helipad apron. He left his Mini-14 with his nephew, deciding he would not need it for this trip. Williamson hollered for Frazier to be careful as he climbed into the waiting chopper.

The night was moonless and star-filled. A warm breeze blew softly in from the Potomac. The helicopter would carry Frazier to Ottawa, Canada, for an appointment with a connecting flight to Belgium. In less than twelve hours, he hoped, he would confront Martin Hastings face to face. He looked forward to the encounter.

The FBI chopper bit into the humid night air and made its way northward at the upper ceiling of its maximum altitude. On the ground, far below, Frazier could see the lights of the many fires that speckled the landscape. How much more, he wondered, could the country stand. Not much, he decided.

Demetrius Galen sat atop the cab of the transfer truck at the edge of the forest just west of Scranton, Pennsylvania and searched the night sky with the starlight scope. He was the last of the eight guardsmen who had deserted in September. The others had died, one by one in the months following the firefight in Chicago. Galen had been wounded, himself. Shot in the leg. He had recovered, but he had a terrible scar. His part in the Revolution had carried him to a dozen different states. He had shown his propensity towards killing in each.

Now, in the night's blackness, the ex-guardsman studied the skies for any hint of aircraft. A few yards away, another member of Galen's revolutionary band reclined against a large sycamore tree, the SAM launcher resting on the ground beside him.

Farther away, in the darkness, Derek Conway slipped along through the trees, a determined look upon his scarred face. He had heard voices. Black voices. Targets. Conway was, with the exception of Chris Hunter, the last remaining NOA soldier and he was tired, tired of cold, tired of hunger. But, he had not, yet, tired of killing. Rifle trained directly ahead, he stalked through the brush.

Galen spotted the tiny speck way up and far away. He watched it with great intent as it grew larger. He whistled softly. On the ground, the SAM carrier bounded to his feet and jogged to the truck, SAM launcher in his arms. Galen continued watching the aircraft.

"It's a helicopter!" Galen announced when he could see the craft more clearly. "And he's way up there."

The SAM carrier strained his eyes against the darkness, but he could not see the reported chopper. Galen continued watching the approaching helicopter through the night vision scope and pointed, with his free hand, upward in its general direction for the benefit of the ready SAM holder.

Derek Conway crouched low and eased forward. He had heard the voices again. They were close. He could see the edge of the clearing ahead. He moved further. There was a truck. A black man was atop the truck looking upward through a night scope. There were other black men gathered various distances from the truck. Twenty in all, Conway estimated. He switched his rifle off of safety and crawled forward.

"Hold it." Galen instructed, continuing to watch the growing helicopter, "Hold it…Hold it…" The helicopter was almost directly overhead now. "Fire!"

The SAM holder yanked the launcher's trigger and the anti aircraft missile leaped from the tube, spiraling upward, accelerating.

Derek trained the cross hairs of his rifle's scope on the black man atop the truck and squeezed the trigger.

Galen, attention still fixed on the helicopter overhead, felt the sudden, burning pain in his side. He spun with the impact. The next round caught him just below the right eye. He collapsed to the truck's roof, then rolled to the ground, dead. Derek shifted to other targets.

The night lit up with the flashes and sounds of the firefight as dozens of blacks returned Derek's fire. The tree behind which Derek was situated was cut to splinters in the onslaught. The solitary NOA soldier downed seven more blacks before the 7.62 mm projectile slammed into his forehead. He died instantly.

Several thousand feet above the Pennsylvania landscape, Frazier saw the strange colored fire and watched it as it grew steadily larger. Realization dawned. Frantically, he slapped the helicopter pilot's shoulder and pointed in the direction of the incoming missile. The pilot swiveled his head downward and narrowed his gaze. He saw the missile, immediately. The color drained from his face. "Hold on!" he ordered. Frazier gripped the sides of the seat firmly and the pilot yanked the collective to the right. The helicopter turned on its side and banked hard, trembling in the buffeting air. The missile tracked its every move. There was no way out and the pilot knew it "Bail out!" he hollered. Frazier, eyes fixed on the rapidly approaching missile, either did not hear the command, or ignored it. At any rate, both he and the pilot died instantly upon the missile's fiery impact with the doomed helicopter. Burning, twisted metal rained down across the countryside.

In a partially burned house in Harrisburg, Pennsylvania, tears dripped intermittently from the edges of Waymon Ryan's eyes. Their course made streaks in the dirt that covered his pudgy, pale face. He lay upon the floor, knees pulled in close to his chest, and rocked back and forth in gnawing pain. The room was thick with his smell.

In September, when the Revolution began, Ryan had just arrived in Boston on a sales trip. The ferocity with which the violence engulfed Massachusetts' capitol made it impossible for Ryan to engage a return flight to his home in California. Desperate, he bought a ticket on a bus. The bus made it as far as Mystic, Connecticut. In the middle of October, Ryan paid a fisherman to ferry him to Maryland. Sea lanes were still relatively safe, then. Ryan hid out in an Annapolis hotel room until late October, when it was no longer safe to do so. Frightened, Ryan left Maryland under cover of darkness and headed northwest, on foot, dodging any and all forms of human contact.

From the start, Ryan was as confused as most Americans. Cut off from human contact and from any forms of news, he received no reports of the violence raging between the coasts, but could clearly see, in the rubble he passed in his journey, the effects the Revolution was producing. Ryan wondered where the government was. Why did they not step in with military force and squash the violence? Maybe, he thought, the whole thing was being run by the government. That was more believable for him than the concept of Washington not being able to do anything to stop the fighting. Ryan had never trusted the government. Ryan had, really, never trusted anyone.

At the end of the second week in November, Ryan began experiencing familiar urges. For the first couple of days, he fought against them, trying to concentrate on his efforts to return home. By the third day, the overweight salesman, yielded to his need for the hunt...a hunt for a young boy.

Waymon Ryan first became aware of his peculiar differences from the average male during his high school years. While the other boys of his age were turning their attention to girls, Ryan found himself aroused by watching the younger school boys during physical education. Nights, in the sanctity of his bedroom, Ryan would achieve sexual release through drawing colorful pictures of young boys in various stages of undress. Ryan was very detailed in his drawings, and especially meticulous in coloring them, sharpening his crayons to a needle point and absorbing himself in the application of colors and shades. Countless hours were spent at the dimly lit desk coloring his drawings.

Ryan had his first homosexual experience during his junior year. By the time he graduated high school, Ryan had had dozens of such experiences. Yet, none of these were exciting for him as his fantasies of young boys. By the time he turned thirty, Ryan's sexual liaisons with other men no longer satisfied him at all. Ryan found himself seeking out younger and younger men and, finally, boys to fulfill his fantasies. Finding such boys, Ryan soon discovered, was not at all difficult. He would hang out around malls, arcades and skating rinks, anywhere youths would congregate in numbers. It would not take him long to pick out a likely subject, approach the youth, befriend him, and invite him for a ride. Once in the car, the boys would have no defense against Ryan's large frame, and he would force them to perform sexual acts. When he was finished with them, Ryan would return the abused boys to where he had picked them up.

On the evening that Ryan was overly rough with one of the neighborhood children and the boy died, Ryan's sexual appetites changed, yet again. The sexual release on that night was like nothing Ryan had experienced before. It surpassed even those achieved at the drawing table. Taking the knife to the motionless child was an afterthought, but that too had aroused him, tremendously. Sliding the crayon in was the ultimate exhilaration. Later, with no hint of remorse, Ryan dumped the mutilated body into a drainage ditch less than a half a mile from his home.

When the murdered boy's corpse was discovered, Ryan's neighborhood became an instant flurry of activity. Normally quiet streets were, now, filled with anxious, confused, and enraged residents. At the ditch where the boy's body was found, yellow crime scene tape affixed to familiar objects outlined the place of darkness. Chalk marked the position in which the body was discovered. Police investigators fanned out from the chalk in ever-widening, concentric circles, searching for clues.

Keeping a watchful eye on the proceedings quickly led to paranoia settling in on Ryan's twisted mind. Tangible fear, ugly and coarse, descended upon him. Chattering demonic voices plagued his every waking hour, which, with time, expanded as sleep came only in snatches. Ryan's appetite left him. Headaches beset him with throbbing regularity. The inevitable happened, and two detectives canvassing the neighborhood knocked upon Waymon Ryan's front door. Ryan, fighting with all his will to maintain his equanimity, invited the policemen into his living room. Following a battery of routine questions, the two men thanked Ryan for his time and departed. Ryan had hugged his stained toilet, violently ill, and stayed in that position for the greater part of an hour, shivering uncontrollably. The stress-induced paranoia tormented him for several weeks. During this time, Ryan was very much like some caged, frightened animal haunted by thoughts too dark for the common man's imagination.

As time passed and the neighborhood lapsed back into normalcy, Ryan's clutching fear, also, gradually, subsided and, finally, disappeared altogether. Coinciding with the diminishing paranoia was the return of an increasing, perverted desire. Ryan's thoughts wrestled with one another. He had no wish to feel, again, the fear that he was, only now, overcoming. Yet, his need to satiate his unnatural lusts cried out for attention.

The idea fell upon Ryan like a bolt of lightening. An invisible burden flew from his shoulders. It was so simple. All he had to do was find a job that involved extensive travel. In the course of those travels, Ryan recognized, he would be free to attend to his special needs with relative anonymity. A faceless stranger passing through an area, he reasoned, would attract little attention and would be able to perpetrate any manner of crime with relative impunity. It was brilliant. He congratulated himself. It was such a simple thing to contrive, he cursed himself for not thinking of it earlier.

Searching the classified section of his local paper, that very afternoon, Ryan found what he was looking for. A phone call, a little paperwork, and a short interview landed him a job as a travelling salesman with a nationwide distributor. After a week of training, he was assigned a route that extended from Los Angeles, California to Portland, Oregon. Ryan could hardly contain his glee as he poured over the road map, the hundreds of miles of lines passing through dozens of cities and towns harboring thousands of potential victims for his nefarious desires. Ryan took to the road with renewed spirit.

On his second trip, at a movie theater in Portland, Ryan found a victim. Once again, the sexual release was overwhelming. He left the body in a tangle of bushes just off the county road and headed south. Ryan was safely back at home in California when the body was discovered. The paranoia returned for about a week, but was not nearly so intense.

In the years to follow, Ryan found more and more victims. Authorities did not have to look far to see the pattern in his murders. In each case, the bodies were always placed in a relatively accessible area, that was no real link, the victims all showed signs of sexual assault, again, no conclusive link, but the presence of the ubiquitous crayon was a dead give away. The police were forced to admit to themselves that yet another mass murderer was prowling among the normal citizens. In their classic 'avoiding panic' reasoning, however, the authorities failed to apprise the public of the suspected link in the dozens of murders of young boys occurring up and down the coast. The FBI was called in.

It had been many years since Ryan had last experienced a panic attack. When the lone FBI agent appeared on his door step in the middle of September, the panic returned. The simple blue jacket which the man was wearing, with the white letters 'FBI' stenciled across the top of the pocket, triggered waves of paranoia in Ryan's troubled mind as cold chills enveloped him in familiar fear. Ryan did not answer the door, but rather, watched the government agent from the shadows, behind the living room couch. After what seemed an eternity to Ryan, the agent departed. Ryan barely made it to the toilet in time.

That night, Ryan fled his home, in panic, and headed east. The boy he found in the Arizona mall and took into the darkness did much to relieve his unease. When he boarded his flight for Boston, Ryan felt like his old self again. The abused, cold body of his victim would be found before Ryan landed.

Now, moving only at night, and oozing from shadow to shadow, searching for food and prey, Ryan made his way west at a snail's pace. Frustration slowly ate at his mind. By December, Ryan's clothes hung loose on his body, as the lack of food, and the almost continuous exercise burned the fat from his frame. The dark desires that plagued him ate into his consciousness. Search though he might, Ryan could find no trace of a young boy to take. The few he did see were always well protected by armed men. His cowardice was far too great to even consider a confrontation. Tormented, Ryan continued to plod ever forward. His skin lost all color, becoming paler and paler, so that, by the time the

Crayola Slasher entered Harrisburg and happened into the former house of Beatrice Washington, he resembled a walking dead man.

Ryan found the unopened can of peaches beneath a pile of shattered wood. Using the can opener on his knife, Ryan ripped into the peaches and devoured them ravenously, syrup streaming past the corners of his mouth and onto his stained shirt. The peaches were the first thing he had had to eat in two days. When the last peach was gone, and the juice thoroughly drained, Ryan rummaged around the rest of the house for more food. There was none to be found, so he moved out into the darkness to continue his nocturnal searching.

Three hours later, the effects of the bacteria began to be felt by Ryan. Hastings' experimentation in poisoning had claimed yet another victim. Death came in slow, agonizing stabs. Waymon Ryan whimpered and rolled about in frenzied circles in his own vomit and defecation as the bacteria continued to multiply in his blood stream. An unopened pack of crayons fell from his crusted pocket as Ryan breathed his last.

"Frazier had all of the evidence he needed to nail Martin Hastings," Williamson announced, "and I'm not talking circumstantial crap either! No, he had no doubt that it was Hastings. Had known it for a while, I guess. Probably, ever since the incident up on Martha's Vineyard." The big man paused, continuing to roll the worn baseball between his thumb and forefinger, turned slightly in his chair so as to have a better view over the skyline and the long shadows moving silently eastward. "And Dave Frazier's not the only one who knew, either. Couldn't have been. And that's what has me shook. That Hastings Bastard is responsible for a hell of a lot of deaths in this country. Black and white, alike. Hell! Millions of deaths. And here's Frazier, one of the best agents in the Bureau, knowing that Hastings is behind the whole shooting match, and he's not telling? It just doesn't wash."

The pain of Frazier's death was still fresh in Williamson's mind. The news had visibly shaken him. He cursed the Revolution for the thousandth time. "I knew Dave Frazier since before he was at the Academy." Williamson stated. "Over the years, I not only watched him develop into an outstanding field agent, but also spent a good bit of off-time with him, too." Williamson pitched the baseball into his in-basket and stood up, stretching slightly. It was he who had broken the news of Frazier's death to Chris. The young man had taken it well, outwardly, but Williamson knew that inside, he had to be torn to pieces. Frazier was the only thing the kid had resembling family in the whole world. Now, Chris was an orphan again. That has to be tough.

"And in all those years," Williamson continued, "close to 30, I guess, never once did I discern any hint of racism or bigotry in the man. And you know, as well as I, that that is saying something in this business. So why wouldn't Frazier bring Hastings in? And if Frazier, who didn't have a prejudiced bone in his body, knew about Hastings and wouldn't turn him, how many others knew?" He looked around the room pausing. "It's my guess that there were a lot of others. Hell, John," He exclaimed, turning his attention to his closest friend, "maybe you knew!" He settled back against the window's sill, "Or you, Frank," He turned to the senior field agent in the room, "you could have known. You were involved in this investigation from close to day one, weren't you? Surely, along the way you had a chance to find out that Hastings was our man. Or, Russell," He shifted his attention to the deputy director, "How about you? You, of all people, should have had access to evidence that implicated Hastings."

The men in the room exchanged nervous glances and an electric energy permeated the silence.

"Any of you could have known." Williamson pointed out. "From what I've seen of the stuff that Frazier left for me before he took off for Belgium, it looks like Hastings wasn't too awful hard to pick out once a man was on the right trail."

The others could only listen, mute. The silence was thick. Think what he might, Williamson was wrong. None of the other agents had known the things that Frazier had known. None had even suspected the enormity of the conspiracy.

"Well, hell!" Williamson interjected. "We're not getting anywhere here. What difference does it make, anyway? Now, we all know. Martin Hastings is our man and I want his ass! I want his ass, NOW! I don't care where he's hiding ,or how many goons he's got protecting him, I want Martin Hastings found and I want him in cuffs. Is that clear?"

A number of 'Yes, sirs' followed and the meeting was at an end. The agents filed silently out of the room, heads full of questions.

The night wind blew in gusts upon the enclosing cordon of black clad FBI special operations agents. The objective, Hastings' manor, was well illuminated against a dark background at the cliff's edge. The last three hundred yards to the objective was being covered in a slow, cautious crawl. At one hundred yards from the front entrance to the manor, the six man entry team assumed defensive positions and awaited the go signal from the second team. Waiting for them there had been the sixth member of the second team. This agent had preceded the other eleven agents by thirty minutes and had neutralized the motion detectors surrounding the perimeter of the manor grounds. Now, all waited for the signal to move in.

The last week of April, a bulletin arrived at FBI Headquarters. The incoming message produced an instantaneous flurry of activity. Martin Hastings had been located. Weeks of surveillance had paid off.

Hastings, the message reported, had arrived at his northern California home, by helicopter, shortly before sunset. No outgoing or incoming traffic had been observed since that time. The FBI's highly trained special operations unit, on standby for six weeks, had been mobilized within 45 minutes of the surveillance team's report. It had taken just over two hours for the unit to arrive at the FBI's command post, located about 18 miles south of Hastings' California home. Surveillance team photos, enlarged now, of Hastings and the others suspected to be present at the objective were taped to the walls of the warehouse-turned-command-center. Alongside these were blue-prints of the cliff side residence, small-scale topos of the surrounding terrain, complete with colorful pins indicating the suspected and, in some cases, confirmed locations of Hastings' security teams' anti-intrusion devices. The plexi-glass status board and individual photos indicated that there were at least eight other individuals, in addition to Hastings, in the manor: A female, Hastings' youngest daughter, and six males, Hastings' personal aide, his bodyguard, the cook, and a four man security team. The four man security team was composed of ex-special forces types who had seen extended action in Southeast Asia and other points of the globe and had excelled in their art. All were expert and well practiced marksmen in addition to being experienced hand-to-hand combat specialists. They were suspected to be highly motivated and well disciplined.

Rebecca, Hastings' daughter, had arrived four days prior to Hastings' return. To the delight of the FBI's surveillance team, she had spent the mornings and afternoons, since her arrival, sunning at the pool's edge. Oblivious to the surveillance, she had the habit of removing her bikini top to enjoy the full benefit of the sun's browning rays. At 34, Rebecca Hastings still retained her youthful figure and the natural beauty of her mother before her. Baby-sitting the manor was much more enjoyable with Rebecca at the pool side. She had met Hastings at the helipad with a big hug the day he arrived. Surveillance photos of the arrival showed that Roger Delong, Hastings' aide, and Pete McNair, Hastings' omnipresent bodyguard had accompanied the billionaire terrorist. All the desirable targets were now present in the manor. Plans were well underway to take them out.

The assault on the manor was expected, by all, to be successful. Martin Hastings would either surrender, or he would die. The objective was simple. The assault was not, however, expected to be simple, and, by no means, easy. Barring some divine intervention, casualties were going to occur, and had been factored in as acceptable, even before the SOPs unit had been placed on alert. Profiles of each of the suspected occupants of Hastings' residence, with the exception of Hastings, his daughter, and Roger Delong, read like a roster of some special forces' elite team.

Eduardo Munoz, the cook, had served two tours of duty, in the soup, in Vietnam, as a marine reconnaissance ranger. Several of the operations in which he was involved still carried classified labels. Discharged honorably in 1985, with a host of decorations, including three distinguished service ribbons and two purple hearts, Munoz returned to college. There he distinguished himself as an all American defensive end for the Pac 10, three years running. Proficient in four languages, an expert marksman, and accomplished martial arts expert, at six foot five, and 260 pounds, Eduardo Munoz was a force to be reckoned with. The profiles for the four man security team were even more impressive.

Thomas Griswold and Randy Harbert were both ex-Navy Seals. Too young to see action in Vietnam, the two had participated in Operation Desert Storm as well as dozens of smaller operations in Central and South America. Few training programs, anywhere in the world, were as thorough and effective as that received by Seals. It is generally accepted that a man has to be a little crazy just to want the job, let alone endure the torture doled out to test that man's commitment. Crazy or not, Griswold and Harbert were, without doubt, disciplined, motivated soldiers.

John Knowles spent eight years with the U.S. Army, two years in the 101st Screaming Eagles and the remaining six in the 1st Special Operations Group. Officially, the non-commissioned officer had an uneventful career, promoted on time, no disciplinary problems, a model troop. Unofficially, Knowles had quite an exciting term of service in the special forces. The operations in which he was involved, the majority of them, will never see the light of day. All records, if there were any, were destroyed about the same time as the operations' executions. It would not do for the American public to know that their military personnel were being subbed out to the Central Intelligence Agency for extremely sensitive, wet, black bag operations. Knowles was no stranger to killing.

The security team's fourth member was the only one with no military ties of any kind. Jared Place was and always had been a civilian. But, he was far from being the normal citizen. Born in Singapore to American parents, his father was a business man. Place traveled throughout Asia and the south Pacific for the first twenty years of his life. He developed an obsession with the martial arts and eastern philosophy. Dynamic mind over matter mysticism coupled with ancient technique and steadfast discipline transformed Jared Place into a most extraordinary individual. The man could do things that were uncanny. He could move with speeds that were close to beyond comprehension. From the age of fifteen onward, Place never lost a martial arts competition in which he participated. The other three members of the security team had learned, each in their turn, that this civilian was, in their vernacular, one bad hombre. It was rumored that Place could dodge bullets.

Less was known of Pete McNair, Hastings' personal bodyguard. What was known about him, however, explained the thinness of his file. Before changing his name in the late 80's, McNair was known as Petyor Vasiliovich, a disenchanted Spetznaz Major, who had staged his own death and slipped away to anonymity in the west. It was believed that Martin Hastings had assisted Vasiliovich in the ploy, and some evidence had been collected to substantiate the belief, but nothing was proven conclusively. Shortly after his defection from the Soviet Union, Vasiliovich, now Pete McNair, was hired as personal bodyguard by Martin Hastings. As far as the Bureau could ascertain, McNair had been by Hastings' side ever since.

"Jaysus!", exclaimed Agent Chappell, one of the SOPs younger members, as the team reviewed the profiles, "How does a guy collect people with peculiar talents like these guys and not draw attention to himself? Aren't we supposed to be on top of stuff like this?"

There was a general murmur of like concern among the other team members. The readiness and dedication of their opposition inside the objective was without question. This element, alone, posed a very significant threat. Although, they were, certainly, highly trained and motivated, the FBI's SOPs unit did not have a single member who had been exposed to any level of combat. The closest any had ever come was the occasional exchange of small arms fire with drug dealers or other such criminals. Team members exchanged nervous glances among themselves. They were an impressive sight, the 13 of them, gathered in the briefing room in their black jump suits complete with the latest in highly technical paramilitary weapons and gear. The nervousness in their eyes, to the man, seemed to question, 'Is 13 enough?'

The assault plan was simple and straight forward. At 0225 local, the two six man squads of the SOPs unit would be dropped off at a designated point two miles north of the manor. The team would then proceed, on foot, to the objective. One team would be responsible for neutralizing the manor's security, to include any persons on the grounds of the manor, securing the helicopter, the parking area, and all entrances to the manor. Once these objectives were achieved, the second squad would make a hard entry into the manor to retrieve Martin Hastings. At the initiation of this latter phase of the plan, other agents and law enforcement units, standing by, would proceed to the objective in a pincers-like maneuver. The ocean element of the planned 360 degree envelopment of Hastings' manor would be provided by three coast guard vessels now standing idle a safe distance off shore. In addition, two FBI helicopters would be on the scene within seconds of the SOPs unit entering the manor.

Final orders were reviewed. Equipment was checked, again, and the FBI teams boarded their transport to the drop off point. Silence descended. Each man's thoughts turned to the operation ahead. Any communication was through eye contact or hand signals. The teams had gone tactical and would not drop their game faces until the assault was over.

There was no detectable activity at the manor, other than the solitary guard who was, at the moment, in the pool area. The team assigned to secure the grounds splintered into three groups and slipped into the darkness among the scattered rocks. One group circled, in a wide arc, to the southern side of the manor to cover all exits from that side. The second group made their way to the rear of the manor. Their job, the most crucial of the preliminary assault; was to neutralize the lone guard, secure the helipad, and cover all exits from the rear of the manor. The third group, a single agent, inched his way closer to the front of the manor to link up with the assault team and prepare for any last minute contingencies.

Agent Chappell, assigned to the first team's second group, slithered, ever so slowly, to a position behind one of the larger rocks just outside the penumbra of light. The second agent continued crawling southward towards the brightly lit helipad. Fully prone, heart racing in his chest, Chappell activated his weapon's night eyes scope and trained it on the manor's solitary guard. It was Jared Place. Place was now wandering in the hedges between the pool and the helipad.

"Shit!", Chappell exclaimed under his breath as his view of the target was suddenly obscured by a line of boxwoods. Silently, he willed Place to move back into view of the night scope. "Get your lily white ass over to the pool, badguy…Get out of those bushes." Seconds turned into a minute, and, then, two. Still, the guard did not reappear. Chappell grew increasingly impatient. "Come on, you son of a bitch! Where are you?"

A sudden noise to his left caused Chappell to quickly shift his aim towards the rear of the manor. The scope's view turned a brilliant green as Chappell, in a move he had been trained not to perform, momentarily pointed his assault rifle directly into the four quartz halogen lamps near the manor's rear entrance. "Shit!!" he exclaimed through clenched teeth. The scope would be useless for several moments. Relying solely on his own eyesight, Chappell scanned the area between the pool and the rear of the manor. There was no movement. After a few seconds of staring, just to make sure, Chappell returned his attention to the maze of hedges. Instantly, he wished he had not fried the scope. Situated between the well-lit helipad and the equally well-lit poolside, the darkened area of the hedges made it impossible for Chappell to discern if the guard was still there. "Shit. Shit. Shit!" he cursed, "This is not good."

To Chappell's right, less than 40 yards away, the second agent was lying prone and completely motionless. His eyes were open and trained over the cliff's edge into the darkness beyond. Protruding from a point in his neck midway between his ear and the top of his collar was the black fletching of a blowgun dart. The dart, poison tipped, had killed the agent almost instantly.

It was a skill that Place had picked up in the jungles of New Guinea. The martial arts specialist had been alerted to the presence of the FBI's SOP team a full hour earlier by radio signal from the manor. Despite the exhaustive surveillance and research, the FBI had failed to identify one of the newel posts of the captain's walk railing, atop the manor, for what it actually was; a highly sophisticated, state of the art infrared camera system that provided detailed computer enhanced images of the terrain surrounding the manor for a distance of, in ideal conditions, a half mile. This night's conditions, although not ideal, were sufficient to allow the camera to detect the slow, northern approach of the agents when they were about 600 yards away. The remaining members of Hastings' security team, inside the manor, had been watching the monitor with interest ever since the lone FBI agent had been detected fiddling with the perimeter motion detectors. There had been several comments about the agent's stealth and method as he crawled about the grounds, pausing here and there to perform his clandestine activity. It had been the general consensus among the experienced men, that, had the sensors actually been turned on, the agent was probably good enough that he would not have been detected. The guards watched as the lone agent took a position about 300 feet to the north of the manor.

"Good!," exclaimed Knowles. "That's an excellent place to hole up there, cowboy."

The others agreed. The infrared camera's effectiveness decreased dramatically as distances from its subjects decreased. Inside of fifty feet from the manor, the guards knew, the camera would be useless. The guards settled back and waited for the computerized camera to detect the inevitable approach of the remaining SOP agents.

Through this entire time, Place, outside the manor, was being updated, via radio. The message "twos" that he received required no interpretation. The FBI agents had broken into two man groups and had begun their move towards the manor. Place was well aware of the infrared camera's limitations once the FBI agents were inside the perimeter, and was resigned to the fact that experience, and luck, were now his only allies. Place passed the first minutes wandering aimlessly around the well-lit pool's edge to establish his position for the benefit of the agents who, he knew, were somewhere out there, moving closer among the shadowed rocks, watching him. Calculating times in his head, times provided by the other members of the security team, and times estimated from personal experience, factoring the minimum safe distance the SOP team would maintain from the manor and the approximate time it would take for agents to maneuver themselves into their desired positions, Place timed his entrance to the relative cover of the hedge maze with uncanny accuracy. Once there, he had carefully slid to one side one of the stone benches near the center of the hedge. The bench covered the entrance to a subterranean chamber. Place quietly slipped into the underground chamber, slid the bench back over the opening, donned night vision goggles, and chose the tunnel leading north.

The agent assigned to securing the helipad, attention focused on the hedge maze, did not notice the large rock directly ahead and to his right as it sunk into the earth, nor did he detect Place inching slowly up through the newly formed hole in the earth. Place almost panicked as he realized how close he was to the agent. A miscalculation on his part, or, more likely, he had failed to factor in the agent's inexperience as he had made his expected position calculations. Fighting back the urge to redescend into the tunnel, Place stealthily raised the four foot length of tubing to his pursed lips, took careful aim, and forced air into the tube. The poisoned dart covered the 30 odd feet separating the two men in less than a second. The agent's body jerked once then went silently limp as the tiny messenger of death burrowed deeply into his neck. Seeing the agent go suddenly limp, Place expelled an inaudible sigh of relief. "Damn fine shootin' in this wind!" As he began crawling westward, he whispered, "Now for our next contestant!"

Less than one minute had passed between the time Place had entered the tunnel beneath the hedges and the time he killed the agent, yet, as he well knew, he would have to move quickly before the other agent starting getting jumpy. Place scanned the ground before him, careful not to allow the manor's lights to enter his field of view. When, after more than a minute of searching, he had failed to locate the second FBI agent, Place decided to resort to another trick out of the bag he had amassed over the years. He retrieved a small slingshot from one of the large pockets on his leg, felt around on the ground beside him, located an acceptable sized pebble, placed it in the slingshot's leather webbing and let it fly towards the manor.

There was a sudden sound to the right, and Agent Chappell shifted his aim, peering through the sight.

"There you are," Place exclaimed, silently, detecting the movement, "You little weasel! Am I good, or what?"

Chappell was less than forty feet away from him, but rocks effectively precluded Place from taking a shot with the blow gun. "Looks like we got to do this the hard way," He thought, removing the night vision goggles and laying aside the blow gun. Place began crawling southward to a position immediately behind the agent.

Agent Chappell felt, rather than heard, the presence behind him. Quickly, he turned, simultaneously swinging his weapon to bear, just as Place, knife in hand, lunged for him. Chappell's finger squeezed off four 7.62 mm rounds into his attacker's chest at point blank range. A look of disbelieving surprise died on Place's face as he was propelled backward by the force of the slugs ripping through his body armor.

Agent Chappell, shaken from the sudden encounter, was, momentarily, oblivious to the calls for status crackling in his headset. He stared at the inert rag doll body of Jared Place lying at his feet, his head already filling with 'what ifs'. Adrenaline rushes surged and shook his entire body. After an instant, the agent returned to his senses and acknowledged the calls in his headset.

"Storm? Two Alpha." Chappell spoke quietly, nerves calming. "Target One down and out."

"Roger. Copy, Two Alpha." Came the instant reply. "Stand-by."

"Two Bravo? Storm", the command post called another agent. There was a moment of white noise, but no reply. The call was repeated. "Two Bravo? Storm. Come in, Two Bravo." This call, also, went unanswered.

Elsewhere on the grounds, the radio crackled meaninglessly in the headset of the dead agent, Two Bravo. Listening to the silence, Chappell gritted his teeth, hoping against hope that the second member of his team would respond. After a few seconds more of silence, a new call came through the headset.

"Two Alpha? Storm."

"Go, Storm." Chappell answered.

"Roger, Two Alpha. We've got negative contact with Two Bravo. Proceed to helipad and secure same. Copy?"

"Roger that, Storm." Chappell acknowledged, digesting the order. "I copy secure helipad. Standby." The radio went silent and Chappell moved like a cat in the darkness to his objective.

Suddenly, all the lights in and around Hastings' manor went out. On signal, the SOP entry team bounded to their feet and rushed the manor's front entrance. The foremost member of the six man team hurled a concussion grenade at the manor's front door. The force of the grenade's explosion blew the heavy oak double doors off their hinges. The gunfire did not begin until all six agents were inside the manor. Two miles away, the go signal was given to all other units to commence their advance upon the objective.

Inside the manor, the six man FBI SOP entry team had stormed headlong into a deadly crossfire. Hastings' guards had been waiting patiently, had allowed the agents to enter the manor unchallenged and then, when all six agents were inside , the guards had opened fire. The white hot fusillade of Teflon jacketed 5.56 and 7.62 mm projectiles ripped the FBI's six man team to ribbons. The cook, Munoz, stationed in a second story window, with two, quick, precise head shots, easily killed the two SOP agents assigned to secure the southern side of the manor. The gunfire ended as quickly as it began. The remaining two FBI agents assigned to security of the front of the manor exchanged nervous glances, aware that the entry team had not been successful. Slowly, the two began to move backward from their positions. Agent Chappell, positioned, now, in the hedge maze, just west of the helipad, listened to the command post's efforts to raise the entry team on the radio. Silent static was the only reply.

"Jaysus Christ!" Chappell muttered in disbelief, fixing his aim on the rear entrance of the manor. "What a circus!" Anger coursed through his veins. His best friend had led the team that had just entered the manor. He was, surely, dead, now.

"You're gonna pay, Hastings!" Chappell promised the night air. "You are going to pay big time, you son of a bitch!"

Bright light suddenly illuminated the manor from above as the first of the two FBI helicopters arrived and battled the gusting winds. The second helicopter arrived seconds later and took a hovering position south of the manor. Above the noise of the helicopters, Chappell could hear the sounds of the approaching secondary units. Their sounds and the dancing of their lights as they neared the manor reminded Chappell of the cavalries in the old western movies he had loved as a child, arriving just in time to defeat the indians and save the wagon train. Only, this time, the cavalry had not arrived in time, and the wagon train was not saved, but was lying, shot to pieces, scalped, drawn and quartered, in the Indian camp. His headset was alive with traffic as everyone, it seemed, was trying to talk at once. Chappell turned down the volume and continued to concentrate on the manor's rear entrance.

The secondary units were close enough now that Chappell could make out individual members running in the darkness. The time for stealth was passed. As the forward elements arrived to within 100 yards of the manor they quickly fanned out, assumed defensive positions and opened fire. The night exploded with the sounds of battle as the lead and steel projectiles poured into Hastings' manor. In the confusion, it was impossible for Chappell to tell if fire was being returned from within the sprawling structure. Twenty feet behind Chappell, one of the stone benches was rotating on its axis. In the chaos of the secondary attack, Chappell did not hear its barely perceptible grate. Pete McNair eased the upper half of his body above the opening and, after a careful 360 degree scan of his surroundings, trained his rifle's tiny laser sight on the back of the single FBI agent's head.

"Hey, Rambo." McNair beckoned, lowly. Chappell froze at the sound, wanting ,but unable, to move. "Chew on this!" McNair's finger tightened on the trigger. Chappell began to roll to one side, but he was too slow. A brilliant, white burning in his skull was the last sensation agent Rodney Chappell would ever experience. His body jerked twice, then, went rigid, lifeless.

The FBI's secondary entry team burst through the manor's entrance and secured a bridgehead among the torn bodies of the first entry team. Other units followed them into the large house. A floor by floor, room by room, inch by inch, systematic search for Hastings was then initiated. Each agent or other law enforcement official entering the manor had to pass the dead bodies of the FBI's SOP entry team. The sight of the dead men enraged the newcomers. To the man, it was clear: Martin Hastings, when located, would not be taken alive.

In the hedge maze, Pete McNair, half in, half out of the underground chamber was busily assembling a collection of circuit boards. He conducted his business unhindered. For reasons that would never be known, none of the secondary assault groups would bother to investigate the pool, hedge, and helipad areas until it was too late to do so. His assembly work finished, McNair positioned a row of toggle switches and dials on the ground before him, cracked his knuckles, breathed deeply, and stated to the guard stationed behind him, "Here we go!"

McNair pressed one of the buttons on the control panel. In Hastings' helicopter, McNair's signal triggered the release of compressed air and inflated several rubber, life-size figures. With the flip of one of the toggle switches, a deafening explosion ripped through the southwest portion of the second floor of Hastings' manor sending debris, shrapnel, and body parts raining over the surrounding terrain. The FBI helicopter hovering in that vicinity was severely buffeted by the shock wave produced by the blast and the helicopter's pilot had to call upon all his skills just to keep the craft airborne. Both FBI choppers pulled away from the manor.

Inside Hastings' manor, the screams of those agents and officers wounded during the explosion punctuated the silence. McNair flipped another switch and Hastings' helicopter's twin engines began to whine. Quickly, McNair flipped two more switches and the entire landscape was illuminated as the second floor of Hastings' manor exploded with a terrifying roar.

"Alright, John," McNair called to the guard behind him as hot air from the blast washed over the two men, "back in the hole!" The guard quickly obeyed, sliding past McNair into the darkness beneath. McNair handed the control panel down the entrance to the underground chamber and, then, descended also. The stone bench rotated back into place. "Hit the light!" McNair instructed Knowles, once the chamber's entrance was sealed. The ex-Special Forces soldier, still holding McNair's control panel, obeyed and the chamber was flooded with a dull illumination.

"O.K." McNair continued, taking a position at a small table, "Let's confuse some folks!" On the table rested a television monitor, a series of gauges, switches, dials, and a joystick. McNair gripped the joystick, activated the monitor, and began flipping switches and turning dials. On the helipad, Hastings' helicopter's rotors began to lazily spin, then, picked up speed and the helicopter slowly began to rise. McNair manipulated the joystick, causing the helicopter to rotate with its nose facing the Pacific Ocean. "And we're off!" he exclaimed as he flipped more switches. The helicopter bit into the night air and leapt over the cliff's edge climbing into the star filled sky.

The FBI net sparked with a new energy. "All stations clear this channel. Repeat, all stations clear this channel. This is Omega Actual. We've got a chopper eastbound from the helipad. It could be the target…Birdseye One? Come in, over."

There was a short pause before the reply, "Roger, Omega Actual. Birdseye One copies and is in pursuit!"

Overhead, both FBI helicopters altered their flight paths and sped off trailing Hastings' fleeing helicopter into the black August night. In the monitor, McNair could clearly see the three coast guard vessels standing off shore. He moved the joystick slightly so as to direct the helicopter over their positions.

Again, the FBI net crackled, "All units in the manor? All units in the manor? You are advised to leave the building at once. Repeat. All units inside the manor are to return to the perimeter at once." The order, however, came too late.

With a swipe of his hand, Knowles, still holding McNair's control panel, flipped the remaining switches. The earth shook as Hastings' manor vaporized with the detonation of nearly 2000 pounds of C4. McNair activated the remote auto pilot switch adjacent the monitor and rose from the table, ears ringing from the massive blast. "Let's get the hell out of here!" he called over his shoulder to Knowles as he entered the tunnel that lead south.

The surface of the objective resembled the Ruhr valley of 1945, or Hiroshima of the same year. All that remained of the Hastings' manor was a crater. Dead bodies and debris were strewn for a thousand yards in every direction around the smoking crater. Nearly every agent and officer within 100 yards of the manor when it had exploded was now dead or dying. Omega Actual, the FBI's on-scene commander, lay beside his radioman, both dead, bodies riddled by blast debris. Beside them, the radio, intact, shielded from the blast by the body of the radioman, crackled.

"Omega Actual? This is Birdseye One. Come in, over." The radio went silent with only the noise of static. "Omega Actual? Come in, over."

Another pause, then, the chopper pilot redirected the transmission, "Storm? This is Birdseye One. Come in, over."

"Go, Birdseye One. We copy." Came the reply from the command post.

"Roger that, Storm." The helicopter pilot continued. "Be advised that I have closed with subject bird. I am reading eight, maybe more, passengers. Over."

"Roger, Birdseye One. Copy eight or more hostiles." The command post responded.

"That's a good copy, Storm." acknowledged the helicopter pilot. "Subject bird is still outbound. Request instructions, over."

"Stand by one." replied the command post.

Silence returned to the radio as agents in the command post hastily discussed their options. Omega Actual was off line. The agents manning the command post had not, as yet, been fully apprised of the magnitude of the blast that had rocked the Hastings manor and had no idea that the on-scene commander was dead. Where was Hastings headed? Under no circumstances could he be allowed to escape. The options were limited. The FBI wanted him alive, but, above all, they wanted him. The decision was made.

"Birdseye One." The command post called. "This is Storm. Splash the outbound. Copy?"

"Roger, Storm." the veteran chopper pilot replied, "Copy splash outbound…standby."

With practiced precision, the pilot's right hand went to the control panel and began flipping switches. A state of the art target acquisition board immediately appeared on the windscreen before him. Hastings' fleeing helicopter made a large target. The experienced helicopter pilot got missile lock immediately.

"Birdseye Two, this is One, over." he spoke into the microphone.

"Go One." came the reply from the second helicopter.

"Roger Two." The first helicopter replied. "Break high and right, I'm going to launch on this duck. Follow it in and see if there are any jumpers."

"Roger, One." Acknowledged the second helicopter's pilot. "Breaking right."

The two helicopters separated as the first stayed in line behind Hastings' chopper, while the second veered to the right and climbed into the night sky. Inside Birdseye One, the pilot's thumb depressed the fire button. With a shuddering 'whoosh', two sidewinder missiles leapt from beneath the helicopter and accelerated towards Hastings' chopper. The explosion was almost instantaneous as the missiles rapidly closed the distance between the two helicopters. Birdseye Two followed the fireball down as it spiraled lazily towards the white capped waves below. There were no signs of any survivors. Coast Guard vessels sped toward the wreckage.

Seven miles away, at the hidden mouth of the tunnel, just over the ridge from Hastings' manor, McNair and Knowles joined Hastings, Delong, Rebecca, Munoz, Griswold, and Harbert in the darkness. All were assembled on a roll of carpet extended from a waiting van. With the arrival of McNair, the eight quickly loaded into the van, pulled the carpet in behind them, and headed west, lights off, into the night. McNair drove using night vision goggles. Forty minutes later, the van pulled to a stop at a secluded farm house. In the pasture behind the barn was a small air field. Quickly, McNair and the guards wheeled two aircraft out of the barn and performed a quick preflight check on each. Ten minutes later the planes took off. McNair and Hastings in one plane headed north. The second plane, containing Rebecca, Delong, Munoz and the members of the security team, headed south. The sky to the east began to lighten.

Investigators discovered the tunnels in the daylight hours following the assault. That the tunnels had been used as a means of escape for Hastings or anyone else that had been at the manor was out of the question. Investigation of Hastings' wrecked chopper had recovered enough vital evidence to indicate that Hastings along with his daughter, Roger Delong and Pete McNair had died in the crash. The other remains, though not identifiable, suggested that at least four other people were on the helicopter when it was downed. With the body of Jared Place being found, this accounted for all the bodies.

The objective had been achieved, but the price had been great. Thirty seven agents and other law enforcement personnel died in the fiasco. Twenty eight more were seriously wounded.

The fighters, wave upon wave, lifted off in the cold darkness and turned south and west. Minutes later, the first of the missiles were also on their way. Closer to the borders, the armored divisions waited silently in the frigid darkness for the order to advance. Eyes turned skyward as the first wave of fighters passed very low, overhead, towards their rendezvous with strategic targets in Europe. Line commanders nervously awaited the 'go' order. Failure was not allowed. It would not be tolerated. All the years of training, the years of deception and secrecy were for this moment. The army poised to strike along the frontier was the greatest ever to form under the sun. The Bear had awoken and it was hungry.

Over two decades of subterfuge and feigned retreat from communism had convinced the world that the Soviet Empire was no more. The carefully planned step backward had allowed the Soviets to refit their armed forces right under the watchful eyes of the rest of the world, packing the ranks with personnel, and the armories with weapons and ammunition at a rate unequaled in their history. Their intelligence gathering agencies, under new names, used the time to intensify rather than decrease their scrutiny of other countries' secrets, their ranks also increased as never before. Proclaiming democratic and humanitarian ideals, the communists were able to build and equip a military, in plain view of any who cared observe, which was unparalleled in history in either size or technological advantage.

Major Kevin George counted the targets on the three dimensional acquisition screen, trying to block out the 'missile lock' warnings resounding in the cockpit. Two of his fighters were already out. He had seen no chutes. That left his and one other plane to face impossible odds. His missiles were gone, fired in the first 90 seconds since takeoff. All that was left was the guns. His and the second fighter rocketed eastward.

He had been stationed in Germany for eight long, anxious months. He had left his wife and three children behind in the states just three weeks prior to the atrocities of Black Tuesday. The absence of information from the States only served to heighten his anxiety. He had not spoken to his wife in over two months. He did not know if she and the children were safe from the violence that was raging back home and, more aggravating, he had no way of finding out. His request for emergency leave had been denied. Under the present circumstances, his commander had explained, any leave was emergency leave. All the airmen had concerns about loved ones' welfare in the states, but there was still a mission in Germany that had to be performed. No matter how painful or harsh it may seem, his commander had reminded him, if the Air Force had wanted us to have families, they would have issued them. Major George had, gradually, understood his commander's position. He tried to block his wife and children from his thoughts as much as possible and concentrate on his duties. His tour, up to now, had been uneventful, even with the barely restrained racial tension at the base. News from the states was very slow and all were certain that they were not being told everything. More was found out in the local papers, and those that could read German had become very popular among the men. No one could believe the reports, regardless of their source.

The klaxon split the darkness at 0319, snatching Major George out of his dreams. "Great!" he muttered sarcastically as he rolled from the bed, "I love these early morning exercises." He peered out of his second story window into the coldness. "Well, at least it's not raining. Instead of wet and freezing, I'll just be freezing!" He half-heartedly, though rapidly, donned his flight suit and was just reaching for his boots when he not so much heard, but felt the first explosion.

The Soviet missile hugged the terrain and sought its target at better than 800 miles per hour. The highly sophisticated navigation chip, potent hybrid of technologies stolen from the U.S. and France during the years of 'openness', guided the instrument of destruction with a precision of less than one quarter inch variation from center per thousand yards traveled, regardless of weather or man made interference. At less than 400 miles away, the Wing Operations Building on Baden Air Base was an easy assignment for the missile's guidance system. The missile's clones, thousands of them, were elsewhere, screaming in the darkness, seeking their own prey. On the air base, radar had detected many of the incoming missiles. Seven automatic launchers were ordered activated by the Command Post OIC in a flurry of orders that included sounding alert, notifying SHAFE, launching the two alert fighters, notifying Security and a number of other checklist items. The nervous Air Force officer moved toward the display board and called for a cup of coffee as the missile made a sudden 60 degree shift, dropped to less than 25 feet from the surface for several hundred yards, then, shifting another 20 degrees and dropping to less than eight feet above the ground, impacted the brick Ops building. The automatic launchers never acquired the incoming missile. The explosion was tremendous.

"Oh shit!" Major George exclaimed, adrenaline beginning to prod his nerves. The second explosion followed the destruction of the Wing Operations Building in less than three seconds and the third, only an instant behind it, as the radar complex and flight tower were destroyed. Major George left his room at a sprint and joined the bewildered scramble in the hall with three other pilots making their way to the stand-by alert bay. The four alert birds were already powering up and were readying for taxi off the alert pad and onto the runway. The other three pilots sprinted to the stand-by pad while Major George made his way to the alert controller's office. From there, George watched the alert flight's four sets of flame doublets roar away and up into the cold night sky.

When the aircraft were no longer visible, George faced the Duty Officer. The ashen look on the latter's face and the fear in his eyes told Major George that the situation was not good. Wing Ops had scrambled the alert fighters to intercept what looked to be incoming missiles. The order had, apparently, come too late. Wing Ops was gone, so was the tower. Nobody was sure, yet, what the third explosion had been, but it was probably the radar clusters on the other side of the base. The installation was definitely under attack and, from the looks of things, the attack was coming from the former Soviet Union.

In the skies above Germany, another Major, the alert flight leader, fought the fear. The 34 year old major had flown missions in the Gulf War and had participated in other, non publicized combat sorties in the middle east and the Balkans. His capacity for reasoning and exceptional hand/eye coordination coupled with his raw nerve made him an excellent fighter pilot. He would get his silver cluster at the end of his short stay in Germany for sure, and, then, it was back to the states for a cushy Deputy Commander job. His thoughts, now, were far from promotion and getting back to the states. His mind was fastened securely upon survival. The targets on his fighter's acquisition screen were too many to count. With uneasy voice, he spoke into the mouthpiece.

"Ready One, Base." the alert flight leader called. Major George, monitoring the transmission, could feel the electricity in his friend's voice. "I've got multiple readings on my board north and east about 100 clicks out and closing." Major George bolted from the briefing room and sprinted to his waiting jet. There were no more doubts. The base was under attack.

The alternate command post's reply crackled instantly, "Roger, Ready One. Can you get a signature?"

"Definitely Soviet class!" the experienced pilot responded, studying the profiles on the display, "Looks like fighters mostly. Closing fast. I read five heavies, maybe transports or tankers…could be bombers. There's mor…" The loud tone was clear over the radio. Missile-lock warning. From 280 miles plus, the Soviet mig fighters had locked on the four American aircraft and had fired air to air missiles.

"Bulldog. Catfish. Launch everything, go vertical and push it!" The alert flight leader instantly ordered and, in the same breath, "Rooster. Stay on my wing!" The 34 year old pilot flipped a series of switches firing eight anti missile missiles, then, twisted the stick slightly and the sleek fighter plane responded smoothly, auguring sharply down and westward. The unnerving warning tone droned in the cockpit. Back at Baden, four more Soviet missiles had found their targets. The base's automatic launchers continued to track, whir and rotate, but failed to fire at any of the incoming missiles.

"Ready One, Base." The alert flight leader called, "We are attempting to evade incoming. Have fired all air to air missiles and are down to guns and cluster bombs. Advise launch of stand-by birds." Major George's flight was already powering up. Ground crews were hastily replacing bombs with more air to air missile clusters. No reply was issued to the alert flight's commander. The alternate command post was a smoldering ruin.

In the seat behind the flight leader, the navigator craned his neck from side to side, continually searching the night sky for the inevitable air to air missiles homing in on them in the darkness. His counterpart in the second fighter did the same. The two aircraft whistled through the night sky, less than 100 feet from the earth's surface, at close to three times the speed of sound. From the east, from a slightly higher altitude, six Soviet air to air missiles tracked them at an even greater rate of speed. 16 American anti-missile missiles charged to meet the closing missiles. Not all of the pursuing Soviet weapons were destroyed.

The other two alert aircraft, after firing all of their air to air and anti missile missiles in the direction of the approaching radar blips, had nosed their aircraft skyward upon the flight leader's orders and had applied every ounce of thrust. Ready One had told them to 'push it', and push it they did, transforming their warplanes into ballistic rockets. Of the six Soviet missiles dispatched in their direction, two were destroyed by the American anti missile missiles and the other four burned out and fell to earth, far below, as the two fighters needled their way to classified heights. The two fighter planes would, after a short orbit and warm reentry, land safely in Iceland.

"I've got visual on two incoming on our six, Grave Robber!" the nervous navigator reported excitedly.

"Roger! Hang on tight!" the flight leader replied, "Rooster, on my mark, climb and head south. I'm flipping the bridge, copy?"

In the other plane there was a short pause before the shaken pilot responded. "Roger, Ready One. Copy that."

Grave Robber paused a moment, milking the time, then spoke the single word into the mouthpiece, "Mark." The two fighter aircraft parted rapidly, the one angling slightly northward, the other turning sharply to the left and flaming skyward.

There had been a lot of talk about 'flipping the bridge' among the fighter pilots at Baden and other airbases. No one had ever 'officially' done it, but all of the pilots knew of the location of the 'bridge'. It was a small, stone bridge spanning one of the many man-made tributaries feeding the Rhine River. The span was right at thirty feet. Twenty-nine feet, eight and a half inches, the rumor reported. On a good day there was at least fifteen feet of clearance between the dark, cold water and the stones which made up the centuries old bridge. To flip the bridge was to pass under it in an aircraft, clearly not an authorized maneuver. With hostile missiles closing on his aircraft at supersonic speeds, Grave Robber was not particularly caring about the rules, his instincts were to survive and those instincts told him to flip the bridge. He had never done so, before. He had, however, flown very close to the bridge, more than once, just wondering. He did not believe the maneuver to be impossible. Tricky, yes, but not impossible. Of course, all of the previous less than authorized passes had been during the daylight hours. The visual cues were gone, now, and the stressed pilot did not have time to wait around on the sun. Rocketing through the buffering blackness, the seasoned pilot had to place his faith solely in the aircraft's navigation systems.

"They're closing fast, Grave Robber!" the navigator warned, watching, with increasing anxiety, the twin trails growing behind them.

"Roger, Cowboy! Just hang on back there!" Grave Robber was only slightly relieved to learn that neither of the missiles had turned south with the second fighter. That had been Grave Robber's plan, to draw the heat away from his wing man. The plan had worked. The small victory was bitter sweet. Grave Robber pulled sharply on the stick and the fighter plane leapt skyward. The two missiles mimicked the action. The bridge was less than nine miles away. Grave robber pushed the stick down and to the left and shot along the highway at just over twenty feet off the concrete. The missiles moved closer.

"We're not going to make it!" the navigator panicked.

"Almost there." the pilot assured.

"Let's punch out, Grave Robber!" the navigator pleaded as the missiles grew larger.

"Almost there." the pilot promised. He could see the moon's reflection dancing on the dark surface of the still water. Biting firmly on his lower lip, he eased the stick forward and to the left bringing the aircraft onto a course just inches above the water's surface in the man-made channel. He hoped it was just inches. It was difficult to tell. He could not see the bridge, but he knew it was close.

The first Soviet air to air missile accelerated into the tail section of the fleeing American aircraft and detonated. The resulting fireball skipped twice on the water's surface before smashing into the stone bridge with an earth shaking boom, raining fire, twisted metal and broken rocks for hundreds of yards. The second missile impacted in the debris for an even more spectacular secondary explosion.

In the sky above, in the glow cast by the artificial light of the crash's flames, twin camouflage canopies filled with air. The navigator, foreseeing the impending immediate impact of the missiles, had activated the auxiliary egress sequence without notifying the pilot. There had been no time. Both airmen had been blown from the cockpit of the fighter only an instant before the missile arrived. The blast wave from the missile's impact had knocked both men cold, but both would survive, albeit a bit scorched and broken up.

In the night sky 100 miles to the northeast, Major George did not share the same good fortune. Both his aircraft and that of his wing man exploded before any chance of ejection for the airmen. The smoldering wreckage rained down upon the frost covered terrain. Moments later, wave upon wave of Soviet aircraft screamed by overhead. Air superiority was theirs.

General Charles Vandiver was jolted from a sound sleep by the incessant pounding upon the chamber's door. Angrily wrapping a robe about his naked body, General Vandiver stomped to the door and yanked it open. The ashen look on the young captain's face prevented the General from bellowing as he had planned.

"What is it, Bob?" he demanded, "What's wrong?" The General's mind conjured visions of some terrible accident involving his family. The Captain shakily handed his commanding officer the coded message.

"Better get dressed, Sir." The Captain announced, "The Soviets commenced an invasion of Europe about 15 minutes ago. The Command Post is receiving hundreds of reports of missile and air attacks, and forward observation posts were reporting unbelievably huge Soviet armored columns on the move before we lost contact."

The years descended with all of their weight upon the three starred General Vandiver and he felt, suddenly, weak as the aide's message filtered into his consciousness. Vandiver's first inclination was denial. The aide had to have the facts wrong. This was only an exercise. Russia was dead. A beaten enemy. They would not dare attack Europe. The General saw that the aide was staring at him peculiarly and snapped, "Alright, Bob. Get the car. I'm ready in five minutes!"

"Yes, Sir!" the aide answered and, saluting stiffly, headed down the hall.

The General closed the door, slowly, tucked the coded message in his military jacket hanging on the hat tree and headed to the bathroom in an almost trance-like state. The denial phase had passed quickly, only to be replaced by doom-like reality. Of course the Soviets would dare attack. What better time would there be to do so? The U.S. was certainly going to be no obstacle. The race war raging back in the states effectively crippled any possible hope of military reaction to a Soviet invasion of Europe. The drastic and continued trimming and cutting of the military budget since the end of the Cold War had resulted in a great reduction in the number of U.S. weapons and personnel committed to NATO and the security of Europe. The General had seen the numbers, saw them daily, of available forces, both American and European, available to contend with any emergencies. If his aides' report was correct, and the Soviets were advancing in force with conviction, Europe was in trouble, if not already lost.

NATO existed in name only and was caught unaware, unprepared and unequipped to slow the Soviet advance. The Soviet missiles and fighter attacks proved very effective in crippling NATO defense force capabilities. Radar stations, anti-aircraft emplacements, anti-armor units and other strategic targets were removed with blinding, furious precision as the vanguard of the Soviet attack ripped into eastern and central Europe. When the order for advance reached the waiting invasion force, the thousands of Soviet tanks, helicopters, troop transports, and hundreds of thousands of soldiers roared across the frontier unhindered. By dawn, forward elements of the Soviets' massive armored assault were sweeping over the landscape, rolling over German and NATO defense forces by sheer strength of numbers and firepower.

Across northern Europe, elderly citizens awoke, in horror, to the sounds of invasion and battle. Some, survivors of a time gone by, were reminded of a similar time, many years earlier, when Hitler's army blitzed across the map. As these few watched, with tear filled eyes, the innumerable masses of Soviet troops and armament sweep across their homeland they were acutely aware that the invasion of so long ago had been but child's play in comparison with the size and technology of the enemy which they now faced. "Where," they asked, "is our army? Where is NATO? Where is the U.N.?" The answers to these questions would have chilled them.

All that could be done, short of nuclear launch, was being done to stem the invasion. None of the efforts were proving successful. The war was over before it had begun. The world had been caught napping as the Soviets took two giant steps forward. In less than two hours, the Soviet Union repossessed all of the real estate it had ostensibly given up in the 1980s under the guise of embracing western ideals. In less than five days, all of continental Europe was under their direct control. England, virtually defenseless without the help of the United States was openly rattling its swords threatening nuclear holocaust should invaders set one foot on English soil. Behind the scenes, the British Prime Minister was desperately seeking to negotiate a truce with the insatiable Soviets.

The winter had been terrible. Spring arrived and the killing had continued to rage, unchecked. The National Guard had proved unsuccessful in putting down the black rebellion and had sustained staggering casualties in the failed campaigns. The Special Forces units committed in December had suffered losses of their own, although they were still at greater than fifty percent of full strength. The Nation tottered on the brink of collapse. The U.S. government, what remained of it, kept watchful, apprehensive eyes on the situation. The revolutionaries' artillery had been, finally, thanks to the Special Forces elements, silenced. No more than a dozen pieces were believed to be still in operation. The black spirit and determination, however, remained and the conflict continued to rage like never before experienced in recorded history. Blount, his advisors, and the Chiefs of Staff were once again reevaluating the military option.

The regular Navy had been activated in late March. The coasts had to be shut down. The supply of arms, especially the SAMs, had to be stopped. The blockade extended from the frozen seas above Alaska and Nova Scotia in the North to the Panama Canal in the south. Mexico had protested vehemently. Its representative at the United Nations had walked out after that group's refusal to censure the U.S. for the illegal blockade. The President's and the Congress's minds had been made up. Mexico would just have to deal with it. The coast was shut down until further notice. The rules were straightforward. Aircraft, ships and boats could pass through the corridor in the outbound direction only. Any surface craft approaching the corridor from the exterior would be challenged, boarded and turned away. Aircraft attempting to enter U.S. airspace would be intercepted. The campaign had been effective. The supply of anti aircraft missiles and other weaponry making it to the front lines slowed to a trickle. More Special Forces teams were working on stopping that trickle.

The killing continued, however, and with such abandon that, in the minds of the President and his staff, the checks and balances begin to weigh on the side of involving regular army and air forces. The whole point of keeping the military out of the turmoil had been to preserve the Nation's ability to meet an enemy in the field. The enemy had always been presupposed to be foreign in origin. The concept of an enemy within was foreign to the military establishment. The mind set had been present, except for a short period in the mid nineteenth century, throughout the life span of the United States. The threat was always expected to be from abroad. April's official estimate of total dead was 43,168,773. The numbers of dead suggested all too powerfully the very real threat which menaced on the inside. What good was an intact armed force, the question was, if there were no nation left to defend?

The events in Europe, made the President's and Congress's minds up for them. With the Soviets threatening takeover of the entire globe, the government was faced with no alternative but to commit regular forces towards ending the Revolution. Early on the morning of May 5, two days after the Soviets crossed the frontier, the long delayed order was finally given. Elements of the U.S. Army, Marines, and Air Force were given the necessary clearance to engage civilian forces. For the first time since 1865, U.S. regular forces undertook full scale campaigns in the continental United States.

The question of loyalty of black soldiers within the ranks of the military was not put to the test. In a sweeping move not used since the Japanese civilian detention camps of World War II, black service-men, those which had not already deserted, were disarmed, placed under arrest and confined en masse in military installations located in North Carolina, Alabama, Missouri, Nevada, and California. Overnight, the U.S. military lost greater than 40% of its effective manpower. The measures, however paranoid or Draconian, were, the President and Congress decided, necessary. Patriotic Blacks loudly voiced their complaints, but the decision was final. The Country could not afford to trust the black soldiers.

Across the nation, regular Air Force fighters took to the air, U.S. Army tanks and armored transports rolled onto the asphalt, and nervous soldiers shouldered patrol packs. Their mission, search and clear. Blacks, every black in the United States, were to be located, challenged, and transported to the nearest regional detention camp. Anyone seeking to thwart the military's efforts were to be likewise challenged and apprehended. In the final analysis, it would stand as 'the event' leading to the end of the Revolution. The mathematics very quickly came to bear.

The introduction of U.S. regular military forces into a conflict which already saw the black forces at more than a 4 to 1 disadvantage proved to be the final death nail in the coffin of the black cause. For the blacks, suddenly, the enemy was everywhere and pressing. Sleep, for the revolu-tionaries, grabbed in small bunches for seven months, now became an unaffordable luxury. Such was the force and effectiveness of the fresh infusion of anti-revolutionary forces that, to the combative blacks, to surrender to the urge for sleep was to die. The constant fighting, con-stant moving, and sleep deprivation withered the already seriously depleted black ranks. The firepower and the technological advantages of the new adversaries ripped at the fabric of the black cause. With their backs against the wall, the scattered, bloodied black armies had nowhere to run, no haven of security. Beginning in the middle of May, all across the country, white flags began to surface with exponentially increasing frequency. The fire died. The killing slowed to a trickle. The Revolution was defeated.

Less than two months from the time that black optimism was at its peak, when victory seemed sure and close at hand, the tide had swiftly and irreversibly turned. Ten days after the commencement of U.S. regular military operations, there was no area of the country where the blacks were still on the offensive.

---◆---

From the sanctity of his Virginia retreat, Reverend Mustafa Ahmet could read the writing on the wall, clearly. It translated doom. Something shrank inside him as he reviewed the reports coming in from field commanders across the country. Hope died. Realization sparked in his tormented mind. The Revolution had failed. On May 12, a broken Ahmet, his family and several of his bodyguards secretly boarded a Saudi Arabian cargo ship in Corpus Christi, Texas. The Nation of Islam, the majority of its members either dead or, like Ahmet, on the run, quickly faded to a memory.

In California, Clinton Farrell, equally broken, sat in the still, darkened silence of his make shift, abandoned command post and stared at the map on the shadowed wall. His forces were, with the exception of only a handful, gone, most were dead. Defeat was no longer a question, it was reality. The question, now, was, what would be the cost of failure? Was the white man capable of forgiveness? Farrell was not optimistic there. In many areas, the whites, showing a reluctance for forgiveness, were not honoring the black forces' flags of truce. Like the Indian wars of the past century, the mop up operations were being conducted with maniacal fervor, no prisoners were being taken. The country Farrell had served for so many years was ravaged, perhaps irreparably. A darker realization tugged at his emotions.

The Revolution, of which Farrell had been such an active part, had severely impaired the U.S.' position as a world power. Taking full advantage of this weakened position, the Soviets had dropped the subterfuge of reform and had pounced with lightning swiftness on their neighbors in Europe. With a trembling born of fury and hopelessness, Farrell could clearly see that his Cold War enemies were in firm control of the European continent and had turned their eyes southward. It was only a matter of time before they focused their expansionist sights across the Atlantic. To the rational, disciplined military mind, the reality was greater than he could bear. Thoughts of a childhood Sunday School lesson found their way into his troubled musings; visions of Iscariot, the traitorous disciple, coursed through the tangled darkness of his consciousness. Like some three dimensional interactive program, Farrell could imagine the scene vividly; the broken Judas wandering in the pre-dawn stillness, mad with despair, searching for a way out. Leaning back in the leather chair, Farrell slowly and deliberately raised the 10mm to his temple and tightened his trembling grip on the trigger, finding his own way out.

The black cause had suddenly metamorphosed, becoming no longer a goal of victory and autonomy but, rather, one of survival. Many enraged whites, fed up with nearly a year of unrest, now that the end was clearly in sight, were not prepared to accept the surrender of black forces. Countless blacks died, unarmed at the hands of unmerciful, vengeful whites in the final days of the Revolution. No distinction was drawn between combatants and non-combatants. In those terrible, final days, to be black was cause enough to lose one's life. Frustration born of eight months of bloody revolution fueled the genocide that coursed through the nation in the final days of May. If not for the direct intervention of regular military forces, which established secure containment camps for surrendering blacks, perhaps all of the blacks in the United States would have been killed. As it was, when the smoke cleared, less than fourteen million Afro-Americans were alive on the first day of June. The Revolution had cost them 82 percent of their former population.

The official estimate, like President Blount had suspected, was indeed a blind eye estimate. The official figure for total casualties through the end of May reported 53,653,925 dead. This reporter's research indicates a much higher, more realistic number of dead and missing for both sides. It is with disturbing chills, even at this writing, that I reveal that the number exceeds a staggering 80 million souls.

In the now empty Virginia retreat, Khalied Humari sat in the chair formerly occupied by the ambitious Ahmet, his feet resting on the ornate desk. A satisfied smile was upon his face. He was the only smiling black man in the United States. It was a smile of insanity. Through it all, Khalied had never once considered himself a traitor. The tremendous numbers of black losses that occurred as a result of the violence of the Revolution had not phased him. The Revolution was Allah's tool to purge the iniquity and Khalied was Allah's blessed assistant. The population had been purged, as Allah had shown him it would be so many years earlier.

When the news reached him of Ahmet's flight from the country, Khalied was ecstatic. He recognized that, with Ahmet gone, the end must be close. The Revolution was over, the seas were calming. A chosen woman would soon appear. Smiling broadly, Humari nestled back in the soft leather of Ahmet's former chair and patiently awaited Allah's next move.

Epilogue

♦

Martin Hastings' plan had been successful in the sense that his ultimate objective of destruction of the black race within the U.S. had, for all practical purposes, been accomplished. The retaliatory fury of the white population, once it gained the upper hand in the conflict, had been almost total. Campaigns of genocide followed the final victories. Angry, vengeful mobs traversed the countryside, rooting out blacks and killing them mercilessly. Through his and the Planning Groups's nefarious manipulation, the ends had been achieved. The campaign was a success. Now, in the icy stillness of the arctic expanse, the fruits of victory were not at all sweet. Through it all, Hastings had been played as a pawn and he, now, recognized that fact clearly. The nation he loved was, thanks in large part to his scheming, in extreme peril. He shook his head slowly. What a fool he had been.

The betrayer, Pete McNair, now Petyor Vasiliovich once more, had joined Hastings on the ice covered deck. An explanation, he had told Hastings, was probably in order. "You were going to hear all of this, sooner or later, Martin. From someone." Petyor declared. "I just thought it would be better for all concerned if it came from me. That is, if you are interested?" Hastings looked at his former bodyguard and shrugged his shoulders slightly, a disgusted look pasted across his deeply lined face.

"I'll take that as a 'yes' under the circumstances," Petyor answered.

Hastings was not, Vasiliovich said, expected to understand it all right away. There would be time enough for understanding later. Right now, it was enough, Vasiliovich assured, just to know the facts. A strange sense of Deja vu enveloped the broken Hastings as his former body-guard sketched the rough details of a mammoth conspiracy. A conspiracy which, without the direct involvement of Hastings, might never have occurred.

The Soviets had, Vasiliovich explained to an expressionless Hastings, watched him closely from very early. The general intelligence gathering arm of the communist giant had first directed their attentions towards Hastings during his early years at the defense consulting agency. Later, as he began to amass a substantial fortune, the KGB had taken a keener interest in the rising capitalist and had stepped up its surveillance substantially on the odd chance that Martin Hastings might be, one day, valuable to the communist cause.

One year after Kelly's murder, when inklings of Hastings' intentions with regards to blacks began to filter in, far sighted idealists in seats of hidden power within the vast government of the Soviet Union sat up and took notice. As their suspicions of Hastings' intentions began to gain confirmation, long range plans were drafted and operations initiated to assist the billionaire crusader. The secrecy associated with the campaign was total; so much so that the plan had remained nameless even now. Those privy to the information, even the barest inklings, were monitored continuously. In the thirty plus years of the plan's molding and implementation several dozen such insiders had been liquidated when they showed the slightest hint of opposition. Hundreds of others had been removed, eternally, without knowing anything of the plan. These were, for the most part, victims of no greater crime than being in the wrong place at the wrong time, seeing or hearing the wrong thing.

Absolute secrecy and devotion were required for the plan to have any hope of survival. The future of the Soviet empire demanded no less than total, unquestioning commitment. The powers that were had gambled in a big way on Hastings. Bankrupt and grasping for life, the Soviets had placed their entire future on the hope of race war and the toppling of the United States. As it became apparent that Hastings was intent on exterminating the black population, the plan had been placed into full motion. Poland, East Germany, the destruction of the Wall, open efforts towards reform were offered to the rest of the world as a token of the Soviet Empire's change of heart. Subterfuge, Vasiliovich admitted, on a grand scale—the effectiveness of which was only now becoming fully evident. Yes, the Russian assured a sullen Hastings, it had been a great gamble and their horse had come in in a big way. The dividends would be paying for years, maybe centuries.

Hastings sat in silence, listening, throughout it all. The words were surreal. His mind reran the events of the preceding years. Nowhere could he see any trace of the Soviet scrutiny. Neither could he discern any area where their clandestine assistance was evident. Evidence or no, it was painfully obvious that he had been used like a pawn, or, more directly, as a puppet queen. Hastings crumbled bit by bit inside.

The U.S. authorities believed Martin Hastings to be dead. The dental records had matched the remains found among the wreckage of the downed helicopter. Hastings' file had been closed. Slicing eastward through the ice, Martin Hastings was on his way to his new home, 'more like prison,' he thought, in the newly expanded Soviet Union—an expansion he had made possible. His two daughters were on another ship, further south, if he could believe Petyor, also headed for a new home in the Soviet Empire. Roger Delong had not been so fortunate. He had died quickly and painlessly, Vasiliovich emphasized, along with Knowles, Munoz, Griswold, and Harbert, shortly after their arrival in Honduras. Their usefulness to the Soviets was at an end. The pain of the loss of his dearest friend was great and taxing to Hastings, yet there was a certain amount of envy mingled with the grief. Perhaps Roger had died mercifully, without knowing the truth.

The world Hastings had carefully constructed since Kelly's death folded in upon itself and the years fastened themselves across his shaken brow. Petyor, friend and betrayer, methodically droned on in the frigid, gray stillness. "You were supposed to die in California." Petyor announced, hurling an iceball across the deck and over the side. "In the house, along with everyone else." Hastings did not reply, continued to stare forward. "It may not mean much to you right now, Martin, but I convinced them to let you live. And Rebecca and Laura, they are alive thanks to me also. The helicopter stunt was my idea, too. Just like the crash in Afghanistan so many years ago. Some tricks are timeless, no? It will take time, Martin, but you will thank me, one day, for your life and for the lives of your daughters."

Still, Hastings did not reply. He was, undeniably, grateful that Rebecca and Laura were alive. One day, he imagined, he might even appreciate the fact that his own life had been spared, but for the moment, he wished he had died alongside Roger Delong.

"I can not blame you for what you are feeling now, my friend," the rugged Georgian sympathized, seeing the torment in Hastings' eyes. "You have been betrayed. The pain must be tremendous. If I were you and the situation was reversed, I would not hesitate to kill my betrayers; slowly…painfully. I can only say in defense, weak though it is, I did not enjoy deceiving you, Martin. You have become as a brother to me." Petyor faced Hastings squarely, but Martin refused to look up. "More than once I have wanted to tell you all; every stinking detail. Ultimately, however, I realized that should I do so, nothing positive would have been accomplished. We would have been both killed. In not telling you, I was able to assist you in your fervent desire to kill the black man. You must realize, Martin, that without our help, you never would have succeeded. Yes, you would have been able to kill many, but, certainly, nowhere near the numbers that are now being reported. Strangely enough, ours has been a completely symbiotic relationship. Your assistance will be, whether you desire such or not, rewarded."

Hastings, eyes set against the cold, remained motionless, hating Vasiliovich, hating the communists, hating himself, hating Kelly' murderers and the race that spawned them.

"As early as 1969," Petyor announced, now pacing back in forth alongside the motionless Hastings, "you had already made a name for yourself along certain corridors of the Kremlin. Though your work of those days was almost a continuous sequence of embarrassments for us, certain high-level party members saw in you a glimmer of hope. Allow me to tell you that, so far as I know, there was never any who were so foolish as to believe that you could be bought or actively recruited as a communist. You were only to be watched, albeit a bit more closely than most."

The Russian squatted down alongside Hastings and leaned back against the dinghy. "The man you knew as Paul Farmer was the first assigned to cover your activities at close hand."

The name was like a sledge hammer blow to Hastings' already pummeled spirit. Paul Farmer had been his neighbor and friend at his Atlanta home for almost forty years. The sudden truth of Petyor's words and the implications of that truth washed across him like a dark, oily tide. He and Paul had been close friends for decades, Kelly and Paul's wife, Joan, had been even closer. Joan had wailed like a banshee at Kelly's funeral, inconsolable. Paul had been angry and had railed at the police for not doing more to apprehend Kelly's attackers. Hastings could only wonder, now, if Paul's emotions were real or if it had all been a cleverly designed and played act. He wondered if Joan had been an agent also. He felt soiled to the marrow.

"After Kelly died," Petyor continued, "we could see the change that took place in you. When you began to look into nerve gases and poisons, naturally our curiosity was aroused. More powerful elements of the Party began to take interest. More agents were assigned to watch you. After your experiments in Washington and New Jersey, it was clear what your intentions were. The possibilities opened like a curtain before us. Clear heads immediately saw the benefit of assisting you in your quest to kill blacks. Those same minds recognized the opportunity for rocking the United States to its very foundations."

The Russian looked down at his former boss, searching for any hint that his words were registering there. Hastings face was blank, his expression emotionless. Petyor continued, "In 1975, an entire branch was delegated to monitoring and assisting your nefarious activities. I doubt that anyone knows exactly how many millions of dollars have been expended over the years in direct association with your efforts, but I can tell you that it is a substantial amount. More money, I would guess, than we have spent on any other single project apart from defense." Petyor mindlessly formed another iceball and flung it arcing across the deck. "We were determined that you would not fail. Our very existence depended on your success."

Hastings broke his silence, "What about Afghanistan? All that intelligence you handed over? That had to hurt the Soviet cause!"

Petyor folded his arms and squinted against a sudden breeze. "Yes, Martin, it cost. It cost dearly, but for the ultimate objective, it was necessary. Afghanistan was a mistake, anyway. We realized that early. If we had possessed sufficient strength, strength to withstand you Americans in a shooting war, we could have dealt with Afghanistan easily. As it was, we had to rely on conventional tactics—tactics which were not at all effective on the elusive Mujahadeen. We had already written off our objectives in Afghanistan, before I ever approached you. The information I handed over simply accelerated the inevitable. The moves we made in the late 80s were much greater, much riskier than anything we did in Afghanistan. The demolition of the Wall was our point of no return. All the chips were riding on you from there on out."

Hastings considered Petyor's explanation, seeing, albeit obscurely, the rationality on the second time through. Finally, he looked directly in the large Russian's clear blue eyes. "But why, Pete? Why did you continue to go along with it? Surely you don't still espouse the communist view of things? How could you after so many years in the west? You would have to be blind? There can be no utopian state."

Petyor answered immediately, softly, straightening somewhat. "It is you who are blinded, my friend. Accomplishing my mission has always been foremost in my mind. I realize that a capitalist such as you will probably never be able to understand, but we communists look beyond the money. With the right people in authority, the communist form of government is, unquestionably, superior to your greedy, self styled democracy." Petyor reflected, perhaps for the first time, on how mechanical his own words seemed. He wondered how truly he actually believed them, how much was him and how much was training and indoctrination. "The bottom line," he continued, without betraying his thoughts, "is the people, Martin—the average man. Look at the products of your government. Of what do you have to be proud. Freedom? What is that? The west's definition escapes me. Yours is a freedom which harbors crime like nowhere else on earth; starving beggars living alongside the extravagantly rich, no fairness, no concern for the masses. The communism you invision, that of the Khmer Rouge, the communism of Stalin, and similar ideologies are not what I represent. I abhor such domineering power no less than you do. Pure communism, the communism that even now is preparing to govern the globe, does not persecute, does not dwarf the common man, but, rather, provides security, nurtures the citizens, eliminates class and places all on equal footing. What, I ask you, sincerely, now, Martin, is so terrible about that?"

The deck shuddered perceptibly beneath them and the conversation ceased as the research vessel came to a slow, crackling halt. The two men could feel the reduction in power reverberating through the deck.

"Ah," proclaimed Petyor, "our rendezvous point."

Hastings turned his head from side to side, scanning the misty horizon, and searched for the other ship. There was none in sight. Petyor noted Hastings' searching gaze.

"They are here, Martin." He assured Hastings. "Patience."

One of the vessel's crew approached Petyor, handing him a sliver of paper—a note. The big Russian accepted the note, read it quickly, then replied to the messenger, "Very good. We'll get our things."

Turning to Hastings and briskly rubbing his gloved palms before him, Petyor announced, "Our ride to your new home has been here, it turns out, for several hours."

Hastings searched the horizon again. Still. Nothing.

"No, Martin," Petyor said, shaking his head, "Down there." He pointed to the ice littered sea lapping languidly at the sides of the boat below them. "They'll surface when we're ready to board. Come on. We've got to get your bags."

Reluctantly, Hastings rose from his position and followed Petyor into the vessel's bowels.

800 feet below the NOAA research vessel, the Soviet submarine's commander impatiently waited to give the 'surface' order. He had always disliked these political runs. He was a warrior. He wanted battle assignments, not diplomatic taxi missions. His father had fought in the great war, had stood his ground in a frozen foxhole at Stalingrad and, later, lead a band of patriots into the streets of Berlin at the close of that war, victorious. His grandfather had died in the mountains of Chechnya fighting to subdue a rebellious population. Now, it was his turn to take the battle to the enemy. The great whore was on her knees. It was time to strike. It was certainly not time to be playing spy games in the middle of a frozen sea. A series of tones echoed across the radio net. The tones were code and the code revealed that the passengers were ready for departure. With semi-forced professional resignation, Vasily Inoyavich gave the orders for the submarine to surface.

"You live in a dream world, Pete." Hastings flatly stated, handing his bag to the attending crew member, "Communism failed a long time ago. I don't know how it stood in there as long as it did." He put his gloves back on, slowly, and stared into Petyor's eyes. "You're an intelligent guy. A bit brainwashed, obviously, but competent enough, I think, to realize that your communism is an unworkable system. Men are not cattle, Pete. They're individuals."

Without reply, Petyor walked out of the cabin and forward towards the stairs leading to the frozen deck. Following, Hastings continued, "Communism denies the individual. It will never work. How many of your own did you kill between your fiasco revolution and you're eventual collapse? Seventy million? A hundred million? More?"

The bitter cold penetrated the exposed skin on Hastings' face as he stepped onto the deck. Petyor faced him there.

"And your capitalism, Martin?" the Russian questioned. "What of it? Where does that lead? How many die to fill the pockets of the fat and lazy? Don't even try to tell me that capitalists are not the biggest exploiters of the masses that have ever come down the pipes! Keeping the rich rich at the expense of the poor is only a favorable arrangement if you happen to be one of the fortunate few."

Two crew members were pointing to the east as others looked on. Petyor continued, "Perhaps you are correct, Martin. Perhaps not. Our taxi is here." He nodded his head in the direction the crew members were pointing. "And, now, we shall see, Martin, how well my communism works. In days, your United States will be relegated to the pages of history texts—a failed endeavor. Who will have the power, then? It is we Soviets that will dominate the globe. There will be no one left to contest us. There will be no repeat of the cold war." The Russian smiled broadly. "Yes, Martin. Now, we shall truly see."

Without waiting for a reply, Vasiliovich turned and slogged off towards the bow.

Hastings moved to the rails and watched the sea's surface bubble as the Soviet submarine nosed its way out of the depths. His transport to his future. What lay ahead? He could not imagine. He stared at the ice littered sea's dark surface rising and falling at intervals. For an instant, Hastings flirted with the idea of hurling himself overboard and ending it all in wet, frozen asphyxiation. But, suicide was not something Martin

Hastings could reasonably embrace. Hastings lowered his head and kicked at the ice building up along the deck with the heel of his boot. His thoughts returned to a schoolyard fight.

Made in the USA
Las Vegas, NV
11 October 2022

57079253R00236